ON and OFF the FIELD

A NEW BEGINNINGS ROMANCE NOVEL

ANASTASIA DEAN

Copyright © 2022 by Anastasia Dean

All rights reserved.

No part of this book may be reproduced in any form or by any electronic or mechanical means, including information storage and retrieval systems, without written permission from the author, except for the use of brief quotations in a book review.

This books is a work of fiction. The characters and events portrayed in this book are fictitious. Any similarity to a real persons, living or dead, business or locales is coincidental and is not intended by the author.

ISBN:

E-book: 979-8-9856806-3-8

Paperback: 979-8-9856806-4-5

Edited By: Shelby Goodwin

Cover Designer: Ebook Launch

For my sister (and best friend!) Maggie. She doesn't read, so she'll never know.

Chapter One

Ofelia Mendez stared blankly at the large cutout of William Shakespeare contemplating where her life went so wrong. She suspected it was the moment she agreed to teach high school. The incessant nagging in her ear belonged to an irate parent droning on about her precious baby boy. By "baby boy" she meant her seventeen-year-old son and by "precious" she meant starved for attention. She desperately tried to follow the conversation, but thoughts of her mile long to-do list plagued her mind.

What Mrs. Davis didn't realize - or care to realize- was that Ofelia didn't *want* to be on the phone with her, hashing out the same conversation she had with Mrs. Davis about her son, Dustin, countless times before. It was her school district's policy to call home each time a teacher gave detention to foster a better parent-teacher-student relationship. She tried very hard not to notice Dustin's outbursts in class or the hallway - like *really* hard - but she couldn't just ignore it when he physically threatened another student. Unfortunately, his mother didn't share her views.

"Mrs. Davis," she said, attempting to sound both kind and unwavering. Mrs. Davis smelled fear. She fed upon emotions like a soul sucking vampire. "I apologize for yet another call. Dustin has actually been a sweetheart in class these past few weeks. However, there was an incident in class today I needed to inform you-"

"Oh, this will be good." Mrs. Davis interrupted in a haughty tone she often adopted when talking to Ofelia. It made her feel like a child and since she was already one of the youngest teachers on campus, she hated feeling inferior because of her age. "So, tell me, what did Dustin do to deserve detention?"

"Well, Dustin yelled at another student and-"

"Oh, bless your heart." Mrs. Davis said in her southern drawl, making the hairs on the back of Ofelia's neck stand up. She only recently moved to Texas, but she understood what that phrase meant.

'Oh, bless your heart' was the equivalent of 'wow, you're a huge fucking idiot.' That was one thing about southerners, they were polite even when they were insulting you straight to your face. If the insult hadn't been geared towards her, she might have been impressed.

"Ms. Mendez, I'm not sure how they ran the schools back where you came from-"

"California."

"-but in Texas, we don't call home after every little mishap. They're children. They are still learning how to socialize and sometimes they do so inappropriately. It happens. I don't see why you needed to call me."

She kept her voice as neutral as possible, continuing before the evil witch could get another word in. "Mrs. Davis, my classroom is a safe zone for all students. Dustin threatened bodily harm on a peer. I had to deescalate the situation before a fight broke out. I do not tolerate bullying of any kind."

"Sounds to me like it was just a case of boys being boys. Let me ask you this Ms. Mendez: do you have any children?" Mrs. Davis inquired.

Gritting her teeth, she responded. "No, I do not."

"I can tell. I'm a boy mom, I have one in college and my youngest is in middle school. They fight - it's what boys do. They don't know how to express their emotions, so they use fists."

"Mrs. Davis, are you insinuating I should have let the students fight?" She shouldn't be surprised, but she was. Did Mrs. Davis really teach her sons to bottle up their emotions and use fists as a coping mechanism? She tried her best not to be the type of person who judged mothers, but this didn't sit right with her.

"Of course not!" Mrs. Davis gasped, sounding shocked Ofelia would suggest such a thing even though Mrs. Davis brought it up first. "What I'm saying is that boys are different creatures than girls and they express their emotions in a way fitting for a young man..."

And that was where Ofelia stopped listening to the lecture because she knew from experience that it was better to just let them talk. She hated how this woman made her feel; small and out of control of the situation. The anxiety Mrs. Davis brought forth would be enough to fuel an entire therapy clinic. She had only felt so out of control twice before in her life and for things much larger than a helicopter mother. Once was at her mother's funeral and then again at what should have been her wedding day. Both monumental parts of her life, and yet Mrs. Davis worked her way into completing the trifecta of misery.

Wonderful.

Instead of listening to Mrs. Davis's ignorant ramblings, Ofelia tried to think of the one positive thing she was looking forward to today. Cheer practice. As a former cheerleader herself, she reveled in the bonds she made with her squad. Now as a coach, she strived to make her squad feel the same meaningful connection. Like with everything else in her life, Ofelia threw herself into coaching with passionate ferocity, spending countless hours creating and perfecting routines.

Although she put an insane amount of pressure on herself, she looked forward to coaching every Monday and Wednesday afternoon where she could hang up her teacher cardigan and don her whistle and yoga pants to coach a tight-knit squad. The stress of the day melted away during each practice.

No one could take that feeling away from her. She just needed to get her cheerleaders whipped into shape before the start of competition season...but in order to do that, she needed to end this phone conversation.

"Mrs. Davis," The woman was still in the midst of her soliloquy, but frankly Ofelia didn't care. She'd heard enough; anymore, and her head would spontaneously combust. "I hear your concerns, but I'm not sure we are understanding one another. Maybe you should contact our principal, Colbie Thompson, for a meet-"

"Oh I most certainly will, Mrs. Mendez. You can count on that. I'm concerned with how much attention you're giving my son. In fact, if I didn't know any better, I would say you were targeting him." With those parting words, Mrs. Davis hung up the phone, leaving Ofelia with her mouth open like a fish gasping for water.

What. Just. Happened?

This was not what she needed today - or any day for that matter. On top of her forever long teaching and coaching list, she would now have to add a meeting with Colbie and Mrs. Davis. She expected the conversation to go south, but she hadn't expected to be accused of "targeting." The call left her uncertain about whether she did the right thing. Ofelia *did* call Mrs. Davis more than the average parent, but according to her school's guidelines, she was simply following protocol.

Though perhaps she was being bothersome...

No. She refused to let Mrs. Davis get under her skin when she knew for a fact she did the right thing. If Mrs. Davis acted upon her threat, Ofelia was certain her principal would have her back. She had a good relationship with Colbie Thompson. If one woman could go head-to-head with Mrs. Davis and end up victorious, Colbie could.

As much as she loved her principal, she couldn't help but feel slightly flustered around the woman. The childhood fear of being sent to the principal's office after acting up in class still lingered, even years later.

Realizing the phone was still in her hands, Ofelia hung up as a knock sounded at her door. It was the end of the day, but she knew who waited at the other end. Bright red curly hair and a freckled face smiled brightly and waved manically in greeting.

Willow Clarke was just the person Ofelia wanted to vent to. Her teacher bestie always had impeccable timing. Ofelia swore she was psychic because Willow always appeared at her door holding chocolates after any inconvenience occurred. This time was no different.

"You look traumatized and in desperate need of wine." Willow said as soon as she let herself into the classroom, shutting the door behind her. She marched over to Ofelia's desk and for a horrible moment, Ofelia thought she had a bottle of wine to offer, but her eccentric friend pulled out a large

Snickers candy bar instead. "You need this more than me," she said by way of explanation.

Willow was in her mid-thirties, married to a German man, and was the most free-spirited person Ofelia knew. The two of them connected almost immediately when she started in her current position as the English III and Creative Writing teacher at McKinley High. Willow said the reason they got along so well was due to their matching energies. Both women were insanely passionate, even to a fault, and preferred the company of each other over a large friend group.

"I think I made the top of Mrs. Davis' shit list." Ofelia groaned and reached for the proffered chocolate.

"Oh, that's right! I forgot you had to call that awful woman. I didn't realize Hell had cell service." Willow deadpanned.

Despite her best efforts, Ofelia laughed. The ball of anxiety brewing in her chest began to dissipate, but she still felt on edge. She was already behind schedule and when she glanced at the clock on her desktop computer, she realized practice started five minutes ago.

"Damn! I'm sorry Willow, I have to go. You didn't need something, did you?" She asked, frantically searching through her gym bag for her yoga pants and sports bra.

"Yes actually, but I don't think you're going to like it." Willow bit her lip, avoiding eye contact with Ofelia.

That was never a good sign.

"What is it?" A million thoughts ran through Ofelia's mind. Had she done her lesson plans? Had she somehow missed an observation or important deadline? She didn't think they were missing any books their English III students were reading because she had counted them herself this morning.

She supposed it was possible that one of them accidentally got taken by a student but-

"It's about the gym."

Ofelia's blood went hot at the mention of her gym. The gym she had booked months in advance by attending every stupid meeting about the school's calendar and promptly submitting facility request forms. She even went as far as bribing the girls' basketball coach with a fresh batch of her famous empanadas, just to obtain an extra ten minutes of practice.

"What about the gym?" She couldn't hide the annoyance in her voice, trying hard not to aim her curt aggression towards Willow.

"Well..." Willow's voice went higher in pitch and suddenly seemed to find the pile of sticky notes on Ofelia's desk to be the most interesting thing in the room. Ofelia was trying really hard to keep her face curious rather than murderous.

"So, remember when you asked me to check if the gymnastic club had returned the blue mats?" Willow asked and Ofelia nodded. "Well, the good news is that the mats are there."

"But..?" Pulling teeth would have been less painful than getting Willow to speak. She loved her best friend, she did, but Willow had a way of dragging out the suspense.

"But...the bad news is that the gym was already in use."

"What?!" Who would have the audacity to take *her* gym during *her* scheduled practice hours? Especially with competition just around the corner. Although the other coaches didn't quite understand the importance of cheer and the scholarships her seniors could win if they placed highly at nationals, they typically respected her allotted time. Maybe if she finally brought home the big trophy, they might rethink their ignorance and even respect her sport.

"I think it was the baseball team because I didn't recognize the coach. You heard we got a new baseball coach, right? Old coach decided on an early retirement." Willow went on, oblivious to Ofelia's scowl. "So to be fair to him, I don't think he's been told about the calendar. Those things typically get overlooked during orientation."

Ofelia could accept that he was new and probably hadn't been told about the schedule, but she wouldn't allow him to take over her practice. The stakes were too high and she didn't need an audience while her cheerleaders were learning a new routine. They'd be distracted by the players and she needed their undivided attention.

"I'll just have to talk to the new coach then." Ofelia said, finally slipping on her yoga pants from behind her desk and discarding her chiffon skirt into her gym bag. "I'll deal with this, but thank you for telling me." She hoped her smile reached her eyes, but the exhaustion from today was pulling her down.

One more problem. She only had to deal with one more problem today.

Willow reached out and squeezed her arm, offering her a kind smile. "You are the most badass cheer coach and teacher I know. Don't let some guy come in and get you all shook up. Go take your gym back."

That was precisely what Ofelia planned to do. She hugged her friend before ushering Willow out, closing the door behind her. She finished changing and flung her gym bag over her shoulder with her head held high. If there was ever a day she needed a win, it was right now because it felt as if she was cursed. Or perhaps today was a test of her ability to keep calm under pressure. Except she felt like she was on the Titanic with no lifeboat and expected to keep the waters at bay. Oh, and just to add insult to injury, it was raining in this scenario.

Bring on the storm, she thought and walked out of her classroom.

The storm came in the form of two dozen teenage boys and an unfamiliar male. True to Willow's assessment, the baseball team - for some ungodly reason - decided today would be the perfect day to use the indoor facilities rather than their own field. Her squad stood outside the door, waiting on her expectantly to fix this mishap.

"Mrs. Mendez, we should be practicing right now." One of her freshman cheerleaders supplied unhelpfully.

"I know. Just give me a moment to talk to him." She said, sounding more sure than she felt. Ofelia instructed her team to wait outside the gym while she went to speak to the coach. The baseball team sat in the middle of the floor staring at the back of the unfamiliar new coach. He sloppily wrote down different dates on a portable whiteboard, captivating his entire audience with the simple mundane task.

Ofelia must have made a sound, for every set of eyes in the room snapped in her direction. The man by the white board suddenly stopped writing to stare at her, giving Ofelia an unobstructed view of his entire profile.

Dear god he was one of the most handsome men she had ever laid eyes on. He was the epitome of "tall, dark, and handsome." His athletic body moved with such grace, reminding her of a sleek, black panther zeroing in on his target. She had never seen him before, because with a face and ass like that, he would have been the recurring star of all her wildest dreams. This man could easily fill in as a Michael B. Jordan stunt double.

He was tall, taller than her previous boyfriends, with

muscles she only ever saw in movies or read about in books. Even behind his navy-blue t-shirt, she could see what lay underneath would be equally delicious. So much so that she wondered what it would be like to run her tongue along his-

No. Hell no. Stop that thought. Ofelia could not be lusting after this gym-stealing man in front of his team of smelly teenagers. This man was the enemy now, no matter how attractive he looked in those gray joggers...

"Can I help you, miss?"

He could do a whole lot more than help, but the words brewing inside her died on her lips as soon as she opened her mouth.

Well shit.

Chapter Two

It only occurred to Ofelia now that she'd been staring at the new coach this entire time, slack-jawed and silent. She hastily closed her mouth, face flushing with embarrassment. The students in front of him all stared expectantly, waiting for her to say something. Anything.

Words - she needed words.

After a few agonizing seconds, Ofelia found her voice. "Actually yes, you can." She tried to keep the full force of her annoyance out of her tone but was unsure how successful her attempt had been.

"I'm not sure if you glanced at the calendar, but on Mondays the gym is reserved for my cheer squad. Wednesdays too. We get the gym from four to seven. I'm afraid you're going to have to find somewhere else to hold your...well I don't exactly know what you're doing, but regardless you are going to have to move."

The man - she still did not know his name - raised a thick brow at her. His lips quirked into a smile, like he found the entire situation funny and didn't take her seriously. He poked the cheer momma bear, and he didn't even realize what he was about to unleash.

"Calendar? What calendar? I got to the gym at four and nobody was here. Figured it was free for me and my baseball team to use." He shrugged.

"Well it's not. Free, I mean." Ofelia said, standing her ground. Every year she fought for her squad to get a practice space. The athletic department loved the funding her parents brought in, but they saw cheer as more of a hobby. Just a bunch of yelling and jumping around, people would say, dismissing everything she and her team worked so hard to accomplish.

"Anyways, wouldn't a baseball team want to practice outside? Where there are literal baseball fields for you to-" she gestured around at the boys' seated positions, "-do this?"

"Except our fields are currently undergoing last minute renovations for our first game tomorrow. So no, we can't do *this* outside. We need the gym for our team meeting and to run through drills." Coach Ass-hat said, not understanding the concept of a scheduled practice written in stone. Or, in her case, the official McKinley calendar.

Ofelia didn't give a damn about his fields. There were other perfectly good places he could go to get his precious practice in. Of course, she supposed he could make the same argument for her squad, but it was the principle of the matter. She had fought so hard for gym rights, and she would be damned if she let Coach Ass-hat waltz in and take her prize.

"I'm not sure how your fields not being ready is suddenly my problem." She said, earning some *ooohs* from the baseball team, their heads swiveling between the two teachers, watching a very chaotic tennis match unfold.

"Damn Ms. Mendez, you got some balls on you." One of

ON AND OFF THE FIELD

the players called out. It was a familiar voice, but she couldn't quite place it.

"Cambridge! Take a lap. Don't speak to teachers that way."

"Aw. hell coach Wilson, I'm just messing around!" Nick Cambridge, who Ofelia knew from her second period English III class, complained as his buddies pushed him to his feet.

So Coach Ass-hat had a name. Wilson. She made a mental note to learn everything she could about this man, one whose sole purpose seemed to be pissing her off.

Coach Wilson waited until Nick took off before parting the sea of baseball players to cross the gym floor and stand directly in front of her. Ofelia had to tilt her head up to see him properly. He was big, bigger than what she expected. He towered over her as if she were nothing more than a petulant child. Honestly, Ofelia sort of felt that way due to his presence. His very handsome and intimidating presence. Still, she refused to back up or give him any indication he affected her at all.

"I know jack about cheerleading, but isn't your season over?" He asked, confused.

That statement alone was far more than many people knew about her cheer season. And although yes, he technically was correct because Ofelia should have been prepping for the final competition, not their first, their season had been pushed back by a few months due to later school start. At first Ofelia had flipped out in the change of schedule, but then - after being reminded by Willow that this would give her more time to prepare - she eventually grew accustomed to the idea. Not like there was much she could do about it anyway.

"Later start date this school year. Competitions were pushed back to accommodate." She shrugged, but Coach Ass-Hat didn't appear to be paying attention to her anymore.

"Listen," Wilson finally said, dropping his authoritative

tone. "I didn't realize there was a calendar. I was just hired and I didn't get the whole run down. Bottom line, I need this gym. The best I can do is split it with you, but I'm not leaving. It's for one practice. Do you really need the entire gym to skip around and belt out ancient cheers? Doesn't seem like that big of a deal."

"Excuse me?" Ofelia's blood boiled. Damn him for being like every other person who didn't see value in what she did. Who was he to dictate the rules of the gym during *her* practice? He might not understand what this meant to her, but Ofelia had a lot riding on this competition. She'd been a cheer coach for the past two years and hadn't placed at nationals yet. This *had* to be her year. "We do not skip or belt. If you believe that is all cheerleaders do, then you are sadly mistaken. You also sound like a misogynist, so please refrain from insulting me and my squad again."

A slight twitch in Wilson's brow was the only indication Ofelia got under his skin. Good. Let him stew in agitation. She had a younger sibling; she knew exactly how to slither under people's skin. Just ask her brother. If Wilson wanted to play the intimidating stare down game all day, she would gladly oblige.

To her satisfaction, Wilson looked away first. Ha! Victory! At least that was how she felt until he turned around and started to walk back towards his team. He cast one look over his shoulder and shouted, "Half the gym! Take it or leave it."

AFTER HER UNSUCCESSFUL attempts to win back the gym space, Ofelia left with what little of her dignity remained. She most certainly didn't look like the weaker dog that lost a fight and now had to retreat with her tail tucked between her legs. Nope, definitely nothing like that.

Except for the fact that was exactly what happened, and she feared it was written across her very tired face.

The moment she walked out of the gym door she stood face-to-face with her entire squad.

"So, why are we only getting half the gym?" Lacey, Cheer Captain and senior, asked. There was an edge of annoyance to her voice, which wasn't unusual for Lacey and her perfectionist qualities, but it still grated on Ofelia's nerves.

Unfortunately, she had no other explanation than the truth. She told her squad, hoping for an ounce of sympathy from the group but the verdict was split. Some looked perturbed and rightfully so, but she wasn't certain if their annoyance stemmed from the intruders occupying the gym or her inability to regain control over the situation. The others looked almost giddy at the thought of sharing the space with the baseball team.

Ugh, hormones.

It shouldn't be a big deal; she could easily waltz back inside and conduct practice like she always did. Except Coach Wilson would also be conducting his baseball meeting. Just the thought of the man sent shivers down her spine, which wasn't all from disgust. Damn, she seriously needed to get out more.

She had no other choice but to put on her big girl panties and take the initiative. Channeling her mother's 'take no shit' attitude, she said, "This isn't anything we can't handle. We'll ignore the boys, and they'll ignore us. It's one day and then the gym will be ours again. Pay them no mind."

There was still time to stick with Ofelia's original plan, which consisted of their series of warm-ups before they moved on running through their competition choreography. Their performance at regionals needed to be nothing shy of fantastic because it would set the tone for the remainder of the season.

Her plan had not come to fruition. The moment Ofelia walked back inside with twelve girls and two boys that made up her entire Small Varsity Co-Ed team, the mood in the gym instantly shifted. If she didn't know better, she would have thought they were the Montagues, stepping into Capulet territory.

Lacey scoffed, shooting daggers at a few of the baseball players unfortunate enough to be within breathing distance. "They aren't even moving and they already smell. Do you think it's a qualification to be a baseball player? You must smell like horse manure at all times."

"Shut up, Lacey, you're distracting me." Tony said, the only junior who could go head-to-head with Lacey and not shrink under her scrutiny. "You're talking is keeping me from admiring the muscled artwork in front of me."

Lacey scrunched up her face in disgust. "God, baseball boys? Seriously? You realize that baseball is like, the most redneck-y sport, and these 'bros' are most definitely exuding toxic masculinity."

"First off, that's an overgeneralization. Right Ms. M?" Tony asked, causing Ofelia to smile despite the situation. At least she knew some of her students paid attention in class. "Secondly, I'm pretty sure the most redneck sport is NASCAR. And thirdly, baseball players are sexy. I mean, think of how well they can handle their ba-"

"There will be none of that." Ofelia piped up before Tony finished his comment. The hardest part about being a teacher or coach was holding back laughter after a student said something funny and wildly inappropriate. She tried to disguise it with a cough, because seriously, didn't she think the same thing when she looked at the major league baseball players? Not that she watched much baseball. Her father and brother were soccer fans but watched the occasional baseball game from time to time.

"You aren't scared of a few baseball guys, are you Lace?" Came a teasing voice belonging to the only other male on the team. Devin was another senior who had been on the team since his junior year. Part of the reason he joined, Ofelia suspected, was to get closer to Lacey. Anyone could see just how bad he had it for her. Lacey pretended to be annoyed by his attention, but her eyes always wandered over to him when she thought no one was looking.

"Please, the only thing I'm worried about is the drool they will inevitably leave behind when they watch us warm up."

That was her cue to start practice, especially considering they wasted enough time dealing with Coach Wilson. Ofelia pretended like she couldn't hear the baseball team behind her as they also began to move into their workout routine, even when the gym grew exceptionally louder with the sounds of grunts and squeaky shoes. It was, however, nothing a little music couldn't dull.

Ariana Grande, to be exact.

The moment "Thank U, Next" hit her portable speaker and engulfed the room with Ari singing of lost love, Ofelia instantly felt more in her element. This was exactly what she needed after a long day of teaching, dealing with a deplorable parent, and fighting with the new hire. When she stretched, she could turn off her brain and let her body move of its own accord.

She led her squad through their normal warm up routine, slowly walking her hands down her body until she placed them firmly on the ground. One of her legs stretched far behind her while the other stayed rooted in front of her, drawing her chest close. Their breathing techniques came into play next. One long ten second inhale followed by a slow exhale while they pressed forward on their front knee, deepening the stretch. Ofelia felt the stretch in her hamstrings, bringing forth a delightful tingling sensation.

She was about to switch legs when the music stopped abruptly. "What-"

But a deep voice cut her off. "What are you doing?" He asked, his voice a mixture of annoyance and incredulity.

Ofelia didn't need to look up to see who stood above her, berating her. She may have only just met him, but the voice was permanently filed away under "Coach Ass-hat." Which is why she took her time getting up, feeling his eyes track her every move until she stood toe-to-toe with him.

Ass-hat's proximity reminded her how gorgeous this man truly was. His attitude should really fit his appearance. He was far better suited as a bridge goblin, or perhaps a lumpy troll.

"Is something the matter?" She asked innocently, getting a thrill from watching the man play through various stages of exasperation.

"Your music's what's the matter. It's distracting my guys. They can't hear me yell orders over the screeching."

"Would you prefer 'Take me out to the Ball Game?' I'm sure I can find a 2-hour loop version on YouTube if I tried."

That earned her a few snickers from both the cheerleaders and a few baseball players. It provided a small boost of confidence she didn't know she needed.

Ass-hat whirled around at his snickering players and ordered them to take a lap around the gym in typical coach fashion. It was so cliché that Ofelia nearly rolled her eyes at him, until he turned back to her and said, "No Ariana. No 'Take me out to the Ball Game.' You might be trying to relive your high school glory days, but some of us are trying to work. Just stick with your vapid cheers, and we won't have a problem."

Without another word, Wilson stormed away, going back to his side of the gym. He didn't glance back once; in fact, he seemed keen on forgetting Ofelia existed. She felt the stinging in her eyes, tears threatening to fall. She wasn't about to cry over some dick who never learned how to share. No, she wanted to cry because she was so frustrated with people always belittling her. This wasn't the first time a man disappointed her. Wilson was her colleague, not her superior. He had no right to tell her what she could and could not do at her own damn practice.

"Dang Ms. Mendez, who peed in his cereal this morning?" Tony asked, shaking his head. "Do you want me to egg his car? Because I can so egg his car."

"You can't egg his car, moron. Especially since you just told a teacher you plan on doing it." Lacey said, no real venom behind her words. Although they may bicker, the cheer squad was a tight-knit group, and no one messed with any cheerleader except for one another. That included Ofelia, which lessened the lump in her throat, knowing her team loved her as much as she loved them.

"As appealing as that offer sounds, Tony. We are just going to ignore him. To use your phrase, I don't know who peed in his cereal, but we aren't going to let that affect us. We can't control his actions, but we can control ours. So let's choose to be the bigger people. Coach ass-Wilson-" She coughed, stopping his nickname she created from slipping out. "- is perhaps having a bad day."

"He's about to have a really bad day when I egg his car after practice." Tony whispered loudly to Devin.

"No egging, Tony. I'm serious. Devin, you are on Tony duty after practice. Make sure he gets home having touched no eggs."

"You got it Ms. Mendez." Devin grinned, saluting her and playfully bumped his elbow into his friend's side. "You heard the teacher - no eggs for you."

Chapter Three

He was being a dick.

Maverick realized this the second he walked away from the wide-eyed cheer coach. If he had been a better man, he would have turned around and apologized right then and there. It was just music for fuck's sake and it wasn't harming anyone. Except she had to be playing *that* song. He didn't make it a habit to hate music, but that particular song had been one of her favorites and Maverick didn't need to be reminded of her. No, in fact, he needed to never think about that woman again.

Not thinking about her was harder these days. Breanna had been such a huge part of his life for so long, losing her felt like losing a version of himself. He did not know how to act. Breanna had called him at least a half dozen times since their highly publicized and messy breakup, but he never answered or listened to any of the messages she left him. Maverick have been tempted on more than one occasion, but it had become easier to delete and forget than rehashing a scenario neither of them could fix.

Instead of taking his anger out on the actual person who deserved every ounce of his vexation, he took it out on the pretty coach. What a way to make a fucking first impression.

Throughout the remainder of practice, or more accurately work out since they couldn't use the field, Maverick continued to sneak glances at the woman. Her students called her Ms. Mendez, and they looked at her as if she hung the moon every night. He wondered if she knew how much her cheerleaders loved her when it was clearly written across all their faces.

Maverick was under no illusion he would ever be looked at by his players the same way the cheerleaders looked at Ms. Mendez. Even though they looked at him with awe, and some with pity, it was never out of love or respect. It was because he used to be someone. But his time in the spotlight had come and gone in the blink of an eye.

A year ago, if someone came up to him and said he would be teaching at a suburban high school in Texas, Maverick would have laughed in their face and then called security to get that person out of his line of sight.

Now he was nothing more than a glorified babysitter. Actually, babysitting might have paid more than this coaching job.

The only reason he came into coaching was due to his former manager taking pity on him. Maverick had been shunned, cast out of the major leagues just as he was working his way to the top. He could have been big, could have made a name for himself if only...

No, he refused to finish that thought. No good came from reliving those memories and opening still healing wounds. Keanon, his former manager, had made sure Maverick didn't fall on his ass when he plummeted from his high horse. "Listen man," he had told him the last day Maverick had been in

Chicago, "I think time away will do you some good. My sister-in-law is an assistant principal or something down in Texas. They are always looking for coaches and I'll put in a good word for you. Don't you worry about housing or nothing. I got that covered too. I want you to focus on your damn self. Okay, man? Can you do that?"

It wasn't until he moved that he realized Keanon had been his only friend. He had people who wanted to be around him, sure. But did any of them ever reach out to him after that fateful night? Or the day after when he found out only seconds before the public that he had been banned from the major leagues?

No. Only Keanon. Granted, Keanon had been his manager, so he was hurting from the ban as well, but the man at least made sure Maverick had other things lined up before leaving Chicago.

Keanon even texted him just to make sure Maverick was okay, but he was the furthest thing from okay. He used to wake up feeling like the king of Chicago. Now he felt very little at all. Each day was a series of tasks to complete, only to wake up and do it all over again.

This wasn't the life he wanted.

Yet he was here, and Maverick had to make the most of it. Teaching high schoolers wasn't glamorous, but it paid the bills and connected him to his past life.

"Coach Wilson." a voice called, drawing Maverick out of the past and back into the present. Damn, how long had he been working on autopilot? Only a handful of his boys were still in the gym. Three remained, his starting pitcher, catcher, and third baseman, sprawled across the bleachers. "You kicked our asses today."

No, he really hadn't, but that's what happens McKinley's

team goes from an incompetent coach who couldn't tell the difference between shortstop and second baseman, to him, a former MLB player. He worked the boys through a series of warm ups mirroring his old routines. It got the heart racing, but wasn't meant to exhaust his players. To his team's credit, not a single one complained.

At least not to his face.

"Coach, do you think any of your old teammates will come and watch one of our games?" Dustin asked. Dustin was the third baseman, a tall, lanky kid who seemed oblivious to the art of proper conversation. His teammate next to him - Maverick couldn't remember the name since all the blonde kids blurred together - elbowed him in the side, a clear signal to shut up. Dustin, being Dustin, couldn't read the fucking room and glared at his friend. "What? Just because he's banned doesn't mean he doesn't have friends in the league."

Maverick wished he could say this conversation was the first time his ban was brought up by a student, faculty member, or any other asshole that stopped him on the streets, but sadly he'd lost count. Surprisingly enough, no one asked why. They were leeches who wanted nothing more than to ride on the back of one man's misery hoping it would make them feel better about their own wretched lives.

Normally Maverick would walk away or tell the person to fuck off but considering he was now employed at a high school; he doubted his administration would look kindly on either option. Also, from what he heard, Dustin had a rather aggressive helicopter mother who enjoyed picking fights with the school staff. Overbearing mothers were a good enough reason to not engage.

"Locker rooms. Shower. Now. I'm sick of smelling the three of you." Maverick ushered the boys along, unable to make out their faint grumblings. Fortunately, they didn't put up much more of a fight, immediately getting distracted by the departing cheerleaders. None of them returned the unwarranted attention, except a short, skinny male who decided to blow kisses in their direction.

High schoolers were a different breed.

Turning back around, Maverick caught Ms. Mendez from the corner of his eyes. She just finished folding up a giant blue mat and now attempted to pick it up. This gave Maverick a perfect view of her ass. The gentlemanly thing to do would have been to look away, but he already established he was no gentleman. The woman before him had a body meant to be worshiped.

No, he couldn't think like that. Not only was he recovering from a messy breakup of ten years, but he already ruined any chances he may have had with this woman. He regretted that now.

"Here, let me help you." The words left Maverick's lips before he had a chance to stop them. In three long strides, he closed the distance between him and Ms. Mendez – he really needed to learn her first name. She wasn't wearing a badge, so his fruitless search looked like he was checking out her chest.

Another dick move.

The cheer coach frowned, noticing where his eyes were currently located. Not only was he a giant ass in her eyes, but he was also a perv now. "I don't need your help, thanks." The woman said curtly, continuing to haul the blue mats to stack them in the corner of the gym. She lifted them high, giving Maverick a good show of her toned arms. How was it that this woman made something as mundane as lifting mats sexy?

Yeah, definitely not helping the perv thing.

Before he had a chance to dig himself deeper into a hole,

she turned around, her hair whipping to attention as if it too were mad at Maverick. If her hair were snakes and she was Medusa, there was a one hundred percent chance that he'd be nothing but stone right now.

"If you ever embarrass me in front of my cheerleaders again, I'll bury you so deep in grievances you'll never see the light of day again." Mrs. Mendez snapped, showing off a different side to the gentle persona she originally gave off. And damn if he didn't like fiery, passionate women. It was one of the reasons he was in his current predicament.

But they had successfully shared the gym, so she couldn't hold this over his head forever. He hoped.

"Noted. Grievances. Deep hole." He listed off, watching the smallest quirk of her lips. If he hadn't been studying her so profusely, he'd never have noticed the almost-smirk he elicited from her. He wondered what it would be like to earn a full smile from this woman for no other reason other than wanting to see her lips stretch into something other than a frown.

Maverick wouldn't be getting anything out of the woman though, for she pushed past him without so much as a goodbye. Her smell, vanilla and honey, lingered after she left. If he wasn't careful, Maverick could easily get distracted by a certain temperamental Latina woman. He made up his mind right there and then that the next time he saw Ms. Mendez, he would get her first name. There wasn't any harm in asking for a name. He couldn't keep calling her Ms. Mendez the rest of his employment.

There was absolutely no other reason Maverick wanted her name other than to get to know his coworkers. No other motive whatsoever.

Oh, how easy it was to lie to himself these days.

Chapter Four

It wasn't every day you got to threaten the gorgeous, but definitely dickish, gym teacher with complaints, but today was quickly becoming a week of firsts. Did Ofelia regret her words or temper when he tried to apologize to her? Nope. The man definitely deserved her anger for how much of a tool he had been in front of a large group of students. It was completely unprofessional.

However, she couldn't help the wicked sense of pride that filled her stomach when she thought back to the way he looked at her. Never in her twenty-six years of life had she been more tempted to look back as she stormed away to check to see if Coach Wilson was checking out her ass. But she felt like that would have ruined the pissed off attitude she was trying to relay, so despite wanting nothing more than to turn around and peek...she didn't.

If that wasn't a testament to her willpower, then it most certainly would be surviving the rest of the week being the bad ass English teacher and cheerleading coach she was.

By the time Ofelia pulled into the driveway of her bright

yellow craftsman Friday evening, all thoughts of Coach Wilson were pushed deep into the recesses of her mind. Mostly. She wasn't blind. The man was sex on a stick, but he'd be one stick she'd stay far away from except when she was forced to cross paths with him in the hallway throughout the week.

Living alone had its perks. For one, no one was there to immediately attack her with questions about her day. Especially a day like today where she would undoubtedly lose the fragile control over her emotions. Ofelia was an ugly crier, the less who saw it the better. Her past roommates compared her to a wailing banshee. Which...harsh, but accurate.

So no, no human greeted her at the door, but two furry creatures did. Leila, a beautiful, chubby calico cat, brushed against Ofelia's leg. No doubt depositing all her fur into that one spot. Her other cat, a beautiful gray tabby named Stella, continued to rest peacefully atop her couch. The only acknowledgement Stella gave to Ofelia's presence was a slight raising of her head, then right back into nap mode.

"Hello, my babies." She spoke in that high pitched voice most people reserved for infants and toddlers. Yes it was annoying, but no one was here to judge her. "Did you miss mommy today? 'Cause I missed you soooo much." She cooed and bent down to scoop up Leila. The cat in question was not light and tried, unsuccessfully, to escape her loving embrace. But Ofelia had a hard day and she just wanted to be loved, dammit! Eventually, Leila accepted her fate and leaned into her nuzzling, purring in contentment.

Yes, she was a crazy cat lady who loved literature. She knew damn well she fit all the cliches, but after moving thousands of miles away from her family, Ofelia was fine taking solace in books and cats. It made the pain of leaving her home state of California a bit more bearable.

Knowing she put Leila through enough emotional abuse, she finally released her onto the couch, where she swatted at her sister until both were curled up together.

Not having the energy to cook, she declared today an Uber Eats sort of night. The question was, what type of food did she want to drown her sorrows in? Mexican food was good for cleansing the soul, but something about Chinese food always provided a certain level of comfort when one was wallowing in self pity.

Hmm, decisions, decisions.

Ultimately, and to no one's surprise, Ofelia went with Chinese food. The only Mexican food she truly wanted was that of her mother's, but her mother passed away nearly five years ago, taking away the most loving and supportive person in her life. Mexican food didn't measure up when her mother wasn't the one to cook and serve it. It made her regret not paying better attention to her mother when she attempted to teach Ofelia how to make some of her classic dishes. As much as she tried to replicate her mother's cooking, it never quite tasted the same.

An hour later, Ofelia was showered, dressed in her coziest pajamas, and lounging on her couch with her shrimp fried rice nestled neatly in her lap. The tv was showing some reality TV series about couples from different parts of the world and the absolute shit show their relationships were. There was something cathartic about watching other people's drama unfold and realizing your life, in comparison, wasn't all that bad.

Ofelia's life wasn't bad. Not really. She had a job that she loved and adored which allowed her to teach a subject she loved. She had friends, or rather *friend*, whom she loved as much as a sister. And she had a cozy home, close to work. She was truly grateful for these positive accomplishments, but that didn't stop the ache in her heart each time she thought about home and all she left behind.

For starters, her father, brother, and two-year old niece still lived in California. Her mother was buried at the cemetery near her childhood home, a quick ten minute walk from her brother's current residence. Family was everything to her and leaving them had been one of the hardest decisions of her life, but a necessary one.

California held memories that she once held dear, ones that now cut like a knife. Because her favorite coffee shop back home was no longer a place she could go when she needed to escape into a book. She couldn't enter the grocery store near her childhood home without looking over her shoulder because she was terrified she would run into *him*.

She was even more terrified when she eventually ran into him – because in her small town it would only be a matter of time – he'd be happy. For her, the pain of the fateful evening still felt so raw, a festering wound too stubborn to heal properly. A wound she could not discuss to even her best friend, despite the fact it had been five years since it happened.

Ofelia shook her head, placing what remained of her dinner on her side table. She would not allow herself to succumb to the sadness haunting her from that day. Not when he didn't give two shits about her and was probably balls deep in whatever body warmed his bed this week.

Fuck, she was doing it again: thinking too hard that she was bound to hurt her own feelings.

Needing a distraction, Ofelia searched the couch for her phone. The copious amounts of pillows and blankets stacked around her like a personal fort seemed good at the time, but now it had eaten her phone.

"Damnit, where did-ah!" She broke her sentence off with a

triumphant yell, raising her phone as if she had just found the holy grail. To her, at least, it was. It provided her a way to see her family and nothing was more important to her.

Scrolling through her contacts, Ofelia hovered over her father's number. She hesitated, wondering whether or not she should call Javier instead. She knew it ultimately wouldn't matter since her father and brother lived at the same house and she would end up talking to her father regardless. She adored the man, but sometimes Ofelia felt that their love only ran surface level. Her father loved her because he was her father and fathers were supposed to love their children. Just as daughters were supposed to love their fathers. It was an easy role that both of them fell into, but provided very little room for anything other than pleasantries.

To hell with it though. After her day, she would be willing to talk to a third cousin, twice removed if that meant she could speak with family.

Ofelia clicked on her father's contact and then pressed the FaceTime button. She watched as her face engulfed her screen, making sure she looked presentable and not like she just had a shitty week dealing with entitled assholes.

It took two rings before her father answered, showing only the top of his head. He sported a new cut, shaved close to his head. He must have dyed his hair recently because there were no longer gray stands weaving throughout the black ones. "*Hola, mija.*"

Despite her earlier uncertainties, Ofelia's eyes stung with tears that she desperately tried to hold back. "Papá." Ofelia smiled widely. "Papá, hold the phone down so I can see you."

"*Qué?*" Her father asked, jostling the phone some before he understood. "Ah, okay. Can you see me now?" He asked, his thick Mexican accent sounding like home. She really needed to go up and visit soon.

"Yes papá, I can see you. How are you? How's work?" She asked. Her father was technically retired but still occasionally took on an odd job and babysat so her younger brother Javier could work. From what Javi told her, Camilia was a full-time job. Much to her dismay, she had only seen her niece through Facetime, but even she knew Javier had his hands full with his spitfire daughter.

"Busy, all day busy. *Ella* is...*cómo se dice salvaje en Inglés?*"

"Wild?"

He nodded, looking very much like a bobblehead as he did so. "*Sí*. Wild. Just like your mother. Scary too when she's angry."

Ofelia laughed at the image of a tiny two-year-old making a grown man cower in fear. Ofelia might have a precarious relationship with her father, but he was a fantastic grandfather to Camilia.

"How are you, my little *maestra*? Are the kids good?" Her father asked and she just shrugged. Ofelia didn't want to get into school.

"Fine. Everything's fine."

Her father nodded, getting distracted with something in the background. Knowing him, some sport was playing. She tried not to let it bother her, but was it too much to ask for five minutes of uninterrupted visiting? She knew they did not have many things in common, but they were still family. That had to count for something.

"Oh hey, don't you have one of your first dance thingies coming up?" He asked and Ofelia did her best not to roll her eyes at his "dance thingie" comment. She had only been going to *cheer competitions* since she was a little girl.

ON AND OFF THE FIELD

"In a few weeks, yeah. I sent you over the dates to all of our competitions. Why?"

"I'd like to come."

Ofelia could not have been more shocked if her dad had burst out into interpretative dancing, complete with a pink tutu and a matching tiara. She was gaping, and almost certain she blacked out for a second because there was no way her father, the man who never made it to a single competition in her life, was suddenly willing to fly thousands of miles to watch her high school team perform. This did not sound like her father at all. Not even a little.

She waited for the *'just kidding* or *got you there!'* But it never came. "You're serious?" She asked, her voice laced with disbelief.

Her father clearly did not realize he successfully broke his daughter with one statement. "Yes I'm serious. Javi said I should go."

She did her best not to deflate after hearing that the only reason he decided to finally come to one of her competitions was because Javi put him up to it. He knew how hard it was for her last year not to have her mother there to support her coaching career. She imagined he spoke at length with her father until he got tired of hearing Javi pester him and just agreed. Still, it was better than nothing.

"O...kay." Ofelia said slowly, allowing him one last chance to back out. When he didn't take it, a hesitant smile began to form on her lips. "Well, wow. Okay, so I'll have Javi help you with tickets. I'll send over information about the hotel. Wow Papá, this is exciting!"

Since moving down to Texas two years ago, none of her family had been able to make it down for a visit. This hurt her in the beginning, but she realized her selfishness. Her brother worked and had a child. It wasn't easy for Javi to do much of anything, much less get time off from work to take the entire family down to Texas. He wasn't in the financial situation to do that and her brother was too stubborn to ask for help.

Stubbornness was definitely a shared family trait.

"Papá, is Javi home from work yet? I want to talk to him, and I'll mention you're interested in coming down to watch the competition." Like he did not already know.

"*Si, mi amor.*" Her father rose from his spot at the table, looking all too eager to pass her off so he could get back to watching whatever game he had on. The screen suddenly went dark as soft and undecipherable mumbles filled the line.

Then a lamp flipped on, illuminating a small bedroom. Javier filled the screen, looking tired and rumpled, as if she had just woken him up from a nap. Before she could apologize, Javi put his finger to his lips in a universal "be quiet" sign. He untangled himself from his bed and only then did Ofelia see a small lump curled up in the blankets.

Camilia.

"Sorry, just got her to bed. Little brat won't sleep in her own bed these days." Javier said, but when he spoke of his little girl, there was nothing but fondness in his voice. It was so beautiful to see her little brother become a father. Camilia had changed him, changed all of them. She also saved Javi after the death of Estella, Camilia's mother.

"She's so big, Javi. How can she be so big when she was so tiny last week?"

Javier laughed. "Shit, I dunno. I ask myself that daily. I feel like I'll be moving her into college next week."

"Oh god, don't say that. Do you know how old I'll be? Forty-three. Forty-fucking-three. I'm not going to be the young, hot auntie anymore."

"I wasn't aware you were the young, hot aunt now." Javi teased.

"First off, *pendejo*, that was rude as hell. And secondly, just because you're somebody's father now doesn't mean I won't kick your ass the next time I see you."

Her very serious threat was meant by a loud snort, followed by laughter. Yup, that definitely didn't help her ego, but it was worth it to hear his laugh. Javi rarely laughed these days. Not since the accident.

"So, what's on your mind? Did you call to threaten me?" Javier asked, his focus back on Ofelia. Typical for him to get straight to the point.

"Not to threaten, but I do have a question. Papá just said he was interested in coming down to my competition this year. He's literally never been. You wouldn't happen to know anything about that, would you?" She stared at him pointedly.

Javi put on his best clueless face and shrugged, though a small smile creased the corner of his lips. He would never outright admit he did something nice for her, but that was all the confirmation she needed. "Any other reason you called?" He asked, clearly not going to answer her.

"I just...missed you. All of my family."

Javi adjusted himself and moved closer to the camera. His eyes bore into Ofelia's, causing her to stir. Damn him. She knew what those eyes were searching for. Breakage. Any signs to indicate that Ofelia was moments away from a full on ugly cry. Even though she was supposed to be the big sister and take care of him, Javi always reversed those roles and did it without complaint.

"Tell me what's wrong." He said, leaving no room for argument.

Ofelia had none. She opened her mouth to speak, but the

only thing that came out was a rather embarrassing whimper. Her warm brown eyes filled with tears. She seriously hated crying, but her emotions needed a release. In retrospect, today hadn't been entirely terrible, but it was the straw that broke the camel's back.

This camel had come to Texas damaged too, so she had already been at a disadvantage.

"Do you think I made a mistake? Leaving town?" She asked, feeling vulnerable and a little silly to finally say the words constantly plaguing her thoughts. "Did I make a rash decision to leave like a coward?"

Javi let out a deep sigh, his face softening at her words. There he went again, being the best damn little brother ever when she knew he was fighting his own demons. Who was she to dump more trauma on him?

"I'm sorry Javi. I shouldn't-"

"You should." He interrupted before she could tell him to just forget about it. "You should come to me and talk about your problems. I'm your brother, Ofi. *Familia*. You know I'm here to listen."

Despite her tears, she couldn't help but let out a weak laugh. "We sound like a scene from a Hallmark channel."

Javi smiled at that and nodded. "Yeah, probably a bit. It's true though. Listen, Ofi. You needed to get out. It wasn't an easy decision, but we all understood why. We wanted to see you happy and if moving to Texas did that for you, we weren't going to stand in your way. It was brave as hell, honestly. Something mamá would have done. You deserve a fresh start."

A fresh start.

That's what she had called it too when she left a little over two years ago. When her life had come to an abrupt stop. She remembered that day vividly, for it felt like an out of body experience. She saw herself in the hotel room, sobbing into her pillow. There were a few others in there with her, mostly family and even his sister. Ofelia remembered *his* sister, Analucia, attempting to comfort her, but she was so lost in her own grief. She snapped at the woman, blaming all of her brother's sins on her.

It wasn't fair and she wasn't proud of her behavior. Analucia didn't deserve her wraith. Her brother Hector did.

"Have you seen him around?" *Is he still hurting or was mine the only heart to break that day?* Was the question Ofelia truly wanted to ask, but she was afraid of the answer.

Javi looked uncomfortable, which only confirmed her suspicions.

So he *had* seen Hector. Why was he so unwilling to talk to her about it? Was it because Hector wasn't alone? Was he with someone else? It had been two years after all, and just because she hadn't dated since the day he left her, didn't mean Hector also stayed single. Did she care if he was dating someone else? Yes...no...fuck she didn't know.

"Yeah, I saw him." Javi finally admitted. "And Analucia a few times. Hector steers clear of me each time he sees me. Which is smart. I swear if I ever get that bastard alone, I'll-"

"Do nothing. You'll do nothing." Ofelia reprimanded. Not out of loyalty to her ex, but out of concern for her brother. "Call him all the dirty names in your mind. Hell, imagine kicking his ass, but under no circumstances will you engage. Do you understand me? He's not worth it. Camilia doesn't need to see that side of her father." Ofelia didn't actually think her brother would lay a hand on Hector...probably. He wasn't a fighter, at least not in that way. He had never been one for petty drama or relish in his own superiority. He was, however, extremely protective and would defend his family. Perhaps not with fist, but if Hector threw the first punch, she doubted her baby brother would just sit there and take the beating.

Despite having her heart ripped out by this man, Ofelia didn't want to see any harm come his way. It was a terrible burden to have such a good conscience.

"Whatever. No hurting that asshole. I'll just glare at him until he spontaneously combusts."

"Seems fair." Ofelia agreed, smiling at her brother.

"Is there anything else on your mind? Or did you call to see my sexy face?"

Ofelia made a wrenching sound, which she was sure made her look like a cat hacking out a hairball. If she were next to her brother, she'd playfully shove him. "No, you dummy. I just had a long day at work so far."

"Evil parents?"

"The evilest!"

"I'm no English teacher like you, Ofi, but even I know that evilest isn't a word."

"Actually it is." Ofelia said, ready to dive into the history of etymology, but Javier pretended to fall asleep. Her useless knowledge on words and their origins never got the proper respect it deserved.

"Anyways," Ofelia continued, her voice raising an octave to get his attention. Javier opened one eye, a smile playing on her brother's lips. "I just called to vent about crazy parents and an asshole coach."

"There was an asshole coach?"

"Yeah. Truthfully he just annoyed me and was being a bit of a jerk. It was just a lousy way to end my day. I probably shouldn't be keeping you any longer though." Ofelia noticed the time at the top of her phone. It was only a quarter past eight, but her brother woke up even earlier than her. His job was pure physical labor. He tried to hide how tired he was, but she had the sneaking suspicion he could fall asleep right now if he tried.

"Give Camilia a big kiss for me and tell her *tía* Ofi loves her so much." Ofelia felt a surge of emotion in her chest, something she always got when speaking about her niece. It was a mixture of regret, longing, and love. Even though she was far away, she wanted Camilia to know she was so important in Ofelia's life. "I love you, Javi. I'll call you soon."

Javi's smile lit up her camera screen. For a brief moment, she could still see the nine-year-old little brother in him that equally annoyed and delighted her. "I love you too, Ofi. I'm just a call away." He winked and then Ofelia was no longer looking at her brother, but the background on her phone.

The ache in her chest eased only a fraction, but it was enough for her to wind down from the day. Getting up, she placed the remainder of her Chinese dinner in the fridge to have for lunch tomorrow, checked her school email once more to make sure nothing urgent awaited her, and finally moved into her bedroom.

Ofelia fell asleep the moment her head hit her pillow, plagued with dreams of a certain hot coach with a bad attitude.

Chapter Five

Sleeping alone was new for Maverick.

He used to have a partner. Now he only had memories of their time together to haunt his dreams. These days Maverick went to sleep alone and woke up alone. There was once a time in his life when he complained he didn't have enough room in bed. Breanna had insisted she needed the middle of the bed, out of fear of rolling over and falling out of bed. Maverick never understood how a grown woman could have problems staying in bed, but he never pushed it.

He grew used to Breanna and her *unique* tendencies long ago. They had grown up together. In elementary, their friendship began, like most childhood friendships do, at recess. Where the other students had cowered at the bottom of the monkey bars, Breanna had been fearless. Each monkey bar she grabbed was like watching someone compete in the junior olympics.

That was all it took for five-year-old Maverick to fall in love.

Of course, his and Breanna's love story didn't start until freshman year of high school. It wasn't until the homecoming dance that Maverick finally got the courage to ask Breanna out. As much as he wanted to say he had game and was smooth with the ladies, Maverick was fairly certain he blacked out when he asked her to be his date. Smooth, he was not.

Even with his piss poor game, Maverick still scored the hottest and smartest girl at school. Their relationship survived high school, moving on to college where he received a full ride to the University of Miami. Breanna agreed to accompany him; she even received her own Volleyball scholarship to the university.

When he was drafted to Chicago, Maverick promised he would make an honest woman out of Breanna, but neither one of them were in a hurry to schedule a date for their wedding. They both agreed the right moment would come eventually.

Except that moment never came.

Looking back, there had been signs. He had just refused to accept them. He didn't acknowledge the way Breanna smiled when she looked at her phone, or the way she started to dress when she went "shopping." No, Maverick could ignore those things as long as the sex was good. Because if the sex was good, then there was no possible way their ten-year relationship was crumbling around them.

He couldn't remember when sex became more of a competition, rather than a form of expression. Or perhaps he did and once again his mind refused to dive any deeper. His brain knew before his heart and tried to protect him for as long as possible.

When the dam finally broke, releasing a flood of secrets and deceit, Maverick lost everything. His life, his future wife, and his career.

So yeah, he was still getting used to sleeping alone. The world spun too fast and Maverick couldn't plant his feet firmly under him.

Rolling over, he reached out blindly into the dark until his hand connected with his phone sitting on his nightstand. He braced himself for the unholy glow his phone cast in the dark before checking the time. It was five in the morning. His body wanted nothing more than to stay in bed, but his mind was alert and functioning on full power. Nothing unsettled him more than being alone with his thoughts. That and the red notification awaiting for him in the corner of his screen indicating he had another voicemail from Breanna.

Over the past few weeks, he had gotten really good at emotional avoidance. Unfortunately, in exchange, he turned into an asshole. Or so people tended to think. Maverick didn't possess the emotional capacity for idle pleasantries and frivolous conversations.

He was tempted to delete this notification along with the numerous other ones she had left for him. Something stopped him this time and curiosity won him over. He clicked on the green icon and it took him into his voicemails. Before he could stop himself, Maverick pressed play and a familiar voice filled the room.

"Maverick. I know you aren't taking my calls, which I get. I'm not even sure if you are listening to these but we have to talk. I don't like how things ended between us and I want to make it right-"

He deleted the voice message immediately. It had been foolish to even indulge himself and for what? To get angry for no goddamn reason? Breanna could want to make it right all she wanted, but it wouldn't change the fact that she not only ended their relationship, but ended his career. Even now he felt his blood begin to boil and knew he needed to get up and use this misplaced energy.

Forcing himself out of bed, Maverick stretched and did his

best to put thoughts of Breanna on the back burner. An early start to the morning wasn't the worst thing. He had spent the weekend being lazy, the least he could do was wake up early on a Monday. For once, he could take a long warm shower without feeling crunched on time. He desperately missed his shower back in his old high rise with its multiple showerheads and settings, but he made do with the new, more traditional shower located at his current residence.

His former manager, Keanon, clearly didn't believe vacation homes should have all the latest updates. People didn't understand what they were missing if they never experienced a deluxe shower. It was heavenly, big enough for at least four people. The amount of times he fucked Breanna against the wall, hearing nothing but the sound of his dick moving inside of her and the breathy little moans she would make right before she-

Fuck.

She always popped back into his mind uninvited. His cock didn't receive the memo they were no longer together because it stood in full attention, hardening against his control. No matter how low he fell in life, he refused to jerk off in the shower with thoughts of his ex.

Fuck that.

Instead, Maverick stood under the shower head, turning the water on as cold as he could bear it. He let the cold water run down his body, watching it pool at his feet as the drain struggled to do its job.

For as long as he could stand, Maverick let the water fall until he trembled from the icy drops. Only then did he reach out and turn off the shower. The one good thing about being a high school coach was that no one gave a shit what he wore to work. When he played professionally, each work outing had an approved outfit, sometimes two, strictly enforced by some unknown assistant tasked to make the team look good.

Funny enough, Maverick was now allowed to wear whatever he wanted. No one looked at him anymore. Not even the tabloids had much to say about him these days. He didn't expect that last one to hurt as much as it did.

Once dressed in clothes he would normally only wear to the gym, Maverick gathered his phone and lunch before heading out the door. He was still early, with some time to spare. At that moment, there was only one thing he desired.

∼

THE SMALL, local coffee shop was located approximately five minutes from the school. It was partially hidden from the road and Maverick only happened to stumble upon the cafe after a sleepless night resulted in a midnight drive to clear his mind. Pecan's Coffee was the only shop in town open twenty-four seven. Maverick had been surprised to see other restless souls taking refuge inside.

Pecan's Coffee always had a steady line of customers, but no drive through. Their motto read, "don't let the little moments pass you by!" Which translated into, come inside and buy your coffee, we don't serve people in cars. As it happens, they were definitely worth getting out of the car for.

Maverick entered the shop, greeted by the warm smell of coffee beans and the soft instrumental jazz humming through the speakers. A few tables were occupied with people, mostly college students desperately trying to finish last minute homework. He was too busy reviewing the day's specials to pay attention to his surroundings.

Maverick collided with a body, tripping over his own large

feet in the process. Instinctually, he reached out to grab the person he ran into before they made contact with the floor. His strong hands fastened around a small waist, bringing a soft body against his chest. The woman's scent hit him, sparking a flame of recognition. He smelled that perfume before. Was it yesterday? It had been on-

"You can let me go now." A haughty voice spoke, breaking his train of thought.

He knew that voice. It was the same voice he thought of last night before he went to bed. Dammit, she was going to think he was following her or something.

Maverick looked down in his arms, only to find a very perturbed woman staring back at him. Ms. Mendez had the stern teacher expression down perfectly. He felt like a student who'd just been disciplined for being in the wrong place at the wrong time.

When he didn't make an effort to move, Ms. Mendez pushed at his chest, putting distance between them. From her expression, Maverick noticed she was just as flustered as him. He watched as she wrapped her arms around herself, forming a protective barrier between the two of them. Their collision caused quite a stir; a few people looked up in annoyance, blaming him for the disruption to whatever mundane task they were working on. Others looked on, wondering if they should intervene.

The last thing he needed was unwanted attention. Maverick was no celebrity, but his name held a new reputation from his abrupt dismissal from baseball. The headlines would read "Former MLB player harasses young woman at local coffee shop." His name would be splattered all over disreputable news outlets again.

He needed to placate the few onlookers. He plastered on

his camera worthy smile, the same one he wore before any press conference or meet and greet with fans. It seemed to work; the few still staring at him nodded in return before going back to their coffee. The only person still glaring at him now was Ms. Mendez.

Realizing he still hadn't addressed her, Maverick promptly said, "I'm sorry. I didn't see you there."

She snorted, and he'd be damned if that wasn't the cutest sound he'd ever heard. "Clearly. I didn't suspect you run into people out of fun. Then again, judging by your behavior last time, I wouldn't put it past you."

She had sass. He liked a girl who could dish it out just as well as she took it...in more ways than one. Not that Maverick was thinking about this woman like that. No, absolutely not.

"Yeah, about that," he chuckled softly, running a hand down the back of his fade. "I need to apologize again. I was out of line. The baseball fields weren't ready for practice and I didn't want my guys missing out on another practice. I didn't realize the gym was a hot commodity."

"It is. I sat through all the calendar meetings battling the athletics department, band, and drama club for time in the gym. You threw me off. I didn't appreciate how you talked to me in front of my squad."

By squad, he suspected she meant her cheerleaders. That was fair, he hadn't exactly been quiet or kind when he addressed her. He knew what it was like to feel out of control of a situation. He hated that he made her feel that way, but also had it been that difficult to share the gym with him? Her squad wasn't exactly large and the gym had ample space to accommodate them both.

"Then I should probably warn you, I'm going to be in the gym again this week."

Shocked silence followed his breaking news. Her slightly parted lips soon pressed into a thin line as her expression changed to full on anger. It was as if he had just admitted to killing her sweet grandmother rather than admitting he'd be using half her gym on one of her scheduled gym days. If he wasn't gearing up for an earful, he might have thought her passion for her sport was extremely alluring.

"But you just apologized for how you acted the last time you stole my gym!"

"I did and I am. But that still doesn't change the fact that I need the workout equipment to get my boys in shape. They've been sitting pretty for too long."

"Can't you just have your team run around your field for exercise?"

Maverick did his best to hold back his laughter. He didn't think she would appreciate that right now. "I need weights. Running is only half the workout."

Ofelia knuckles whitened around her cup, dangerously close to snapping the styrofoam in two. Between her manicured nails, Maverick could make out a word written on the cup in black sharpie. *Ofelia*. It had to be her first name. Ofelia Mendez, the teacher who wanted to bury him in grievances. Fortunately if things worked out like he wanted, he wouldn't be around long enough to receive them.

More people came through the door, exactly where Maverick and Ofelia stood in their silent battle. He was getting more glares from the coffee addicts and he knew from personal experience that nothing good came from getting between a person and their caffeine for the day.

"If it helps at all, we will only be there until six on Wednesday. You say you have the gym until seven? That's one glorious hour without us." He tried to raise his brow in a teasing gesture, but it did not land well with her.

Ofelia bristled with annoyance. It was clear she had not wanted to negotiate her time in the gym at this godforsaken hour. Maverick couldn't blame her. Neither one of them had their coffee yet.

"Just make sure to stick to your side of the gym and don't interfere with my practice. We have competition coming up and my squad needs to focus." She relented.

"Wouldn't dream of messing that up for you, coach." He winked and swore she saw her tremble. "Have a good day, Ms. Mendez. I look forward to avoiding you in the gym tomorrow."

Ofelia mumbled something unintelligible under her breath, but Maverick was pretty certain it was not flattery at his expense. She stormed past him, her damn hair hitting his shoulder as she left the building.

He was fairly certain that was strike two for him. Without another word, Maverick got his coffee and headed out to another full day of coaching.

Chapter Six

It was a rare day in public education when every single student actively paid attention, but one swift glance around the room confirmed just that. Each group formed a circle and was passionately discussing *Fahrenheit 451*. Ofelia's little teacher's heart swelled with pride. English wasn't everyone's favorite subject, but the times she managed to enrapture her students made her feel successful. It proved that her efforts weren't fruitless after all.

Specifically for her English III class. Her students were a diverse group, each ranging in their learning abilities and interests. They weren't easily won over and getting them to talk proved nearly impossible. Who would have thought *Fahrenheit 451* would be the solution to all her problems? Her dystopian unit was one of her favorites; she looked forward to it every year.

Every year this book was a mild success. Her students seemed to like it and the themes sparked conversations, which is why she kept the book in her curriculum. However, she never received a reaction quite like this and from a typically silent class, nonetheless! Damn, she actually felt like a good teacher.

"The bell is about to ring." Ofelia hollered over the chorus of voices to get their attention. "We are going to have to finish up tomorrow." she grinned, causing the class to groan. Only this time they complained because they didn't want to stop.

"Mrs. Mendez! You can't have a book end like that!" A student called from the back of the room.

The bell rang just as she said, signaling the end of class. "Alright everyone, go ahead and leave your books on your desk. We will continue next class." Ofelia called out over the rumpling of papers being squished into already full backpacks and the scrapes of chairs on the worn off-white vinyl flooring. Most students rushed past her, eager to visit with their friends for a brief moment in the hallway. A few others lingered behind to ask questions or to talk about theories.

When the last student finally left, Ofelia felt as if she could float. She did that! She made her students care about what they were learning. If only the evil Mrs. Davis could see her now.

Ha! Suck it, you witch!

Ofelia took a seat behind her desk, surveying her classroom. From her assessment, all books were accounted for and her room wasn't a complete mess. She looked over at her computer, happy to see that no emails were awaiting her either. Yes, today would be a good day, she thought to herself, reaching for her mocha. Her coffee had cooled to room temperature, but she was still milking the last few drops.

Her mind wandered back to the strange encounter with Maverick this morning. She was still bitter about it, but had he seemed nervous to talk to her? Of course not. Men like Maverick didn't get nervous around women. He held himself

ON AND OFF THE FIELD

like a man used to getting what he wanted. He knew he looked good and used that to his advantage.

"Ofelia?" A familiar voice called out, startling her out of her chair. Ofelia had been so immersed in her own thoughts that she hadn't heard her principal, Colbie, walk in.

"Wow, really? Usually the keys are a dead giveaway." Colbie laughed, gesturing to her jostling key ring that held far too many than any normal human should ever need. "Sorry about that. I wanted to touch base with you about Mrs. Davis."

No, no, no, no. Ofelia groaned inwardly because her day had been going so well! If you discounted the Maverick situation, that is. She had been riding a teaching high, but just the sound of that woman's name sent her falling fast into the ground. Today's lesson almost made her forget about Mrs. Davis's claim of targeting her son.

Colbie took her earpiece off, disconnecting her radio. "I need people to stop needing me for two seconds." She said and planted herself down in the seat in front of her. To say that Ofelia's heart beat a little faster than normal would be an understatement. As much as she liked Colbie, being around a principal was still an intimidating experience.

I'm not in her office. She is in my classroom. Completely different. Normal even. Her brain attempted to rationalize.

"Anyway, I thought I would come by rather than say this all in an email. I got a call from Mrs. Davis." Colbie started as Ofelia's heart sank to the floor. Something in her expression must have alerted Colbie to her dread, and she quickly hurried on. "I know how much of a hassle she's been this year. I also know what type of teacher and person you are."

"Did she demand my head on a stake?" That was the only option that would remotely satisfy that woman.

Colbie's hearty laugh echoed around the room. "Get in

line, Mendez. There's a whole fleet of poor saps ahead of you." Well, at least she wouldn't be headless alone. "No, I think I talked her off a cliff, mostly. I informed her that you were doing your job and notifying home when a problem arises, just as you do for any student. I also let her know how much progress he's made in your class."

"Why do I feel like there's a but at the end of this sentence?" Ofelia asked, knowing Mrs. Davis wouldn't drop something so easily.

"Fantastic question. I think it's time for some restorative practices. Now hear me out-" Colbie said, putting her hands up to stop Ofelia's eyes from rolling. "It wouldn't hurt to try to restore the relationship between you and the Davises. I'm aware that you are not at fault here, but I'm hoping you and I can be the bigger person in this situation."

Ofelia would rather do anything else, but she had to be willing to give this shattered relationship one last ditch effort. "Okay. Do you have any suggestions? Because I'm honestly at a loss of what I can do at this point."

"Actually, I do." Colbie grinned. She got the distinct impression she would not like whatever Colbie had planned. "I hope you don't have plans tonight because I have the perfect solution to your Mrs. Davis troubles."

As Colbie told Ofelia what she needed to do, she knew tonight would test her very soul.

Universe, you son of a bitch.

∼

OFELIA STOOD in the school's parking lot, measuring the distance between her car and the baseball field. Maybe if she walked at a snail's pace, she'd make it just in time to see only the last inning. No one could say she wasn't there because she had undeniable proof her car was parked, and her body was near-*ish* the fields. That had to count for something.

There was the slight problem of her cheerleaders waiting for her to arrive and Willow doing her best to corral a bunch of teenagers. Football games were a given for cheerleaders, but baseball? What the hell were they supposed to do at a baseball game? Wave their poms in the air until someone in the crowd got fed up and threw lukewarm hot dogs at them?

She understood why Colbie suggested Ofelia attend tonight's game along with her squad, but it didn't mean she was happy about it. For one, Dustin was on the team, and she wasn't mentally prepared to see Mrs. Davis. Secondly, the cheer moms were finally showing their claws and questioning Ofelia's coaching abilities and choices about tonight's event. Honestly, she was surprised it had taken this long for any of the cheer moms to start complaining about her.

She could do this. She needed to do this. Colbie assured her this would bring in more school spirit and wasn't that what she wanted? The alternative meant dealing with Mrs. Davis' absurdities all year. At this point, she was willing to try just about anything to get the woman off her back.

With that in mind, Ofelia made her way towards the bleachers. Dozens of people were already seated, talking animatedly amongst their family and friends. A few younger kids stood by the dugout on their tiptoes, trying to get the attention of the baseball players. The other team, a high school from about thirty minutes away, warmed up on the field, throwing balls back and forth.

In the middle of it all sat her squad, all tightly pressed together at the top of the bleachers.

After Colbie left, Ofelia immediately called Willow to help

gather her cheerleaders. Willow took it as far to make sure they stayed in her classroom after school until the game started so Ofelia could attend her department chair meeting.

Willow spotted her first and sighed in relief. "Thank goodness you're here! Get up here, now." Willow waved her arms frantically, gesturing for Ofelia to get her ass up the bleachers.

Ofelia picked the wrong day to wear her brown, heeled boots. Her feet screamed in protest with each clunk of her heel as she maneuvered around families and various other obstacles. The last thing she needed was to take a header directly into the bleachers. There would be no living that down.

Willow reached for her at the last step and pulled her up. Her friend wore her hair in a twisted knot atop her head, a telltale sign she entered panic mode. From what she could see, all her cheerleaders were here, albeit looking aggravated, no pissed off parents stood nearby, and no one was bleeding. So what was the problem?

Judging by the look on her best friend's face, Ofelia prepared for the worst. But Willow just gestured wildly at her squad, as if she should have picked up on this problem too.

"Words, Willow. I need you to use your words." She loved her friend dearly, but sometimes it felt as if she were communicating with a toddler.

"You don't see it? How do you not see it? Look at them!" Willow gestured in the general direction of the squad. "Their clothes! I remembered where you keep the uniforms in the gym, but when I checked they weren't there."

"Okay, first breathe." Ofelia said, going into cheer coach mode. As far as problems went, this hardly qualified. "I only keep the uniforms in the gym at the beginning of school. The squad all have their uniforms, but I didn't think it necessary to dress out. We didn't know we'd be asked to come and support the baseball guys tonight. You managed to get everyone in a McKinley High shirt, which is uniform enough."

"Uh, Ms. Mendez? What is it that we are doing here?" Ofelia looked past Willow to see Devin leaning forward. He sat at the end of the bench, next to Tony and Lacey. Tony looked to be the only one of her cheerleaders excited to be here. He spoke to another cheerleader, no doubt ranking the hotness of the baseball players.

"We are here to support our team! That's why we're here!" She pushed the enthusiasm a little too much, but she needed them to buy in.

"Okay, but why?" This time Lacey spoke, her cheer caption. If Ofelia could get her on board, she knew Lacey would get the others to participate. "We've never cheered at a baseball game before. Is that even a thing? This definitely isn't a thing."

"Of course it's a thing! We're making it a thing. All I'm asking is for you to cheer when they hit the ball and run the little...squares." Ofelia encouraged, getting snickers in return.

"Oh no. You did NOT just say little squares. Ms. M, seriously? Do you even know baseball?" Nadine, one of her new freshmen, giggled.

It was blatantly obvious that Ofelia knew very little about baseball. In her defense, growing up her house only had two sports. Soccer and cheerleading. Watching the former was a religion. The TV was on nonstop during soccer season. Her father and brother tolerated cheerleading because it meant a great deal to Ofelia and her mother.

Baseball was rarely, if ever, on at the Mendez house.

"Apparently I don't. I need everyone to be my hype squad. When it seems appropriate, cheer loudly for our players. Can you do that? I'm not above bribing you with donuts."

"Donuts?" Tony grinned, tearing himself away from his

conversation. "I will do anything for donuts."

"Jesus Tony. You're so weird." Lacey rolled her eyes. There was no real malice behind her words, everyone knew Tony was her best friend. "Fine, Ms. Mendez. It's only because we love you and donuts."

"Pretend I'm hugging all of you really tightly right now. I love you!" Ofelia beamed, giving her squad a dorky thumbs up before Willow pulled her down into the open seat next to her. In a matter of minutes, the bleachers filled with people. A dozen or so more brought their own chairs, propping them up in the grass, while more seemed content to stand.

"Why are there so many people here? Is this normal?"

Willow gave Ofelia a strange look. "Sweetie, do you think I frequent boys' baseball games? Because I don't. I'm only here because my best friend needed help."

"You owe me, by the way." Willow continued, giving her a pointed look. Her wild red hair, stacked high upon her head, illuminated by the bright lights of the field, giving her fire goddess vibes. "But I suspect they're here because of the new coach."

"New coach...you mean Maverick?" She asked, unable to keep the confusion out of her voice. Why in the world would so many people want to show up to a high school game to see a coach?

From her spot in the bleachers, Ofelia squinted to make out the faint shadow of Maverick. If the surplus of fans in the audience concerned him, he did a great job of concealing it. In fact, Maverick wasn't paying the crowd any mind at all. He stood in deep conversations with his players, rubbing his shadow of a beard, and Ofelia couldn't help but admire him in his coaching uniform.

Uniform was a loose term for what he wore. He wore slim

fit pants, the color reminding her of a dusty desert. His black top stretched across his chest in a sinful manner, doing little to hide the chiseled muscles laying underneath. McKinley High Baseball was embroidered into his polo, complete with a matching hat.

This man was the definition of delicious. If he were ice cream – and not her biggest rival at the moment – she'd have her tongue all over his-

"Did you hear what I said? Are you paying attention to me?" Willow's voice cut through her scandalous thoughts. She flushed with unexpected heat, and she silently cursed her body for betraying her. There was no other reason for this lust other than she had not been with a man for two years, her body ached for touch. Her lady boner seriously needed to get a hold of itself *now*.

Crossing her right leg over her left, she smiled sheepishly at her best friend. "Sorry, my mind is all over the dam-dang place."

"You can say damn, Mrs. M. It's a damn good word!" Tony piped up from behind her, causing her to jump. She hadn't seen him move. "Sorry - sorry I'm not listening! Carry on!" He grinned before pushing past them to talk to a few other cheer-leaders.

"I said that I heard some hot gossip about our new baseball coach. I told you that eating in the teacher lounge pays off occasionally. They hold nothing back in there." Willow laughed and then pointed a slender finger at Maverick. Ofelia leaned in, like they were about to share a secret. "Apparently the new coach used to be a professional baseball player. Up until recently. But people are saying he got kicked off the team. Or banned...I don't remember the correct terminology, but you get my point."

Despite Willow's serious words, Ofelia couldn't hold back a

laugh. The news was absurd! Maverick? A baseball player? Or, rather, a former baseball player? Because according to the rumors, he no longer played professionally. Willow did not appear amused by Ofelia's outburst and narrowed her eyes slightly. "Laugh all you want, but it's true. Get out your phone and look it up. Actually, here."

Instead of waiting for her to take her phone out from her purse, Willow thrusts her bright yellow one into Ofelia's lap. With one of her rainbow nails, Willow tapped on the phone screen, gesturing for her to hurry up.

"Fine, fine." Ofelia acquiesced. "What do I look up? Also, this feels a little creepy. He's literally right down there."

"So? You think his Spidey-Sense will start tingling, and he'll run up here to confiscate my phone? Just like, google his name. Maverick...uh, I don't know his last name."

"Wilson." Ofelia said automatically, earning a raised brow from Willow. "I only know because he was a bit of an ass-hat yesterday when he took over my gym."

"Hold up. What?!" Willow's raised voice stirred unwanted attention. "He was an ass-hat? Did he apologize? Why am I just hearing about this? Oh my god, are you keeping things from me? You're keeping things from me. I'm shaking right now."

God, if anyone ever missed their calling, it was Willow. With her constant display of dramatics, she could have pursued a career in acting. After all, Willow never got upset with her or jealous when Ofelia forgot to share something. She liked making a scene; this outburst was purely theatrical.

"Would you keep it down? Yes, he kinda apologized at the coffee shop I ran into him at. Right before he told me he'd be using my gym again. That's it, nothing exciting, so you see why I didn't tell you. I honestly forgot all about it!"

Okay, that was technically a lie. Every moment her brain

wasn't in teaching mode, it switched over to the Maverick station. But that was not something she was willing to tell Willow...or anyone for that matter.

The answer placated Willow, and she nodded, giving Ofelia the opportunity to pick up her friend's phone. She knew the passcode by heart and unlocked the phone, only to be greeted by a cute picture of Willow and her husband, Karl. What disturbed her though were the number of red notifications clogging every app. Ofelia would have a heart attack if her phone had so many messages, emails, and voicemails she needed to catch up on.

Ignoring the clutter for now, Ofelia touched the internet app, pulling up the search bar. Her fingers hesitated over the keyboards as she mulled over what she should do. It felt like an invasion of privacy to search up details about a person, especially when they were a few yards in front of her. If what Willow said was true though, would it really be an invasion of privacy if his business was on the internet for anyone to see?

Her curiosity won out and Ofelia quickly typed in Maverick's name and pressed enter. She watched impatiently as the blue bar slowly loaded. And loaded. And loaded.

"Ugh, Willow, your cell service sucks." She held it up above her head as if the cellphone gods would cast their light upon her, giving her the 5G she rightfully deserved.

What felt like an eternity later, the screen finally lit up with unfavorable news articles and pictures. "Aha!" She brought the phone back down and quickly scanned the first page. Headline after headline greeted her.

He's Out! Former MLB Player Hangs Up Bat
Maverick Wilson: What Went Wrong?
Banned in His Prime: What's Next for Chicago Baseball Player?

More of the same articles came up, some with small pictures of Maverick decked out in his Chicago uniform smiling at an invisible audience. Others showed a stern looking Maverick in dark clothing, eyes black with malice. Yet there was also sadness behind his expression, if one stared long enough. This was the man she was familiar with, the man she had met just a day ago in the gym, who used his dickish behavior as a shield.

What surprised her most is that none of the articles listed the same reason for his ban. Some said it involved an altercation between him and his coach, going as far as obtaining statements from said coach's publicist. One claimed Maverick went berserk after his fiancée broke up with him that he destroyed an entire locker room, accidentally hurting teammates in the process. The only common denominator in the articles mentioned the ongoing investigations into this incident.

"Holy shit." Ofelia whispered once she closed out the last article. "Have you read some of these?"

Willow nodded, tucking a strand of hair that came undone from her bun. "I did. Yesterday, after one of the math teachers mentioned it. Turns out, a few parents made a stink about it and complained to Colbie. I think she listened to appease them, but there's no reason he can't be coaching. No legal reasons anyway. Besides, I think he is winning over parents by the looks of this crowd."

Ofelia swore the crowd had nearly doubled in size since she had started diving into the articles over Maverick. She didn't know what to make of the situation. It explained why he was such an ass to her the other day, though it did not excuse his behavior. She would be wound tight too if she had to deal with the details of her life plastered all over the internet.

"This is a lot to take in. It's also making me hungry. How

bad do you think the concession line is right about now?" Judging by the size of this crowd, she assumed the line would be astronomical.

"The game is about to start, so it's probably dying down. Will you get me a sausage wrap? Thanks." Willow smiled, giving her air kisses. "Oh, and a diet coke? I need caffeine if we're staying here for the next few hours. I'll save your spot!"

Ofelia nodded, giving final instructions to her squad, reminding them to cheer energetically when the game began and to make sure they enunciated their words. Nothing worse than a cheer team that sounded like dying cows.

Weaving through the wall of people had not been one of her best moments, but she managed to reach the bottom without tripping or falling to her immediate death. She turned back to give Willow a thumbs up before making her way to the concession stand. Willow had been right. The line wasn't wrapped around the field as she initially pictured. Only half a dozen people stood in front of her, all on their cellphones.

Ofelia took her place at the back of the line, reading over what they offered...which wasn't much. Luckily, they had Willow's sausage wrap. There was nothing worse than a hungry Willow. She needed to keep her friend fed for both of their sanities.

As Ofelia looked over the menu, she felt someone come up behind her. She didn't think anything of it until she heard a long exhale with a voice that could curdle milk. "Ms. Mendez, funny you should be here, of all places."

Oh fuck. Oh no, no, no. Think happy thoughts. Puppies. Rainbows. Unicorns.

When Ofelia turned around, she wore her best 'I'm Totally Not Afraid Of You' expression and the biggest fake smile she could muster. "Hi, Mrs. Davis! How are you?"

Chapter Seven

There were a lot of damn people.

You would think he'd be used to the crowd by now, but Maverick felt each set of eyes on him, heard every hushed whisper said between friends, and he couldn't shake the feeling of multiple phone cameras pointing directly at him.

He schooled his face into the most neutral expression he could produce, but if anyone looked close enough, they could see the cracks in his armor. Clenched fists. Stiff shoulders. Eyes that couldn't focus on one thing for longer than a few seconds. The evidence was right under everyone's noses; they just had to care enough to look.

"I've never seen so many damn people." A short, stout man named Benny Sanders said, working his way over to Maverick.

When told he would be given a coaching assistant, Maverick expected someone less...Danny Devito-esque. Benny barely reached Maverick's chest, so he had to look down when they spoke. Benny was older than Maverick by at least twenty-years, meaning Benny pushed fifty. He was balding, with small tufts of salt and pepper hair on the sides of his head. His tiny legs made it hard to keep up with the baseball players and Maverick couldn't help but imagine a waddling penguin amongst sea lions.

What Benny lacked in athletic ability, he made up in spirit. He never once balked at a single task given to him, even when it was clear he struggled. He was the first to cheer on the team and made sure each victory, however small, was celebrated. Ironically, Maverick supposed they made a good team. He was the rules, tactic, and leader, while Benny provided encouragement and...that was about it. Still, it worked.

"I take it this isn't a normal Tuesday night crowd?" Maverick asked, though he already knew the answer.

Benny snorted. "Are you kidding me? We can barely fill up a third of the bleachers. Now there's not a single spot open and people are spread out across the grass. They are here because of you."

"Yeah, that's what I was afraid you'd say."

But Benny had stopped listening to him, far too enthralled by the size of the crowd to hear what Maverick had to say. Another stark reminder people cared less about what he said and focused more on what he could offer. Apparently Maverick offered a big ass crowd.

For the first time that night, he let himself take in the crowd, never lingering on one face for long before he moved on to the next. It took him a moment to realize he was looking for someone. His damn brain couldn't shake off his earlier encounter with Ofelia at the coffee shop and the dreaded practice they'd have to endure together. It did not seem rational, but his mind flipped through many things right before a game.

Just as that thought crossed his mind, Maverick caught a glimpse of two people walking back from the concession stand.

He swiveled his attention back, noticing one middle-aged woman and a familiar younger woman.

Ofelia.

Maverick puffed out his chest like a damn peacock attempting to lure in potential mates. The sight of Ofelia both excited and terrified him. It was like he wanted to impress her, but he didn't understand why. They'd had nothing but complicated encounters since their gym run in.

Ofelia didn't seem to notice him staring. She was locked into an intense conversation with the older woman. Maverick thought she might be one of his player's mothers, but he wasn't sure. He had not been formally introduced to the parents and hadn't made it a priority to remedy that.

Ofelia, to her credit, looked engaged in the conversation. She nodded along with whatever the woman said, but her smile was set in a thin line. She looked uncomfortable, eyes darting around, as if looking to make a swift exit.

"Hey, Benny." Maverick called, nudging his assistant in the shoulder. Benny had been with the school district for twenty years which resulted in making many friends in the community. If anyone would know who Ofelia was talking to, it would be Benny.

"Yeah? What is it?"

Maverick tilted his head up and gestured to Benny's right where Ofelia rounded the dugout to head back towards the bleachers. "Do you know who that is?" Benny had been in the district for years and lived in the town even longer than that, if anyone would know, it would be him.

"Ofelia Mendez? Yeah, she's the Eng-"

"No, not her." Maverick did his best to hide his annoyance. "The woman next to Ofelia. Do you know who that is?"

Benny squinted his eyes and took off his hat, as if that

would make him see any better. "Oh yeah." He grimaced. "That is Cheryl Davis. Dustin's mother. She's a *real* Karen, that one."

"Karen?"

"Yeah, you know, a 'let me speak to the manager' type of person. An 'I'm holier than thou' type of person. A-"

"Yeah, I got the idea." Maverick interrupted before Benny went on. "Is she friends with Ofelia?"

"Ha! Friends!" Benny barked out a laugh but Maverick couldn't see the humor. "Sure, they are as friendly as the Starks and Lannisters. That's a *Game of Thrones* reference, by the way. Which is to say, no they aren't friends. But hey, no bloodshed between them yet. That's a good thing!"

Maverick should have left it alone. He didn't know Ofelia well enough to insert himself into the situation. Not to mention he was minutes away from the start of the game. His players were finishing their warm up and slowly trickling into the dugout. He needed to get himself ready for the game, which was the logical thing to do.

But he had not been logical a day in his damn life, so why start now?

"Hey, make sure the guys read the lineup. Have the first three get their helmets and bats. I'll be right back." Without waiting for a response, Maverick found himself jogging towards the fence nearest first base. *Stupid, this is stupid!* The rational part of his brain chanted like a mantra, over and over again. He pretended like he couldn't hear it as he approached the fence.

The tone of the crowd shifted, changing from curiosity to excitement with Maverick within speaking distance. A few tried to grab his attention, but he ignored their calls. Especially when the one person he wanted to talk to turned around and saw him. Ofelia's eyes widened in surprise.

"I'm just saying it's extremely odd that you happen to show

up to Dustin's game, a day after our phone call. I have a right to be concerned. You-"

"Excuse me," Maverick spoke confidently, falling easily back into an old role. Mrs. Davis's attention snapped to the side, an angry retort on the tip of her tongue until she saw who spoke. It was almost comical to watch such an angry woman turn into a gaping fish, moving her lips but no sound coming out. "I'm sorry for interrupting. I wanted to make sure I got the chance to thank Ms. Mendez."

It was Ofelia's turn to gape. "You...what?"

He had no idea what he was saying or doing, but he also didn't want to give Mrs. Davis any other opportunities to berate Ofelia. Benny hadn't been the first person to warn him about Mrs. Davis' helicopter mom tendencies. He hoped she would play along.

"I said I wanted to thank you." He reiterated, staring her down. He willed his eyes to speak what his mouth could not. *I'm trying to save you, go along with it!* "For making sure all my guys had water before the game." It was the only thing that came to his mind. He had watched her walk back from the concession stand, which inspired his lie.

Ofelia didn't answer for a second, her eyes moving back and forth between Mrs. Davis and him. If she didn't speak soon, she would make them both look like idiots. "I uhm," She started, her hazel eyes finding Maverick's dark one. "Right, yes, yes of course. It was my pleasure."

Smart girl.

"And thank you for showing up to support the team. I know you probably have a family who needs your attention."

Shit. It never occurred to Maverick that Ofelia might have a family. Did she have a boyfriend? A husband? No...not husband. He didn't see a ring on her finger. That still didn't mean she was single.

But the slight wince from Ofelia, as if he had physically struck her, told him all he needed to know. She was alone. Like him. A ghost of a smirk crossed his lips. There was absolutely no reason for him to be this pleased about this new discovery, but he was.

"It's really not a problem." Ofelia smiled, recovering from earlier words. "My cheerleaders are here to pump up the crowd and show their support?"

Mrs. Davis had been surprisingly silent throughout the exchange. It could be all in Maverick's head, but he swore he caught her looking at Ofelia with a newfound respect. He blinked and the look vanished, replaced with a frown. "Seems out of place for cheerleaders to come to a game."

Shit. He hadn't thought about that, but Mrs. Davis was right. Baseball didn't have cheerleaders. They had mascots that would occasionally pump up the crowd, but that was the extent of their cheer section.

Luckily Ofelia's brain worked faster than his because she recovered faster. "No, it's definitely unique, but we want all of our student athletes to know their peers and teachers support them."

All Maverick could do was nod his head like a lifeless bobblehead.

Mrs. Davis eyed them both, sizing them up. They apparently passed her inspection because she nodded and said, "Yes, very sweet of you. Let's hope this new streak of honorable deeds remains. Good luck coach Wilson; us booster club moms are rooting for you."

With that, Mrs. Davis walked away, towards a group of women that all shared the same haughty expression and haircut. No doubt they would dive into gossip the moment Mrs. Davis arrived. When she was out of ear shot, Ofelia mouthed "Why?" Which was a fair question. He had gone out of his way to help a stranger. No matter that he thought of her constantly since meeting, Ofelia was still a stranger to him.

"Payment for the gym." He winked, watching her roll her eyes at him, but he didn't miss the small smile she tried to hide. She turned from his gaze before he could properly commit that image to memory, climbing back up the bleachers and straight towards a red-headed woman.

"Mav!" Benny screeched, drawing Maverick's attention away. "Let's go. Game is starting!"

Knowing Ofelia was in the crowd, a new swagger appeared in Maverick's walk to third base. His cocky demeanor stayed firmly in place throughout the entire game, even when his team was down in the 5th inning.

The excitement of the crowd was palpable during the 6th inning, with bases loaded. Maverick assigned a senior as his clean up batter, knowing this player had a reputation for his home runs. Just as expected, the senior hit the first ball out of the park, earning the team's first grand slam of the season.

During the 7th inning, the opposing team wasn't able to bring any runners home, ending Maverick's first game in a victory. Mckinley's first victory in the past few years.

After his team stormed the field, jumping up and down like a group of overly caffeinated toddlers, their attention moved to Maverick. Two dozen teenage boys sprinted in his direction. There was no escape. Maverick had no other choice but to let it happen. Somehow Benny got swept up in the tsunami of teenagers and was half dragged, half carried towards Maverick. He had never seen someone so happy being manhandled.

In a matter of seconds, twenty-four bodies crashed against him, nearly knocking him down onto the golden dirt of the field. He didn't even need to move his body, the movement of his team propelled him off the ground as they jumped in celebration. It was like they had just won a war, rather than a high school baseball game. It made him grin like a fool.

The celebration continued off the field. The moment he got away from his team, their parents struck. He couldn't help but notice that in front of the parent line, was his apparent new best friend, Mrs. Davis. A foul ball must have hit her square in the head, changing her entire personality. It took him closing his truck door for Mrs. Davis and her son, Dustin, to finally leave him alone.

For the first time in a long time, Maverick felt happy.

∼

MAVERICK DIDN'T RETURN HOME until close to midnight. After their victory his entire team stormed the field.

Flashbacks of his time with his former team plagued his thoughts, reminding him he too once had friends as close as family who celebrated every victory and mourned each loss with. Very few relationships came close to that of a well-functioning team. It took every player and every coach to create an atmosphere where everyone felt valued and appreciated, no matter how small their role.

Maverick fucking did that.

He took a group of a few dozen dysfunctional boys in a matter of weeks, and he made them a damn team. They weren't perfect, but their strengths outweighed their deficits. Their first game put things into perspective for Maverick. He now knew they needed to work on infield plays and batting practice. Despite this, his guys played hard, and it paid off in the end.

By the time he stumbled into his rental, Maverick's adrenaline died down. He took the fastest shower known to man, mostly, so he could scrub sweat and dirt off his body before falling face first into his bed. He didn't even bother getting dressed first. The moment his head hit the pillow, he was out in a dreamless, blissful sleep.

Until his phone rang early the next morning. He apparently remembered to put it on the charger but neglected to silence the damn ringer. Before he reached it, the ringing cut off abruptly, and he sighed in relief. He could get a few more moments of uninterrupted sle-

Riiingggg. Riiinggg.

Dammit. Why he ever thought an old-fashioned ring tone would ever be soothing or pleasant was beyond him. He flopped around ungracefully until his naked body unwound from the blanket burrito. Once he freed his hand, Maverick reached for his phone. His annoyance from being awoken unexpectedly went away when he noticed the caller. A new emotion took its place, and his heart began to race in anticipation. "Hello?" He answered, holding his breath.

"Mav! How are you, bro?" Keanon's overly jovial tone came across his speaker.

Maverick released his hold on his breath and sighed. Trust Keanon not to check the goddamn time before he called. "Exhausted. It's six o'clock in the morning. Do you not own any damn clocks? I know your lame-ass has an Apple watch. I was there when you bought it."

"I always love catching you in a good mood, but to answer your question, yes. I know it's early, but don't you work today? Teaching the youngins."

"Not until nine."

"Oh." Keanon paused, papers shuffling filled the line. No doubt his friend and former agent had printed out the school's bell schedule and was now confirming Maverick's words. "Oh, I see that. My bad, man. I just wanted to make sure I caught you before you went off to work. I have some news about your case."

And there it was. The reason Maverick's anxiety spiked the moment he saw Keanon's name flash across his phone screen. He knew Keanon referred to the appeal. Before Maverick left – more like fled – Chicago, Keanon agreed to help him overturn the ban. Maverick hadn't put too much stock in it, but his friend was adamant he could find someone to help plead his case. Keanon was the only person who knew the entire story and wholeheartedly believed his removal from the MLB was wrongfully sentenced.

Now after months of radio silence, Keanon had information, but was Maverick ready to hear it? Did he *want* to? A few months ago, he would've jumped on the chance of any news about the future of his career, but now? Perhaps not knowing made him believe in a future. If he got a definitive answer, there was the potential of him realizing baseball would never be something he'd get back to. He would forever be a disgraced household name.

But if there was a chance that someone would take his case, where did that leave him? Would he be investing in a fruitless journey where all that waited on the other end proved more disappointing? There was always the alternative, which was the possibility of winning the case. He would have his old life back.

"Mav? Are you there?" Keanon asked, sounding like this wasn't the first time he called for him. Maverick had been too distracted with his own thoughts to realize his friend continued to speak.

"Yeah, sorry. What'd you say?"

"Remember that lawyer I was trying to contact? The one who has taken on many professional athlete cases and has a reputation of being an overall badass?"

Keanon had mentioned a lawyer by the name of Lloyd Gilmore who specialized in sports law. Out of desperation one night, Maverick googled his name and found a case from ten years ago where he defended a baseball player who had been banned for allegedly violating his contract. The details of the article were fuzzy, probably because Maverick had been highly intoxicated while reading it, but he remembered Gilmore had found a loophole, proving the player in question did not violate any parts of his contract.

Maverick was under no delusions that his case would be simple, though. Still, his curiosity got the best of him, and he answered. "Yeah, Gilmore. What about him?"

"I just got a call from his secretary. I sent over your information and gave him a quick rundown on your situation. He says he is willing to meet with you, but he wants to know more before he takes that case." A new excitement laced Keanon's tone that hadn't been there prior. "This is a good thing, Mav. A damn good thing."

"When does he want to meet?"

"I think his secretary will reach out to you soon. They have your information, so it's only a matter of time. Listen Mav, I gotta go. Meeting in five, but keep your head up, man. We got a fight ahead of us." Keanon said goodbye and then the line went dead. Maverick dropped the phone back onto the bedside table.

His groggy and sleep-deprived brain was slow to process

the entire conversation. On one hand, hearing they potentially bagged a big time lawyer like Gilmore would be a huge step in getting back everything he lost. Yet he couldn't silence the insistent whisper in the back of his head telling him he didn't belong in that life anymore.

Why wasn't he more excited? This was everything he hoped for.

For now, Maverick needed to silence all thoughts, good and bad. He kicked off the last of his blanket and got out of bed. There was nothing quite like a good morning run to clear his head. Since Keanon got him out of bed so early, he had time to get two miles in before returning home to shower and get ready for work. If the universe wanted to throw him another bone, he would have time to stop at Pecan's Coffee.

The thought of a fresh brew was enough to get him out the door.

Chapter Eight

Wednesday practice brought with it a new level of comfortability and unity that had been lacking previously. Not even Maverick was immune to the positive energy encompassing his team. A newfound respect began to mold and even Benny had commented on the functionality of Mav's team after their first game. He said he'd never seen the guys work so hard together. They had never been a sloppy team, or so Benny believed, but they also hadn't been polished. Winning their first game of the season provided the confidence boost his team needed.

The lists and sets he had written across the old-school white board did not intimidate his team as he thought it would. At the very least he was expecting a few groans or push back, but was instead greeted with a chorus of 'yessirs' and 'you got it, coach!' He felt as if he were living in The Twilight Zone.

He was halfway through helping his third baseman with proper lunge form when the side doors to the gym burst open. Ofelia strutted in as if she owned the place, which she technically did at this time, with her hair pulled back in a high ponytail, bright neon pink leggings and a black tank top with the words "Cheer Boss" across her chest. Her gaze met Maverick's for a beat before going back to the female student next to her, nodding at whatever Ofelia said.

"Damn, is this our present for winning, coach?" Dustin asked as he watched nearly a dozen girls and two male cheerleaders walk in. The urge to hit the back of the boy's head was strong, but willfully Maverick stopped himself. He didn't think his mother would take kindly to that, even if she was his current bestie after last night's game.

"Don't be a creeper, Davis." He barked at Dustin. "We're sharing the gym one more time, so you boys better be on your best behavior." Maverick said to the group within earshot. He got a few grunts of confirmation, all too focused on their sets for the day to pay him much mind right now.

He needed to heed his own advice about not being a creeper, especially once Ofelia began to lead his team through stretches. He was no better than a teenaged boy, but at least he pretended not to stare at a certain English teacher's ass. He wasn't completely without class. It was much easier to keep his mind engaged with his team when he had to coach them through certain exercises, correct their form, or help ease sore muscles by showing them what stretches they could do to help the affected muscles.

It was sweet torture, but for an hour practice went on without a hitch. Even the music Ofelia started to play did not trigger him like it did the first time he heard Ariana Grande play through the speakers. This time he was listening to snippets of their competition music and Ofelia's voice yelling out orders.

It wasn't until the second hour he noticed their side of the gym had mysteriously shrunk in size. He was constantly running into boys and his team had little room to devote to their training. Sometime within the hour, the cheerleaders had managed to push his baseball players into the corner. The cheerleaders were sitting pretty with over half the gym at their disposal. Alas the fragile truce between them had crumbled. He needed to speak to a certain cheer coach about it. And Maverick definitely shouldn't feel as excited as he felt to rile up Ofelia.

Excusing himself from his team, with orders to stay on task, Maverick crossed the invisible line into enemy territory. Ofelia's back was turned to him, but her cheerleaders noticed his arrival. As if sensing a disturbance, Ofelia turned around and visibly groaned when her eyes locked on to Maverick. "Lacey! Take over the counts for me. This will be one second." She called and a girl - presumably Lacey - began their counts from the beginning.

"Hello, Coach Wilson, to what do I owe this pleasure?"

So she wanted to do it like that. He could entertain her sass.

Plastering on what he knew from experience was a 'panty-melting smile,' Maverick watched her stiffen. Good, he wanted her on pins and needles. "Ms. Mendez, I'm afraid we have a problem."

"Yes, we do. I'm glad you finally realized that. Are you going to leave now? Maybe do your practice, oh, I don't know, outside?" She said, a false sweetness in her voice.

"You would like that, wouldn't you?"

"Very much so. In fact, I would personally escort you and your boys outside so you don't get lost." She said and fluttered - actually fluttered - her eyelashes at him. A fire roared inside of him and Maverick licked his lips.

Ofelia took in a deep breath of air, her eyes traveling down to Maverick's lips. He watched her breath hitch before she pulled her gaze back up to his, but by then it was too late. He had seen the desire etched across his features. Her cute blush as she avoided him made Maverick feel far too many unsuitable for work feelings. The air around them was thick and he had to remind himself they weren't alone. And she didn't like him.

Though that wasn't the truth, was it? At least not entirely. Ofelia might have found him annoying or an asshole, but her body felt very differently.

"Anyway," Ofelia said, taking a step back slowly. The tension still lingered, but it was not as all-consuming as it had been only seconds before. "What is that problem you wanted to talk to me about?"

Problem? He had a problem. Oh, right, his cozy corner. Seemed rather unimportant now, considering he could hear his team doing just fine in the space they had. So what if a few elbows touched during weight lifting? They'd survive. Instead, now that he had her attention, he needed to ask her about something that had been on his mind since Monday night. "Why were you at our game?"

The look of confusion that crossed Ofelia's face indicated she had not thought he would ask about it. Honestly neither did he, but her being there had been a surprise. Especially since she brought her cheerleaders.

It only took her a moment to recover before she reluctantly said, "Colbie asked me to come."

Colbie. Their principal Colbie. "Why?" He had no business asking, and yet he still did.

Instead of telling him to fuck off like he expected, Ofelia sighed. "Because of restorative practices."

He blinked once. Twice. But nothing. "Is that supposed to make sense to me…?"

"Well it should, but you probably haven't been versed in the fun world of restorative practices. Basically I'm trying to get on a certain parent's good side. He happened to be on the baseball team and Colbie suggested I take the squad."

"Would that person happen to be the woman I saw you walking back from the concession with? Mrs. Davis?"

Ofelia nodded. "Yeah, and you did manage to help some. So...thank you for that."

Because he was an asshole and couldn't just accept the thank you, Maverick found himself smirking, "How badly did that suck to say?"

"Honestly I feel like I need a cleanse after that." She deadpanned, earning a wolfish laugh from him. "But in all seriousness, it got the desired effect so thanks."

"Happy to help. Besides, we won the game so it's sorta like you and your squad are our good luck charm."

"Don't expect that to happen again. There's no way I'm ever going to get my squad back out there. Except for Tony, he'll be your one-man cheerleader."

He opened his mouth to say something else, but one of his players called his name. "Looks like you need to head back." Ofelia said, already looking towards her squad. "Will this be the last time we share the gym?"

"I believe so." And for some reason that thought saddened him. "Benny found some equipment out in the shed we can use on our fields. We won't need the weights in here anymore."

"Perfect. Enjoy the rest of your practice, Coach Wilson. I'm sure you have a lot on your plate right now." She said the last part as if she had personal experience with it. Once again his curiosity got the best of him and his mouth responded before his brain could.

"Know something about being busy?"

The smile that came across her lips was purely self deprecating with no signs of humor. "Between parents, teaching, cheer, and cheer moms...yeah, I would say I know a thing or two."

He wanted to pry more. He felt like a baby bird who was just offered his first worm. He needed more to be satisfied. Yet before he could ask more, he was called again by one of his players.

"I'm on my way!" Maverick said, hopefully not too bitterly. He offered Ofelia an apologetic smile but she had already started walking away from him to rejoin her team. He sighed and tore his gaze away, finally rejoining his team. Yet all throughout practice, he couldn't help but wonder what responsibilities were weighing so heavily on the all star teacher.

Chapter Nine

Ofelia could count on a single hand how often she had been late for work. She couldn't remember how many times she snoozed her alarm, only that she remembered picking up her phone and shooting out of bed because she had exactly thirty minutes before she needed to be on campus.

Which meant no makeup, no hair products, and absolutely no coffee. If Ofelia could get away with wearing leggings, she would. Instead, she found burgundy pants that she paired with a mustard-colored top. It was all she could gather this Friday morning after neglecting laundry all week. She slipped on the closest pair of shoes she could find, checking twice to make sure they matched before running out to her car. In the seconds it took her to walk from her front door to her car, she managed to put her hair up in a messy bun.

It would have to do.

Since she arrived so late, the parking lot was already crowded with staff and student cars. Ofelia had to forgo her usual front parking for one all the way in the back. Which would have been fine if her room wasn't on the complete other side of the building and on the second floor.

By the time she reached her door, her breath came out in short, labored pants. She doubled over in attempts to get her breathing under control before fumbling with her keys. She found the right one and pushed open the door when Willow rounded the corner. Upon spotting her best friend, Willow laughed at her disarrayed appearance.

"I would say you had a good night last night and are now suffering from the D effect, but I know you too well." Willow smirked.

"D effect? Really? You sound like the students." Ofelia pushed her door open but didn't shut it behind her. Willow followed. Since she ran so late, she silently thanked whatever divine entity listening that she set out all her materials the previous day. At least she wouldn't have to scramble like a chicken with its head cut off while making copies.

"So, I thought of a way you could repay me, your best friend, for helping you out on Tuesday."

Ofelia raised a brow, wondering why Willow felt the need to add in the best friend qualifier. Knowing her, it wasn't anything good. "Okay," she said slowly, "What are you thinking?"

"We're going out!"

"Come again?"

"Ofi!" Willow said dramatically, perching her ass atop the closest desk. Ofelia gazed longingly at the coffee in her friend's hand as if it were the last drops of water in the middle of the desert. "When was the last time we went out?"

"Uh, never. That's why we are friends. We don't go out. We have pizza nights where we drink too much wine, eat too much, and watch crappy hallmark movies. It's kinda our thing."

"So I'm proposing we do something different tonight." Willow said matter-of-factly, like she was commenting on the weather rather than a nighttime activity that involved being social after a day of teaching high schoolers.

"Karl left for a business trip and will be gone for a week. He wants me to pick up someone at the bar for a one-night stand and immediately FaceTime to tell him all about it. Don't worry though, he's planning on doing the same."

She would never quite understand Willow and Karl's swinger endeavors, but she didn't need to understand to support her friend's interests and kinks. As long as both parties were consenting and into it, Ofelia saw nothing wrong with it. Not that Willow needed her approval for what she did in the relationship or in the bedroom.

"We'd need to go shopping after school because I feel like going out in a new outfit. Plus, you haven't bought anything nice for yourself in God knows how long. We are getting you something sexy and slutty, but classy because you are an educated lady."

"Willow." Ofelia groaned inwardly. "This is so much more than what I asked you to do! Are you crazy? Do you know how tired I am? I'm late because I physically could not get out of bed. This week I've dealt with practice, parent meetings, and tutoring. Now you want to not only go shopping, but go out clubbing-"

"Oh god no. Not clubbing. To a bar."

"Fine, a bar." Ofelia rolled her eyes. "No. I love you, but no."

Those words woke the dragon in Willow. She narrowed her eyes, putting her hands on her hips, staring down Ofelia. Ofelia flinched under her scrutiny. "First off, it was a courtesy I even asked. This isn't up for negotiation. We are going, and secondly, you are going to have so much fucking fun, you aren't going to know what to do with yourself. Maybe some good dick would perk you up a bit."

"You did not just say that."

"Yes, I did, and I'll keep saying it until you agree. Good dick good dick good dick good dick good di-"

"Okay!" Ofelia shouted, throwing the first thing she found, an expo marker, directly at Willow. "You're seriously so annoying."

A devious smile played across her friend's lips. Willow knew she bested her. "So you're in?"

"Clearly. I don't get a choice."

"Nope, you do not." Willow squealed, unable to hide her excitement. "Okay, we'll take your car after work and go shopping and then tonight we'll hit the bar. Ah! I'm so excited. This is going to be fun! You'll see."

Famous last words, Ofelia thought.

∼

WHEN WILLOW WALKED out of her classroom, exclaiming she would meet Ofelia as soon as the bell for the last period rang, she pushed all thoughts of shopping and bar visits to the back of her mind. Maybe, if she hoped really hard, Willow would realize how tired she was after a long day's work and their typically Friday night pizza binge would be back on the table.

For the rest of the day, Ofelia threw herself into her lessons on *Fahrenheit 451* and the needs of her students. During her planning period, instead of taking a nap like she really wanted

ON AND OFF THE FIELD

to, she started making her lecture slides for next week. What she couldn't finish, she knew Willow would piece together. She also made sure that all the copies needed for next week were on route to the school. How she managed to function at all without coffee was a mystery to her.

When the last bell rang signaling the end of the day, Willow burst through her classroom doors faster than her students could leave.

"How do you have all this energy still?" Ofelia groaned before sinking onto her pink swivel chair as the last of her students filed out. "I feel like I was run over by a bulldozer."

"Because I'm about to go shopping with my best friend! Then I'm going to get absolutely wasted at a bar. We are in our twenties and deserve to let loose." Willow was already tidying up Ofelia's classroom without being prompted.

Seeing her friend so excited over something so small made Ofelia feel a little guilty that she wasn't as into it as Willow.

Willow had a point. They were still young, and it had been a long time since Ofelia did anything for herself. Yes, she was tired, but nothing a strong cup of coffee wouldn't fix. Maybe subconsciously she was avoiding bars, not because she didn't like to go drinking every now and then, but because it was where she had met her ex. Hector had loved going to bars for playoff games, friend's parties, and after work to unwind. He would often drag Ofelia along and she would go without complaint because she wanted to be close to him.

Then he started leaving her behind. Slowly at first, giving Ofelia excuses about wanting a boys' night. She remembered the moment he stopped bringing her entirely. They had a huge fight over something trivial, probably about the laundry since he was so careless with his, and Hector stormed out saying he needed a break. Ofelia took that as a break from their relationship. She remembered sobbing in the kitchen, elbows on the table with her head in her hands.

That was how he found her, eyes puffy from crying and hair disheveled from anxious fingers. Hector swayed, clearly so drunk that even standing proved difficult. He had apologized and said he didn't want to fight. Ofelia had been young and her love for Hector clouded all her better judgment. She allowed Hector to take her back to bed and make love to her. He had passed out, arms holding her tightly as if he were afraid he'd lose her.

Or afraid she'd run.

But Willow didn't know that. All Willow knew was she left California after separating from Hector before their wedding. Because she was still too scared to tell her best friend what really happened. It was silly, she knew, to completely avoid bars simply because it reminded her of him. This could be her one opportunity to reclaim that part of her life, the life where she didn't fear going out with friends and hanging at bars. Willow, her best friend in Texas, would be there too.

She could do this.

Ofelia, now determined to make the most of tonight, stood up. Perhaps a little too abruptly because she caught the attention of Willow. "Is everything okay?" She asked hesitantly.

"Everything is perfect. I'm just ready to go, but our first stop has to be coffee."

Willow cocked her brow and stared at her like Ofelia had just been abducted by an alien. Ofelia could practically see the thoughts going through Willow's mind right now. *Who are you and what did you do with my best friend?*

"O...okay." Willow said slowly, elongating the "oh" sound. Realizing that Ofelia was actually serious Willow beamed, her smile lighting up the room. "Right! Okay, let's get some coffee!"

One hour, two long red lights, and one frantic coffee stop later, Ofelia and Willow arrived at a small independent boutique. The store was packed full of clothing all ranging from evening wear to sleepwear. Immediately several dresses caught her eye and she imagined slipping a few on, just to take a look. If she got a new dress, then she would obviously need to get a new pair of shoes...and accessories. If they were going out, she might as well go all in.

"Those print jumpsuits are calling my name." Willow maneuvered her way through the racks of clothing, leaving Ofelia by the entrance. The older woman by the register smiled at her with kind eyes. "If you need any help sweetie, you just let me know. Changing rooms are in the back."

"Thank you." Ofelia returned the woman's affectionate smile before wandering off towards the back. The entire left side of the boutique was full of dresses for every occasion. What she needed was something she could wear out that didn't look like the rest of her teaching attire. She didn't want to go out looking like Ofelia, the teacher, but rather Ofelia, the single woman.

All of the maxi dresses were cut from her list, even if they were adorable. She had plenty of those back at home. The dresses that hit mid calf would also not work, but she was getting closer. The dresses left fell under two categories. One being the "legs for days" and the other being "did my ass just pop out?" She wanted to look sexy, but not at the expense of flashing half the bar in the process.

"Legs for days" dresses would have to do. She jumped through one hurdle only to come across another. What color of dress did she want? She could go with a fierce, loud pattern that demanded attention. Or she could choose a solid color that wasn't quite as loud but provided a level of mystery and sophistication. She knew exactly the dress she would have chosen if she were still dating Hector, the bold cheetah print that hugged her ass a little too tightly, pairing it with red pumps.

But she wasn't that person anymore and she didn't want to choose a dress in hopes a man would notice her. She wanted a dress for herself. To look and feel good. She deserved that, dammit!

Her mind made up, Ofelia picked out a little black dress and headed back towards the fitting rooms. Willow was already there, holding a very Willow-like jumpsuit in front of the mirror and inspecting it. "What do you think about this?" She asked, turning around only to notice the dress in Ofelia's arms. "Hell yes. I don't even need to see it on you to know it's going to be your dress."

There was no way Ofelia was leaving with a dress she hadn't tried on. The last thing she needed was buyer's remorse. Still, she appreciated Willow's enthusiasm. "Let me take a look at yours." She said, instructing her friend to hold up so she could look it over. It was a vibrant green jumpsuit with jaguars and roses as the print. It shouldn't have worked as well as it did, but instead of looking tacky, the jumpsuit looked chic and trendy. It also screamed Willow. "I actually love it."

"I actually love it too!" She shrieked, her voice raising an octave as she did a little happy dance. "Wait, wait." Willow stopped suddenly, mid dance. "We need to try them on first. Let's not get too excited until we see how we actually look in them."

Ofelia didn't mention how she thought Willow was already too excited, but instead smiled and nodded. They took up the only two changing rooms in the boutique and Ofelia shut and locked the door behind her before turning her back to the mirror. She didn't want to spoil the look before it was completely on. She stripped out of her clothes, leaving on her bra and panties, and placing them in a neat pile on the bench.

Now to tackle the dress.

There was no zipper, so she pulled it over her head and shimmied inside of it. Once her head popped free, and she could see again, she made sure to adjust the bottom of the dress so it hit mid-thigh. It was short, but she didn't feel in danger of it accidentally showing off her goods. With only the briefest of hesitations, Ofelia turned around to see how she looked in the mirror.

The dress hugged her body tightly, framing her curves in the most delicious way. She was a proud Mexican American woman, so she had ass, tits, and hips and nothing was going to hide that fact. She embraced those parts of her body long ago. What she liked most about the dress though was that it wasn't sleeveless. The sleeves billowed around her arms in sheer fabric giving the illusion of sleeves while putting more skin on display. It cuffed at her wrists, small black satin ties to keep the ends in place.

She was completely and irrevocably in love.

"Ofi, you done? Come out, I wanna see." Willow called impatiently on the other side.

When she opened her changing room door, Willow had her back turned to Ofelia, checking herself out in the full-length mirror. Ofelia had been correct in her assumption that the jumpsuit was made for Willow. No one else could pull off a bold animal print jumpsuit quite like her and look hot doing it. The moment Willow's eyes met Ofelia's in the mirror, however, her friend stopped what she was doing and immediately turned around to gap.

But she didn't say anything. Ofelia was starting to feel like a circus attraction. Maybe the dress didn't look as good as she thought. In her worried state, she quickly tried to rationalize her choice. "I know I'm not wearing the right bra for this, and the sleeves are probably not everyone's cup of tea, but-"

"Shut. Up."

Ofelia did happily.

"Shut up!" Willow said again, girlish giggles leaving her lips. She circled Ofelia like a farmer assessing his prized sheep. It did nothing to quell the nerves inside of Ofelia. When her friend made a full 360, Willow finally said, "You look so hot right now. Like, so so hot. Am I tearing up? I feel like I'm tearing up. You just look so incredible and ugh! Okay, no, I am not going to cry in the middle of a boutique. Stop it, Willow!" She scolded herself.

It made Ofelia's heart warm with love for her best friend's giddiness at that moment. "Thank you." She said, trying to convey so much in those two words. Thank you for being my friend. Thank you for taking me out. Thank you for getting me out of my comfort zone. "You look so incredible too. I'm sure if Karl were here, he wouldn't be able to keep his hands off you."

"That will be someone else's job tonight." Willow winked, clearly still set on her plan to find a hookup partner. "So it's settled. We are both buying these. But a sexy little black dress needs an equally sexy pair of heels. Oh, and accessories."

"You are speaking my language, bestie. Those black strappy shoes on display demand my attention." Ofelia beamed. For the first time today, Ofelia was excited for tonight. She still wasn't ready to invite someone back to her house for a one-night stand, but she was ready to let loose. Just a little bit. Because she deserved it.

Chapter Ten

Her mirror was broken. That was the only explanation she could come up with. The woman looking back at her was not Ofelia. Maybe Ofelia's long-lost hotter sister, but definitely not her. The woman looking back at her had prominent cheekbones and sultry hazel eyes. Her lips were the color of a freshly ripened apple, full and pouty. In her ears, Ofelia chose a set of silver hoops and a matching elegant silver necklace to wear. The strappy black heels completed the look.

"So, what do you think?" Willow asked from the perch of her bed, barely concealing her excitement.

After shopping, they agreed to head back to Willow's home and get ready. It came down to who had the bigger bathroom and Willow's house undoubtedly won out. Which was fine by Ofelia because cramming into her tiny bathroom would have been a nightmare. Plus, Willow had more makeup and transporting hers would have been a pain.

"I've never felt more beautiful in my entire life." Ofelia admitted, blinking back the stinging sensation in her eyes. The last thing she needed was to cry and ruin an hour of Willow's hard work. "Thank you, Willow. For everything."

"Don't you start. If you start, I'm going to start." Willow waved her hands rapidly in front of her eyes, as if the constant air motion would hold the tears at bay. "You deserve this." Willow fluffed her already bouncy, red hair, giving herself a quick look over in the mirror. "No more crying, it's time to drink."

Because they were both two responsible adults, Ofelia ordered them an Uber. "I don't recognize this address, where is it again?" Ofelia asked.

"It's new, I think it opened a month or so ago. It's one of the few bars in the area that isn't a sports bar. I think it's more upscale." Willow replied, grabbing a tiny white purse and stuffing her wallet and phone inside. "Do you think I should take my can of pepper spray? Yeah, I will. Better to be safe than sorry." She answered her own question and stuffed her blue key chain pepper spray into her purse.

"Car's here. You ready?" Ofelia received the notification just as a blue Camry pulled into Willow's parking lot. Her friend nodded and ushered them both out of the house, locking the door behind her.

"I sent a selfie to Karl earlier to let him know we are about to go out and I am determined to give this man some major blue balls. He wants me to text him a play by play." Willow said as she slid into the back seat, followed by Ofelia. "Not for long though, we have an old college friend he's seeing tomorrow that's also into-" she cast a look at their driver, a middle-aged Asian man, before whispering. "You know."

Ofelia loved the wild, care-free spirit of her best friend and the relationship she had with her husband. It was one of the healthiest she had ever seen, even though it wasn't considered traditional. "Of course he will. You look so good. Make sure to send him many pictures and videos from tonight."

The drive to the bar – Willow called it Cloud 9 – only lasted ten minutes. Their driver pulled up to the curb so they could get out. "Thank you." Ofelia smiled, making sure to remember to go back and write a good review for this man because he had to listen to Willow babble on and on about her plans for tonight.

Cloud 9 was located on the edge of a large shopping outlet that catered to both high end and every day shopping. From the looks of people entering the bar, they catered to an eclectic clientele, ranging from people in their early twenties, all the way to mid-fifties. The building was a large one story, with cute black and white brick covering the exterior.

As soon as they walked inside, Ofelia realized too much time had passed since her last girl's night out. Her belly bubbled with a mixture of anxiety and excitement. Her body buzzed, unsure whether to throw up or start dancing.

Inside the bar, top hits played loud enough to dance to, but not so loud that someone couldn't hear the person next to them. It was still relatively early in the evening, about seven, so Cloud 9 was only starting to liven up.

Willow found them a high top table towards the bar area, big enough for two people to sit comfortably. It took some skillful maneuvering for Ofelia to climb the tall chair without exposing herself to the crowd. Luckily the lighting was somber, and she doubted anyone would truly be able to see up her dress.

"I'm going to buy our first round of drinks in celebration of doing something outside of our normal Friday night routine." Willow declared, grabbing her wallet from her purse.

"I'll leave this here and be right back." She blew Ofelia a kiss and headed off towards the bar.

Ofelia took the moment alone to breathe.

She was out and determined to have a great time with her best friend. Didn't she deserve that? Two years was a long time to get over someone, perhaps too long, and in that time she neglected this part of her. The fun, easy-going socialite who enjoyed entertaining and hanging out with friends. She found it easy to lie to herself these past two years by pretending she was introverted and suppress her extroverted tendencies by hiding inside, away from people.

Although that was half true, it wasn't entirely who she was. She would never be the girl who wanted to go out every weekend, but she was a girl who liked having a tight-knit friend group who planned the occasional outings and trips together. She could have that again, if she stopped letting her past haunt her. Part of healing was finally telling her best friends of two years why she really left California two years ago. At that moment, she felt the last chain holding her back began to crumble. She was finally ready. She had needed this final push from Willow to get out of her comfort zone and tonight had done just that.

Ofelia had been so deep down into memories that she didn't hear Willow approach until she placed a giant frozen strawberry margarita in front of her. "You're thinking really hard over there. Should I be worried? You aren't about to ditch me, are you?" Willow asked, her smile not quite reaching her eyes. "Look, if this isn't your thing, we can leave after-"

"No." Ofelia stopped her before Willow could finish her thought. She reached across the table, grabbing for Willow's cold hand. "I'm so happy you made me come out tonight. Not just now, but after school when we went shopping. Then getting ready and listening to old boy bands. I can't tell you the last time I've done any of those things."

"It's a typical Wednesday night for me."

Both women laughed, the tone shifting into lighter and easier territory. Ofelia took the first sip of her margarita and moaned. "Ugh this is the most delicious thing I've ever had in my mouth. Don't make a dirty joke out of it." She said before Willow could make a crude comment.

Her friend only smirked. "Wouldn't dream of it." She said, feigning innocence. "I'm curious about what you were thinking so hard about. If you wanted to share, that is. I won't push you, of course. Just know that I'm always here to talk to. And not only about school stuff. Anything."

Willow's words sounded almost shy, bordering on cautionary. Ofelia felt her heart lurch in her chest. How many times had Willow poured her heart out to Ofelia? Entrusted her with information she probably didn't give to many others aside from Karl? What had Ofelia given in return? Not a whole lot.

Willow knew of Hector and their messy break up, but Ofelia never went into detail. Most of her life was still a secret from Willow and it wasn't fair. Willow would never demand details about Ofelia's personal life, but she realized she *wanted* to tell her best friend everything. To lessen the burden and get it off her chest to someone other than her family.

"I was thinking about my ex." she confessed, searching Willow's face for surprise, but all she found in her friend's expression was compassion. It gave Ofelia the strength to carry on. "We were engaged, you know."

But of course she didn't know. Ofelia never told her. Willow sipped her margarita with wide eyes, speaking only when she pulled away from the straw. "I didn't want to pry.

You always tensed up when I mentioned any of your old relationships, so I just let it be. Damn. Ofi. What happened?"

Two years ago, that question would have nearly incapacitated her with grief for the life she thought she lost. Now it only filled her with shame and embarrassment for falling prey to Hector's game. She couldn't blame him for everything; a small part of her had been aware their relationship wasn't working. Ofelia desperately wanted to ignore all the red flags and believe love would overcome everything. Love conquered all in books, so why not real life too?

"We were having problems. I was trying to get through college to become a teacher and my last few semesters were really stressful. He was used to having my attention all the time and I couldn't give that to him anymore. Hector had the emotional range of an egg; he couldn't process not being my number one priority. Which resulted in him going out...a lot. Sometimes he'd drag me to bars, but then he started going out more often and coming home drunk. We would get into the worst shouting matches and-"

Willow's hand shot out, gripping Ofelia. She hadn't realized she had a death grip on her drink. Slowly, Ofelia released her glass, pulling back but not out of Willow's grasp. "Did he lay a hand on you?"

Ofelia's eyes went wide. "Oh god, no! Nothing like that. Sorry, I know it sounds that way. No, Hector never hit me." Ofelia quickly assured, watching Willow visibly relax.

"Thank god. I was about to drive up to California and kick some deadbeat's ass."

The image of an eccentric Willow who preached love and self-expression, beating up Hector who stood six feet tall with tattoos covering his arms, was comical to Ofelia. She laughed, unable to unsee the image. "He's a jerk, but he isn't physically abusive. He respects women, having grown up in a household of only women. They would skin him alive if he ever touched a woman aggressively. Trust me, he wouldn't dare."

Estella had been a single mom, raising two kids. Her twin sister, Maria, moved in when Hector was eight and his sister Analucia was four, to help raise her niece and nephew. Estella and Maria had been good to Ofelia, even after they broke up. It devastated her more than anything that she wouldn't be marrying into his family. She adored Hector's family, and they tried to reach out when she moved, but Ofelia ignored all their calls, unwilling to bring her past to Texas.

This was the embarrassing part, and it still left her sleepless on rough days. The pain healed long ago, but the shame and distress lingered. Telling Willow felt like the final stage in the healing process. The baggage she carried for so long could finally dissipate.

"Despite all the fights, he proposed. We both thought that was what we needed, and I couldn't have been happier. On the day of our wedding, I was getting ready with his mom, aunt, and Analucia, while my brother and dad were supposed to be getting ready with Hector. When we were the first to arrive at the chapel, I knew something was wrong. Analucia tried calling Hector and I tried calling Javi, but neither of us could ever get anyone to pick up.

"Until about an hour later when Javi and my father walked in, both staring at me the same way they did when mom died. Sadness and a little pity. I thought something happened to Hector. I remember demanding they tell me or take me to him. But neither of them said a word. I think they were silently trying to decide who would be the bearer of bad news.

"In the end, it was Javi who told me Hector left. Gone. He told Javi he couldn't do this, couldn't go through with marrying me. He didn't love me and wasn't willing to give up his fast lifestyle to settle down and start a family.

"So instead of doing the right thing, Hector ran and left me at the altar. His mother and aunt were crying, and Analucia tried to comfort me, but I couldn't look at them. I didn't have anyone to blame, and I took it out on them. It's not one of my prouder moments, but at that moment I was nothing but rage and despair."

There. It was out. Willow knew everything and the last few walls Ofelia erected around her best friend had finally been breached, as they should have been years ago.

Willow didn't speak for a few, long moments. She took everything Ofelia said in. Which to be fair, was a lot. Especially at a bar. She didn't plan to tell her best friend her tragic left at the altar story here, but the moment appeared, and Ofelia seized it. It felt damn good to get that off her chest too, having someone else to confide in.

On the opposite end, Willow looked close to shedding a few tears for Ofelia's ruined love life. "Oh, Ofi. That is so awful. I hate that you went through that, I can't even imagine how you felt. I'm so sorry."

"I'm not." It shocked her, just as much as it did Willow, to say those words. Where would she be now if she had married Hector? Not happy, she knew that for certain. They were two different people and were going to extreme lengths to make their relationship work. Trying to get blood from a stone was fruitless and ineffective.

"I'm not," Ofelia repeated herself. "Him leaving saved me from a life of a loveless marriage. I got the opportunity to figure out who I am and what I'm capable of. I was heartbroken at the time, but I can't help but be proud of the woman I've become. I've made a life for myself and worked my ass off to achieve what I have in my career and personal life. I found the best friend a girl could ask for." She smiled at Willow. "So yeah, I'm not sad about it anymore. Maybe a little embarrassed, but I think that will fade in time as well."

"Thank you for trusting me." This time Willow got up, fighting back tears, and hugged Ofelia, who happily accepted. "I'm so proud of you. Ugh, I'm not going to cry. No, I worked too damn long on this mascara to mess it up." She said and untangled herself from Ofelia. "But I will get us more to drink."

Ofelia must have been chugging her margarita during her story since it was completely empty minus a small puddle at the bottom of her glass. "Fine, but the next ones on me."

"Oh honey," Willow laughed. "If we have to buy any more of our own drinks tonight, then we are doing something wrong." With that, Willow fluttered away, back towards the bar.

After the second drink, Ofelia started to feel a warm tingling in the pit of her stomach. She felt lighter and found herself laughing louder each time Willow told a funny story about Karl or work. Cloud 9 continued to fill up as people and friend groups trickled in. They had been lucky enough to secure a table because now people were claiming wall space to visit and drink with others.

The first time a round of drinks was delivered to their table, Ofelia had been shocked. Neither her nor Willow ordered from the bar. "A round of beer from the two gentlemen over there." The waitress had pointed vaguely over to the corner. The cramped area was dimly lit, making it hard to make out faces. She thought she saw someone raise their hand and give her a wave, but she wasn't sure if it was meant for her.

"You like beer?" Ofelia asked when Willow picked up the glass.

Her friend shrugged and said, "I do when it's free." Then brought the glass to her lips and drank.

Now they were on their fifth round and somehow Willow coerced Ofelia into dancing. Cloud 9 played a killer soundtrack, full of old pop hits she loved in middle school and high school. It would be a sin not to dance when they played Usher. Instead of feeling insecure about dozens of eyes on her, Ofelia didn't hesitate when Willow dragged her over to a small crowd of people.

Song after song, Ofelia danced like nobody was watching, even after Willow was whisked away by an eager dance partner. The dryness in her throat eventually couldn't be denied though, and she made her way through the dancing bodies to quench her thirst. If she remembered correctly, there had been a self-serve water station at the end of the bar. She could feel the alcohol getting to her head and it made the room spin.

When she located the water station, she was happy to see an open bar chair next to it. Her feet cried out in pain. The damn shoes were cute, but her feet throbbed with each step. Beauty is pain had never been a truer statement.

Ofelia filled up a cup of cold water, chugging it down in one go. Her dry throat satiated at last with the cool liquid. Filling it up once more, she took a seat in the unoccupied bar stool, hoping to take a few moments alone to sober up.

Her precious break was cut short when a shadow darkened her view. Ofelia looked up through half-lidded eyes at the strange man before her. He was taller than her, but still on the shorter side. His brown hair was shaggy and cut close to his shoulders. He wore form fitting blue jeans and a collared black shirt he tucked in for some ungodly reason. He wasn't unattractive, per se, but not Ofelia's type. He also seemed to be older than her by more than a few years.

Ofelia offered him a tight smile, one that she hoped convey she wasn't interested in whatever he had to say. She went back to sipping on her water, which she pretended was the most interesting thing in this bar. Unfortunately, black shirt didn't get the memo and plopped his body down on the seat next to her, scooting close. Way to close for comfort.

That was when she realized she was alone. *Fuck! So stupid!* She thought to herself. That was the number one rule in outings! Don't separate from your friend group. She was on the opposite side of the bar, and she couldn't make out her friend's red hair amongst the sea of dancing people. If she walked away, she had the feeling the creep would follow her.

"What's a pretty lady doin' all alone in the corner over here? Tryin' to hide from me?" Mr. Creepy asked, offering her a smile that matched his nickname. She watched as his eyes raked over his body, taking in every inch of her bare skin. Ofelia felt like she stood naked in front of him and did her best to pull her dress lower down her thigh.

"I'm here with someone, just getting water." She said curtly.

The man laughed, a low throaty sound that made her think of nails on a chalkboard. "Don't see nobody here, sweetheart. I guess it's my lucky day. Say, how 'bout you let me buy you a drink? What's your poison, darlin'?"

"No, thank you. I'm fine with water."

Fuck! This was bad. So, so bad. Of course the bar creeper would hit on her. She just had to wander away from Willow to find water. Her heart pounded harder in her chest, signaling a flight or fight response. But the bar was so crowded, there was no way the man would try anything...right?

"Awe, come on, sweetie! Let me buy you a little somethin'. How about a shot then?" This time when he spoke, he placed his hand on her thigh. Her bare thigh. She tried to pull away from him but his hand gripped her tighter, causing a tendril of pain to shoot down her leg.

"Don't touch me." She growled, trying to put on her best pissed off expression. She narrowed her eyes, but she felt like a frightened animal cornered by prey. Her body wanted to run, but her tipsy brain was still trying to process the severity of this situation. It left her immobilized, unable to do more than scream internally.

"Don't be like that sweetheart. I just wanna buy you a drink." Mr. Creepy grinned and leaned closer.

Fear overrode every sense in her body, making her helpless to do anything but stare at the man. Before he could lay another hand on her though, a deep voice sounded from behind Ofelia. "You have exactly one second to take your hands off her." The hairs on the back of her neck stood on end. She knew that voice! His deep, sensual baritone sent shivers down her back, sending warmth between her thighs. She pressed her knees closer together. Not once since they met did she ever think she'd one day be so thankful for his presence.

When she turned towards Maverick, she was greeted by the full wrath of his stare and *oh god* it did wonders for her nether regions. Because not only did Maverick look ready to draw blood, but he was doing it all for *her*.

She was in so much trouble.

Chapter Eleven

Maverick deserved a drink.

Baseball practice ended up running an hour past what Maverick originally intended. They were finally out in their fields and time had gotten away from him, but none of his players noticed either. Maverick only realized the time when a few freshmen parents started to show up looking frazzled and impatient.

Benny and Maverick began to load up the school's golf cart so they could transport their practice equipment back to the storage room in the gym. Benny, who insisted on driving the damn cart, waited for Maverick to take the spot next to him. "Why do you always insist on being the driver?" Mav asked, once inside.

Benny shrugged. "I don't know. It's fun." Maverick couldn't argue with that solid logic, so he nodded as Benny began to drive them back towards the gym. "So, Friday night, huh? What does a young single man do for fun on a Friday night?"

Maverick resisted the urge to roll his eyes. He liked his

coaching assistant, but Benny saw anyone ten or more years younger than him as a child. He had a grandfatherly quality about him that was both endearing and slightly bothersome. "I think I'm going to find a spot for a drink. Any recommendations?"

Benny seemed to light up when Maverick asked for his opinions. He doubted they would frequent the same place, but since Benny was a long-standing member of this town, he should be able to recommend a place with good drinks.

"I don't take you as a western saloon type of guy?" Benny pondered, looking over at Maverick's scowl. "Ha! I'll take that as a no. Okay, well there's a few restaurants in town that serve drinks, but if you are looking for more of a bar scene, I'm not entirely familiar. Wife and I don't often drink and when we do, it's at home."

Well, that was slightly disappointing, but Maverick could easily google bars in the area.

"Oh wait!" Benny piped up once they stopped at the back of the storage room. Maverick hopped out to open the overhead door. "I read in the paper about a new, modern bar that just opened up not too far from here. It's supposed to be hip and trendy with young folks. I think it's called Cloud...something. Cloud Sign? Cloud Five? Damn, I forgot, but I know that it started with cloud."

Of course Benny would still get his news from a printed paper. Everything about the man screamed dated. Still, Maverick liked Benny. Even if he was a bit dated.

"Cloud something. Got it." Maverick said, committing it to memory.

He finished lugging the last of the equipment inside the storage room. It was as if a damn tornado went through this room, several times, obliterating everything in its path. One of his biggest pet peeves was disorderly sports equipment, but there was no way his ass was going to sort through all the football mess piled next to his baseball equipment. He made sure his small corner of the room was orderly, all his equipment packed up and readily accessible when he needed it.

"Alright, Benny I think we're done." Maverick said, stepping out of the garage to shut the door. He made sure he secured the lock before pocketing the key. "Imma hit the showers, so I'll lock down the gym tonight. And thanks for the rec. I'll see if I can find the bar you mentioned."

"Sounds fine to me boss. I better get home to the misses before she sends out a search party." He laughed good-naturedly and for a second Maverick wondered what it would be like to have a love like that. To be excited to go home because you knew the person waiting for you loved you with every fiber of their being.

Mav once thought he had that.

"See ya Monday, Mav!" Benny called, waving goodbye. He made sure Benny got to his car before heading inside.

It was a known fact that schools at night were creepy, especially with no one else around. Maverick walked a little faster than normal to the gym showers, half expecting a murderous clown to pop out and chase him. Luckily, none appeared as he stepped into the boys locker room for a quick shower.

Once finished, he grabbed a pair of light-colored jeans from his gym bag. This morning he had worn a button up white shirt, with a gray blazer over top. They weren't his usual attire to work, but the Yearbook class had wanted to take pictures of the team after their second win last night. Mav had wanted to appear professional in the photos, even if his team teased him mercilessly about it.

Those fuckers, he thought fondly, bringing a smile to his lips.

Maverick slung his training duffel bag over his shoulders, searching through it for his phone and keys. The crisp chill in the air assaulted his skin the moment he walked out of the building and straight to his truck. Yes, truck. A Huge, almost luminescent white pickup. It wouldn't have been Mav's first, or third, choice in a vehicle, but Keanon insisted Mav borrow his truck while he stayed at his home, since Breanna kept the car.

Which meant Mav's latest drive was The Beast, as he dubbed it. If he weren't tall, he'd need a running start to pull himself into the monstrosity. Keanon was six or seven inches shorter than him. He couldn't imagine how his friend managed to pull his body into the driver's seat.

Now, Maverick needed to figure out where to go in this town for good booze. What had Benny suggested? Maverick vaguely remembered and began to type in cloud on his phone. A few results quickly came up. Cloud Dreams, which happened to be a sex store, Cloud Knight - they sold insurance - and finally Cloud 9.

Cloud 9 was the obvious winner, so Maverick let his GPS navigate him. When he arrived twenty minutes later, Mav was surprised to see a packed parking lot. The thrumming music hit his senses instantly once his door opened. It had been a long time since Mav was in a crowded place, outside of school functions. In the back of his mind, he wondered how many people would recognize him and how to handle it if someone approached him in a negative way.

Gathering all the swagger of his former self, Maverick put on the face of a confident man and walked inside. Judging by the parking lot, he had expected bodies to be packed close together, but that wasn't the case. There were a lot of people in

Cloud 9, but the bar was spacious and provided ample space for drinkers and dancers. All the tables were currently occupied, but he didn't need one. Maverick didn't plan to stay long; he just wanted a sense of normalcy and a strong whiskey.

The bar was dead center, and he had to weave his way through dancing bodies and full tables. A few times he thought he heard his name, but no one tried to come up to speak to him or ask him for a selfie. Fading into obscurity was something he had not expected to like as much as he did.

With the bar only feet in front of him now, he scanned the chairs for an open seat. There was one tucked away in the corner, next to a couple. At first glance, they seemed enthralled by each other. The man leaned close, hand resting on her thigh, laughing at something she said. Mav thought the woman, just from a quick glance, was far too pretty to be with a man who looked as if his mother still picked out his clothes. But who was Maverick to judge? Love happened in mysterious ways, or some shit like that.

However, the longer he stared, the more he noticed the woman's rigid posture. She leaned away from the man, not towards him. The hand on her thigh, which Maverick had interpreted as affection, was an aggressive attempt to keep the woman from moving. Her body language screamed her discomfort and Maverick knew he needed to step in; he just didn't want to scare the woman any more.

There was also something extremely familiar about the woman too. Deep chestnut colored hair, hanging in spirals down her back. Long, gorgeous legs that came from years of athletic training. Curves he could lose-

"Don't fucking touch me."

Everything inside Maverick tensed, heat flashing through his body at Ofelia's voice.

How dare the man think he had the right to touch a woman, especially *this* woman. His body reacted before his brain contemplated a course of action. He zeroed in on the fucking bastard touching Ofelia, and Maverick found himself moving forward at a brisk pace. The man noticed him before Ofelia did, and he saw the flicker of fear in the man's eyes. Maverick's own voice was foreign to him, husky and full of disdain for a man he didn't know. "You have exactly one second to get your hands off her."

Ofelia's head shot back, looking at him with a mixture of shock and something else he couldn't quite place. He didn't have time to analyze that now though. Mav stepped in front of her, putting his body between Ofelia and the man in front of her. The pervert took his hand back, stumbling back like a coward. "I..it was nothin' man...I was just messin' around. Didn't know she had a boy-"

"Doesn't fucking matter." Maverick was done listening to this pathetic excuse of a man. "You shouldn't have touched her, period. I swear to God if she's bruised from your touch, I'll-"

"Maverick." Ofelia's soft voice called out in warning. She reached for his hand, trying to uncurl the fists he didn't know he made. He relaxed, but only slightly, as she slipped her hand into his and squeezed. "Don't make a scene. Just let him go."

Let him go? That was the exact opposite thing he wanted to do to this perv. He wanted to take away the man's sense of safety as he did with Ofelia and countless other women before her. The man was weak, trying to make himself seem superior by scaring women into submission. Yet when Maverick turned his head, Ofelia looked at him with worry in her eyes. Worry that he caused. It was like icy water being poured over his head, alerting him to Ofelia's needs.

Only because Ofelia was safe and unharmed did Maverick

take a step backwards, casting one last heated glare at the perv. The stranger turned around, taking this opportunity to leave before Maverick changed his mind. Smart guy. Maverick's eyes followed him until he got lost in the crowd; lost in the sea of bodies.

"Are you okay?" Maverick finally asked, once capable of speech that wasn't laced with profanity. His eyes dropped down to where she still held his hand.

Ofelia must have realized at the same time as Maverick because she blushed before letting him go and tucked a strand of hair behind her ear. "I'm okay. Thank you. He didn't hurt me." They both heard the unspoken *yet*, but Ofelia didn't seem like she wanted to push the matter. "Why are you here?"

Maverick laughed, letting the air in his chest deflate some. His body still felt ready to take care of a threat, even though Ofelia was safe now. "Me? I should be asking you that. Why are *you* here, Ofelia?" More importantly, why was she dressed like she was out on a date? That black dress did all sorts of things to his mind and body. She could stab him with a bar knife and Maverick would thank her. That was how much this damn woman affected him.

Ofelia looked a little offended by his question; he saw her tense up and fold her arms over his chest. Which was a terrible move because it only pushed her large breasts up, causing Maverick to exert all his focus on keeping his eyes from glancing down. "I'm here with Willow. She's dancing and I was thirsty. I didn't ask for that man to harass me, Maverick."

No, of course she didn't. Logically, Maverick knew that. The last thing he wanted to do was blame her for the actions of another. There were far too many men that blamed women for what they were wearing, or their levels of alcohol consumption and Maverick refused to be that person. The anger built up in his chest began to subside. He let out a deep breath, sounding like a kettle letting out steam.

"I'm sorry. I know. I'm sure you could have handled him yourself but-"

"No, no, thank you." Ofelia cut him off, shaking her head. Her beautiful curls bounced around her face as she moved. "To be honest, I was getting worried. I can usually hold my own against assholes, but my body froze. I think I was in shock. So, thank you for stepping in. I feel like I owe you a drink." She laughed, trying to break the tension between them.

"Nah, you don't owe me anything. Mind if I sit here?" He indicated to the seat beside her. When she nodded, Maverick pulled the seat close, but left enough room to give her personal space, as he waved down the bartender. "Are you drinking anything?"

"I really shouldn't."

"But if you were?"

"It would be something light, like a mojito, but I'm buying."

Maverick ignored the last part and turned his attention towards the bartender he flagged down. "Your best whiskey and a mojito." He asked and quickly threw in a "please." Once gone, Mav swiveled his body to face Ofelia, resting his arm on the bar to prop himself up. This was the first time Maverick was able to get a good look at the woman. Before, his thoughts were preoccupied with making sure the man got his hands off her. But now...

Now he indulged himself.

Ofelia held herself with confidence he hadn't yet seen from her. That dress demanded it. There was no way anyone could wear that sexy, form fitting number and not feel anything less than a goddess. He hadn't considered himself a leg man before, but damn if he didn't want to run his hands up and down them. "You look fantastic." The words slipped out before he stopped himself. Sexy was the word he wanted to use.

"Don't I, though?" Ofelia beamed and God if that wasn't the single fucking hottest thing he had ever heard. He loved a woman that owned her own sexiness. "You don't look half bad yourself. You clean up nicely for a...what sport do you coach again?" There was no mistaking the sly look on her face as she spoke.

"You know exactly what sport I coach."

"Do I?" A teasing smile played on Ofelia's red lips. "Hmm, must have slipped my mind."

Maverick knew damn well that it didn't. Was she flirting with him? No, of course not. Why would she? They hardly knew one another. And yet...

"Your drinks." The bartender said, placing two glasses in front of them. "Holler if you need anything else." He smiled before moving on to the next customer.

"You never answered my questions." Ofelia said, reaching for her martini, soft pink nails reflecting in the light. "What are you doing here? Waiting for someone?"

Mav shook his head. "Not exactly. I came because it's been a roller coaster of a week. I don't know how teachers like you do this every day, year after year. I'm exhausted and it's only been a few weeks."

Mav earned a laugh out of Ofelia. He found that he liked the sound, low and seductive without trying. "Teaching isn't for the weak, but you've seemed to pick up coaching well. I've heard a few students say some pretty nice things about you. Trust me, coming from a high schooler, that's like an academy award."

"Glad to know they don't think I'm completely incompetent." Mav mused. "Your turn. What are you and Willow doing here?"

"Ah, well." Ofelia's eyes flickered down, and Maverick heard the slight hesitation in her voice. "Willow thought we needed a girls night. Something other than sitting at home and eating pizza. We went shopping for new outfits, got ready, and came here. She's somewhere..." Ofelia gestured to the crowd dancing. "Over there. I think she's been hitting on the same woman since we've been here."

"Sounds like Willow's getting a lot out of tonight. And you? What are you getting?"

Ofelia looked over at Maverick with confusion etched across her features. "What do you mean?"

"Well, Willow seems to be here to have fun and maybe more. Why did you come here? Boyfriend gone?" It wasn't the most eloquent way for Maverick to ask if she was seeing someone, but he was rusty. How did he use to pick up girls? Didn't people come to bars if they were looking to meet people? Maybe that's why she was here.

His question clearly flustered her. "B..boyfriend?" She said the word like bitter vinegar on her tongue. "Oh, no. No boyfriend. No. I don't date."

"Correction, she doesn't date yet!" A familiar voice rang shrill behind them. Then arms wound tightly around Ofelia, familiar red hair catching Maverick's attention first. He was happy to see Willow tear herself away from her dance partner long enough to come and find Ofelia.

"Maverick!" Willow greeted him as if they were old friends rather than coworkers who have had only a few interactions during lunch duty. She untangled herself from Ofelia and then went over to hug Mav like it was the most natural thing in the world. He awkwardly patted her back, thankful she moved away quickly.

"If we are talking about Ofelia's love life, then as her best friend, I must be here." Willow declared to no one in particular.

"We are most certainly not talking about that, or lack thereof." Ofelia said, thrusting water into Willow's hand.

He didn't have any right to know, but it didn't stop the seed of curiosity planted within him. "Why not? Sounds like a delightful topic to me."

Ofelia glared at him. "Because it's none of your business!"

"Ofi!" Willow whined, dragging out the last syllable. "Let loose, just a little. You deserve it." Willow said, sloppily kissing Ofelia on the forehead. "Gotta go. I got a sexy brunette waiting for me. Enjoy the rest of your date."

"Oh my god, Willow, this isn't a date!" Ofelia shouted after her friend, but Willow no longer paid attention. She groaned, rolling her eyes. "Ugh, sorry about her. She becomes overly affectionate when she drinks. This is why I keep her corralled at my house on the weekend. Wait, why are you smirking at me like that?"

Was he smirking? Yes, he most definitely was. He needed to remember to thank Willow later, for inadvertently giving him the perfect opening. "Nothing, it's cute that she thinks this is a date."

"Yeah, she's a mes-"

"Because I would never bring you to a bar for a first date. That dress is wasted here."

"What?" He watched Ofelia straighten up, his words slowly washing over her. He scanned her face carefully for any hints of anger or fear, but he found none, only shock.

This made him brave. He played a dangerous game, one

that had the potential to end badly if he didn't play his cards right. They had played this game before, but under different circumstances. Now he was going to push her like he always wanted to. Not a teenager in sight. "You heard me, Ofelia. I said I wouldn't take you to a bar and call it a date."

"Why would you think I'd ever let you take me out on a date?"

She was toying with him. Good. He piqued her interest, despite her hesitation. He fucking loved that she knew her worth and questioned his. As confident as she appeared, Maverick couldn't help but notice the apprehension in her gaze and the way her eyes darted around nervously. This was new to her as well, or so Willow implied. They were both in a strange limbo, uncertain what the other thought. He hoped he gave her the same butterflies she had been giving him since he arrived.

"Because you're curious. You'd want to know what a date with me entails."

Maverick watched Ofelia bite her lip. He couldn't help but think about what it would be like if he was the one biting her lip, sucking, and tasting her. What sounds would she make when he kissed her, pulling her close to his hard body? He bet they would be the sweetest damn sounds he'd ever heard.

"You are awfully cocky for someone who doesn't know a thing about me." Ofelia said, spinning in her chair until she faced him. Her knee brushed against his and she left it there. He'd place a wager that it was purposeful. "I don't like cocky men, Maverick. That's a strike against you. Three strikes and you're out." She held up a finger, signaling his one strike.

Fuck, she wanted to do baseball references now? He hadn't been this aroused and intrigued by a woman in so long. Even with Breanna. Towards the end, they had lacked the spark they

ON AND OFF THE FIELD

once had and Maverick craved a woman who could not only please him physically, but mentally and emotionally as well.

"I'm not cocky, sweetheart. I'm confident and I know what I want. I suspect you do too, deep down." Maverick said. "I'm also attracted to confident women. The way you wear the dress, how you command your cheerleaders so effortlessly, it's an amazing quality about you. How am I doing?"

"Not bad." Ofelia tried for nonchalance, but Mav saw the smile quirk her lips. "Tell me about this date you'd take me on if I were to agree."

"Where do you take any English teacher? The bookstore." He grinned and Ofelia laughed. He felt that was a safe answer, but what else would he do? Mav was rusty when it came to dating, but he wanted to impress this woman. "After, we'd head to a restaurant and-"

Another finger went down, leaving only her pointer finger up. "You were doing so well with the bookstore, but a restaurant? That's not very original of you. Try again but be careful. You only have one more chance to impress me."

This woman was evil. Pure, and unadulterated evil. But he loved this game they were playing. It was fragile and could break at any moment, but he wanted to play it until the end. "Did I say restaurant? You must have heard me wrong. I meant to say that I'd cook for you."

"You cook?"

"Not a bit, but I'm a fast learner." Maverick smirked, earning a laugh from Ofelia. Good, he wanted her to enjoy herself and see him as a possibility. What did either of them have to lose?

"So, a bookstore and homemade dinner. How could a girl pass that up?" Ofelia asked, her ring finger swirling over the top of her empty glass, as if pondering something. Maybe the fake date scenario?

Before he could ask more of her, Willow chose that moment to make another reappearance, slithering in between them. Maverick had to move back in his chair to make room for her. She seriously had the worst timing ever. "We have a major problem. Ofi, we need to leave. Now."

"What?" Both Maverick and Ofelia said at the same time. Ofelia pulled Willow to face her, running her eyes up and down her friend's body. Not in the way Maverick had looked at Ofelia earlier. She assessed her friend for any signs of maltreatment. Exactly what Maverick had done to Ofelia after the man harassed her.

"My contact! Mascara got into my eye, and I tried to rub it away, but I ended up ripping my contact in half and now my eye hurts." Willow's voice turned whiny. He didn't know how many drinks Willow consumed, but he assumed more than her body could handle.

Ofelia seemed to sense the same thing and got up. "Yeah, that's awful babe. I'll get our ride here. We'll take you home." She already had her phone up, clicking through the app.

Maverick was not about to let two young women get into a stranger's car while intoxicated. Even if Ofelia wasn't as drunk as Willow, she had still had a few drinks. "I'll drive." He offered, waving down his waiter to pay and close their tabs.

"You really don't have to do that."

"I'm not letting you walk out of here without me. I don't trust a stranger to get you both home safely. It's not up for discussion; I'm taking you home." Maverick didn't wait for her to argue. He paid his bill and dug his keys out of his pocket. "Bring her to the front, I'll bring the truck around."

Not wanting to leave them alone for too long, Mav jogged to his car and soon pulled up at the front doors. Ofelia had just gotten Willow through the door. Mav left the truck on and hurried to help Ofelia lift Willow into the back seat. Willow flopped on her back, giggling and murmuring unintelligible words. Ofelia struggled with her buckle, but eventually clicked it into place.

"She's going to have the worst hangover in the morning." Ofelia said, shaking her head. "Willow isn't a lightweight. I can't begin to guess the number of drinks she had."

"We'll get her home safely." Maverick assured.

The drive back to Willow's house was silent, minus the incoherent mumbling from Willow in the back. The silence in the car wasn't awkward or tense, but comfortable. Maverick liked not having to fill the time with idle small talk. Even though there was still so much he wished to know about Ofelia, this was not the time.

When they pulled up to Willow's house, only a five-minute drive from his own, Maverick cut off the engine. "Do you want me to help you carry her inside?"

Ofelia shook her head, unbuckling her seat belt. "No, I can do that. But can you help me get her out?"

"Of course." Maverick met Ofelia on the passenger side. She had the door open, attempting to coax Willow out like a child with promises of pizza and cupcakes. He reached in to unbuckle her seat belt. Between the two of them, they were able to pull Willow out of the car and plant her feet firmly underneath her.

It then took her approximately two seconds to escape their grasp and run towards the door. "I'm going to be sick!" She yelled, stumbling inside. Maverick was amazed at how fast a drunk Willow could run.

"I should probably go check on her." Ofelia said after a beat passed between them.

A wave of disappointment overcame him. He had been enjoying his night and then it had been cut short. He felt like he missed his moment. "Yeah, you probably should."

Ofelia began to walk away, but when she made it halfway to the house, she turned around and looked back at him. "You never told me how that date would end? The hypothetical one."

A smile crossed his features. He wasn't the only one that had been thinking about the fake date. "I'm a gentleman when the time calls for it, Ofelia. I would take you home and walk you to the door. Before you turned away from me, I'd pull you to my body and kiss you like you deserve to be kissed."

He swore he heard an intake of breath. It was too dark to see her expression, but he imagined her flustered. When she spoke, her voice was a little breathy. "That's your idea of a gentleman?"

"Sweetheart, if you read my thoughts, you would see that is the most gentlemanly thing I want to do right now."

"Oh." Was all she said and for a moment, Maverick thought he lost her. Then her voice pierced through the silence. "When would this date take place?"

As much as he wanted to say tomorrow, Maverick didn't want to rush her. "Next Saturday?"

"Can I have a night or two to think about it? Before I give you my answer?"

"Yeah, of course." He would have preferred an answer now, but he was thankful it wasn't a no. "Let me give you my number."

They exchanged numbers in the dark. Ofelia handed him the phone back first, his fingers lingering a second longer than normal, before pulling back. "I'll hear from you soon?" He asked.

"You will. Goodnight, Maverick."

"Goodnight, Ofelia."

He waited until Ofelia locked herself inside the house before getting in his car and driving home.

The smile he wore the entire way home never once disappeared, even as he slept soundly that night.

Chapter Twelve

Willow had not been a fun friend to be around last night. As soon as Ofelia came back in from saying goodnight to Maverick, she found Willow hunched over a potted plant, puking her guts out. "Oh Willow! That's not...oh, never mind." Ofelia had said before coming up behind her friend and pulling back her hair. They stayed like that for an hour, Ofelia rubbing her friend's back as Willow apologized profusely.

She wasn't upset though. She was worried about her friend, but mostly her head was still clouded with thoughts of Maverick. Hot, sexy Maverick. The same guy who had been a dick to her the first time they met, but had been nothing but sweet since. Was she actually considering a date with Maverick Wilson? Was she crazy not to?

Luckily Willow had needed her full attention last night and Ofelia's mind had no time to think about just how yummy Maverick looked. She was definitely not thinking about the way he stepped in to rescue her from Mr. Creepy, feeling his hard chest against her back. She would also not think about the palpable chemistry brewing between them and the way he ignited a fire in her core.

No, those were things she definitely wasn't thinking about as she helped Willow get herself showered and hydrated. Many times her friend tried to apologize, but Ofelia was hearing none of it. They had a great time and she was happy they went out, but she did lecture her friend on knowing when it was time to switch over to water. They weren't in college anymore and couldn't drink like they used to.

After making sure Willow was tucked into bed with water and ibuprofen on her bedside table, Ofelia meandered into the guest bedroom down the hall. Since their usual Friday nights took place at Willow's and Ofelia typically had one too many glasses of wine to safely drive home, she began to store some clothes over at her friend's house. Within twenty minutes, Ofelia had showered, brushed her teeth, and put her phone on the extra guest room charger before slipping into bed. The moment her head hit the pillows, she was out.

It was only when her body rested and her thoughts roamed freely, that Ofelia dreamed of Maverick. Her thoughts started innocently enough, simple things like getting coffee with him or what it would feel like to cuddle on the couch. Her mind drifted into more dangerous territory when she thought about the strong, protector side of Maverick and how that would transfer to the bedroom. Her dreams quickly become R rated when she pictured them in bed together; her writhing and begging for more. Just as Dream Maverick was going to give her exactly that, a vibrating sound rattled the bedside table, causing her to wake up.

Dammit! She had been in the midst of probably getting the best orgasm of her entire life and her damn phone ruined it. Yes, it had been a dream but it felt so real. Her body was on high alert, aware of every tingling part of her. She wanted nothing more to take care of the ache between her legs, but her phone vibrated once more, signaling an incoming text.

Curse her curious nature and her inability to not obsessively check her phone as soon as a notification came in. She groaned and reached for it, seeing a missed FaceTime call and a text, both from Javi. There was nothing more of a buzz kill than having your brother interrupt your sex dream. It was exactly the cold water she needed dumped over her body to kick the horny demon to the curb.

Ofelia pushed herself up into a sitting position on the bed. She was sure her hair was a crazy mess; it was the reason why she hated going to sleep with wet hair. Her head was pounding slightly from the alcohol. Even though she hadn't been wasted, she still had more alcohol than she normally did. Poor Willow, her friend must be absolutely miserable. She hoped Willow saw the medicine she placed near her bed and took it as soon as she woke up. Knowing Willow, it would be a few more hours.

Her brother would just have to deal with her looking like a swamp monster. She clicked on her brother's missed FaceTime call and her face, a very tired and slightly hungover face, stared back at her. It only took two rings until her brother picked up, Camilia snuggled up happily in her daddy's arms.

"Oh my goodness, is that my Camilia? Hi, baby girl!" Ofelia cooed, unable to stop the warm smile her niece brought to her lips. There was still an ache in her heart each time she saw Camilia because her niece was so far away. She felt like she was missing out on her life.

"Tía Ofi!" Camilia said and pointed to what Ofelia guessed was the tv. "I watch Bluey!"

She had no idea what the hell Bluey was, but Ofelia smiled all the same. Her sweet niece climbed off her father's lap and ran off screen, Javi pointing at some toy she was asking for. "Sorry, sis. She's on to her baby dolls now."

"Well, I can't compete with baby dolls." Ofelia laughed, before asking. "So, what's up? Why did you call me at the butt crack of dawn?"

"It's 10am." Javi laughed, rolling his eyes. "And I wanted to make sure you didn't wake up dead or with a weird ass guy you met at the bar last night."

"Javi, you can't wake up dead. You're dead. But also, how did you know I went out to the bar last night? Are you tracking me?"

Javi didn't look apologetic as he shrugged. If anything, her brother looked smug with his cocky grin. "I have my ways and of course I'm tracking you. I didn't want you to end up in a ditch somewhere." It was Ofelia's turn to roll her eyes, but secretly she liked that her brother loved her enough to make sure she got home safe. "But no, Willow told me." He said, stunning Ofelia.

"W...Willow told you? As in my best friend Willow? Since when have you and Willow talked?" Ofelia was honestly confused. She had mentioned her friend a few times to her brother and introduced them over FaceTime a year ago, but that was the extent of their communication. Or so she thought.

"Don't be so shocked, Ofi. You think I'm going to let my sister move across the country and not check in on her from time to time? You got it twisted. Besides, it is hella easy finding people on social media."

Well, that was new. Ofelia wasn't sure how she felt about her brother and Willow talking behind her back. Of course she understood the need to make sure she was okay, Ofelia felt the same way about her family. She couldn't get mad at him for caring, but she could be bothered by the secret exchange. This was definitely something she was going to grill Willow about later.

Since he knew, she supposed there was no harm in telling him about last night. She could actually use his advice on the whole Maverick issue. "It was really fun." She admitted, running a hand through her highly matted hair. "It had been a long time since I allowed myself to let loose and have fun. But, something did happen. And don't freak out!"

She knew immediately she said the wrong thing. Javi's relaxed posture on the couch grew rigged as he sat up straighter, bringing the phone closer to his face. "What the hell happened, Ofelia?"

Yeah, she definitely shouldn't have phrased it like that because she alerted the guard dog inside of him. Too late to take it back now. "There was a creepy guy hitting on me at the bar and getting a little too handsy."

Javi cursed under his breath and Ofelia heard Camila "ooh" in disappointment. "Sorry baby. Papa will put a quarter in the jar." He said to his daughter, before giving his attention back to his sister. "Did he hurt you? What happened?"

"No, Javi. No one hurt me. Or at least no one got the chance to hurt me. Maverick stepped in before the guy could do any real damage."

"Maverick. Who is Maverick?"

Oh right. She hadn't really kept her brother up to date with what was happening in her life. She knew that was common in most siblings, but Javi was one of her best friends and she told him everything. It was unusual that she kept anything from him. She blamed this on her busy cheerleading schedule that consumed her every free minute.

"Maverick was the asshole I kinda started to tell you about, but it's good now." She said quickly, before more steam could pour out of her brother's ears and nostrils. "He's apologized since then. Anyway, he happened to be there that night and scared the jerk away. Then we sorta ended up talking for the rest of the night. Actually, I think we were flirting. No, no we were most definitely flirting."

"Oh." Javi said, his shoulders relaxing. He didn't look ready to fly down to Texas and tear the dude's head off, so Ofelia took that as a win. "Wow, that's great Ofi. Do you like him?"

If that wasn't the world's most loaded question. Yes, she did like him. Maybe. But did she like him enough to end her two year dry spell? Was she really ready to get back out there? "I...yes? Maybe? Fuck, I don't know." She groaned miserably. "Help, Javi. I haven't been in the dating scene for years. I'm rusty as hell. Not to mention jaded."

"You are preaching to the choir, sis." Javi laughed, but his smile didn't quite meet his eyes. Instantly, Ofelia felt guilty for complaining. She was only left at the altar. Which sucked and she wouldn't recommend it, but Javi had found his person. He created life with her and was getting ready to plan their wedding. Until Camilia's mom got into a horrible car accident and died on scene. So yeah her situation was shitty, but what right did she have to complain when Javi's love died?

As if knowing what she was thinking, Javi shook his head. "Stop it. I can handle you complaining to me about things like this. I'm just happy that you are even considering dating again. That's a big step, Ofi."

This was why she loved talking to her brother so much. He knew exactly what to say and what she needed to hear. He could be her light in the fog and she really needed that right now. "I'm scared." She admitted.

"What are you scared of?"

"I...I guess I'm scared to open myself up again. To go on a

ON AND OFF THE FIELD

date, which is essentially like a job interview. First dates are the absolute worst things in existence. There is so much judging going on. What if he's not the person I thought he was? What if he is and I really like him but he doesn't like me? There are so many unknown factors and it's driving me a little crazy." Ofelia said, words pouring from the deepest parts of her insecurity.

Javi didn't judge; he just nodded. "Yeah, I think those feelings are natural though, you know? Dating is fucking terrifying. But that just means you like this person and want to see where it can lead. Maverick is obviously interested, which is why he asked you out. The hard part is out of the way. The date is something you both can enjoy."

"What if he turns out to be horrible? Or thinks that a microwavable dinner counts as a meal? What if we have nothing in common?"

"But what if you do?"

Ofelia groaned. "Javi! You can't answer my question with a question. I need you to tell me what I should do!"

"You know I can't make the decision for you, sis." Javi laughed as Ofelia deflated. Things would be so much easier if people could just make all the hard choices for her. "But I can support you in whatever you choose. I don't think there is any harm in going on one date with Maverick. But if you don't think you are ready to hit the dating scene yet, then that's also fine. There's no timeline that you have to follow."

Just the one that she set for herself. At twenty-six, Ofelia thought she would be married by now, with a child. Her life had changed so drastically from the girl who wanted that life. She enjoyed the path she was on now and knew if she had gone through with her marriage to Hector, she would be miserable. Maybe now was the perfect opportunity to see what other options she had. Like Javi said, she didn't have to put any expectations on the date. She could just see where things went.

"How about this." Javi spoke again, after a beat of silence passed between them. "You go on the date with Maverick. An hour in, I'll call you with some fake emergency. If you feel overwhelmed or things are going badly, answer it and I'll make up some reason for you to leave. But if things are going well and you are having a good time, just ignore my call. I'll take that as a sign that everything is fine."

"Javi, you are a genius!"

"About time you picked up on that." He smirked.

Ofelia loved the idea of having a choice to leave the date if things weren't going as she wanted them too. This would make the anxiety she felt about the date lessen considerably. "Okay. I think I made my decision. Holy shit, I'm going out on a date!" Ofelia said with a sense of giddiness. Yes she was freaking out, but she couldn't help how excited she was about it. This just seemed like another step in the right direction for her. Like she was finally in control of her life again. She just needed to text Maverick that they were on for next week.

"Thank you, Javi. You're the best. I think I should go and text Maverick back-"

"I'm proud of you, Ofi. I'm glad you are doing something for yourself for a change." Her brother cut in, smiling. Ofelia felt her cheeks flush as pride swelled in her chest. "Listen, I gotta take Camilia to the park, but tell me how things go. Keep me informed."

"You know I will. Thank you, Javi. For everything. Wait! Before you go, how's dad? He's still coming to my competition, right?" Ofelia wondered, since the last time they spoke her father had shocked her by dropping that bombshell.

Javi looked confused. "He talked about going?"

Dread began to set in, but she kept it at bay. If there was one thing her father was bad at, it was communication. "Yeah, I was under the impression you put him up to it honestly. But he said he wanted to fly down to see my competition. I think he feels bad since I don't have mama to come watch me. I sent him all the information."

"Right." Javi said slowly, still confused but plastering on a smile. "I'll talk to him about it later and see what's going on. You just worry about your date, but I gotta go before your niece destroys my house due to her impatience." Her brother offered her one last wink before ending their conversation.

With newly found elation and slight trepidation about her father, Ofelia got out of bed. There was one thing she needed to do before checking on Willow. She grabbed her phone and scrolled through the contacts until she landed on Maverick's name. Her fingers flew across the screen without hesitation. She pressed send, watching the blue line move across her screen, disappearing once it was sent.

'You've convinced me. I would love to go out next Saturday."

Ofelia didn't wait to read his reply. She tossed her phone on to the bed and went off to tell a very hungover Willow all about her exciting morning.

Chapter Thirteen

The new school week went by in a blur. Maverick finally found his footing and developed a routine. He juggled between coaching off-season boys and mentoring his baseball team. Both were rewarding in their own way but left him with little time to do anything else during the actual school day. He never realized how needy teenage boys could be. They were like chicks to a mother hen, flocking to him each time a problem arose.

And Maverick loved every fucking second of it.

Since when did he become such a damn softie? He not only helped teenage boys run through workout routines or baseball plays, he also helped them in their personal lives too. Sometimes his players would come to him when they had homework. Maverick didn't know shit about algebra, but he knew how to google. At times, he would have the whole damn team in the gym, sprawled out across the floor and working on their core classes. If they didn't pass, they didn't play. He couldn't preach the importance of academics without supporting their studies.

His office in the gym turned into therapy sessions when his guys needed someone to talk to. They told him far more than he would have ever told any of his teachers or coaches in high school. Maverick didn't think he was qualified to give high school boys relationship advice, but he could listen and impart some wisdom from his own experiences.

Over a short period, he had been able to make strong impressions and relationships with his students, but it also meant he rarely left the gym. It killed him knowing he worked in the same campus as Ofelia but was unable to see her during the day. After her text accepting his date, Maverick's mind hadn't been able to think of little else.

They started texting each other more and on Wednesday, Ofelia had sent a picture of her, draped dramatically over a stack of what he presumed to be student essays. She had that sexy librarian look going on again, with her hair styled in a messy bun, wearing a sweater dress he hadn't seen before. She looked beautiful and Maverick had to do everything in his power to stop himself from finding her room and kissing those pouty lips until they were both breathless.

The only thing keeping him sane was their date on Saturday. An entire day to impress her and finally spend time alone that didn't involve needy teenagers or drunk friends. He wondered if she thought about him as much as he thought about her, since she plagued his every dream.

More than once this week, he woke up hard and had to relieve himself in the shower. It was pathetic, but also incredible. If just the thought of Ofelia made him throb with need, what would it be like when, or rather if, he got her into his bed?

Maverick was getting ahead of himself. He needed Saturday to go well before he started down this road he'd be unable to turn back from. For now, Mav, like many other important things in his life, packed Ofelia and their upcoming date into a neatly wrapped box, shoving it far back into his brain. If he agonized over this, no work would get completed. There was only an hour left in the school day and he wanted to make sure he completed all of his tasks.

Maverick sat down in front of his computer, fully set on updating his grade book and making sure everything was in order for their game next week, when his phone rang. He groaned, fishing around in his pocket until he found it. Breanna's number flashed across the screen and he saw red.

It had been several weeks since she tried reaching out and he had naively thought her calls were finally going to stop. Clearly he needed to take care of the problem himself and it did not involve answering the phone to rehash the past. No, his method was quite simple. He blocked her. He wasn't entirely sure why it took as long as it did, maybe he had been holding on to a pathetic hope they would rekindle once he was ready.

But he knew he never would be ready, so he went back through his call log and finally blocked Breanna. A sense of peace came over him and he was about to put his phone down when it lit up again.

An unknown caller flashed across the screen with a Chicago area code.

He frowned. A part of him wondered if a reporter found his number and was looking for an easy story. It had happened so often directly after his ban, but had slowly become less frequent. Normally he'd ignore it, but he remembered Keanon mentioning someone from Gilmore's firm might be reaching out to him about his case. Or maybe it was Breanna again, calling from a new number, but that didn't seem likely either. She had never once tried contacting him by any other number other than her own and her area code had never switched over to Chicago.

At the last possible second Maverick picked up the phone. "Hello?"

Someone cleared their throat on the other side, away from the speaker. "Maverick Wilson?""

"Speaking."

"Mr. Wilson, this is Lloyd Gilmore from LG Law Firm. A Mr. Keanon Jermaine contacted my firm last week regarding your case. Is this a good time to talk?"

Holy shit. Maverick thought he'd speak to a secretary or an intern. Not Lloyd fucking Gilmore himself. He definitely wasn't prepared for this phone call, but he couldn't demand Gilmore call him back at another time. Maverick's body tensed as he spoke. "Yes, of course. Thank you for taking the time to look at my file."

"It's been a long time since I've dealt with an MLB ban, so I'm intrigued. I had some questions for you before I agreed to take on your case. Now, from what I'm seeing in your file, the reason for your ban is disorderly conduct with a coaching professional and conspiring to fix the game outcome. Is that correct?"

Maverick gritted his teeth. He heard the reasoning a multitude of times, but it never got easier to hear. Gilmore was one of a handful of people who could read the charges without disgust or superiority in his voice. Mav couldn't help but to be a bit unnerved, even though it was quite literally, the man's job to be neutral until he accepted his case. "That is correct."

"This was brought to the Office of the Commissioner by Grant Adams, coach of Chicago Rays, after an altercation took place between you, your former fiancé Breanna Homes, and said coach."

It wasn't a question but Maverick answered anyway. "Yes, sir."

"There isn't a detailed record of what transpired between the three of you. This may be hard to talk about, but it is important for your case. I don't need the long, drawn out story, but I do need the important facts. Do you think you can give me that?"

Did he? He wasn't sure he understood that night and it had been replaying in his head almost daily since it happened. It had gone so wrong, so quickly. If Maverick hadn't stayed late. If he hadn't gone in search of Grant Adams. If he didn't bring Breanna to his practices....so many ifs and all completely out of his control. He could, however, control his own narrative of the sequence of events that happened that night. He needed to get his thoughts in order because they were racing as fast as his heart.

"I understand this is hard to talk about, but it is really important. I could call back later-"

"No, no. It's okay." Maverick assured, not wanting to agonize over this for any longer than he had to. Gilmore was his best shot at getting his old life back; he needed to play along. "Coach Adams had the team come in for conditioning training. My fiancée at the time, Breanna Homes, came with me so she could hang out with the other wives and girlfriends. I was already hesitant to go because I was getting over a mild case of food poisoning and I didn't want to push my body."

"Did Breanna go with you to all your practices?" Lloyd asked. Maverick heard the click of a pen and knew the man was writing down their conversation.

"Not at first. She didn't like one of the other wives, but my last three months playing was when she really started to come to each practice."

"I see. Continue." Lloyd said.

"I started to feel nauseous and my trainer told me to hit the showers. He didn't want me to push myself anymore. So I left practice early and headed down to the locker room."

"Is there an office in the locker room?" Lloyd asked, interjecting again.

"There is, though Adams rarely used it." He said, remembering how his coach hardly visited the locker rooms. "But when I got down there, I saw the light on in the office and then I heard a grunt. I thought someone was hurt or in trouble. When I walked in..." Maverick stopped. This was the hard part. A piece of him died that day, perhaps his innocence. He had been naïve enough to think love was enough, but it wasn't. And it hadn't been for a long time.

When he continued, he closed his eyes and remembered the scene. "Breanna was bent over his desk, naked minus her bra. Grant Adams was behind her, pants down around his legs. He was...inside of her, and they were in the middle of having sex and neither noticed me. Breanna saw me first and-" He would never forget the look on her face. It shattered any hopes of a future with her and this team. "She looked part relieved and part smug. I got the sense this had been going on for a long time, but I was too much of an idiot to notice."

Lloyd didn't change his tone as he spoke, but Maverick detected a softness to his voice that hadn't been there before. "According to the report, you attacked Grant Adams and struck Breanna? Is that true?"

A bitter laugh left Mav's lips. "Hardly. The man attacked me first. He had the audacity to be pissed at me when I walked in on him fucking my fiancée. He lunged and I defended myself. Breanna tried to pull me off, but she got caught in the crossfire. I'm not sure which one of us pushed her back, but I didn't slap her. She hit her face on the desk when she fell. I screamed, said things I'm not proud of. I was angry and hurt. Breanna told me they'd been sleeping around behind my back for months."

"And Grant Adams, he's a married man is that correct?" Lloyd asked.

Maverick nodded, even though the man couldn't see him. Grant and his wife had been married for over twenty years. She was a former beauty pageant queen turned doctor. Arguably more of a success story than her husband. "He's married to Geneva Adams."

"I see. This is starting to make more sense. Adams claims you forced your fiancée on him, to manipulate him so you have more field time. Not sure how that equates to fixing the outcome of the game, but I'll dive into that. The other claim, disorderly conduct, will be harder to overturn. But from what you've told me, I think we have a pretty strong case in your favor."

"Wait, are you saying you'll take my case?" Maverick was stunned. At the beginning of his fall from grace, Maverick had reached out to countless lawyers. Only a handful ever got back to him and only to say they wouldn't represent him. Grant Adams was so lawyered up that no one was willing to risk their career for a case that seemed like a losing battle. Yet Lloyd offered his services, despite the risk to his career.

"I'll be honest, Maverick. Your file interested me and believe it or not, you have not been the first to reach out about Grant Adams. You are, however, the first I see with a solid case. If you are willing to proceed forward, then so am I." The man said, throwing the ball back into Mav's court.

Maverick had waited to hear those words for so long. He had a case. *Finally.*

He thought he would feel a sense of satisfaction, but he just felt slightly queasy, and he couldn't understand why. Still, he knew, even if his body said otherwise, this wasn't an opportunity he could afford to pass up. "I'm ready. What do you require from me?"

"In about a day or so, I'll have my assistant send over a contract and a few other documents I'll have you read over and sign. I don't need anything from you right now while I start building your case. When it's time, you'll need to come back to Chicago for your hearing.

"Once the process starts, it can go fast. I reckon Grant Adams's lawyers will be eager to get this case out of the way in a hurry." Lloyd said and then went over a few details of his contract and payment plans. Once he finished describing the nuts and bolts of the contract, Lloyd finished by saying, "I'll be in touch. Keep an eye out for my call and check your email."

The call ended, leaving Maverick in a stew of his own mixed emotions. This is what he wanted. He wanted to clear his name and get back to the life he had worked so hard to obtain. Baseball *was* his life. His purpose. So why did he have to convince himself of that?

Maverick started to pack up his duffle, unable to think about work now. He needed to go home and call Keanon about what happened. Slinging his duffel over his shoulders, Maverick headed for the door. He looked back once, to make sure he didn't leave anything behind, before turning off the light. He shut his door, locking it before turning around, preparing to walk out to his car, and...

He ran straight into Willow, startling her. "Oh! Maverick, don't sneak up on me like that! You nearly gave me a heart attack."

Maverick just stared. "Willow, you're in my gym. Quietly

stalking outside my door. How is it that I'm the one getting yelled at?" It was strange to see the woman here. Maverick had only ever seen her come in here with Ofelia, but even then Willow never stayed long, and she most certainly didn't come alone. "Did you need something?"

"Actually, I did, and I know you are eager to get home, so I'll be quick." She said as her face changed from friendly to what he assumed was meant to be intimidating. It was as effective as a puppy with a knife, cute and maybe a little spooky, but mostly comical. "You're taking Ofelia out on Saturday-"

"Yes, I'm aware of that."

"I'm not finished." Willow did not appear pleased at being interrupted. "Let me start over. What I came down here to say is that Ofelia is very special to me. I love her like my own sister. I don't know if you know how big of a deal this is for her to agree to go out with someone. I don't want to see her get hurt. You understand?"

Maverick did. He smiled, trying to reassure her friend. Willow looked on the brink of crying, and he didn't handle tears well. "Willow, calm down. I know Ofelia is your best friend. I wouldn't do anything to intentionally hurt her. I like her and I want to see where this goes. I promise, I'll be a perfect gentleman." Well, mostly. There were a few things he wanted to do that were not very gentleman-like.

Thankfully his words seemed to ease Willow. She let out a deep breath and the tension in her body visibly eased. "Good. That's good. Because if you hurt her, I will sic my husband Karl on you and....actually no. Karl would think you were cute and then I would have another problem on my hand. My point is, don't hurt her or I'll make sure you get bus duty for the rest of your days."

"You wouldn't dare." He smirked.

"Oh, I dare! I dare so hard. I'm watching you Maverick." She did a weird hand gesture, signaling she had her eyes on him. "Also don't tell Ofelia I threatened you. Make sure you pick her up at her house. Don't have her meet you anywhere, that's not classy enough for her. I have a few ideas on where you can take her, so I'll be in touch."

With that last ominous threat, Willow gave him one last piercing glare before walking out the gym. She stopped when she got to the double door to scowl at him once more for good measure and then disappeared entirely.

Today was shaping up to be more eventful than he anticipated. He didn't think he could handle another intense phone call or strange encounter, so he walked to his truck a little faster than normal and drove away without looking back.

Chapter Fourteen

Ofelia was sweating. It was so damn hot in her bathroom. Not only were her mirror lights shining spotlights on her but coupled with the heat of her curling wand, made the space unbearable. Also her arms hurt, like a lot. Which was pathetic but they burned from exertion. *Note to self, stop skipping arm day in favor of butt day.*

"You should have gone with the curlers." Willow said unhelpfully. "I told you it will save a lot of time and you'd be on to makeup by now. But no one listens to me."

"You have my curlers, Willow!" Ofelia glared at her phone. "And besides, I'm almost done. Stop distracting me."

"Why did you FaceTime us both if you don't want us talking to you?" Javi asked, distracted by his video games. She knew Camilia was napping because there was no way her brother could play his games in peace.

"Because," Ofelia threw her arms down, a bit too dramatically because her phone fell into the sink. "Ah shit. I just needed to give my arms a break, not drown you both in my sink." She mumbled, grabbing her phone to perch them up against the mirror once again. "Sorry. Anyways, I called you both because you are the two people I love most in this world and I'm fucking nervous. I need to see friendly faces while I get ready and I need you both making sure I don't talk myself out of going."

Today was her first official date with Maverick. The nerves set in the moment she woke, and they nearly consumed her. It didn't make any sense, since this was the first time all week she started feeling anxious. She talked to Maverick daily since last Friday night. Never on the phone, but rather they texted each other dumb memes and mundane life events. It was so easy to talk to him, but it was easy to talk to anyone with a screen dividing them.

Today Ofelia wouldn't have the luxury of a screen between them; a concept that both thrilled and scared her. It was silly to be this nervous, especially since they had spent a great deal of time together last Friday night. It still didn't have the "date" word attached. Now she actually had to try putting herself out there. What did one talk about on a date?

"Your arms have rested enough. Now back to curling. You are almost done. Maverick should be there in thirty minutes." Willow piped up after she deemed enough time had passed.

"Thirty minutes! What the hell! I don't have time....wait." Ofelia paused, narrowing her eyes into little slits as she glared back into the phone for the second time in five minutes. "How do you know what time Maverick is coming?"

"You think I'm going to let my best friend go out with a stranger, albeit smoking hot, and not get his number? Javi has it too." Willow smiled triumphantly.

"Javi!"

Javi threw his hands up in a 'don't look at me' gesture, feigning innocence. "Hey, don't be mad that we care for you."

Despite her best efforts, Ofelia couldn't stay mad at the two of them. Annoyed...but not mad. "Do not text or threaten him. I don't need him thinking I associate with crazy people."

"Sweetie, he saw me shit faced and crying over my contact. If he doesn't think I'm crazy by now, nothing will." Willow had a point. "There's nothing wrong with us having his phone number. Just in case."

"Fine, whatever." Ofelia acquiesced, finishing her hair. "Let me go get dressed first. Stay here."

"Where the fuck else would we go?" She heard Javi calling after her, but Ofelia was already deep within her closet.

It wasn't a particularly cold day, but a slight chill hung in the air. A skirt was out of the question...unless she paired it with one of her thick tights. That could be cute, if only she could find her brown corduroy skirt. It only took a few moments of searching before she found her skirt and the long sleeved, black bodysuit she typically paired it with. Would it be a pain in the ass to pee today? Yes, yes it would. But she also looked cute as hell, so she was willing to risk it.

It took Ofelia approximately five minutes to get dressed, which she hoped left her enough time to apply some makeup. When she walked back into her small bathroom, she was surprised to hear her brother and Willow chatting about the best toppings for pizza. She had no clue how they arrived at this conversation, but it was cute to see her best friend and brother getting along.

"So how do I look?" Ofelia asked, hating to interrupt their very intense conversation on whether pineapples went on pizza. They didn't, in Ofelia's opinion.

Willow and Javi looked over at her at the same time. She watched as their eyes widened, looking at her as if she just sprouted angel wings on her back. Neither one of them spoke though and it didn't help her nerves one bit. "Someone needs to say something now before I call this off."

"Ofi, you look beautiful, just like mama when she was younger." Javi's voice spoke up first, sending unexpected emotions coursing through her body. Hearing that made Ofelia feel like her mother was still here, that she carried her wherever she went. She fought back tears at his comment.

"Sweetie, you are beautiful, but you have about ten minutes until Maverick gets there. No time for tears! Makeup. Now!" Willow's command ended the sweet moment. Her friend smiled at her encouragingly as she started listing off what Ofelia needed to do. Brows, concealer, mascara, and blush. She didn't have time to do a full face, but she could enhance her natural beauty.

Ofelia finished applying her lipstick when her doorbell rang. She let out a sound of surprise, eyes wide in terror. "Holy shit, he's here! What should I do?"

"Well, personally, I'd answer the door, but that's just me." Javi said, smirking. He was trying to lighten the mood, but Ofelia felt on the brink of a panic attack. Was it normal to be this nervous before a first date? Was it too late to cancel?

"Yes! It's very too late to cancel and I wouldn't let you do that!" Willow said. Ofelia hadn't realized she said that out loud.

"Remember Ofi, we have a plan." Javi spoke, his soothing voice was exactly what she needed. "In an hour, I'll call you. Then you can decide if you want to answer or not. You have options, don't forget that. Now hang up and go answer the door. Remember, have fun."

Both Javi and Willow waved goodbye before disconnecting, leaving her alone. She could do this, deserved to do this. It would be a shame to waste a good outfit and hair day. She repeated her silent pep talk as she walked to the door.

Taking a big breath and before she could chicken out, Ofelia opened the door a little too forcefully because Maverick took a step back in alarm. "Uh, sorry. Hi." *Great start*, she thought miserably. "I guess I don't know my own strength."

Maverick chuckled, probably at her expense. "No worries." He assured as his eyes swept down her body. His gaze landed on her feet and slowly made their way back up until he met her gaze. He looked at her as if she were art on display, his smoldering gaze hot and assessing. "You look beautiful. Wow."

His words brought on a faint blush but also boosted her confidence. Since he allowed himself a once over, it was only fair she did the same. She had never seen him outside his uniform or work out gear. Today he wore faded jeans that looked expensive, but Ofelia couldn't be sure. She knew virtually nothing about men's fashion. His black and white shirt fit his torso nicely. He paired it with an oversized army green jacket. When she finally reached his eyes again, Maverick was smirking.

The man exuded sexual energy, leaving her hot in all the right places.

Heat soared through her body, going directly to her core. Great, now she was nervous and horny. If she made it out of this date alive, it would be a miracle. "Are you ready to go?" Maverick asked.

"Let me go get my purse." She said, disappearing back into her house and returning a moment later with a small, over the shoulder purse. "Now I'm ready."

As they walked to the truck, Maverick's hand hovered near the center of her back. She could feel his phantom touch, and she had the urge to stop walking entirely so she could feel his body against hers. She resisted though and Mav opened the door to his truck for her. She didn't remember the vehicle being this obnoxiously tall. Maverick had to give her a little boost before getting in on the driver's side. "I didn't take you as a truck man."

"Trust me, I'm not. I hate this damn truck. The gas mileage on it is shit and I feel way too tall when I'm driving." Maverick said, buckling up. "It's not mine though. It belongs to my friend Keanon. I, uh, am currently living in his vacation home and this happened to come with the house."

That was an interesting tidbit about Maverick. She wondered if she could ask more about it, but maybe they weren't in the hard questions portion of the date yet. She could file that for later. For now, she suspected it better to keep the conversation light. "So, do I get to know where we're going today? Or are we sticking to the fake date scenario we made up last week?"

"So I should probably get this out in the open before we officially start our date." Maverick said, causing Ofelia to raise a brow. Nothing in his tone raised alarms, but the statement piqued her interest.

"Okay...should I be scared? If you are about to tell me you have a furry kink, I'm going to have to leave this truck. Not to kink shame you or anything, live your true self."

Maverick's expression turned positively wicked. "Are you already thinking about me in bed, sweetheart?" He all but purred, melting her panties right off her.

Oh shit, she definitely walked into that one. Her cheeks flamed with heat because she *had* thought of him in bed. Multiple times. Having him so close brought back those dirty dreams and the bleak reminder that she hadn't had sex in two years. "No! No, of course not. I was just-"

"I'm messing with you, Ofelia." Maverick laughed, stopping her babbling. "For the record, no. That is not a kink I have but maybe I can fill you in on those later." He winked and Ofelia felt like she could explode at that very moment. "What I was going to say is that I was completely on board with the whole cooking thing even though I'm terrible at it. So I bought stuff to make pizza."

"Sounds easy enough."

"That's what I thought!" Maverick agreed. "But just to make sure, I decided to make a tester pizza, to see if I could do it. And...let's just say I'm so glad Keanon has a fire extinguisher under the sink because it could have ended badly."

Ofelia stifled her laugh with her hand. A cooking Maverick was an adorable image but hearing he nearly burned down his entire house because he was attempting to make pizza for her, was both incredibly hilarious and sexy. Why was burnt food turning her on? She seriously needed to get her priorities sorted.

"So, to spare you from any fire damage, I am going to have to insist that I take you out somewhere. This way, I can assure your safety and your sated appetite." He grinned, showing off his white teeth.

Ofelia pretended to think about it, biting her lip in concentration. "Hmm. I accept. However, I insist that for our next date, I will cook you an authentic Mexican dinner. I haven't had the chance to cook for many people since I've moved to Texas and I miss it."

"Second date, huh?"

"Of course that is what you got from that." Ofelia rolled her eyes but couldn't hide the smile twitching at the corner of her lips. "Do we have a deal?"

Maverick didn't hesitate. He put his truck in drive and took it out of her driveway. "Sweetheart, if that means more time with you, I'll agree to just about anything."

Chapter Fifteen

Maverick had been nervous about picking Ofelia up. He couldn't remember the last time he felt so tongue-tied around a woman, but Ofelia rendered him senseless. He was surprised he had the capacity to string two words together, let alone a sentence.

Was it cliché to say she took his breath away?

Ofelia rested her arm on the middle console, right next to his. A few times, Maverick ran his knuckles against hers and from the corner of his eyes, he swore he saw her smile. It made him feel bold and like he actually might not seriously fuck up their date.

Their first stop was an indie bookstore Maverick extensively researched last night. It took up most of his time because only big book retailers popped up in his search, but Maverick didn't want to take Ofelia somewhere she had been a dozen times. He wanted a spot that would be more cozy and intimate, where he wouldn't have to battle crowds for Ofelia's attention.

Which is why he settled on a family owned bookstore called Quills, Books, and Coffee. He knew he'd made the right choice when Ofelia's beautiful face lit up in wonder. "I've never been here before. Oh my goodness, it's so cute!" She said and exited his truck before he could cut off the engine. By the time he was out of the car, Ofelia waited at the front door for him.

"You are about to let a bookworm roam freely in a cute little bookstore. Are you ready for that responsibility?" Ofelia asked. Maverick thought she was teasing, but she waited expectantly for his answer.

Maverick patted his jeans pocket and gave her a thumbs up. "My wallet and I are prepared for this. We've been preparing all week actually."

"Oh, I don't mean you have to pay-"

Maverick reached for her hand, effectively silencing Ofelia as she glanced down at their interwoven fingers. Her hand was warm in his, molding perfectly to his own. He half wondered if she would pull back, but Ofelia seemed to relax her body after the initial shock passed through her. "I know you don't mean for me to pay. Despite my current job-" he faltered, unsure how much she knew about his time before coaching. It was something he would need to bring up when they were at dinner. "-I have money. And I would love nothing more than to buy you tattooed shavings of dead trees."

That earned him a laugh and a playful shove. "Oh hush. But don't say I didn't warn you." She teased before leading him inside, their hands still clasped firmly together.

He couldn't boast about not being strapped for cash because he didn't want to come across as cocky, but Maverick didn't hurt for money. He made a decent amount from baseball and his sponsors. Even though his current income was only that of a high school coach, he had enough money to live comfortably for the rest of his life.

It was only when Ofelia began to take books off the shelves

that his hand fell to his side as she paged through a thick book. He wasn't much of a reader. He had never enjoyed it as much as some of his other friends and family. Part of his lack of reading stemmed from his short attention span and the need to be moving and doing something. When he played baseball, his mind and body were always occupied, and he felt completely at peace. He missed that feeling.

As Ofelia browsed, Maverick soon became the designated book carrier. Which he didn't mind at all. He liked seeing the various titles and covers she enjoyed. Most of the covers she put in his basket were colorful with cartoon people on the front. "You really like these types of books. What are they?"

"Romance books." She said, tossing another one in the basket. "I find them empowering and a way that I can freely express my romantic needs. I've learned a lot about myself from reading romance books. Like the fact that I cannot stand miscommunication. It happens a lot in some romance genres and it frustrates me beyond belief each time."

"My ma has a huge stack of romance books by her bed. She calls them bodice rippers." He shuddered.

"Then your mother is an empowered sexual lady and should be proud of that."

Maverick didn't want to think of his mother as anything sexual and left the comment at that. Ofelia took that moment to enter a new book section. "Fantasy?"

"Oh yes. I love a good fantasy in between my romances. The world building is spectacular and I love quests. Game of Thrones is my all time favorite fantasy series, but they are massive."

"I've only seen the show."

This time it was Ofelia's turn to cringe. "Oh Mav, there is so much I need to teach you."

He smirked. "Word around town is that you're a pretty good teacher, Mrs. Mendez."

She beamed with pride which made Maverick want to make her feel like that always. "Aren't you lucky?"

He was. Oh so very lucky.

They continued like that for a while. He'd ask her questions each time she handed him a book and she would go on a long tangent of how excited she was to read it and what drew her to the book. The way she described her stories and reading was nothing short of magical. He hung on to her every word, finding himself agreeing or nodding as if he too were a reader.

By the time they finished, Maverick held nine books and a bullet journal as Ofelia fussed over which books to put back because she couldn't possibly let him spend his money on so many. Maverick did what anyone in his situation would do: turn towards the register and ignore her protests.

By the time Ofelia approached him, the cashier handed him his large bag of books. She tried giving him a reproachful glare, but he wasn't buying it. Her bouncing feet and cute lip bite said differently. "Thank you." Ofelia murmured, giving him a swift hug before taking the bag.

They headed back to the car and thirty minutes later found themselves sitting at a locally owned, authentic Italian restaurant. Admittedly, this place had been Willow's suggestion. After the fiasco of his pizza, Maverick wanted to make sure he took Ofelia somewhere she liked and Willow assured him Ofelia would melt. The interior of Stefano's Italian Cuisine was cozy. It was small, but intimate. Each table had a thick white tablecloth with flowers and wine waiting for them. The lights were low, giving off a romantic ambiance.

Hanging on the walls were intricate art pieces by Italian artists, family photos, and photography of Italy. A small fountain decorated one of the few free walls. Small stone cherubs forever immortalized in dancing positions lined the edges. Their table sat directly in front of the fountain and Maverick noticed the abundance of coins littering the bottom.

"I have been dying to come here." Ofelia said once they were both settled at the table, a fresh basket of bread was placed in front of them, alongside a small plate of olive oil. "I'm so okay with you burning the pizza now."

"If I knew a burnt pizza would get you out on a date with me, I would have burnt hundreds by now." Maverick mused, reaching for the bread. He wanted to know more about the gorgeous woman sitting in front of him, but he didn't know where to start. He couldn't ask her anything he was unwilling to answer himself.

Maverick landed on the safest option he could think of and asked. "So, I heard you lived in California before Texas? Why the switch?"

Apparently that was the worst fucking question he could ask because he watched Ofelia tense up. She seemed locked in a silent battle with herself and Maverick mentally kicked himself for asking such a dumb question.

Why do people move, dumbass? To start over. He never wanted to take a question back so badly, but before he could dig himself into a deeper hole, Ofelia surprised him by answering.

"To escape. I was engaged at the time, but my ex left me on our wedding day." She admitted, looking at him as if he were the one that needed pity.

A pang of jealousy shot through him upon hearing Ofelia had been so close to getting married. Anger for the stupid prick who left her came next. It was illogical for him to feel jealous and angry when he had also been engaged to someone else.

Even so, he wanted to throttle the man that broke this woman's heart, but also thank him for getting himself out of the picture.

His brain was a confusing place.

"Sorry, I didn't mean to make things awkward. I'm over it! Mostly, but definitely over *him*." Ofelia said quickly, probably thinking she was the reason for his silence.

"No, please don't apologize. I was just thinking about how idiotic this man sounds. I hope that isn't too forward of me to say."

Ofelia waved his comment away. "You're right, it took me a while to reach that mindset, you know? So long in fact that you are the first guy I've been out on a date since."

He liked knowing that he was the first person she had dated since her breakup. She trusted him enough to agree to this date and Maverick couldn't help but feel prideful along with a fierce sense of need. "I like knowing that I'm your first, sweetheart." He said it because he knew she would blush and it would color her cheeks like he liked it. She did blush, but this time she never took her eyes off him. Her comfort around him was growing. Good.

"What about you? Any skeletons in your closet, Mav?" Ofelia bit her lip and Maverick felt it straight down to his cock. She looked so fucking sexy, biting her lip and looking at him as if she knew exactly what she did to him. Under the table, he swore her legged rub against him. All the blood from his body headed south.

Trying to readjust himself covertly, Maverick leaned against the side of his chair. She had given him the perfect opportunity for him to talk about his past. He wanted to be able to clear up any misunderstandings. "Did you know I used to be a Major League Baseball player?"

She nodded.

"So you also know I got banned."

Another nod.

"What exactly have you read about me?" Maverick shook out his napkin, giving his nervous fingers something to do while he waited for her answer. He smoothed the cloth over his lap, trying his hardest to keep his expression unreadable.

"Just that. I know that you were in the MLB, but I'm not clear on the reason. You have to forgive me because my knowledge of baseball is nonexistent. The more I looked into it, the less everything made sense. Then I realized how much of a creeper I was being, so I stopped looking. I figured I didn't need to know." She shrugged, offering him a sympathetic smile. "I heard that you were good."

A wave of sadness overtook him, darkening his features. Maverick didn't think it would ever get easier to think about his past, but the pain had dulled to a slight ache rather than a sharp cut. "I was." He said after a moment, not fully present. Ofelia didn't try to stop him or encourage him on and Maverick liked her all the more for that. She was willing to sit there and listen. The only comfort she gave was placing her hand over his, squeezing it gently as if to say, *I'm here.*

After that, the words began to tumble out of Maverick. He told her everything. How he met Breanna to how they became high school sweethearts and eventually engaged. He spoke about slowly losing the love between them and the fateful night he found Breanna with his coach, leading to his downfall. And how he finally began to work with a lawyer in attempts to right the wrongs of his situation.

When he was finished, he dared to look up and noticed the entire time he had been talking, Ofelia had tears in her eyes.

"Mav," she started gently after Maverick poured his heart out. "I'm so, so sorry. I can't imagine the pain the situation has caused and the anger you must carry because of it. What happened to you is wrong and you were unfairly pulled from a game that means the world to you. Please don't feel like you need to carry this baggage alone. You aren't alone. If there is anything I can do while you are dealing with the legal actions, let me know. I can make some pretty fantastic comfort food if you want to eat your feelings."

No one had ever said those words to him before. Keanon was the only other person who understood Maverick's struggle and offered up his home and car. Maverick would never forget his kindness, but they didn't talk about how Maverick felt. Not past surface level emotions, at least. Ofelia offered the emotional piece he had been missing for years, a confidant he could bare his soul to. This beautiful woman couldn't possibly understand how much those words touched Maverick.

"You don't know how badly I want to kiss you right now." He said unabashedly, his piercing gaze staring into Ofelia's hazel ones. She didn't look away or blush like Maverick expected her to. The magnetic pull between them became almost palpable.

"Perhaps you should show me then."

Fuck yes. He would jump across this damn table, pull her lips to his and kiss Ofelia until she was breathless. Until she begged him for more. Maverick wouldn't stop until she was unable to take any more pleasure. He desperately wanted her in his arms, bodies melding together until they fit perfectly as one.

Except none of those things happened. Reality came crashing down when their waiter, a portly man with a thick mustache, placed their dinner in front of them, breaking the spell they were under. Maverick didn't remember ordering, but they clearly had.

Dammit! He had never been cock blocked by food before,

this was a first. Luckily, he wasn't the only one that was disappointed. Ofelia grimaced when the waiter chatted with her briefly, eyes flashing back to Maverick in silent apologies.

Even though the raw sexual tension between them simmered down to a light flame, their conversation didn't stop. It flowed freer and without restraints now that their past was laid out on the table. Never before did Maverick find himself wanting to learn every small detail about a person before. Where did she go to school? Did she always want to be a teacher? What music does she listen to? Maverick asked all these questions, soaking up the new information like a sponge.

Ofelia asked him questions too, mostly about his baseball career and his family. He surprised himself by finding he wanted to talk about growing up with baseball. How he started when he was only four years old in T-Ball and how that slowly progressed into his full time career. She was a good listener, always nodding and smiling at the appropriate times and laughing at his dumb jokes. She would take time to ask him questions as well as answer a few of his own.

The food in front of them lay untouched for quite some time. When Maverick finally remembered he had a bowl of pasta, it had already gone lukewarm. Neither of them seemed to mind, far more invested in learning about each other's lives than the delicious food they ordered.

By the time the check came, two hours had passed by in a blink of an eye. Their date was reaching an end, but Maverick wasn't ready to say goodbye. When they got up to leave, Ofelia reached for his hand, a simple gesture but one he didn't take for granted. He leaned down, pressing the faintest kiss to the top of her head, letting his lips linger for a second longer than necessary. Ofelia leaned into his touch, and he silently cursed the fact they were in the middle of a restaurant.

"I guess I should get you home." Maverick said, pulling back just enough to see her face.

The idea didn't seem to thrill Ofelia either, but she nodded reluctantly. "Yeah, I think you're right." She said, but made no movement to start walking first, so Maverick took the lead.

This time when he helped her in the truck, his hands lingered on her hips, feeling her soft curves underneath. He let go all too soon and made his way over to the driver's seat. He tossed Ofelia his phone, already unlocked. "You pick the music this time."

Her eyes lit up, and he saw her instantly click on his Spotify. From the corner of his eyes, he saw Ofelia scroll through the music before landing on her chosen song. Or so he thought a song would start playing over his car speakers, but he was greeted by haunting music and then a crisp female voice.

Ofelia laughed at his expression and put his phone down in the console. "I do like music, but I also love murder mystery podcasts. This podcast is about a serial killer that got away with his crimes for two decades, even though the people of his small town suspected him for years. So many were terrified to speak up because they thought they'd be next."

Morbid, but damn if he didn't get sucked right in the crazy story, hanging on to the woman's every word of the bizarre and frankly fucked up descriptions of the man's poor victims. The podcast made their twenty-five minute drive back to Ofelia's home pass too quickly. By the time he pulled into her driveway, the episode was nearly finished. Naturally, they both sat for another five minutes to see how it ended.

"Okay, I'm hooked." Maverick said as soon as it ended. "I didn't expect to hear about chopped up remains on our date, but you know. First time for everything."

"I already favorited it for you, but you need to go back and listen to the first two episodes and report back. Hearing about the man's upbringing is honestly outrageous and makes so much sense as to why he turned out the way that he did."

The truck then grew quiet, both of them realizing they were completely alone and in close proximity. Both unbuckled as soon as Maverick put the truck in park. Maverick's hand was close to Ofelia's thigh. Just a few more centimeters, and he could have his hand splayed across it. The same heated urgency from earlier hit him in full force.

Maverick cleared his throat, needing to break the tension before he did or said something out of line. "I should-"

"I want you to kiss me." Ofelia blurted, stunning them both into silence. She bit her lip, as if contemplating what to say next before she did. "I want it, but only if you do. And if you don't want it that's cool too, but I-"

His mouth was on hers, cutting off the last of her ramblings. She squeaked when his lips pressed against hers and his large hands cupped her face in a feathery light caress. Ofelia didn't kiss him back right away and for a second, Maverick thought he might have scared her. Until she leaned into his touch and kissed him back, sighing softly.

The sigh was enough to drive Maverick crazy. He deepened the kiss, his tongue running along her bottom lip. When she opened for him, Maverick wasted no time exploring her mouth, needing the taste of her on his lips. His tongue flicked across hers and elicited the quietest of moans. Ofelia moved her hands up to rest on Maverick's chest, rubbing her hands along his shoulders.

"Fuck, baby girl." Maverick panted. "I need you closer."

"You, wha-?" Ofelia said breathlessly, but Maverick was already pulling Ofelia over the middle console and into his lap. She giggled in surprise, but eagerly helped move her body closer to his. Soon her legs straddled his thighs and his hands moved down her back, hovering over the curve of her ass. Ofelia shifted her body, grinding down over his hardness.

If she noticed his hard cock against her ass, Ofelia didn't say anything nor did she pull away. Instead, she leaned down and kissed him this time, putting her entire body into it. They groaned in unison, Maverick bucking up, creating more fiction between them.

The woman was going to be the death of him. Or his rebirth. He was still unsure of which.

"Mav," She moaned his name, so breathless and full of lust. Fuck he was never going to get the sound of her moaning his name out of his mind. Her flushed cheeks, looking as turned on as him, made his cock harden painfully in his pants.

"Tell me what you want, baby girl." He murmured against her smeared red lips. No doubt he was supporting his own set of red lips as well.

She did that thing again, where she bit her lip and looked at him like there was nothing in this world she wanted to devour more than him. "You." She whispered.

With every fiber of his being, Maverick wanted nothing more than to indulge Ofelia's request. He wanted to hear her moan his name again. To feel her tongue all over his body. He wanted to look into her eyes as they reached their peak and came down from their high together. And if Ofelia were anyone else, he wouldn't hesitate taking her to bed, no problem.

But she wasn't anyone else. Ofelia was someone who was starting to mean a lot to him, and he didn't want her to get the impression that he only wanted a quick lay. "Ofelia, I think-"

"Oh shit." Ofelia lurched back, hitting the steering wheel. Her eyes were wide, full of panic. "I messed this up. I pushed too hard, too fast. I'm sorry, Mav." Tears were pooling in the corner of her eye as she frantically reached for the handle, attempting to flee Maverick.

Maverick reached out, placing his hand over hers to hold her in place. "There is absolutely nothing more I want than to take you inside, strip you naked, and taste that sweet little pussy, baby girl." Ofelia sucked in a breath, eyes fluttering close for a brief moment. "But, and I hate myself so much for saying this, I don't think either one of us is ready.

"When I take you Ofelia, it's not going to be in the front seat of this ridiculous truck. It'll be when you are truly mine and we are both ready for it." Maverick finished, leaning in to give her a soft kiss on her lips. "Tonight when I get home, I'll think of all the ways I wish to ravish you as I get off to the thought of your legs wrapped around me, moaning my name."

Ofelia shuddered and warily nodded her head in agreement. He should leave it at that, but he had a clearly needy female on his lap and if one of them didn't come in the next ten minutes, it would be a waste.

He could give her exactly what she needed, a final thing to remember him by, all while not lifting a single finger.

Ofelia went for the door, prepared to leave his car, but Maverick was faster. He grabbed her wrist, holding it in place. "Do you want to get off, baby girl?"

"I thought you said-"

"I know what I said. Answer my question. Do you want to get off?"

She was already so close as it was, he could see the way her chest heaved and the flush along her cheeks and down her neck. Slowly she nodded. "Yes," she whispered.

He waited for her to change her mind, but Ofelia continued to stare at him expectantly. He brought her hands to the hem of her skirt. "Let's see how well you listen." He murmured. The moonlight hit her so perfectly that he could make out just enough of her. "Push up your skirt."

"You aren't going to do that for me?"

He smacked her ass, causing her to gasp in surprise. "I'm not touching you, baby girl. But I'm going to watch you get yourself off for me before I drop you off at your door."

She glared at him, but he could see the eagerness in her eyes. Maverick normally wasn't this dominant and he doubted Ofelia was one to fuck her date in the front seat of his car on the first date, but there was an undeniable rightness about this moment.

She did as she was told, pulling her skirt up around her waist. She had on leggings, but didn't ask her to take those off. He wanted her to have some semblance of modesty in case they were caught by a nosy neighbor. "Show me what you would do if you were alone." He said.

Ofelia's hand shook. For a moment he thought that she would call this off and Maverick would have stopped immediately. Except she didn't do that. She moved her hand and let it disappear into her leggings. He knew the moment she touched her clit because a low moan left her lips. His dick had been hard before, but now it painfully pressed against his jeans and her ass. "Tell me how wet you are."

She did not hesitate this time. "Very. Very wet." She moaned, as her hand moved faster underneath her leggings. It was a new kind of torture to watch someone masturbate before you, but not actually being able to see it happening.

Her needy moans began to increase and Ofelia moved her head to rest against his forehead. "Mav…"

"Let it out, baby girl. Make yourself come." He whispered, unable to stop himself from bucking up against her core.

That was exactly what she needed because he watched her body tense up, her breathing hitch, and listened as she moaned longingly in his ear as she came for him. They stayed like that, pressed together, forehead to forehead, and breathing heavily for a few minutes.

"You didn't get off." Ofelia said after a moment, breaking the silence.

"This wasn't about me. It was about you."

"But-"

"Next time." He assured her, silencing any more protests with a swift kiss to her lips. He then began to help her fix her clothes, just enough so that she could walk out of this truck without it looking too scandalized. He found her blushing each time he would look at her, but he did not see regret or embarrassment in her eyes.

"Do you regret it?" Maverick asked, needing to be sure.

Ofelia shook her head, loose curls falling down her face. "Not even a little bit."

"Good." He smirked before finally opening the car door to let them both exit.

They walked in peaceful silence to her door, Maverick stopping at the entryway. Ofelia turned to him. "I had such a fun time tonight, Mav. And...thank you for stopping us before we got too carried away. I am not a one night stand type of person. I wouldn't have wanted you to feel that way. What we did was incredibly hot and enough."

Maverick also didn't want one night with her. He wanted plenty...when they were both ready and knew what they had between each other was more than lust. "I only hate myself a little for stopping us, though I did enjoy the show immensely." Maverick smiled and laughed with Ofelia.

"Goodnight, Maverick. I'll text you tomorrow?"

"I'll text you tonight." He winked and stepped forward. He leaned down, bringing his lips to hers one last time. He kept it light, knowing he wouldn't have the strength to stop himself for a second time. "Goodnight, sweetheart."

"I prefer baby girl." Ofelia quipped.

"Noted." He said, grinning like a fool. He lingered while she opened the door and led herself into her house. Ofelia gave him a small wave goodbye, which Maverick returned, before closing the door.

As Maverick walked back to his car with a newfound lightness to his steps, he realized that he was still smiling so hard his cheeks were hurting. Ofelia Mendez was one of the first good things that had happened to Maverick in this new post baseball life. Tonight had been just a taste, but he was determined to see where this could lead.

Chapter Sixteen

Two days later, Ofelia's lips still tingled from Maverick's warm kisses and her body heated each time she thought of his commanding tone. She had waited to feel some sort of guilt or shame over their intense interaction in his truck, but it never came. At work today, she all but strutted in, stopping by the teacher's lounge to leave a box of donuts she bought for no particular reason. She told herself that she most definitely didn't buy the donuts for the lounge because it was located across the hall from the gym. That was only a bonus. If she happened to spot Maverick from the door window, it would simply be fate's doing. Not her own.

She was not ashamed to say she peeked inside the gym when walking by. The basketball team was running drills while Coach Campbell blew his whistle to bark orders. *Damn.* Not the coach she wanted to see. Her good mood faltered, but she knew coming by would be a long shot. Instead of pouting, she decided to head back to her room and-

The air rushed out of her as she ran directly into the person

who silently stood in front of her. Strong hands came up to grip her arms, keeping her from embarrassing herself even more. "Ugh, I'm sorry! I wasn't-"

"Were you looking for me, baby girl?" A low whisper tickled her ear. A pleasurable shiver went through her body as she timidly looked up at the man she ran into.

She sent up a silent *"Thank you, Fate!"* as she met Maverick's deep brown eyes. He smelled of peppermint mouthwash and fresh laundry. He wore his standard black joggers and an old school shirt someone from the office must have given him. This man looked delicious enough to eat.

"Why would I be looking for you?" Ofelia played coy, wiggling out of his grip. Maverick gave her one last squeeze before taking a step back, putting some distance between them. It was for the best; she didn't need to jump his bones at work.

"Because you were staring pretty hard through that window. Unless you're checking out Campbell over there, I'd say it's safe to say you were looking for me."

"Maybe I was looking at Campbell. Would that make you jealous?"

"Incredibly so."

Ofelia beamed. "Then I totally checked out Campbell. It's the salt and pepper hair and the beer gut that get me going."

Maverick sighed melodramatically. "It's always the beer gut." He made an adorable drama queen and Ofelia couldn't help but laugh.

"Maybe I hoped I could catch a glimpse of you, so I brought donuts. They're in the teacher's lounge if you want one." She said, noticing a few students began to trickle in. The first bell was still forty-five minutes away, but she had a few coming in for tutoring this morning. "I need to head back to my room, but if you have C lunch today, you can join Willow and I."

Maverick gave an apologetic smile. "B lunch. Let's have dinner after school?"

Ofelia felt her heart race in excitement. Could someone die of giddiness? Was that a thing? If it were, she'd be patient zero. "Perfect. I have a cheer meeting after school, but I was hoping to have dinner together tonight?" She suggested, thrilled with the prospect of potentially seeing Maverick later.

"Of course, where would you like to go?" He asked, sliding his hands into his pockets.

"Actually, I was hoping I could cook for you." She said, her cheeks warming.

Maverick raised a brow, a slight smile pulling at the corners of his lips. "I would love that."

"Great!" She said a little too loudly, earning weird looks from a few passing students. "I uh, will text you tonight."

More students began to filter in, walking towards the cafeteria for breakfast or headed to teacher tutorials. She couldn't kiss him goodbye and had to settle for an awkward wave with their hands brushing as they walked past each other. She didn't look back, even when she felt eyes watching her as she made her way to her room.

The kiss would wait until later. She had writing workshops and cheer moms to get through first. Upon entering her hallway, Ofelia was shocked to find ten students waiting outside her door. "Oh my goodness, I'm sorry y'all. I didn't mean to keep you waiting." She fumbled with her key and unlocked the door, immediately turning on the lights. Her students all filled in behind her, slugging their backpacks down on desks and rifling through them for their work. One by one, Ofelia went to each student, going over what each needed to work on and answering any questions they had. Five more students entered and waited patiently for their turn with Ofelia.

It was the start of a long day.

By the time the last student left her morning tutorials, Ofelia's first period class began to trickle in. The cycle started anew because this week was every English teachers' nightmare. Essay writing week. A minimum of five paragraphs over a subject the kids knew well, but when presented with the prompt, everything they learned magically disappeared.

At Lunch, Ofelia took slight comfort in seeing Willow come into her room looking like a walking corpse. Her classes weren't going much better, and she had an angry email from a parent stating that their child is grievously injured from the amount of writing this school was forcing upon him. "What does that even mean?!" Willow complained. At the end of the day it was Ofelia's turn to deal with parents. Not just any parents, cheer moms.

Back in December when Ofelia scheduled the parent meeting, it seemed like a great idea. Her dumbass-self believed she was being proactive. Ofelia would lay out exactly what their first tournament would look like, detailing everything out from the expense to the time they left for San Antonio, and ending with competition schedules. Now she knew it was only an added, unnecessary task she put upon herself.

After changing into her cheer coach uniform and putting her hair up in a bun, Ofelia started down to the gym. There was nothing terrifying about these mothers. They were just...a lot. One wrong move meant an unflattering post on their not-so-secret Facebook group. Since she was already running a few minutes late, she had minimal room for error.

Parents were still making their way into the gym and on to the bleachers by the time Ofelia arrived. Lacey sat in the front row with her mother, a woman who tried a little too hard to cling to her youth. She wore a top, one likely stolen from Lacey, with a plunging neckline. Her boobs spilled over the top and Ofelia wondered what type of bra she wore and where she could get one of her own.

"Ms. Mendez." A high-pitched southern voice called, effectively dragging Ofelia's eyes from Mrs. Steward's cleavage. Inwardly Ofelia groaned when she caught sight of the woman standing in front of her; the cheer mom's fake southern charm in full effect. One would think it was snow storming outside rather than a crisp seventy-degree day, for Mrs. Roberts was decked out in her best winter attire. Long sleeve shirt with a white, pleated vest over top. Dark jeans with tall brown boots.

Mrs. Roberts was the mother of one of Ofelia's juniors, Gabbie Roberts. Without her mother's influence, Gabbie could be a sweet girl if she weren't weighed down with crippling anxiety and the need to always be perfect. It was obvious to everyone but Mrs. Roberts how badly her daughter craved her approval, but Mrs. Roberts was obsessed with her family's image. If they weren't the best, they were nothing. It pissed Mrs. Roberts off that Gabbie hadn't made cheer captain when she tried out at the beginning of the year.

Because Ofelia was nothing if not classy, she smiled at the woman. "Mrs. Roberts, it's so nice to see you again. I'm glad you could make it."

"You know I never miss an opportunity to hear the latest news firsthand. Besides, I have a few questions and concerns I was hoping you'd be able to answer."

Shocking, but Ofelia kept her expression neutral and nodded. "Of course. There'll be time for questions at the end. Go ahead and take a seat, and we will get started immediately."

She could tell that Mrs. Roberts wanted to argue, but

Gabbie pulled her mother into the stand. Ofelia waited as the last few parents took their seats, waving at Tony's mom as she entered. Gianna was the only mom Ofelia was on a first name basis with and the only mom that supported anything Ofelia planned.

Why was it so easy to talk in front of a group of teenagers but debilitating when it came to talking in front of peers? She had to emit queen bee energy, even if these bees stung back. A lot.

"Hello McKinley cheer parents. Thank you so much for taking the time to be here today so we can discuss our first competition in San Antonio this upcoming weekend." Ofelia took a moment to pass out the itinerary to all the parents and cheerleaders. Her squad already knew this information, so really it was for their parents and their need to track every minute of every day.

Ofelia walked them through the detailed four-page document; she even color coded the schedule. She made it idiot proof so none of the parents could come back and blame her for not knowing time or location.

They would meet at school on Friday morning at 5am. From there, the squad would board the charter bus and take the two-hour drive down where they would immediately check into their hotel. At ten, they would walk across the street to the convention center and sign in. Their performance time wasn't until 2:15pm so the team could go for brunch before warming up.

Ofelia walked the parents through the second day as well, making sure they realized they performed twice that day. "Then on Sunday we get our results and see if we placed. We will start heading home around one or two." Ofelia took a deep breath; mouth dry from talking for the last thirty minutes. Miraculously not a single person interrupted her. Unfortunately, she would still have to take questions. As soon as she asked if anyone had any, most hands went in the air.

"Yes, I do." Mrs. Roberts piped up disregarding every hand in the air. There were a few glares from some other parents as their hands slowly went down. "Will you be asking for parent volunteers? Some of us have a lot of experience with these things and it might be beneficial to you if you had some of our expertise."

Ofelia pursued her lips. She couldn't jump a parent, that was unprofessional and wouldn't set a fitting example as a leader. But seriously, Mrs. Roberts always had to flaunt her knowledge of cheerleading and overlook everyone else. It didn't matter that Ofelia had been in cheer since she could walk. It didn't matter how many state championship trophies she won or that she went to college with a full scholarship for cheer. She could hold up all her awards and accomplishments, but none of that would phase Mrs. Roberts. She would still find fault in something.

Ofelia had to brush her comments off and deal with the question laced between the sass. Admittedly, she asked an important question because she did need parent support. "Of course, I'm so glad you brought that up." She praised, as she would with any challenging student. Mrs. Roberts looked pleased with herself. "Parent chaperones are highly encouraged. All our fundraising efforts only provided us with enough money to cover the hotel rooms for the team and me. If any parent would like to attend, they would need to purchase their own room. They can, however, ride up with us in the charter if they want."

"Oh, that shouldn't be a problem for most of us, Mrs.

Mendez. Don't you worry about that. Where do we sign up?" Mrs. Roberts asked, a big, fake smile plastered across her face.

"You'll see a QR Code on the last page of your schedule. Just hover your camera over it and the website will pop up. Fill out the information and you'll receive a text message confirming your sign up."

Much to her squad's dismay, almost all the parents flipped to the last page and scanned the QR code. It was a relief to have this many hands-on-deck, even if those hands belonged to some questionable characters. Mrs. Roberts was tolerable at big functions, as long as they were winning. It was poor Gabbie who would have to suffer her passive aggressive attitude if she didn't perform at top tier.

"Mrs. Mendez, can you give me more information about the hotel? Is it the one directly adjacent to the convention center? How will the girls - and Tony and Devin - room?"

For the next hour, Ofelia fielded questions from all the parents. Would dinner be provided? Did the parents have to pay for admission? What happens if there is a wardrobe malfunction? Ofelia answered to the best of her abilities, even if some questions seemed improbable. Mrs. Roberts and Mrs. Steward grilled her the most. Lacey ended up dragging her mother away from the conversation. "Seriously, mom. You'd think this was your first damn competition." Lacey growled.

Mrs. Roberts finally ran out of obscure questions and Ofelia adjourned the meeting. She smiled and said her goodbye to each parent. There was no way they were going to write a shitty post about her on Facebook after this.

Gianna was the last to walk down from the bleachers with Tony. "You handled that excellently, Ms. M. Totally crushed it." Tony said, sipping on his iced coffee.

"He's right, those parents were out with claws tonight. You'd think this was a Botox convention."

"Mom!" Tony said but giggled. "Okay true. Those foreheads weren't moving!"

Gianna rubbed her son's head affectionately. "I'll be coming along as a chaperone, so I'll run interference. Don't stress about that. You're doing great. Tony tells me all the time you are his favorite teacher. It's so easy to see why your team loves you. Plus, it takes a special type of person to deal with these cheer moms. I think the only thing worse would be dance moms. Maybe football moms."

"I understand. They want what's best for the kids, they just don't have the best ways of approaching." Ofelia said, not able to blame the parents for their consistent nagging. It stressed her out to no end, and she vowed that she would never be that type of mother, or at least she hoped she wasn't the type of mom most teachers avoid. "Even Mrs. Roberts, as...difficult as she is. I know deep down, very deep down, she loves her daughter. She just shows it differently."

"Girl is two types of crazy, no sir. Her husband must be-" Tony started but was cut off by his mother, nudging his shoulder.

"Hush boy. That mouth of yours is going to catch up with you one day."

"And it will land me a fine husband and I'll finally live out my dream of being a trophy husband." Tony smiled, looking all too smug about his future. He winked at his mother before strutting through the door, leaving Ofelia and Gianna as the last two remaining.

"Love that boy, but he's going to be the death of me." Gianna shook her head, but affection colored her face. She loved her son, and it showed in everything she did. "Anyway, I know you are eager to go home. This momma has your back this weekend. Let me know if you need anything."

Gianna hugged Ofelia goodbye, leaving her feeling good about the meeting, even if only one person thought so. Everything was planned to the T, her father would come, and she had enough chaperones to lighten her load. So tonight she could simply enjoy her evening with Maverick.

Chapter Seventeen

The pop of the sizzling grease made Maverick jump back despite her many warnings to stand clear. "Listen, if you want to get burned, keep it up." Ofelia smirked and nudged him out of the way of her stove with a light hip bump. A deep laugh caressed her senses, sending a delicious tingling sensation straight to her core. Something that happened a lot when Maverick was around.

"Maybe I like knowing you'd nurse my wounds if I get burned." He said and Ofelia rolled her eyes. He had her pegged though; it was exactly what she would do. Any excuse to have her hands all over him again. Thoughts of their time in the car rushed back and she blushed for a completely different reason.

"So how do you make it so the corn tortilla doesn't fall apart when you roll it?" Maverick's question brought her back to the moment. Just in time too because the flautas she was currently cooking reached the desired golden brown color, signifying they were ready to take out. Maverick stepped back as she maneuvered the hot flautas to a napkin to drain all the excess oil.

"You just put the tortillas in the microwave to let them warm up before you try handling them. My mamá taught me that." She said, creating four more corn tortillas stuffed with shredded chicken and dropping them into the pan. Maverick had offered to help, but she had watched him demolish and shred two tortillas already and burn their first attempt at spanish rice.

A chef he was not.

Not that Ofelia minded. She loved cooking and it had been a long time since she had someone other than Willow to make dinner for. Although she forbad Maverick from touching any food currently out on her counter, he watched the process and asked tons of questions. She liked answering them and sharing a bit of her culture with him.

After another fifteen minutes, she finished dressing up their flautas with pico de gallo and Mexican Crema while Maverick set the table. She soon joined him, pushing his plate in front of him. This was her favorite part. The part where she watched someone try her food for the first time. She liked seeing the different emotions play across their faces as they took their first bite.

Sensing her anticipation, Maverick didn't hesitate when he took the first bite of her meal. A low groan left him as he licked off sour cream from the corner of his lips. He took another bite, this time shoveling rice in his mouth. He made sounds this time which Ofelia believed to be words, but she couldn't decipher their meaning.

"I'm not fluent in stuffed mouth language. You are going to have to translate for me." She laughed, watching as he quickly chewed the remaining food.

"I said," he coughed, clearing his throat. "That this is the best damn meal I've had in a long time. Thank God I didn't have this food around me when I was in the major leagues. I would have pissed off my trainer and nutritionist." He laughed, but soon stopped as if realizing what he just said.

This thing between them – whatever it was – was still new, but Ofelia quickly learned that Maverick didn't like talking about his baseball life. He would share a few details of his time playing, but the conversations never lasted long and she got the sense he didn't want to talk about it with her. It stung a little, but she understood his need for privacy, especially when half of his life was plastered on the internet for anyone to see.

"You really miss it, don't you?" She asked softly, afraid that Maverick might close up on her. She saw him tense slightly and noticed the rapid tap of his finger on the table while he tried to decide what to say.

"I do." His voice was barely above a whisper. "It's what I know. I dedicated my entire life to baseball and I just wish..."

What did he wish? Ofelia wanted to know so badly, but she could see Maverick deflecting with a slight shrug to his shoulders. "I suppose it's in Lloyd Gilmore's hands now. But enough about me. I want to hear about your cheer meeting. How'd that go?"

Ofelia highly doubted he wanted to talk cheer, but it was clear Maverick was ready to change the subject back to something safe. She obliged him, if only to see the lingering sadness leave his eyes.

"I regret holding a meeting instead of sending out the competition information in an email." It had been so foolish to think she'd be able to run a quick meeting and be out in time to get her house cleaned before Maverick came. But of course the mothers had kept her for over an hour past the scheduled ending time.

She told him all about the snide cheer moms and their

obnoxious questions about her preparedness thinly veiled behind fake concern. Of the countless reminders that Ofelia hadn't been able to obtain a win at nationals yet and the pressure the parents placed on her this year to be perfect. Maverick nodded and commented at the appropriate times, actually listening and taking an interest in her day. It was...refreshing.

"The one good thing that came out of the meeting is now I have chaperones for the competition and one of them is Gianna, Tony's mom. She helped me deal with the high demands of the parents last year and kept me sane throughout the entire competition weekend." It was a small relief a friendly face would be joining, but a relief all the same.

"You're amazing." Maverick said after a beat of silence between them. His words were so unexpected and she didn't know how to respond. Surely he couldn't be talking about being amazing from simply dealing with parents? It wasn't that impressive, but she appreciated the sentiment.

"It's really noth-"

"No, it's not nothing. You are amazing." His words came out strong and he stared at her as if daring Ofelia to argue with his assessment. She didn't. "It's not just the meeting, though I could never deal with that many mothers at once. No, you're amazing because of your passion and dedication to your students and squad. You make a difference in countless lives every day. That's why you are so well loved and respected by those who have the honor of knowing you. I won't be convinced otherwise, baby girl."

When he spoke like that, a weird fluttering sensation happened in the pit of her belly...or was it her chest? Maverick rendered her speechless with the naked honesty of his words. He actually *did* think that about her. How he saw her each time he looked at her.

What did one even say after such high praise? Thank you felt inadequate and no other responses came to her. She hated that they were separated by her kitchen table when she wanted nothing more than to use her body to convey how she felt; to say the words she couldn't.

Luckily she didn't have to try coming up with a suitable comment because Maverick soon continued. "And you mentioned your father would be there, yeah? That's kinda a big deal, isn't it?"

It was a huge deal and she had mentioned that to him before. Maverick didn't know all the details about her strained relationship with her father, but he did know that she struggled to connect with him. Growing up it had been a constant fight for his attention and even when she got it, it was never undivided. Sports, Javi, or work would take precedence over her. She was made to feel inadequate and that she didn't deserve her father's love.

"I just hope it works out and we can finally spend some much needed time together." Before her thoughts spiraled into anymore gutters, Ofelia cleared her throat and smiled, wanting to change the subject. Clearly Maverick wasn't the only one avoiding hard topics tonight. She glanced down at his plate, realizing he must have finished sometime during her story and she hadn't noticed. "Oh. Are you still hungry? There's plenty more."

"Nah, I'm good, but I'll take leftovers." Maverick said. She liked that he enjoyed her food enough to have it for lunch the next day. She could get used to cooking for him if it meant she got to share her kitchen with him and learn more about Maverick.

"Where are you going?" Maverick asked as Ofelia got up to find Tupperware for the leftovers.

"I'm just going to tidy up the food really quick and make you a plate to take home. It'll only take a moment." But Maverick was already shaking his head before she finished talking, wrapping his hands around the arms of her dining room chair and pushing himself to his feet.

"Later. Right now I would very much like to sit on the couch and put a movie on so we can pretend we are actually watching it, but really we are just waiting for the other to make their move so we can make out like teenagers."

Ofelia let out a bark of undignified laughter. His words were not only funny but true as well. How many times had she thought about kissing him each time his tongue licked his lips clean? Far too many for one night.

"I'll help you clean up before I go. Just give me an hour?" Maverick stuck out his bottom lip like a child begging his mother for the shiny new toy. How could she say no to that face?

She couldn't.

She allowed herself to be led into her own living room and pulled down next to Maverick on the couch. They lasted approximately five minutes before Maverick initiated the first kiss.

And the second.

And the third.

Despite the stress from the day and knowing that tomorrow would be the start of her weekend tournament, Ofelia had never felt more at ease. Not only did she have this amazing night with Maverick to replay over and over again, she knew everything was planned to the T. She had all her ducks in rows for the first time in a long time, everything was working out perfectly.

Chapter Eighteen

Everything was going wrong.

Friday morning arrived like an unexpected house guest, far too early and full of complications. For starters, Ofelia slept past her alarm clock and woke up with only thirty minutes before she needed to leave. She hadn't packed her suitcase yet. She had every intention of doing that last night, but dinner with Maverick consumed most of her evening.

She thankfully remembered to do her laundry the other morning and began to toss unfolded, wrinkled clothes into her small suitcase, not caring how disorderly she was being. Ofelia mentally went through her checklist, knowing she had her clothes, but needed her bathroom accessories. She darted into her bathroom, nearly slipping on the title but righted herself by holding on to the sink.

Ten minutes later, with only two to spare, Ofelia ran to her car, like an overzealous Olympic runner. She tossed her suitcase and purse in the backseat and placed her phone in the console.

It had been vibrating for the past ten minutes and Ofelia knew parents were wondering where she was. If she wasn't fifteen minutes early, she was late.

Major panic sat in when Ofelia pulled up to the school and no giant white charter bus awaited her. "What the hell?" She hissed, gripping her steering wheel hard. She grabbed for her phone only to realize now that the charter company tried to contact her. Several times and left a voicemail, which she promptly listened to. Apparently there had been miscommunication about the bus's arrival time. They promised to have a bus out ASAP, but it could be another twenty minutes.

This was fine. Totally fine. No reason to freak out. She needed to remain calm when she told the news to her squad, half of which already stood on the curb waiting for Ofelia to hop out of her car. Devin gave her a tentative wave as Lacey glanced up briefly before putting her nose right back into her phone.

After returning the call from the charter company and hearing a bus was in route, Ofelia felt more confident walking over to her team. From the squad, she received a lot of smiles and a few hugs. The only person missing was Tony and his mother, but Gianna always ran a little later than everyone else.

"Mrs. Mendez, where's our bus? My mom is having a meltdown, so I made her wait in the car." Lacey questioned, clearly the adult in the situation. If it weren't for her cheer captain, Lacey's mother would wreak havoc, more so than the other two moms on her list.

"So I got a call from the bus company, and they said there was a bit of a mix up." She started as the protests began and the panic started to seep in. Sometimes she wondered if she directed the drama troupe rather than coaching cheerleaders.

"But your amazing coach, AKA me, planned for some delay in our schedule. We will still get to San Antonio with enough time to check into our hotel rooms and change before we need to be at the convention center."

"You are sure we will make it on time?" Gabbie asked, looking around nervously.

"Of course we will. If worse comes to worst, we will check into our hotel later. Don't panic." She said, just as Gianna's car pulled up.

Tony ducked his head out of the window with a big grin. A song from *Hamilton* loudly played on the speakers as Gianna tapped along to the beat. Tony paused for dramatic effect before saying, "Ladies and Devin, we brought donuts."

Suddenly everything was better.

Twenty minutes later the charter bus arrived and everyone piled in while the parents loaded the luggage. Ofelia counted heads, making sure everyone was there. Only a few parents wanted to ride up with the bus while the rest promised to follow along in their own cars. It was quite the parade as a large white charter with six various cars and trucks followed close behind. They were finally on the road.

Now that she had a moment to herself without teenagers or parents breathing down her neck, Ofelia texted her father. She knew he would be boarding his plane in an hour and wanted to catch him before he got on. "I'm so excited to see you, Papa! Call me when you land." He hadn't responded since last night, but that wasn't unusual for her father. He was notorious for ghosting his children and then having the gall to get upset when people stopped texting him. She spoke to Javi as well, but he had not seen much of their father due to his busy work schedule.

The next message was for Maverick, just saying they took off and that she missed him. She debated that last part, not wanting to seem clingy. She decided she didn't care and sent it anyway. Almost immediately, Mav responded with "Stay safe. I miss you too." He included a green heart emoji at the end, which made her inexplicably happy.

For the duration of the ride, Ofelia popped her earbuds in and listened to a fantasy series Willow recommended to her about ancient vampires and gods. Romcoms were more her speed, but she promised Willow they'd discuss it soon. Ofelia retreated into her imagination for the next two hours, only stirring when someone poked her. Nila, an upbeat freshman, looked down at her, as if waiting for Ofelia to answer a question.

"I'm sorry, what did you say?" Ofelia apologized, stopping her book and removing her earbuds. The bus was stopped, which explained why Nila was up and walking around. She straightened up in her seat to peer out the window.

"I said we're here. The bus driver wants to know if he should park or wait." She said before bouncing back to her seat, joining the rest of the squad in an off-key rendition of Justin Bieber's classic, "Baby."

"We can park. Thank you." Ofelia said to the driver, who nodded and made his way to the parking garage. The bus zone was bare, meaning they had to be one of the first schools to arrive, which pleasantly surprised her. She was glad that they made it early, even with their late start. By the end of the day, the zone would be filled with various buses from all over Texas. The same thrill Ofelia got before each performance started racing through her body, making her giddy. It was amplified now that she coached a kick ass team.

Said kick ass team were quickly becoming squirrelly and impatient. "Does everyone remember who they are bunking with?" Ofelia asked, rifling through her oversized purse in search of their reservations and school credit card. Of course it hid all the way at the bottom of her bag, causing a near mini heart attack. It would have been just her luck to leave the important documents at home, even though she checked her bag religiously the day before to ensure they were in there.

"Yes, Mrs. Mendez." A chorus of voices said. The bus was a whirl of activity as everyone gathered their personal items. The parents sitting in the back of the bus began to shoo her cheerleaders forward, getting them off the bus.

"When everyone has their suitcase, meet me in the lobby. I'm going to go check us in." Ofelia called over the noises of moving bodies and luggage, making her way towards the hotel, seeing a steady line of patrons ready to check in.

This year's hotel was a big upgrade from last year because Ofelia actually knew what the hell she was doing. She booked their rooms at the end of last year, as soon as she got approval from administration. She learned waiting a few months before a huge cheerleading competition to book a hotel left very slim pickings, which resulted in her finding one thirty minutes away. It had been hell packing up each time they needed to go anywhere near the Riverwalk or the convention center.

By the time Ofelia made it to the front of the line, most of the squad had wandered over towards her. An older gentleman greeted Ofelia as she placed the yellow folder full of their reservation information on the table. "You must be here for the competition?" He asked pleasantly.

"We are. I've bet you've seen a lot of us." She said conversationally, handing over her ID when he asked for it.

"Y'all have been arriving steadily, but I suspect it will pick up in an hour or so." The man typed a few things into his computer, taking her reservations. It took only ten minutes to sort out the rooms and the keys. "Your rooms will be located on the tenth floor, but we couldn't arrange six rooms right next to each other. I did my best to make them all relatively close. If you have any problems or questions, the front desk is open twenty-four hours. Feel free to come down or call. Oh, room 1045 is the only room with a single bed."

Which made it her room by default. When they got back in the evenings, she would make sure her squad was locked in their rooms, and she could hide away in her fluffy hotel bed and read whatever romcom she had loaded on her kindle. "Thank you for all your help." Ofelia smiled and went to rejoin the rest of her team.

Her squad all looked at her with the same expectant expression when she made her way towards them. "Alright squad, gather round." Ofelia gestured for everyone to move closer, so she didn't have to yell. "I have our keys, and we are on the 10th floor. It is currently-" she checked the time on her phone. "9:25. We need to be at registration by ten. Let's be ready to head over to the convention center in an hour."

"What about brunch, Mrs. M? I am two seconds away from being hangry." Tony said.

"And nobody wants to see that." Devin agreed. "Especially me. I'm rooming with him. A Hangry Tony is a Scary Tony."

"Of course, we will pick up food after. There are places in the convention center to eat, but they will probably all be crowded. We can walk the Riverwalk and find the food court by the mall. They'll have plenty of options for everyone." Ofelia suggested knowing her team was full of picky eaters. For dinner, they were going to have to split up with their parents and go to different restaurants because Ofelia didn't want to fight that battle.

"So meet back out here in thirty?" Nila asked, arm and arm with her best friend Faith. "In full uniform?"

"Yes to meeting back in thirty minutes and no to the competition uniform. Wear our cheer shirts and the black wind joggers. Hair needs to be competition ready and full face of makeup. Pack your competition outfit and your makeup in a duffle. We will lock it in our assigned room."

After handing out keys to the assigned roommates, her squad all made a beeline to the elevators, but Ofelia stayed back. By now, her father should be in the air, only an hour before landing. She hadn't heard from him yet and worry started to settle in. It wouldn't be the first time her father left her high and dry. Much of her childhood had been a sequence of disappointments when it came to her father attending her cheer events. Work always took priority for him. It was why she was closer to her mother than anyone else.

Ofelia was still going to give her father the benefit of the doubt. If he said he was coming to support her, then he was. She would allow herself to be excited because she was no longer a child anymore, and he no longer had work obligations. At least not a full time job. For some ungodly reason, his father still liked picking up odd contracting jobs from time to time. For now, she checked her phone for updates and hoped her father would show up in the nick of time.

∽

Registration was much more of a streamlined process than last year. Getting her team out of the convention center and across the street to take the stairs down to the Riverwalk had been something else entirely. She felt like a rancher, wrangling in her unruly animals and trying to get them to the same location at the same time. Honestly high schoolers were just larger toddlers with more attitude.

At the food court she released her squad and many flocked towards Starbucks and McDonald's. Ofelia decided on Little Tokyo and found Gianna sitting away from the rest of the parents. Tony's mom was young and many of the other mom's looked down on her since she had Tony when she was fourteen. Ofelia admired the woman's tenacity and ability to raise another human being when she was still being raised herself. To her, Gianna embodied strength and perseverance.

"Thank you again for agreeing to chaperone." Ofelia said once she sat across from her. "It's nice to see a friendly face amongst-"

"The sharks?" Gianna supplied.

"Well...yes. That."

"It's cool. Tony is so excited and it was cute, you know? I wanted to be here and see him perform. I didn't get to come last year and I know he was super bummed about it, even if he won't admit it. Bad mom move."

"Hey, you're here now and you helped out so much last year." Ofelia encouraged. Gianna's eyes flickered over to Tony who was deep in conversation with Lacey. It still shocked her the two of them were best friends, but Ofelia loved that. Lacey needed a Tony in her life. "Tony is thriving. So you are doing a good job, mama."

Gianna smiled and it only enhanced the woman's natural beauty when she did, making her appear younger than her early thirties. Many people thought Gianna was Tony's sister. "Thanks, Ofelia. You're doing great too. Seriously, you are handling these parents with so much patience. I know you don't see it, but they truly respect you. Before you came here." She shook her head, letting out a low whistle. "Let's just say the poor woman couldn't leave for summer fast enough. I'm fairly certain they ran her out of town."

The parents were difficult, yes, but she had grown up in the cheer world so many of their comments and attitudes didn't phase her as much as they would someone who hadn't been part of this world since childhood. When she didn't run away after one year, Colbie knew Ofelia belonged in this position.

Was she thriving? Ofelia wasn't sure thriving was the right word, but her team was damn good and worked as a unit. They teased each other and fought occasionally, but at the end of the day they were family. Family took care of one another and that was what her squad did too. It wouldn't have been possible without her gentle push.

So maybe she *was* thriving. It certainly felt like that at this moment.

While Ofelia ate, Gianna talked about her job as a correctional officer. Ofelia was content to listen while her friend spoke. Every so often, her father would pop into her mind and the string of anxiety wound its way a little tighter around her heart. Judging by his flight schedule, he should have arrived thirty minutes ago. There was still a chance that he would come, but hope was fleeting.

After two years of not being able to see her family, Ofelia had let herself become excited with the notion she would soon be reunited with her father. It would be the first time he saw her coach and for inexplicable reasons, she wanted his approval. It was such a childish thing to want, but Ofelia craved it.

As if he knew she was thinking about him, Ofelia's phone went off. Her heart lurched as she looked to see who called. Her father's picture illuminated the screen. "I'm sorry Gianna,

I need to take this. I'll be right back." Ofelia said, all but jogging away to find a more secluded and quiet area to answer.

"Papa, hi!" She answered with too much enthusiasm, denying what her gut told her was coming. "Did you land yet? Do I need to send a car?"

"*Mija,*" Her father spoke, and she could hear people in the background talking in Spanish. It sounded like he was outside, surrounded by a lot of commotion. "I am sorry, *Mija,* but I'm still in California."

As soon as he said those words, her heart shattered. The hope she dared to have died, leaving a heavy sadness in its wake. Breathing became harder because she felt the sob trying to break free. If she let herself cry, she didn't think she'd ever stop. The only thing her body knew as a defense mechanism was to go numb. Numb off all feelings and emotions. If she didn't feel the pain, she couldn't hurt. It was as simple as that.

She didn't need to listen to her father as he gave her another bullshit excuse as to why he couldn't be here. She caught a few words, "exchanging tickets," "job," and "bad cell phone service." He chose a random job over her and didn't have the common decency to tell her beforehand. She was two seconds away from a mental breakdown in front of her kids during one of the most stressful times in her career.

Her father was still talking when Ofelia cut him off, no longer caring to hear his pathetic excuses. "You know what papa? I don't care. I don't care that you picked work over your own daughter again. I don't care that you never gave a shit about my life. I shouldn't have even asked you to come in the first place. It was always mama supporting me, and I was foolish to think you would give up one weekend for me."

She hung up and immediately silenced her phone. It took everything in her power to hold back the angry tears ready to fall. Later she might regret her harsh words, but right now she meant what she said. This was so typical of her father, but she had still fallen for one of his neatly dressed lies! She would pay for her foolishness later, but she had to put on a smile to go out and be a coach to her cheerleaders. Her problems would have to wait until later.

Doing a quick glance in her phone's camera, Ofelia made sure she looked presentable and not the miserable mess she felt on the inside. There were cracks in her barrier, her eyes were watery and her smile didn't quite meet her eyes, but otherwise she appeared fine. Gathering the last of her strength, Ofelia held her head high and walked back over to the rest of her team.

Not many of them saw her leave to take the call, but Gianna had. She clearly had been watching and noticed something was wrong. "Is everything okay?"

And damn if Ofelia didn't almost break her fragile composure and let the tears spill. She swallowed back a sob and controlled her face into what she hoped was a reassuring smile. She failed because Gianna winced, looking even more concerned.

"Everything's fine. All good." She said, her voice sounding strange to her own ears. "But we should go. It's time to start warming up and I'm sure you all want to find the best seats to watch the performance."

"Are you sure-"

"Yes." Ofelia said too quickly, loving Gianna but wanting to throttle her at that moment. She just needed to keep busy and not think about the horrendous phone call she just had. "Will you help me gather the team? Thanks."

She didn't wait for Gianna to reply. She simply left her behind, pushing the pain deep, deep down and focusing all her attention on her squad. Ofelia didn't need her father to be the best coach she could be for her team. She just needed to be here and clear-headed.

If there was ever a time she needed comfort, it would be now. She wished Maverick was here.

Chapter Nineteen

Over two hundred schools traveled for the cheer competition, raising the stakes from one hundred fifty teams last year. They needed to do more than shine to get the judges' attention, especially since they wouldn't be performing first. The judges had to sit through nearly three dozen schools before McKinley would enter the stage.

Normally, Ofelia found herself giddy with anticipation right before her team took stage. She was a picture of perfect composure because her squad depended on her to be their rock during their storm. After her phone call with her father, Ofelia found it difficult to muster up a smile. Her father's words played through her mind on repeat, reminding her why she shouldn't put her faith in him, knowing it was in his nature to disappoint.

What was worse, Ofelia started to feel bad about some things she said to her father in the heat of the moment. Years of pent-up resentment came to the surface, and she spoke without thought to his feelings. But what about her feelings? Didn't he give a damn about how his actions affected her? Maybe he was so used to disappointing her he was unconcerned with how she would take the news. Fuck her conscious and its inability to stop caring.

Right now, her cheerleaders needed her full attention.

Tears came to her eyes as she watched her babies, aka full grown high schoolers, run through the routine so flawlessly and effortlessly. Tony landed his tumbling pass perfectly for the first time. Faith finally nailed her two-to-a-standing-full instead of her usual layout. Lacey's smile illuminated her entire face, looking entirely the cheer captain she was meant to be. The squad's pyramid stunt sequence went off without a hitch and their cheer section bursted with crowd-leading energy.

All the moving parts to the routine Ofelia spent countless nights meticulously creating came together in a way she couldn't imagine. Even if the judges hadn't seen the great strides her cheerleaders made this year, Ofelia could, and she was going to make sure each of them knew how incredibly proud she was to be their coach.

Ofelia screamed the loudest, to the point her throat became scratchy with overuse, at the end of their routine. So much pride radiated off her body.

When she found her squad after, Ofelia jumped, hugged, and cried along with them. Not once did she think of the heavyweight burden on her heart placed there by her father. She didn't think about him when the team went out for dinner, all miraculously deciding on one location on the Riverwalk. Nor did she think of him when she told her team how proud she was of each and every one of them.

She didn't think about the ache in her heart as parents took pictures of the squad, nor when they complimented her,

ON AND OFF THE FIELD

suggesting they always suspected Ofelia would lead their team to victory. She didn't think about it even when they made it back to the hotel and locked the students into their room for the night.

She only allowed herself to give into the sadness once back in her room, showered and changed into her fleece pajamas. Ofelia had half a mind to call her father up now and demand answers. Anger wouldn't accomplish anything other than making her feel better.

She could call Willow, but Karl recently came back from working out of town. She knew her best friend, and they were probably going at it like rabbits, potentially with another couple in their bed. Good for them. Her brother Javi would also be asleep or getting Camilla down, and she didn't want to interrupt their nightly routines.

Then her finger hovered over the last name. She stayed up well past ten to text Maverick before; he was a night owl like her. He would be awake and would answer.

Yet she wondered if he really needed her drama at the moment? She didn't know what they were yet or if calling him would even be appropriate. What they had was new, and she desperately wanted to continue the dinner dates, the lingering kisses, and the deep conversations where everything else faded away, leaving only the two of them.

Ofelia wasn't willing to let that go. Still, for every reason she shouldn't, a reason she *should* also came to mind.

Before she could talk herself out of it, Ofelia pressed Maverick's name to video call and her phone started to ring. As she suspected, Maverick was still awake and answered after two rings. His gorgeous face and torso filled the screen. He was shirtless and looked so fine. He laid in bed, the light from the

TV in his room lit half of his face. He smiled up at her as if he had been waiting for her call all day.

Something on her face gave away her emotions because Maverick's smile instantly faded, and he sat up. He momentarily went out of frame and soon a light brightened the room. When he looked back at the screen, Ofelia saw worry crease his brow. "What's wrong?" There was no hesitation in his voice, only the need to try and fix whatever was broken.

He couldn't fix this though, no matter how hard he tried. Ofelia lost her last bit of composure, and the tears started to fall freely until they turned into heaving sobs. She couldn't form words to tell him what was wrong. All her body seemed capable of was trembling and crying. A dam broke inside of her, and she didn't know how to fix it.

To Maverick's credit, he didn't shy away from Ofelia's ugly crying face. He murmured soothing words, not asking her to talk about it or telling her to stop crying. He promised not to get off the phone until she felt better, even if he needed to stay on all night. Ofelia wanted to thank him, but each time she opened her mouth to talk, another sob came out.

God she was so fucking pathetic. He probably thought someone in her family died or she got fired. Not that her dad stood her up. Without context, it would seem like she was overreacting, but this was something Ofelia had dealt with her entire life. Her mother had always supported her, up until college when she passed away from breast cancer. She had been her comfort and security and without her mother, she hoped her father would pick up the role in her absence.

So no, she didn't cry simply because her father didn't show...again. She cried because she no longer had someone to share this huge part of her life with. Last year Javi was able to video chat in. He couldn't be there in person, but he promised

Ofelia he'd still be here for her in this form. That had been enough then. This year, she wanted more.

Fifteen minutes of waterworks, Ofelia's crying turned into small drunk-sounding hiccups. She had a tentative grasp of herself, or at least she didn't feel like she was about to start sobbing again. Small victories.

"Just breathe, baby girl. That's great. You are doing excellent." Maverick encouraged, breathing with her. Each time she tried to speak, Maverick would shake his head and make her continue the breathing exercises until the small hiccups went away and her cheeks dried of all tears.

"Good." He said at last. "Now you can tell me what happened. If you're able to."

When Ofelia spoke, her voice sounded small and scratchy. "He didn't come."

Maverick cursed under his breath; she didn't even have to say who *he* was, she knew he already guessed. She mentioned countless times about how excited she was for him to come and admitting he didn't show was embarrassing. "My father didn't show up because he chose to pick up a random job over me. Again. For once in my life I just want someone – other than my mother – to show up and support me."

"Did you call your brother?"

"No. I didn't want to talk to Javi." An unspoken, *'I wanted you,'* hung heavily between them. It scared her how much she needed Maverick's comfort, especially when she didn't exactly know where they stood yet.

Maverick looked like he wanted to jump through the phone and pull her to his chest. She would gladly take solace in his arms. "I'm sorry, sweetheart. I know how much you wanted him to show up. I have half a mind to go pick up his ass and drag him to San Antonio."

A small smile crept across her features. "I wish you could."

"I do too." He admitted. "Fuck, I would do anything to see you smile. He would have been proud to see you shine today. How did your squad do, by the way?"

Ofelia was thankful for the change in topic because she didn't have any more energy, or tears for that matter, to continue to discuss her father and his lack of commitment. He was not going to ruin the amazing performance her team put on.

Instead of dwelling any longer on her father, she told Maverick all about her day and how proud she was of her cheerleaders. She explained all the amazing comments from the judges, mostly about their contagious energy and the execution of their pyramid stunt.

"Damn, I didn't realize I'm talking to a badass coach." Maverick grinned once she ran out of steam. "Did you record it?"

"Uhm, of course I did. This isn't my first rodeo. I had a parent record them. Why? Did you want to see it?" She asked hesitantly.

To her surprise, Maverick nodded eagerly. "Of course I do. I want to see what your long nights resulted in."

Seriously, she could kiss him right now. Why hadn't they'd been able to go out again so she could do just that? She desperately wanted to kiss his sexy face until they were both breathless and in need of much more. Damn her horny thoughts when he was so far away. "I'll send it to you as soon as we hang up."

They talked for an hour about nothing and everything all at once. When their conversation came to a natural end, Ofelia couldn't hold back her yawn. She had another early morning tomorrow, and she needed sleep. "Maverick? Thank you for letting me ugly cry to you, and thank you for listening."

"I like being the one you called, baby girl. Regardless of the reason. Call me again tomorrow and tell me about your day?"

"Of course. Bye Mav."

Ofelia smiled when she hung up her phone and put it on the charger. The moment her head hit the pillow she fell into a peaceful sleep with thoughts of Maverick's voice.

Chapter Twenty

The following morning, Ofelia awoke before her alarm. Much to her surprise, she didn't wake up with any residual sadness from yesterday's disappointing call from her father. A familiar excitement crept in, stemming from today's events. Crying to Maverick had been the best thing for her, who knew! She couldn't remember a time when she felt this good after a phone call.

A low rumble from her stomach reminded her of how little she ate yesterday. She'd kill for a few breakfast tacos at the moment but would settle for the continental breakfast her hotel offered. As long as they had something hot and savory, she couldn't complain. Oh, and coffee. A lot of coffee because today would be the longest day of the competition.

Bring it on.

Stretching out her long, tired limbs, Ofelia groaned as she worked the knots out of her body. Her dirty mind thought of a few ways Maverick could work the knots out of her body...and speaking of Maverick, she needed to text him a "thank you" for last night. He had no obligation to listen to her pitiful story, but he stayed on the phone through it all.

For now, Ofelia needed to focus on feeding herself before her stomach went on strike. She kicked the feather down comforter off and rolled out of her bed. Today's coaching outfit consisted of a navy-blue polo shirt with cream colored pants. She dressed pretty modestly compared to some of the extravagant outfits coaches wore.

By the time she made it down for breakfast, Ofelia was surprised to see that everyone else beat her there. She thought she got up early too, but she hadn't been the only one starving. "Y'all better have left some food for me."

Devin, whose plate was piled high with eggs and bacon, spoke between bites of food. "No promises, Ms. M. Tony-" he glared at his friend, who wore a *'who me?'* expression, "-woke up in the middle of the night and ate all my snacks. All of them. Do you understand how much I brought? He saved me one pop-tart, but he even took a bite out of that!"

"Yes, I did, and I would do it again. Next time don't challenge me by saying I couldn't eat half the snacks you brought. Let the record show, I, in fact, ate all." He said smugly, looking around as if he had adoring fans and not just Lacey who laughed at Devin's expense. "But don't worry, I promised I would buy him lunch. So he can't stay mad at me."

"I'm pretty sure I still can."

"But you won't. We are too sexy to be mad at each other."

Devin shot Tony a confused look. "What does that even mean?"

"As exciting as this conversation is," Ofelia interjected, stepping away. "I'm going to grab my plate before Tony eats my food too. Lacey, hold him back." She said to her cheer captain, but apparently 'holding back' meant attack, because Lacey threw herself at Tony, so he wouldn't run for more food.

"I'm not seeing what I'm seeing." Ofelia threw her hand up and walked away from the unruly children. The smell of sausage and eggs permeated the air around her and once again her stomach gave a loud grumble. "Alright, alright, I'm feeding you." She mumbled, grabbing a disposable plate and piling it high with potatoes, sausage and gravy on biscuits, and a fruit salad. She made her coffee, adding a little cream and sugar, before taking a seat with her team.

Per Ofelia's orders, everyone at the table had studied the schedule numerous times, but Gabbie asked if Ofelia could go over it one more time. A few of the others groaned, but she shot them a look to quiet them. "That's a great idea, Gabbie. Let me walk you through our day one more time. There's been a slight change." She said and upon hearing that, her team all scooted in a little closer.

The change wasn't a major one, but required them to sign in at ten today, rather than eleven. They would be performing at one and their last performance wouldn't be scheduled until midday if they advanced. Lunch would be provided by the convention center, though Ofelia didn't know what that entailed. She would find something she wanted to eat, she wasn't picky, but she hoped the rest of the squad would also find something. If not, the parents would have to make a food run.

Day two would be their most physically demanding day, but she hoped today would also be the most memorable for her team, especially her seniors. If they didn't place in the top fifteen percent, they wouldn't be on the track to nationals. Their year would end abruptly, and Ofelia wanted so much for her seniors. If they didn't advance to the finals, she would have all four of her seniors to console.

After her last bite of eggs, Ofelia looked around the table only to notice she had been the last to finish and everyone waited for her to leave. "Alright team, I think this is the time I give the big pep talk before we sign in, yeah?"

"You could." Lacey said, elongating the final syllable. "Or I could." She said it nonchalantly. Ofelia blinked slowly, making sure she heard Lacey correctly. The girl wasn't one for big declarations of teamwork, though she was great at inspiring the team individually. Ofelia couldn't help the pride that began to swell in her chest.

"Okay, go on." she encouraged, allowing the captain to take over. Every eye turned in Lacey's direction, waiting expectantly for what she had to say.

To Lacey's credit, she didn't shy away from the attention. She thrived. Inwardly, Ofelia did a little 'yaasss queen' dance as her second in command began to speak. "So, I'm proud of us, or whatever. We did a great job yesterday and that set the bar for today. We can't screw it up now, because us seniors aren't ready to put up our poms quite yet. Right, guys?" Two senior girls and Devin nodded, all giving her thumbs up. "We gotta be better than we were yesterday and play on our strengths. We go in confident, like the badasses we are – sorry Ms. Mendez – and we leave those judges wanting more."

As far as speeches went, it wasn't earth-shattering, but clearly got the job done. A chorus of "McKinley High" chants erupted around Ofelia, much to the dismay of the handful of guests who unfortunately booked the hotel over competition weekend. They were probably seriously regretting that choice now.

"Okay, okay!" Ofelia laughed once the chant started to die down. "Let's sign in. Battle faces ready, team."

Chapter Twenty-One

Maverick made up his mind the moment he hung up the phone last night. She didn't ask him, he wasn't entirely certain she'd want him there, but he knew one thing for certain. There was no way in hell he'd let his woman suffer another day.

His girl needed him, so he'd show up.

Fuck her father for not understanding how lucky he was to have Ofelia as his daughter. He didn't deserve her, but Maverick would prove that *he* did. He'd fix the man's mistake.

Everything Maverick needed for a night away fit in a small duffle bag that he threw in the backseat of his truck. His plan, one he thought of last night, was to sweep into the competition unannounced and then attempt to locate his girl. If Ofelia needed someone to show up for her, he was going to be that person.

He would need to ask around to see where McKinley practiced and if he was allowed backstage. He'd have to play it smooth so the parents or her cheerleaders didn't think much of it, other than Ofelia called in Maverick for backup.

Believable? Maybe.

Okay so that part was weak, Maverick was going to have to improvise. Who knew romantic gestures took so much time and careful consideration? The men in the movies made it seem so effortless, while he tried to remember if he packed a toothbrush. He was fairly certain he did.

The drive down to San Antonio wasn't bad. The problem came when he found the convention center and realized quickly how much of a nightmare parking was going to be.

The first two parking garages were completely full, causing him to drive further away in desperation, hoping some unlucky fool would give up their parking. Eventually Maverick did find parking, in a sketchy McDonald's parking lot. He paid the man sitting outside twenty dollars to allow him to park, and he couldn't be certain that was even the man's job. It made the man leave him alone though, going off to find his next victim, so Maverick thought it was a twenty well spent.

He'd have to come back to his truck at some point, so he left his overnight bag inside, shutting and locking the door. In the far-off distance, he could still see the convention center on the horizon, but he had to be at least a mile away. Nothing like showing up to his own romantic gesture smelling like sweat. If he was lucky, Ofelia might be into the smell of a musky man.

Maverick hoped he wasn't making an ass of himself. What if when she saw him, Ofelia looked horrified? Or worse yet, she might stare at him with pity. Here comes Maverick, the dumbass that thought he could play the hero. Hadn't he learned his lesson on surprising people at inopportune times? He refused to let his mind drift off into that dark place, so he picked up his pace. No sense in chickening out now.

As expected, the convention center was flooded with people, an introvert's worst nightmare. Even Maverick, who

ON AND OFF THE FIELD

was used to stadiums full of people, couldn't help feeling out of his element within the sea of cheer fanatics. But nobody paid him any mind. He may as well have been a ghost for all the attention he got. Many people around him were primarily female, young and old, all clumped in groups talking amicably to one another or consoling crying cheerleaders.

No signs indicated where he needed to go, and if there were, they were covered up by groups of people. Maverick needed to locate the damn sign-up station so he could ask....well he wasn't entirely sure what he would ask yet. The more he thought about his plan, the less confident he was about surprising Ofelia. He knew from experience how testy she got during practices.

Not to mention he was fairly certain the sign-up station, if such a thing existed, would not let a random man know the whereabouts of a group of high school students. If he were still somebody, he could have cajoled someone into giving up that information, but even that would have been risky.

Maverick needed a new plan of attack, one that required a lot less unknowns. He first needed to get out of the middle of the damn convention center so another person wouldn't "accidentally" bump him as they walked by. Navigating through the crowd proved easier said than done. It wasn't so much where he wanted to go, but where the mass led him, and they led him straight towards a small cafeteria area.

He decided to just text Ofelia and hoped she had her phone with her. If not, his search would continue. He quickly typed out a simple message, hoping it got a prompt response. "Where are you?" He pressed send. There, now he just needed to wait on-

Immediately his phone began to buzz. "Fuck, she's fast." He murmured, since her name, along with the picture she sent

this morning, filled his screen. There was no way in hell he could hide from the cacophony of sounds around him, but maybe she wouldn't notice if her side was equally loud.

Maverick answered and put the phone to his ear, trying to cup his hand around the speaker and his mouth to keep the sound at bay. Before he could speak, Ofelia beat him to it. "What do you mean, where am I?" She sounded confused and slightly apprehensive. There was definite apprehension in her voice. *Fuck.*

Ofelia wasn't buying his bullshit. Maverick heard her whisper something to someone and moments later the surrounding sound all but vanished. Had she walked into a utility closet or something? "I feel like I should ask where *you* are, Mav."

So much for surprise, but Maverick thought this might be better. He could at least find her without having to walk every square inch of this place. "Oh, you know, San Antonio."

"What?!"

"I'm in San Antonio."

"No, I heard, but...*what?*"

"I'm not sure how to answer that." Maverick laughed awkwardly. "Uh, I guess more specifically I'm at the convention center."

"You did not drive two hours to come to our competition. Tell me you didn't do that."

Maverick still couldn't tell if Ofelia was happy or furious and it unnerved him. "I mean, I did, but if you'd rather I not-"

"Tell me where you are! Now. I'll come find you."

Chapter Twenty-Two

Maverick was here. *Here.* As in he drove all the way to San Antonio on a Saturday morning after she sobbed her eyes out to him last night. Who the hell does that? Maverick, apparently. Ofelia needed to see him this instant to make sure this wasn't a dream because there was no way Mav came. Right?

Ofelia had no problems leaving her team in the capable hands of the parents. She told Gianna an impromptu coach meeting sprung up, which was the quickest lie she could produce. Thankfully, Gianna didn't question her; if she had, the lie would quickly unravel.

Maverick described his location next to multiple vending machines and self-serve pizza stands. Ofelia knew right away where he was. The convention housed many small eateries, but only one served pizza on the first floor. She clutched her phone tightly, as if it were a lifeline connecting her to Maverick as she raced to the escalators. The first teams of the competition had already begun to perform, making this area less busy than usual.

When her feet touched down on the bottom story, she went through a mental map of the layout. Yes, she had memorized the entire layout of this damn building in case she lost a cheerleader or needed to get them from point A to point B as fast as possible. She didn't also know that it would come in handy now.

As she got closer to where Maverick should be, her heart began a funny lurch in her chest. She was feeling a mixture of emotions, most notably one she had not experienced in years. Ofelia couldn't put a name to it, not yet. She wouldn't allow herself to think of that word now. Still, she felt deeply and eventually she would have to face her emotions.

Ofelia finally arrived at the eatery, stopping dead in her tracks as all the breath in her lungs left her. Standing only a few feet in front, with his back turned towards her, was Maverick. He'd come. He showed up after one of the most important men in her life let her down. She couldn't begin to form words now because she nearly burst with emotions.

Maverick must have sensed a presence behind him because he turned around. The moment their eyes met, he beamed at her, a rare smile he reserved solely for her. One minute he was across the shop and the next Ofelia was in his arms, kissing him passionately. She didn't know who moved to whom, but she frankly didn't care. All she wanted was her lips on his with her body planted firmly against Maverick, creating a new type of heat.

Maverick let out a low chuckle from the back of his throat, vibrating through their kiss. "Shit, baby girl. I take it you're happy I came?"

"Happy? Maverick I'm fucking losing my mind. I don't know if I want to kiss you, or cry, or climb you like a tree!"

Maverick's eyes went dark, and Ofelia swore she saw lust

within him. "Hmm, if I had known that was an option, I would have waited for you in your hotel room."

"You're staying? In my room?" Ofelia didn't care if she sounded over eager. She had no sense of chill, and she was okay with that. Maverick didn't seem to mind.

Maverick didn't want to assume, but he would also need to find a hotel fast. Booking a room hadn't been part of his grand gesture plan. "I can find my own room, but yeah, I wanted to stay and make sure you had someone here for you." He said softly, reaching out to tuck a stray curl behind her hair. She leaned into his touch, closing her eyes to let this moment truly sink in.

"Nonsense. You'll stay with me." Then, almost reluctantly Ofelia pulled back, but just enough to look into his eyes. "But I won't be back in my hotel room until tonight. I can give you a key if you want, I have an extra. My squad is probably performing twice today, so I'm not sure when I'll be back in the room. You can wait in there for me though. You'll just need to be kinda secretive. I can't have the parents finding out I'm housing a man in my room."

Maverick looked at her as if she were speaking a different language. "Sweetheart, I'm going to watch your cheerleaders perform. I came here knowing you'd be busy, but I wanted you to know there was someone in the crowd for you. I'll take that key though, for later. I'll make sure no one sees me sneaking into your room."

It was official. Ofelia was never going to let Maverick get away from her. He officially proved himself to be a permanent fixture in her life. He didn't know how wonderful he was. "Thank you. Here, take my room key." She said, fishing through her back pockets to hand it over. "The room is written on the back. I'm on the tenth floor. Are you serious about staying to watch?"

Maverick nodded and Ofelia thought he looked genuinely excited. It was cute. "Yeah, I am. These people look like they are going to go to war, and I don't want to miss that. Where should I sit?"

"Just take this escalator up and head right. You can enter the arena from there and find a seat with a decent view of the stage. My phone is with me if you need me. Tonight is all yours, I promise." Ofelia grinned, lighting up like a kid on Christmas, except instead of a Barbie as her gift, she had a super-hot baseball player. Honestly, it was the definition of an upgrade.

"Don't worry about me today. I'm here for support. You text me if you need me. I've got nothing but time."

Speaking of time, she was quickly running out. Her team would be expecting her back soon, and she still needed to run through the first routine once more. Even though she wanted nothing more than to stay next to Maverick, she was needed elsewhere. One last time before tonight, she leaned up to press a soft, yet deep kiss to his lips. "Tonight. And remember, don't let anyone see you." She promised, basking in his piney scent, before reluctantly untangling her arms from around his waist.

"Tonight." Maverick repeated.

When Ofelia walked back to her team, she did so knowing the man she was falling deeply for would be sitting in the audience.

Chapter Twenty-Three

Maverick had never seen anything quite like this. Baseball tournaments were a given because of his familiarity with them. The crowd would burst with pent-up energy as they waited for their favorite teams to enter the field. Each play would be taken to heart and if the desired outcome wasn't achieved, the umpire was bound to hear a chorus of boos and threats.

None of that compared to the utter spectacle taking place in front of his very eyes. This crowd wasn't just invested; they acted like their very souls were in the hands of Lucifer, and if they didn't give the perfect performance, a giant pit would open in the center of the floor and drag them down to the fiery depths of hell. That wasn't an exaggeration either. Maverick witnessed plenty of interactions between cheerleaders and their overly involved parents to make him want to call up his own parents and thank them for never becoming *those* parents.

Maverick understood the dedication and pressure these young people put upon themselves. Didn't he do the same thing when he was their age? He hustled and worked his ass off to be the best. It paid off in the end, but the small voice he was seriously beginning to despise reminded him that he lost it faster than he earned it. He wondered how many of these young cheerleaders would watch their dreams slowly fade away into obscurity.

And that was enough self-deprecation for the day.

Luckily the dark place in his mind didn't stay active for long; it soon became enamored with the routines he witnessed. These squads didn't come to mess around and Maverick began to worry slightly for Ofelia. His girl was good, but he hadn't seen her team in their elements. They would have to be completely badass to stand a chance against some of their opponents' routines. He was fairly certain one team had their own blow horns and Bluetooth speakers.

As it turns out, Maverick had no reason to worry about Ofelia and her team. When McKinley walked on stage, owning it like a damn catwalk, Maverick was glued to their every movement. So much happened, and he didn't know whether to look at the ones back flipping or the ones soaring through the air after being tossed by their teammates. Gravity evidently hadn't been invited to watch their routine. There was no physical way the squad could pull off so many flips, flies, and jumps if Newton's law of universal gravitation was involved.

When McKinley's first routine ended, Maverick sprung to his feet, cheering like a proud father. Apparently, he was no better than the loud mothers sitting around him, for many of them turned to give him a look indicating their annoyance. Not that it mattered much to Mav. It felt like the right type of justice after what those very moms put him through only minutes ago with their loud wails and obnoxious crying.

After McKinley's second and final routine of the night, which was somehow even more impressive than their first,

Maverick's stomach began to protest. He heard a deep rumble despite the cheering crowd. He hadn't eaten since that morning and Maverick was ready to consume an ungodly amount of calories. He quickly sent off a text to Ofelia, letting her know he was going out to pick up dinner for them and would meet her back at the hotel.

Dinner wasn't a hard choice. Since he was in San Antonio, a place full of amazing Mexican culture, he needed authentic food. Maverick settled on a restaurant called *Mi Tierra*, a place that not only sold amazing Mexican dishes, according to the online reviews, but also a variety of baked goods. He made sure to stock up, knowing Ofelia liked to sample a mixture of foods and Maverick was hungry enough to eat the entire restaurant.

Getting back to the hotel was simple enough. It was located directly across the street from the convention center. Finding parking for said hotel was a different story. He should have remembered the parking fiasco from this morning. It took an entire thirty minutes of driving through the garage, getting frustrated and cursing like a sailor before he found a car finally pulling out of a spot.

He wasn't surprised he beat Ofelia back to her room, but was glad that he didn't run into anyone from McKinley. When he checked his phone, she had texted him only ten minutes ago saying she was picking up pizza for her squad and would be back after. Her parents offered to arrange a movie night for the teens in the hotel's media room while Ofelia got some much-needed rest. If things went the way he hoped they would tonight, Maverick didn't expect either of them would be resting much.

He couldn't deny wanting Ofelia. The need to have her in every way possible only strengthened from their first night in the truck together. He had done the right thing when he said they should go any further that night, but the feel of her soft skin against his and her sounds of pleasure had stayed with him ever since. He wanted to know what she sounded like when she came undone in his arms and not just by her own hand. When she withered in pleasure as he moved inside of her, moaning his name. When she...

Fuck. He was hard again. His body heated at the mere thought of her and him together. He needed to cool himself down before she got here and saw him sporting a hard on while he sat in her bed. Fortunately for him, his stomach took this opportunity to growl in hunger again, giving him something new to focus on other than Ofelia's naked body.

Thirty minutes and four barbacoa tacos later, Maverick heard a faint tapping sound of a key before Ofelia peered inside. Her face instantly lit up when she saw Maverick. She was glowing from today's achievements. At that moment, hair slightly askew and clothes rumpled, she looked more beautiful than Maverick had ever seen her.

"Are you hungry?" Was all he was capable of asking. All other words left him when he realized he was alone with Ofelia in a room with a bed. He reverted to a caveman, only able to think in simple sentences. *Man have woman. Man have bed. Man take woman to bed.*

Ofelia shook her head, coming into the room and shutting the door behind her. "I had a slice of pizza, but I'll definitely be taking some food later." She said, shrugging off her bag and kicking her shoes off. She crossed the room in a few long strides before dropping herself into Maverick's lap. Her ass ground down on him until she was comfortable, and Maverick had to hold his breath for his body not to react to her.

"You came." She whispered, snuggling up to him. It was only two simple words, but they packed a punch. He had come when her own father let her down. This wasn't a simple act and whether he meant it or not, it spoke on their relationship and how much Ofelia meant to him.

"I came." He repeated into her hair, moving his hand to take out the elastic. Her bun toppled over, and he ran a hand through her hair, working out any tangles. "And you were brilliant. Your squad was amazing. I don't think you understand how impressive you are." He murmured, hoping his breath didn't smell like onions.

If it did, Ofelia didn't seem to mind. She tilted her head up and leaned forward until their lips touched. It started off tender, simple with no real heat behind it. It was perfect. She was perfect. Ofelia didn't know it, but she had Maverick securely under her spell. He'd do anything for her, including but not limiting to driving two hours to sit in a massive crowd so she knew someone was there for her.

"Thank you." He heard himself say the moment Ofelia's lips moved away from him.

She looked at him oddly, tilting her head to the side and flicking her tongue out to lick her bottom lip. Maverick had half a mind to bring that lip between his teeth and suck on it until she begged him for more.

"Thank you? For what? I should be the one thanking you." She asked, bringing his attention away from her lips and back up to her eyes.

"For..." Maverick hesitated. The words were on the tip of his tongue, he tasted them, but something held him back from effectively communicating the raw emotions he felt. How could he say what he needed to without scaring her away? What were they to begin with? Maverick wanted to be more than a guy she casually dated, but was Ofelia ready for that?

The words soon began to tumble out of him, unexpectedly

and without hesitation. "For being you. For listening. For trusting me enough to call me when you were at your lowest. God damn, Ofelia, for just existing. When I took this job, I was miserable and couldn't see past my own pain. I gave up, and I was going through the motions of day-to-day life, but I wasn't living.

"The moment I saw you at the coffee shop after our first encounter, I left feeling something for the first time in God knows how long. When I saw you at the bar with another guy, all I could see was red. I hated that man because I wanted to be the one next to you. After our first date, you were all I thought about, and I haven't been able to go a single day – no, a single moment – without thinking about you. You provided the sun when I was in the storm and when you called me, I felt like I could be your sun. Like I could be worthy of you."

For a long moment after he finished his emotional soliloquy, Ofelia didn't say a word. She looked at him with wide eyes, eyebrows raised nearly to her hairline. Then she did something unexpected, causing Maverick's heart to lurch. She pushed off him and stood.

Fuck! He blew it. He word-vomit scared her. He couldn't take back the words even though he desperately wanted to turn back the clock and go back to their kiss. Back before he screwed it up with his fucking feelings and his inability to read the room. "Ofelia, I'm sorry-"

Ofelia shushed him by holding out her hand, looking down at him. Now he saw the tears in her eyes and his increasing anxiety only heightened. How could he say so many wrong things in such a short amount of time? Was he truly so unlovable or intolerable that the thought of him caring about her made her want to cry?

"Come here." Ofelia said when Maverick made no attempt

to get up or speak. This time she smiled at him, and he swore there was a new warmth in her eyes that hadn't been there a moment ago. "Please Mav. Come here. Stand up."

He wasn't going to argue with that. He stood, nearly bumping into her with how quickly he picked himself up from the chair. Ofelia stepped forward and wrapped her arms around his waist. "Remember when we were in your truck?" She asked. Maverick nodded because it never strayed far from his mind. "You asked me what I wanted, and I said you. But you said you didn't want our first time to be in your truck and not until we were both ready."

Maverick watched as Ofelia took a step backwards. The dim lights in the room made her look ethereal, playing on her skin to illuminate the best parts of her. She locked her eyes with him and didn't hesitate as she lifted her polo shirt over her head, tossing it down on the ground. She stood in her white bra, showing off her toned stomach. "Well, I'm ready. I think you might be too. And if memory serves, I remember you saying you wanted my legs wrapped around you while I scream your name. Is that still true?"

Maverick's entire body heated up. His cock strained against the front of his pants uncomfortably. For a brief moment, he saw Ofelia's eyes dip down, taking in his bulge. Color reddened her cheeks before she looked back up, waiting for Maverick to speak. Although she looked confident, there was a shadow of insecurity in her eyes, and he wondered if she thought he'd reject her.

"I believe my words were something along the lines of needing to taste you when your legs are wrapped around my shoulders." His voice was deep as he took a step forward. Ofelia shivered. She stood abnormally still as he circled her; a hungry wolf ready to taste the little lamb. He stalked up behind her, placing one large hand on her lower abdomen and the other on her hip. "Tell me what you want, baby girl."

He said those words before, but this time he wasn't planning to stop. He intended to devour her if that's what she desired. Ofelia leaned back against him, and Maverick was certain she felt his erection pressing into her ass. "You." She said breathlessly.

They had been down this road once before, but neither had been ready to take the plunge. Until now. Maverick dipped his head lower, his lips finding the crook of her neck and nipped. Ofelia let out a little frustrated whimper, causing Maverick to chuckle at her impatience. "Don't be a brat, baby girl. I already told you that when I get to have you, I'm taking my sweet time with you."

"Mav-"

Maverick located the clasp to her bra and undid it. He slid the straps down her shoulders until the bra was nothing more than a discarded memory on the ground and her soft brown breasts were bared to him. He brought both hands up, taking her breasts into them and squeezing gently. Ofelia gasped softly, her sensitive nipples pebbling at his touch. He ran a thumb over her delicate flesh, earning himself another moan.

"I always pegged you as an ass man." Ofelia said, attempting humor but Maverick heard the shakiness to her breathing.

"Would it be cheesy to say I'm 'your' man?" Mav smirked.

"A little. But it's working for me." She laughed as Maverick spun her around. He took in the beautiful woman and once again thanked his lucky stars for putting Ofelia into his path. He kissed down her collarbone until he got to her breast. He pulled her nipple into his mouth, running his tongue along the hardened nub. She arched into him, and Maverick wrapped an arm around her waist to keep her up.

ON AND OFF THE FIELD

"Why are your pants still on?" Maverick murmured around her nipple. Ofelia's eyes flickered open, looking over Maverick who was still fully dressed. He read the question in her expression, but he shook his head. "No. My clothes stay on. For now. Take off your pants, baby girl. Let me see what you are hiding underneath."

Ofelia splayed her fingers out across her waistband. Her thumbs dug into the sides, waiting for his reaction. Maverick didn't give any, he simply waited, motioning for her to continue. "Pants, Ofelia. Off."

"You are bossy in the bedroom." Ofelia giggled and Maverick thought she didn't know the half of it. If she knew the dirty things running through his mind right now, she would call this request vanilla. Ofelia did a cute little shimmy as she pulled her slacks off. She then stood in nothing but a lacy black thong. Maverick raised a brow in question and Ofelia shrugged. "Thongs don't leave panty lines in pants. Plus, I paid way too much for these and I'm going to get my wear out of them."

"Trust me, baby girl, I'm not complaining. Those are going to stay on. For now." He said, getting a full view of her body. Her body was soft and toned from years of cheerleading. She was what he liked to call "thicc," plump in all the right places with thighs for days. How one woman held so much power over him was beyond him. The tentative control he had over this situation was slipping rapidly.

Still, he needed to remember this wasn't about him right now. It was about pleasing the goddess of a woman in front of him. He closed the distance between them, leading her back until the back of her legs hit the bed, and they both stumbled into it, Maverick on top. He pinned Ofelia underneath him. She was so small compared to him, but not meek.

In fact, he'd never seen her look stronger than in this moment.

"I've been thinking about how you taste, sweetheart." Mav purred. Ofelia tried to reach under his shirt to feel his torso, but her hands kept getting stuck in the fabric. Her attempts amused him, so he took pity on her. "I think you've earned this." He lifted himself up momentarily, stripping himself off his shirt before laying back on top of her. "Better?"

"It would be better if you were naked. I want it, Mav. Please." She begged him, reaching for the fly on his jeans. She managed to get it halfway down before Mav playfully swatted her hands away.

"Soon." He promised her, kissing his way down her stomach. He slowly made his way further down, kissing the apex of her panty covered thighs. They were drenched and Maverick inhaled deeply, taking in her aroused scent. "Beautiful." He whispered. "And entirely mine."

"Yours." She echoed as Maverick hooked a finger through the crotch of her panties and pulled them aside. He was serious when he said he wanted those to stay on. He wanted to enjoy them a little longer before he ripped them off her body.

Maverick took a slow, long lick down her center before parting her and flicking his tongue out to meet her clit. "Holy shit!" Ofelia gasped, clutching the bedding as her body spasmed under his first touch.

"I couldn't agree more." He smiled mischievously, taking her clit between his teeth as his tongue relentlessly teased her. She tasted sweet, like he thought she would. He moved to swipe one finger through her wetness, rubbing it against her lips, spreading her arousal all over her bare pussy. Maverick groaned before pushing in a single finger, feeling her tightness. "So fucking tight baby girl."

Ofelia said it had been at least two years since she had been with a man and Maverick was also going through a dry spell. This felt like coming home, buried deep between her legs. When he felt her adjust, Mav then pushed in a second finger, groaning when she tightened around them.

"Mav!" Ofelia moaned, rubbing her sweet pussy in his face. "Yes, please, please don't stop! Don't stop...yes!" Her words ended in a scream as he tongued her clit again, feeling her squeeze around his fingers. "Maverick...don't stop...don't stop! I'm going...going to..."

Mav was relentless with his sweet torture. He took care of her clit while finger fucking her until she became a puddle underneath him. When Ofelia orgasmed, she screamed out his name as she came all over his tongue. He licked her until she came down from her high and immediately Maverick pushed away to claim her mouth.

Their lips met in a warm, wet embrace. Ofelia's climax still on Maverick's tongue, but she didn't shy away from tasting herself. "More. Mav I need more. I need you." She pleaded and this time when she went for his pants to finish what she started earlier with his zipper, Maverick didn't stop her. Ofelia clawed at his jeans until he helped her kick them off. The last to go was his boxers and her panties, joining together on the floor.

They were both naked, laying flushed against each other. Ofelia reached down to grip Mav's cock in her hands, moaning. "You're so fucking big." She panted, each stroke driving him absolutely wild. "I want it. Please Mav." Her begs were like candy to him, sweet and addictive.

"What do you want to do with this cock? It needs you." He wanted to be inside of her, but he wanted to do it in a way that she liked. He hadn't had to learn what someone liked in bed in so long, it was actually fun discovering what made Ofelia moan.

There was no shyness in his girl's voice, only complete understanding of what she wanted and needed. "I want to ride you."

How could Maverick say no to that request? He would be a fool otherwise. They moved together until they switched positions. Maverick was laying on his back, his head on the pillow as Ofelia climbed on top of him. His cock was throbbing, painfully so, but he needed to last for her.

"Do you have a condom?" She asked like the question just dawned on her.

Maverick came prepared. He reached for the bedside table, grabbing his wallet. He opened it up and pulled out a silver wrapper. Ofelia immediately stole it from him, ripping it open with a devious smirk. "I want to do the honors."

"You don't need an excuse to touch my cock, baby girl. Touch away." He winked. Then watched as she took the condom out and rolled it down his impressive length. He took the base of his cock into her hand and hovered over his length before slowly bringing herself down.

Ofelia hissed as the first few inches went inside of her and Maverick reached out to grab her hips, stopping her before she could go any lower. "Are you hurt? Did I prep you well enough?"

Ofelia's features softened as his concern, but she shook her head. "You're so big, Mav. Just give me a minute. I'll adjust." She murmured and leaned down to plan a soft kiss to his lips. Ofelia kept his lips on his, inching herself down on his cock. When he was fully seated inside of her, she gave off a soft gasp. "I've never been this full before." She panted gently.

"Move when you're ready. I want to see you please yourself

on my cock." Maverick couldn't keep the moan out of his own voice. It was enough to make Ofelia start to move for him. It took everything for Maverick to remain focused and not let his lust consume him out of fear he would take over in a frenzy. He didn't want to hurt her.

Ofelia seemed to be playing a battle of her own, shifting on top of him so he rubbed deeper inside of her. He watched transfixed as she rubbed herself against him, the movement providing a natural up and down movement. Her eyes flickered halfway closed and soon Maverick's name was leaving her parted lips in a series of moans. Maverick's own face mirrored her own.

He couldn't stay still anymore though. On their own accord, his hips lifted and slammed into her. He felt himself hit deep inside of her and Ofelia cried out. Not in pain but pleasure. "Yes! Oh, Mav...rough. I want it rough."

She knew what she liked and Maverick was going to give her just that. He met her thrust for thrust, a string of colorful expletives leaving his lips. Ofelia was on top, but Maverick oversaw their pleasure. Her hand snaked between her legs and began rubbing her clit. Maverick tsked. "Fuck no, baby girl. When you are with me, I take care of your clit. Do you understand?"

"Yes. Oh, fuck yes I do." She nodded enthusiastically and all but grabbed Mav's hands to move between her legs. He began to stimulate her clit, giving more pleasure. His own began to build, and he didn't know how much longer he could last in this state.

"That's my girl. Fuck, you drive me crazy. That tight little pussy of yours is going to be the death of me. I'm so fucking close." He opened his eyes, making sure she was as consumed as him.

She was.

"Mav...oh god, Mav-"

"God has nothing to do with this, baby girl. It's my cock that is making you crazy. My cock that is nestled deep inside of your pussy. Cum for me baby. Cum all over my cock." The dirty words left his mouth just in time for her to scream out as she toppled over in her orgasm. Maverick finally let himself go, coming hard inside of the condom.

Ofelia milked him until he went soft inside of her and then pulled out of him before falling into his arms, panting. "That was..."

"I hope you say nothing short of amazing." Maverick's own breathing was labored from their activities.

Ofelia grinned and kissed his chest. "Exactly that." Then a sly smile crossed her features. "And to think, it's only the start."

That made Maverick cock his brow. "The start?"

"Oh yes, the start." She said as if it were the most obvious thing in the world. "You awoke something in me, Mav and I want to make you feel as good as you've made me feel. I hope you'll be ready for another round...after tacos of course."

And damn it if his cock didn't twitch in anticipation at her words. "What can I say, I'm captive to your every need. We have all night."

That was precisely what they did too. They finished off the last of the food Maverick had bought before going in for another hot and sexy round between the sheets. When they finished for the third...or was it fourth?...time, Maverick held Ofelia as they fell asleep with their limbs still entangled.

Chapter Twenty-Four

Ofelia woke up with the most delicious ache between her thighs, a parting gift from last night's activities. Her body was extra sensitive; she felt the soft caress of the sheets against her naked body. Big, strong arms held her tightly against a firm chest. Maverick's chin nestled atop her head and Ofelia wondered if his mouth was full of her unruly hair.

Last night was nothing short of spectacular. Maverick worshiped her body, treating her like a sacred deity he wanted to please. And please he did, many times. To say her sex life previous had been lacking, even when she was with Hector, would be an understatement.

For so long Ofelia believed something inside of her was broken. Hector and her had good sex, but it had taken her so long to reach orgasm and it hurt Hector's feelings. It wasn't that she wasn't attracted to him, she had been and loved him desperately, but Hector struggled to reciprocate in bed. Often Ofelia ended up working out her own tension.

Her lack of orgasm hadn't been ideal, but Ofelia had

thought the problem was entirely her own fault. If she gave Hector pleasure, then her own didn't matter. How stupid her thinking had been back then. Maverick, in only one night, had found the most sensitive spots and drew out her cries of ecstasy.

Sex wasn't supposed to be like that, was it? Fucking spectacular and earth-shattering. Hadn't Ofelia read countless books and spoken to a few friends who all agreed their first time with their significant other was less than stellar? Ofelia had thought that until Maverick completely rocked her world.

Home run. Knocked it out of the park. Grand slam. All puns included.

Maybe they were just the rare match that instantly clicked. There was no embarrassment or shame Ofelia felt during or after, quite the opposite. She felt empowered and sexy, capable of bringing grown men to their knees. Maverick falling between her thighs would be etched deeply into her brain for the rest of her life.

The thought made her smile and cuddle back against Mav, her back resting against his chest. She wiggled slightly to readjust herself, effectively grinding into his crotch. Something was definitely awake, even if Maverick was not. His morning wood pressed against her ass, and she nudged back against him again, biting her lower lip.

"If you keep doing that, I will be forced to retaliate, baby girl." Maverick gruff voice whispered into her ear. So, he was awake, not just her new favorite part of him.

"Who, me? I'm afraid I don't know what you mean." Ofelia feigned innocence and moved back against him again. Which promptly earned her a low groan and a swift spanking on her ass, causing her to yelp. "What was that for?" She asked as if she didn't know. Ofelia also made a mental note that she really liked being spanked, and she would need to demand more of it the next time.

Maverick didn't answer her. Instead, he rolled her around until they were chest to chest. He snaked an arm around her thigh and hiked her leg up around his hip. The head of his cock pressed against her entrance, teasing since Mav made no attempts of pushing in further. "Good morning, beautiful." His voice was deep and husky with sleep. She didn't think she had ever found him more attractive.

"Morning." The word came out more breathlessly than she anticipated. Maverick must have noticed for he reached down between them and dragged the tip of his cock down her seam. A moan escaped her lips, and she suddenly no longer cared that she was still sore from last night.

Ofelia had the foresight to grab their last condom from the bedside table before reaching down and halting his movements, a sly smile on her lips. "Did you sleep well?"

Ofelia didn't give him a chance to answer as she ripped open the condom, rolling it over his hard length. He plunged his thickness deep inside of her, filling her up completely. They both hissed in surprise and pleasure, Maverick squeezing her thigh draped around him.

"I could get used to this." He murmured as he started moving. These were not the hurried, almost frenzied movements from last night. No, this morning Maverick moved almost lazily with no regard to time. Ofelia found that she liked it a lot.

"Waking up with my hair in your mouth?" She grinned, feigning naivety.

Maverick chuckled and shook his head. "Your hair is beautiful and none of it got in my mouth. I'm talking about waking up with you next to me."

"It's...nice." Ofelia's last word left her lips in a soft moan. Maverick had quickened his pace but kept his movements gentle. Nice didn't describe how she felt, not even close. She couldn't yet put those feelings into words, but the thought of waking up alone or with anyone else other than Maverick caused a deep ache in her chest she didn't want.

"Nice is one way to describe it. Fucking euphoric would be another." That's when their conversation ended, and their lips met in a passionate embrace. The kiss communicated far more than Ofelia could articulate; she only hoped Maverick understood what she conveyed in that kiss.

They made love slowly and fervidly. The searing caresses started a flame deep within her belly and it built and built until the flames erupted into a full-on inferno. They toppled over at the same time, holding on to one another until their fire fizzled out, leaving nothing but immense satisfaction in its wake.

Again, just like last night, three tiny words played at the tip of her tongue. Small in stature but heavy in meaning, they begged to be released, but her fear of ruining this precious thing between them stopped her from voicing how she felt. In time, she would work up the courage. She wanted to be sure anyway, perhaps when Maverick wasn't seated inside of her, and her brain wasn't full of lust and satisfaction.

Ofelia's alarm began to go off, ruining the moment. "Damn." She muttered, untangling herself from Maverick to reach for her phone. It occurred to her that in an hour, Ofelia would have fourteen cheerleaders and their parents starting to wake up, and it seemed incredibly salacious to have a naked Maverick next to her. Slight panic began to course through her body. Maverick needed to leave.

As if reading her thoughts, Mav rolled to the edge of the

bed, bracing his feet firmly on the floor as he stretched his back. "I suppose that's my cue to leave."

"I'm so sorry Mav, it's just that if anyone found out we were together right now-"

Maverick silenced her by reaching around to pull her in for a quick kiss. "Trust me, I'm not offended. I know I'm not your booty call." He winked and stood. His entire body stood on full display and Ofelia thought she'd get used to seeing all the hard lines and strong muscles, but she definitely wasn't. The man was built like a damn gladiator and Ofelia had rode that man! Multiple times!

Damn it felt good to be her right now.

Ofelia blatantly and unabashedly stared at her man as he got dressed. Maverick seemed to eat up the attention, winking at her as he slid up his jeans. "Do you want me to stay around for the results?" He asked.

He was sweet to ask, but Ofelia knew nothing exciting happened today. She could easily text him if they were moving to nationals. This competition was a stepping stone to bigger things. "No, it's fine. Go home and rest. I'll text you later and let you know how we did."

Maverick was fully dressed and disappeared momentarily to brush his teeth. When he finished, Mav walked out carrying his overnight bag. Ofelia still laid in bed because she desperately needed a shower so she didn't reek of sex. Not that she was complaining, of course.

"Thank you again, for coming. I'm so happy you did." Ofelia tilted her head up as Maverick walked over to her, stopping in front of her. "Does this mean we are serious?" Ofelia wasn't sure what prompted her to ask the question right then, but she needed to know. She didn't make it a habit of sleeping with men that didn't mean anything to her, not that she was against hookups. Mav meant something to her, and she needed confirmation he felt the same.

"Baby girl, I've been serious. I'm glad you are finally on board." He grinned and leaned down to kiss her gently. "You're mine, Ofi. You're mine and I don't like sharing what is mine. And I'm yours. You are stuck with me."

"I wouldn't say stuck. Happily committed, more like." Ofelia smiled like a fool but didn't care. She was happy, happier than she had been in years. All because of a stupid gym fight. Amazing how that could be the best thing to ever happen to her. "Text me when you are home?"

"Not a minute later." Maverick agreed, hovering above her. Unsaid words hung heavily between them and for a second, Ofelia thought Maverick might say what she couldn't. The stretch of silence lasted only a few more seconds until broken by a kiss from Maverick. "Bye, Ofelia." With that, she watched her man walk out of the room. An embarrassing giggle left her lips the moment she was alone.

She had it bad for Maverick Wilson.

Chapter Twenty-Five

Happily committed was the perfect way to describe how Maverick felt. The ridiculous grin he wore hadn't left his face since he left the hotel. Stranger yet, Maverick couldn't shut the hell up when he passed someone walking back to his car, forcing polite conversation with everyone he passed.

There was only one reason he acted like a social butterfly starving for attention and that was because of what transpired last night – and this morning. It would have been easy to slip back into bed and spend all day together wrapped up in each other. They were both adults and had adult things they needed to do, but Maverick wouldn't mind ignoring the outside world for a little longer.

The drive home wasn't bad. Maverick only stopped once for gas and to pick up a gas station burrito he was certain he'd regret later. Traffic was nonexistent, but he pitied the poor souls who would leave once the competition ended. He imagined that would be one hell of a nightmare.

As soon as he walked through his front door, Maverick

texted Ofelia knowing she wouldn't answer until she was on the way home. He tossed his overnight bag by the door leading into the small laundry room.

As Mav moved further into the house, passing the small office and the guest bathroom, he headed straight for the living room to relax as his phone started to vibrate. He figured Ofelia texted back, but the vibration didn't stop. A Chicago number glowed across the screen. Through all the excitement of the past couple of weeks, Mav had nearly forgotten about the lawyer Keanon set him up with.

Before the screen flashed to black, Maverick answered by clearing his throat and saying, "This is Maverick Wilson."

"Mr. Wilson, glad I caught you. This is Lloyd Gilmore again. Is this a good time to talk?" Even without introducing himself, Mav remembered Gilmore's voice. Just like the first time they spoke, his body grew tense. He felt like he navigated life as two different people, baseball star Maverick and humble Coach Maverick. Gilmore served as a reminder that his old life was still within reach.

"Yes, hello Mr. Gilmore. Now's a perfect time." Mav said as he moved to sit on the couch, legs wide apart as he leaned an elbow on his thigh. Whatever Gilmore was about to say, Maverick braced himself.

"Fantastic. I took the liberty of moving ahead with your case and I must say, we have solid evidence in your favor. Remember when I said that you weren't the first of Grant Adam's unfortunate victims? There seems to be a connection between you and the two other banned players because of a complaint posed by Adams.

"Unfortunately, there's not much I can do for the others, but this does help your case. The petition we filed has been accepted, which means our case is eligible to be brought in front of a judge. Are you with me, Mr. Wilson?" Mr. Gilmore paused since Maverick hadn't made so much as a noise.

To say Maverick was stunned was an understatement. He wasn't privy to the dealings of court, but he didn't expect his case to be picked up so quickly. It felt like yesterday he was signing contracts for Mr. Gilmore for the man to represent him. Though looking back, he supposed a few weeks had passed since then. Still, everything was moving so fast. "I...think so." Maverick said hesitantly. "But I guess I don't understand what happens next."

"Ah yes, well that's why I'm calling. I've already gotten multiple letters from Adams lawyers, and they want to flush this out quickly and privately." Meaning that they didn't want the press to catch wind of this. Even if Maverick lost, it would still reflect badly on Grant Adams.

"I must request you fly back up to Chicago at your earliest convenience." Gilmore continues as if he were commenting on a weather change rather than asking Maverick to jump on the nearest plane to get his ass back to Chicago. "The proceedings will take place in two days' time, and you are required to be there, as is Grant Adams. If this time frame doesn't work for you, I could try to change the date, but I highly advise against it. The sooner we get this done, the better. We've taken his legal team by surprise in getting this far. What would you like to do?"

The pitch was on the table and Maverick had to be the deciding factor. The best option, at least according to Gilmore, was to get to Chicago as fast as possible. Was he prepared to face his past? His coach? Worse yet, would Breanna be there? He wasn't sure he could see her and face all the emotions he buried so deeply. It wasn't a clean break and Maverick was content with leaving it as is, even if a small part of him would have preferred closure.

"Mr. Wilson, are you still there?" Gilmore asked, making Maverick realize he had been quiet for longer than appropriate.

He wished he had more time to make the decision, but he wasn't given the luxury of time. Waiting any longer would only postpone the inevitable. It was better to jump in feet first and hope for the best.

"I'm in. I'll be there by tomorrow night."

"Wonderful." He heard the smile in the man's voice. "I'll have my assistant give you the details about our meeting and perhaps help arrange a flight." Gilmore paused before adding, "You are making the right choice, Mr. Wilson. Be ready to fight like hell. Your name and your career are on the line."

Not to mention Gilmore's career as well, but Maverick didn't think he needed to point that out. Losing this trial wouldn't damage Gilmore's name and reputation but winning could skyrocket him further.

"Thank you so much, Mr. Gilmore. I'm eager to get this over with." Maverick said and Lloyd said his final goodbye before switching Maverick over to his assistant. She helped coordinate their meeting times and locations. She went as far as helping him find the first flight into Chicago, a flight that would be leaving at six the following morning, and a room at a hotel located in the center of downtown.

It was done. Just like that. He felt like he should be more excited about this, or at the very least relieved. He did feel a sense of excitement, but it was mixed with conflicting emotions of indecision. Gilmore said he needed to make sure this, meaning lifting the ban and getting a chance at his old life, was what he wanted.

If someone asked him a month ago, there would be no hesitation. But now? Now he felt as if he finally started to connect to his new team. The small suburb of Austin was growing on him, and he liked the atmosphere of it.

Plus, there was Ofelia, his main reason for the hesitation.

It was silly to base his entire life on a new relationship, but he couldn't deny he was falling for her. Hard and fast. Yet...there wasn't any harm in going through with the proceedings. At the very least, he could clear his name and wouldn't be looked upon as a failure. Baseball would be an option again, not a distant memory. He could make that choice when he heard the final verdict.

He would need to let his work know he'd be out and try to find a substitute. Laundry needed to be completed and then packed. He needed to call Keanon and fill him in on what was happening.

And finally, he needed to let Ofelia know. He regretted not having enough time to tell her in person, but he'd be gone early in the morning. Gilmore said Adams' team wanted to get this over quickly, so he hoped that meant he wouldn't be gone for more than a few days.

He hoped his new streak of luck wouldn't run dry now.

Chapter Twenty-Six

The weekend came and went like petals in the wind, disappearing before Ofelia could appreciate its beauty. San Antonio had given her what she needed and provided her with so much more than she hoped for. Her cheerleaders far surpassed her expectations and performed their little hearts out. She could see all the hard work her squad put into their season pay off in their performance. They never lacked in school spirit or camaraderie. Seeing their smiles when the judges announced McKinley would be moving on to nationals fed her soul (and her energy) on their ride back home.

From there, everything else was much of a blur. She texted Maverick they'd placed and headed to the next competition in about a month. When she arrived home, Ofelia stripped out of her clothes to change into something more comfortable. Then thought to herself a nap was exactly what she needed and put her head down on the pillow. The next thing she remembered was waking up to the sound of her alarm.

Perhaps it should have worried her that she had slept her entire Sunday away and didn't stir once during the night. She hadn't stopped to think about how much she did this weekend. From shuffling kids around, making sure her cheerleaders felt prepared for their routines, placating parents, and her time with Maverick, Ofelia had to be constantly "on." Her body needed to crash and recoup.

Especially since she experienced a marathon of sex with Maverick and each time more intoxicating than the last. She so desperately wanted to spill, in great detail, everything that transpired between them. Willow would freak out and demand a play by play, which Ofelia would gladly provide. Over the past two years, she heard all the dirty details of Willow and Karl's sexual endeavors, so it only felt right she returned the favor. Now that she finally had a sex life to talk about.

Unfortunately, her mood changed once she picked up her phone and saw she had a notification from Maverick. The time stamp was around nine last night, meaning Ofelia had been dead to the world. It was a short message, but still shocking.

She typed out a quick response and although she had a million questions, she didn't think Maverick needed any extra stress while he was dealing with his unjust ban proceedings. A small, selfish part of her wished he asked her to go along, even though that was utterly crazy. Not just because he received the news last night, but also because Ofelia was nowhere prepared to leave her class in the hands of a sub.

Still, Maverick was all she could think about on the ride to school. He hadn't texted back yet, but he had mentioned his plane took off at six. She didn't expect a response until he arrived safely in his hotel room. It wasn't as if she had ample time to check her own phone at school. Especially today when she would be in the midst of essay revisions, also known as her own personal purgatory.

Even if she wouldn't be seeing Maverick's beautiful face

today, she knew she had the next best thing: a quirky best friend she was ready to divulge all her secrets to.

∽

"Shut up! Shut all the way up!" Willow screeched, looking like a flightless chicken as she flapped her hands in excitement. Ofelia had to admit it was nice being on the receiving end for once. Usually it was Ofelia getting excited over Willow's sex adventures. She resolved herself to a lifelong term of being the single friend. Until today.

Thank God that ended.

Ofelia had been bursting with the news of her and Maverick all day, but she had been unable to catch her friend's eyes. Willow was called into a student meeting before school and they didn't share the same off periods on certain days. Lunch was their only time to catch up and Ofelia wanted to tell her so much about her night (and morning) with Maverick and his hasty departure to Chicago.

When Ofelia finally got her best friend alone, she shut her door to ensure their utmost privacy before immediately jumping into the events of the weekend. Willow's jaw dropped to the floor and in a very Un-Willow like fashion her friend didn't speak once while Ofelia shared every juicy detail of her night with Maverick. It wasn't until she recounted the morning he left did Willow find her voice.

"Was it good? Can he locate where the clit is? Maverick seems like a guy who could but looks can be deceiving. Oh! Please tell me you little love birds were safe, because-"

"Willow, oh my god." Ofelia couldn't help it. She busted out laughing. "I'm not some horny teenager who hasn't been taught about contraceptives. I'm on the pill and Maverick used a condom. Well, all his condoms actually."

"SHUT UP!"

"Willow!" Ofelia hissed but couldn't conceal her slight smirk. "Use your indoor voice, please."

"Don't use your teacher voice with me, Ofi." Willow said but made a show of lowering her voice down to a reasonable level. "I can't believe you had sex with a steaming hot baseball player! Or former, but you know what I mean. Ofi, do you know how freaking cool you are? How many women would die to have their chance with Maverick?"

Willow paused for a second before her face scrunched up in something that could only be read as disgust. "Ugh, I take that back. Does Maverick know how lucky *he* is to have *you*? You are smoking hot and have the perkiest ass I have ever seen. You are a freaking catch! Maverick better understand what he has. As your best friend, I am obligated to beat his ass if he hurts you."

Ofelia looked over her petite friend. Willow didn't scream threat, especially when Maverick stood well over six feet and had at least sixty pounds on her. Willow was, at best, an angry teacup chihuahua; small but packed a mighty bark. Ofelia wouldn't want to be on the receiving end of that.

"Well thank you and if he does, I'll let you loose on him. But I hope it doesn't ever get to that point. I really like him, Will. Like a lot. Far more than I should. Like I feel I'm moving too fast."

"Pfft!" Willow rolled her eyes dramatically. "It's not too fast at all. I'm honestly surprised it has taken you this long to get some D from him. Trust me, girl, you aren't moving fast."

Easy for her to say, considering Willow married Karl after three weeks of knowing him. Willow and Karl's romance was the kind authors write about. Several summers ago, Willow took a summer vacation to Germany with a few friends. The first night there, she met Karl in some dingy pub and fell in love. Right then and there. Willow described it as coming home after a long and strenuous journey. When their eyes met for the first time, Willow claimed the room parted, giving them space to run into each other's arms.

It was all very fairytale and fantastical, but Ofelia liked to believe it happened exactly as Willow described. Where her friend was more of a dreamer, Ofelia usually kept two feet on the ground. She wasn't ready to go off and profess her love for Maverick yet, even if her heart delt sure.

"So where is he today, anyway? I had to make copies after my meeting and when I walked by the gym, I saw an ancient looking grandpa as his sub. Did you bang him into a coma?"

Despite her best efforts, Ofelia barked out laughter at the absurdity of Willow's statement. "You are so vulgar sometimes." Willow didn't even attempt to look contrite, not that Ofelia expected her to. "No, Maverick texted me last night when I was asleep. He left for Chicago."

Willow's eyes widened at that. "Chicago? What's he doing there?"

Ofelia realized she hadn't been keeping Willow in the loop. To be fair, Maverick didn't talk to Ofelia much about his sudden departure. From previous conversations, Ofelia knew Mav had been contacted by a big shot lawyer named Lloyd Gilmore to represent him in his ban appeal. However, for Willow to understand the severity and unfairness behind his band, she would be required to tell Mav's story, even though it wasn't her story to tell.

Willow was her best friend though. Ofelia told her everything and if anyone would be on Mav's side beside herself, it would be Willow. Besides, his business was already out into the world, albeit wrongly reported, so it seemed only fair that Willow knew the true story.

"Fuck that guy and his cheating fiancée! That is absolutely deplorable. No wonder why Maverick was such a hard ass before. It makes so much sense now." Willow exclaimed as soon as Ofelia finished retelling the events. As expected, Willow reacted as Ofelia thought she would.

"Right? But I guess Mav was just as shocked as I was when he told me he had to leave. They want to settle this quickly and his lawyer feared that prolonging it wouldn't work in his favor."

"Wow. This is...a lot." Willow seemed to deflate into her swivel chair. She plucked a grape from her bento box, popping it into her mouth. "So how do you feel about all this?"

"I mean, I want to support him of course. This is all new territory for me, so I'm just trying to keep an open mind. Mostly I want to make sure Mav is okay. I don't know if he's thought about it, but there's a good chance he will see his ex. I don't know what type of emotional toll that will take on him, but I want to be prepared for anything."

Willow nodded, seeming to consider everything Ofelia said. She appeared calm on the outside, but her insides were churning with worry and self-doubt. Worry because she didn't want Maverick to feel like he needed to go through this ordeal alone and self-doubt because she was unsure if she was doing her part as a supportive girlfriend.

How much did he need from her? She didn't want her presence to become overbearing, but Maverick shouldn't feel isolated either. Plus, and she would never admit this part to Mav, she was a little concerned about Mav seeing Breanna again.

Okay, maybe a *lot* concerned.

Maverick would never do anything to violate her trust, but

she didn't trust Breanna. There was no telling what that woman was capable of. In her mind, Breanna was a beautiful seductress keen on making Mav as miserable as possible. Whether that was the truth was completely irrelevant to the unease beginning to blossom within her.

"So, let's say that the judge overturns the ban and Maverick is then allowed to play again. Where does that leave you in this equation?" Leave it to Willow to ask the very question Ofelia tried to avoid. Those thoughts had crossed her mind one, two, or ten times since Mav texted her this morning, and she honestly didn't know how to answer that question.

Luckily, Willow appeared to realize the question struck a nerve with her friend, so she waved it off, downplaying the severity of it. "You know what? It doesn't matter. That's a 'cross that bridge when you get there' sort of thing, yeah? Anyway, I wanted to ask you what you were planning to do for Spring break. It's coming up in a few weeks. Freaking finally."

Ofelia appreciated the subject change and the light tone that came with it. "Well actually, I planned on finally going back to California to visit Javi and Camilia." She conveniently left out her father because she was still upset about his last-minute ditching.

Willow choked on the grape she was eating, having to pound her chest and chug water to stop the coughing hysteria. When she composed herself, Willow melodramatically said "I'm sorry. I just thought I heard my best friend say she was going to go to California. The same California she has been avoiding for the past two years. Are pigs flying?"

"Yes, why I just saw a few fly over my car this morning." Ofelia deadpanned.

Willow looked around her desk, probably trying to find something to throw at Ofelia, but she came up empty-handed.

"You make fun, but this is a big deal. You've never talked about going back, only trying to get your family here to visit. What changed suddenly?"

Saying Maverick would have been too cliché and made Ofelia seem like she was only willing to change for a man. Maverick had unknowingly been a big part of her decision, but Ofelia had been the one to break free from the fear that consumed her so viciously for the past two years. It had kept her from her family, and she didn't want to go another year without seeing them.

"I guess I just realized the reasons for not going weren't as important as the reasons to go. I'm tired of letting something hold me back and it's a lot easier for me to travel than it is for them. I'm just one person and Javi is dealing with a toddler and my father, which is essentially the same thing as a stubborn toddler." Even if she was pissed at him, a large part of her wanted nothing but to be wrapped in his warm embrace and smell the scents of home on his t-shirt.

Willow finished her last grape and stuffed the bento box into her lunch bag. They only had a few more minutes of peace before their students began to fill the hallway at the sound of the bell.

"I think that's wonderful, and I fully support this. Are you going to bring Maverick with you? You know, meet the family and such." Willow pretended to ask casually, but Ofelia could see the wicked glint in her eyes.

Her cheeks reddened as she shook her head adamantly. "Of course I'm not. I know you literally fell in love and married your husband in less than a month, but we don't all have Disney love stories. It's too soon. I want to be one hundred percent certain this man will be in my life for the long run before I commit to anything. Besides, he does not need to experience the knockout my father and I are destined to have."

Willow nodded in understanding. What she liked most about her talks with Willow was that she'd actually listen and give great advice. She wouldn't just say what Ofelia wanted to hear. At one time that annoyed her to no end, but now she enjoyed getting another perspective. Even if it sometimes hurt.

"Even though I think it is more than appropriate to take Maverick to meet your family, I also agree you deserve this time alone. I know how much you miss them and I'm just incredibly happy you've decided to go back home for a few days." Even though a whole desk sat between them, Willow leaned over and reached for Ofelia, bringing her in for a hug. "I'm so proud of you."

Ofelia's eyes began to sting, the threat of tears nearby. She hugged Willow back a little harder than normal and if her friend noticed, she didn't comment. Instead, she hugged Ofelia back a little tighter too. "Good things are happening for you and I couldn't think of a more deserving person."

If the bell didn't ring at that exact moment, Ofelia was certain she'd cry. Since it did, she let go of Willow and ran a finger underneath her waterline, wiping away tears that fell in the process. She smiled at her best friend, thanking her again before she headed to her room, prepared to sit through grammar revisions for another three hours. Tonight she would get to talk to Maverick and hopefully learn more about what was going on in Chicago.

Chapter Twenty-Seven

Mav regretted leaving so suddenly and without seeing Ofelia once more. It wasn't as if he had much choice on the matter though; he had needed to get to Chicago and put this case to rest as quickly as he could. Still, he would have liked to hold her once more before he had to pack up and leave abruptly for an unknown length of time. He was hoping his stay wouldn't extend past a few days, but even he knew that was wishful thinking.

Maverick landed in Chicago around eight thirty in the morning and was promptly whisked away to his hotel. A man in an expensive looking black suit drove him to a ritzy hotel nestled deep within downtown Chicago. It was the type of hotel his team might have stayed at if they were having a stellar season, where the interior was impossibly white and complimentary champagne awaited in every room.

Unfortunately, Maverick didn't get to explore the hotel past his room. He only had enough time to change for his meeting with Gilmore. He had talked to many attorneys over the years, mostly dealing with his baseball contracts, but never something as world changing as this meeting.

Maverick was nervous and several other emotions he couldn't quite place since arriving back in Chicago. He turned every corner with trepidation, wondering if this would be the moment he ran into someone from his old life. To Adams or Breanna.

It was the first time his old life had mixed with the new Maverick and already he started to see some substantial changes. For example, his old self wouldn't have thought twice about having a personal chauffeur drive him to and from an overpriced hotel to a prestigious law firm. He definitely wouldn't be as unsure and anxious as he was now. No, his former self was a bit arrogant, if he was being honest. The world revolved around him and baseball...until it didn't.

Until it started being about coaching his high schoolers, supporting his off-season athletes in their wellness journey, and spending as much time as he could with the woman who was consuming his life.

Mav's phone buzzed, effectively reminding him he needed to be at the law firm in the next fifteen minutes. He grabbed his wallet, phone, and hotel key before leaving his room and heading down the long, dimly lit hallway that reminded him of a modern castle: sleek and the color of stone.

He made it back to the lobby half expecting professional dancers to burst out from one of the expensive vases and began a slow waltz. Sitting patiently on a sofa was Jared, his driver. "Ah, are you ready to go, Mr. Wilson?" The man asked, pushing himself up.

"Call me Maverick and yeah, I'm ready." He said. Jared nodded, though Mav had the inkling suspicion the man would continue to call him Mr. Wilson. He opened the back door for him again, even though Maverick was very capable of opening his own door. Since Jared seemed almost eager to do it for him, Maverick kept silent.

Jared ran around the black car and got into the driver's seat. He glanced up, meeting Mav's eyes in the mirror and smiled. "A Mr. Keanon Jermaine will be meeting you at your destination." He informed him as he started the car.

It shouldn't have shocked Maverick that Keanon would want to be in there for the meeting, because of course his agent would. Keanon often said Mav excelled at tuning out what he didn't want to hear and only relaying the information that behooved him. Which was...accurate. Knowing his friend would be there lessened some of the knots in his stomach.

Jared, somehow miraculously, made the drive through downtown as painless as possible, getting Maverick to the firm with three minutes to spare. "Damn, you're good. That traffic was no joke, man."

Jared tilted his head back and winked. "Thank you, Mr. Wilson. Driving for as long as I have, you pick up some tricks along the way." He said, pulling up as close to the curb as possible. He put the car in park and before Mav could argue, Jared was out of the car and opening his door, holding out a small card. "Here's my number, sir. When you are done with the meeting, just send me a text and I'll be right back here to pick you up."

"Thank you." Mav pocked the man's card, tilting his head in goodbye. The firm was exactly as Maverick pictured it, a tall executive building, bustling with interns eager to get their foot in the door. The first floor was spacious and quiet, with a bulky secretarial area, a sitting room, and a small coffee bar. Seated on a large leather couch was Keanon. His dark complexion contrasted starkly with the white interior. In fact, the only color in the room was Keanon and Maverick, which shouldn't have surprised him. True to form, Keanon was busy responding to something on his phone. It took him a few moments to realize he was being watched.

Keanon's gaze traveled from his phone to land on Maverick, still standing in the doorway. His face changed instantly from serious businessman to excited friend. "Mav man! My dude!" He hopped up, crossing the room to pull Maverick into a one arm embrace. "It's good to see you. You look good. Really good." Keanon said as he pulled away.

Despite his reservations and anxiety about the meeting, Maverick smiled. It was good to see one of his oldest friends and the person who had continued to be a friend even after Mav lost everything. "You have a good feeling about this?"

Keanon's smile soon turned into a smirk. He was all predator at that moment and Mav wondered if his friend knew something Maverick didn't. He was almost certain he had stayed connected with Gilmore, not trusting Mav enough to fill in all the information.

"I do, Mav, but we need to prepare for war. Let's talk to Gilmore and see where we're at. Is it cool if I come in with you?"

Maverick didn't want to face this alone and was grateful Keanon had probably cleared his busy schedule to support his friend. Money aside -Maverick had been the one bringing in the most money for Keanon - he knew his friend was there for support rather than obligation.

"Fine by me. You can keep up with all the boring legal shit."

"Glad to see you haven't changed a bit." Keanon teased.

The men then walked up to the receptionist behind a large desk with "LG Law Firm" plastered in front. She directed the man to the eighth floor and promised to inform Mr.

Gilmore they arrived. Maverick and Keanon took the elevator up, only to be greeted by another woman once the doors opened. She was an older lady, if Maverick had to guess, he would assume she was in her sixties, but looked like the no nonsense type. She strangely reminded him of his grandmother, not that Mav would ever tell this woman that. He valued his life too much.

"Mr. Wilson. Mr. Jermaine." She greeted them stiffly, but not unkindly. "My name is Constance Barber, head assistant to Mr. Gilmore. Would either of you want something to drink before I bring you back to Mr. Gilmore?"

Maverick shook his head, but Keanon asked for a coffee. Constance Barber looked down her wire frame glasses at him, her expression not changing as she pointed to a small coffee station. "Then make it yourself, young man and make haste."

Both men exchanged a quick glance. Maverick unsuccessfully tried to hide his smirk as Keanon whispered, "Oookay..." Constance Barber continued to stare at him pointedly until she compelled Keanon over to the coffee pot, leaving Maverick alone with the woman. Maverick didn't know what to say and Constance didn't seem like the chatty type, so they stood there in tense and awkward silence.

Silence that broke once Keanon rejoined them. "Good, good." Constance Barber said and turned on her heels to walk in the direction of Mr. Gilmore's office. She was a petite woman, but insanely fast. Her sensible heels clicked behind her as Maverick and Keanon struggled to keep up with her. She soon stopped in front of a door located at the end of the hallway and knocked twice. A gruff voice answered, and Constance took that as permission to open the door.

"Mr. Gilmore, your ten o'clock is here." Constance said once the door opened. Neither man moved until the woman shot them a glare that could have turned them to stone. "Please, Mr. Wilson and Mr. Jermaine, do come in."

Maverick quickly entered, too intimidated by Constance Barber to disobey. Keanon looked much the same, nearly jumping when the door shut abruptly behind him. Mav wished Mrs. Barber was his lawyer because no one would want to challenge that woman in court, if they showed up at all.

Lloyd Gilmore's office was nothing short of spectacular. The room was spacious, filled with bookcases full of pristine books, half of them with no titles and the other half not in English. Mr. Gilmore sat behind a grand mahogany desk with a glass top. Two comfortable looking chairs sat unoccupied in front while Mr. Lloyd Gilmore sat in the expensive looking swivel chair behind the desk. Behind Mr. Gilmore was the best part of the office, in Maverick's opinion. The entire wall was constructed with floor to ceiling windows, giving a breathtaking view of Chicago.

Lloyd Gilmore wasn't what Maverick expected him to look like. Mav had imagined a heavy man in his mid-forties, balding with an impressive mustache. How he conjured that image, Maverick didn't know, but the Lloyd Gilmore sitting in front of him looked nothing like the man Mav envisioned. This Lloyd Gilmore was not balding, but in fact had a full head of perfectly shiny black hair, styled back. The man looked extremely athletic and prided himself on his appearance. He also had no facial hair and Maverick spotted a tattoo creeping up his neck.

On Mr. Gilmore's desk, Maverick saw a few personal photos. One of a big, but friendly looking greyhound with a brindle coat. Two other photos were of Gilmore and another man, holding a little girl. They were both in the other picture as well, but on the beach this time. He suspected they were his husband and daughter.

"Maverick Wilson." Gilmore said in a way of greeting, a smile curling at the end of his lips. Even his voice, which sounded so gruff on the phone, held a lighter, more friendly note in person. "It's a pleasure to finally meet you in person." He got out of his chair to reach across his desk to shake Maverick's hand. Then turned his attention to Keanon. "As well as you, Keanon. Good to put faces to the men I've been talking to. Please, sit down." He gestured at the two chairs in front of him.

Maverick took the chair on the left, his body molding to the soft backing and cushion. He felt at ease in Gilmore's office. It wasn't stuffy or daunting, which he suspected was the point. Gilmore looked like the type of man that wanted to make sure his clients felt comfortable and relaxed in his office.

"Shall we get started then? I'll have you fellas out of here by lunchtime." Gilmore assured, rifling through some folders on his otherwise meticulously organized desk.

"Before we start Mr. Gilmore-"

"Lloyd, please. Call me Lloyd."

"Lloyd." Keanon nodded, offering a small smile. "Does my boy Maverick stand a chance? I don't want to cause anymore unnecessary drama and drag his name through the news again. I would rather you tell us straight, so we don't go into this without a chance."

Lloyd nodded in understanding. Instead of addressing Keanon, his gaze flickered over to Maverick. "Listen Maverick – is it okay if I call you Maverick – good. I don't often deal with MLB bans because most cases wouldn't stand up in court due to lack of evidence. But I firmly believe that Adam's legal team is going to have a tough time digging themselves out of the hole we are about to dig for them."

Both men's attentions piqued. Mav raised a brow. "So there's a chance we can win?"

Lloyd didn't answer. Instead, he laid out four manila folders on the desk before them. He pointed at each one and began to name them off. "Harvey Black, 2000 for assault against a team member. Issac Rodriguez, 2005 for conspiring to fix the outcome of the game. Donnie Wellbringer, 2011 for substance abuse, and Tito Walker, 2017 for violating contract. Do you know what all these men have in common, Maverick?"

Maverick didn't, so he shook his head. "I don't. Is this relevant to my situation?"

"Oh extremely." Lloyd said, with a certain flair that made Maverick wonder if he rehearsed this speech before. "You see Maverick, these men were coached by Grant Adams. All star players in their prime who fell from grace abruptly. Just like you. Grant Adams is named as the accuser and witness of the deeds in which they were tried for, and each man banned from baseball; their contracts voided immediately. And each time, Mr. Adams came into a healthy chunk of money from the MLB for his part in it."

Keanon was thinking the same thing as Maverick because he spoke up first, voicing Mav's thoughts. "So they were set up?"

"Hmm, seems like it. Doesn't it?"

"And no one seemed to have noticed this? No one thought it was odd that this happened every few years and Grand Adams got a payout?"

"Oh, I'm sure one of these men did. Which is probably the real reason a few of them aren't playing today. I'm sure others started to notice as well, but like I said, Grant Adams' legal team is nearly indestructible." Lloyd shrugged, looking relaxed and completely at ease. Not like a man who just suggested they would be going against a dragon with nothing but steak knives.

Maverick began to get nervous. Adams had a team and he had Keanon and Lloyd. They were good, but they were two people against an entire legion. Maverick was the only one showing any outwardly dejection though. "I don't understand. You say I have a chance, but then claim that Adams' legal team is indestructible-"

"Nothing is indestructible." Lloyd said, not reassuring Maverick at all. "I'm not saying this is going to be easy and I can't guarantee a win, but what I can guarantee is a chance. A pretty big chance at clearing your name. I'm poking holes in the narrative his team tried to spin, but there are so many inconsistencies and coincidences that can't be overlooked. Plus, you've never fully told anyone your side of the story, and this will give you a chance to plead your case in front of the big wigs on the MLB panel."

Maverick was still skeptical, and rightfully so. What made Lloyd think he stood a chance when so many others failed? Was Maverick just asking for more drama when he could be saving himself a lot of media attention? And how would this affect his life going forward?

No one spoke for a moment, all giving Maverick a chance to come to terms with what would soon take place. Keanon only waited a beat longer before saying, "Remember when I told you that this man-" he pointed to Lloyd, "-was good? I wasn't lying. He can prove that you and the other banned players were used as a money tactic. People love a good scandal and there's money in that kind of exposure. You were used to line Adams' pockets and now Lloyd is willing to fight for you. I'm willing to fight for you too. But we can't do anything if you aren't one hundred percent on board with this. It's your call, man, but now you have people who want to see you succeed."

This was no longer just about Maverick, though his name would be attached. This was about righting a wrong that went deeper than just him. Yeah, he was scared shitless. He didn't like not knowing how this would play out, and he hated knowing the press would catch wind of this. He would be the center of the sports news again. Mav barely made it through the first time, could he seriously go through that all again? But could he also stand to walk away because he was afraid?

He thought of Ofelia. His beautiful, level-headed woman. If there was ever a time he needed to talk to her, it was now. He wanted her opinion, but a part of him wondered if she would understand his situation. She had never been with him while he was in the spotlight. Could she handle that life? Especially since there would be reporters itching to learn more about her when they got wind of their relationship.

No, he needed to make this decision by himself and owed it to himself to at least try to clear his name, even if that was all he did. He missed playing and his team. He missed the life he once had, despite finding happiness in his new life. If he didn't take it, he would always wonder if he would have been able to clear his name or not.

Lloyd and Keanon still waited patiently for his answer. He put the poor fools out of their misery by nodding his head and saying, "I guess we are going to do this, aren't we?"

A collective sigh of relief went around the room and both Lloyd and Keanon smiled. Keanon patted Maverick on the back, assuring him he was doing the right thing. "Good. This is going to be fast and furious. We are waiting for approval for the court date, but it will be this week. You are going to have to stay in Chicago until the end of this. You haven't bought a plane ticket home yet, have you?"

Maverick had thought about it, but he decided against it. He was now glad he did. "No. No return ticket."

"Great. Then I will have Mrs. Barber get into contact with you and Keanon tomorrow by mid afternoon. We should have a date set by then. Before you go, do you have any questions for me?"

Maverick did. But just one. "Will I see Grant Adams?"

Lloyd looked like he expected this question, and he nodded slowly. "Yes. Not for long, but you will see him in court."

Maverick expected as much, even if he had naively hoped against it. He suddenly wanted a glass of whiskey so he could take all this information in. Keanon stood and shook Lloyd's hand. "Thank you again Mr. G-, Lloyd," he corrected. "Mav and I will leave you for lunch, but we will eagerly be awaiting your call."

Maverick stood up last and shook Lloyd's hand. Gilmore looked directly at him and said, "Things are going to change, Maverick – because of you. After this week, this will all be behind you, and you can rest assured that you did everything in your power. If we are lucky, which I'm hopeful we will be, you'll have your old life back by the next game."

That was the thing though, wasn't it? Maverick now had to decide what version of himself he would choose after this week.

And come to terms with the idea of losing something he loved, regardless of the outcome.

∽

APPARENTLY KEANON HADN'T JUST TAKEN the morning off to attend the meeting with Maverick. The man had completely cleared his schedule and took it upon himself to drag Maverick around town. It was as if Maverick had never set foot in Chicago, despite having lived in the area for several years. When he asked why they were playing tourists, Keanon just shrugged him off and demanded he enjoy himself.

That was exactly what they did, and it had taken his thoughts away from the upcoming week.

Nothing had changed in Chicago over the last few months Maverick had picked up and left. Keanon desperately wanted to take him to a new jazzy brunch place a client took him to. He liked it so much he came back once a week and even had his own table. Maverick wasn't much of a brunch person, but he even had to admit the food was fantastic. Bottomless mimosas didn't hurt either. Keanon drank his weight in them, and Mav was happy they had a driver.

After brunch and countless hours exploring Keanon's favorite spots around town, he finally released Mav back to his hotel. It was close to eight at night and Mav felt as if he'd been run over by a dump truck. Repeatedly. He was both emotionally and physically exhausted, but he remembered his promise to Ofelia.

He was still torn about what would happen after the hearing, but he didn't want to think about the complexity that would undoubtedly follow if his ban was overturned. There was nothing he wanted more than to hear her voice at this moment.

First, he needed to get out of his suit. He grabbed a pair of sleep pants and hung up his suit after stripping. He didn't bother with a shirt since he often slept without one. He hated the way it would bunch up in the middle of the night and rub his skin the wrong way.

After completing his nightly routines, Maverick stepped

out of the bathroom and into the main room. There was a small kitchenette with a table set for two. Past this room was his bedroom with a decent sized TV mounted on the wall.

The king-sized bed was piled high with a multitude of blankets. Maverick peeled layer by layer back until he reached the sheets and slid in, working up the nerve to call Ofelia. Deciding on a video call, Maverick dialed. Almost immediately, she picked up and Maverick stared into what he guessed was the ceiling. He heard another voice whisper, "Is that Maverick?" Followed by Ofelia shushing them.

From the corner of the screen, he saw a head peak over and recognized her as Willow. Her curious expression turned into a full bloomed grin as she said, "It *is* Mav! How cute...wait. Are you naked? Oh my god, is he calling for phone sex! Ofi, am I cock blocking you?!"

"You are literally so embarrassing right now, you know that." Ofelia hissed and Maverick could imagine she was blushing. He didn't know for sure though, because Willow had stolen the phone.

After a few moments of phone wrestling and the sound of a door locking, Ofelia's beautiful face illuminated his screen. He couldn't help but smile though she looked thoroughly scandalized.

"Are you in the bathroom?" Maverick laughed, thinking he caught a glimpse of her shower curtain.

Ofelia groaned. "Unfortunately. Willow is trying to sabotage this call. I had to lock myself in the bathroom, and we only have a few minutes before she finds a way to break in."

"Damn, I guess no phone sex." Maverick teased, but it got a pretty blush from Ofelia. She sputtered something unintelligible, and Maverick took pity on her. "I'm just playing, baby girl. I like the real thing better."

"You are a tease, Mav." Ofelia said, finally able to find words. "How is it going? How are you?"

Leave it to Ofelia to make sure he was doing okay. He quickly filled her in about his meeting with Lloyd. Avoiding all discussions on what would happen if he won. He didn't want to go down that path yet.

After taking a moment to process everything, Ofelia let out a long exhale. "Wow. That's a lot...but good. Right? It seems like this Adams guy has been a problem way too long and it's time for him to deal with the consequences of his own actions. Your name would be cleared. That's amazing, Mav. It really is."

He wondered if Ofelia was thinking the same thing he was but unsure of how to ask. The "what happens next" discussion hung heavy between them and Maverick knew this would be his opportunity to bring it up and invite her into the conversation. Yet, he couldn't quite bring himself to broach the subject.

Coward.

There was a loud knock on the door, and it took Maverick a moment to realize that it came from Ofelia's end. "Oh my god." She groaned dramatically. "Willow is about to break down my door. I should go, and it looks like you could use the sleep. Text me tomorrow?"

The moment to talk about the future passed and Maverick sighed in relief. "Sure. I'll catch you up when I can."

Ofelia seemed ready to hang up, but then stopped, looking back at the camera. "Oh, and Mav? Please don't think you need to go through this all alone. I'm here for you. We're a team, okay?"

A team. He wanted that to be true, wanted that more than anything, but he couldn't shut up the annoying whisper in the back of his mind that said Ofelia held no place in his old life. He saw firsthand how it corrupted people and he didn't want that for Ofelia. He also didn't want another Breanna situation for himself. He tried to keep out the uncertainty in his voice as he repeated. "Right. Team."

Ofelia looked as if she wanted to say more but the pounding came again, only louder. "Oh my god, Willow!" She yelled, saying something in Spanish he didn't understand but would have guessed wasn't pleasant. "I'll check in tomorrow."

Then the phone went blank, leaving Maverick to stew in his own troubling thoughts until sleep finally claimed him.

Chapter Twenty-Eight

It was Thursday evening and Maverick was still in Chicago. Ofelia did her best to be there for him, even though they were states apart, but the conversations between them dwindled from video calls to the occasional text message. Logically, she understood Mav was caught up with his legal team and didn't have much spare time to sit and chat with her. He needed what little time he had for himself to sleep, or so she told herself.

But she was worried.

On her first and last video call with Mav, she told him they were a team. Maverick could get in his head and because he was prideful, he didn't always know when to ask for help or when it was okay for him to lean on other people. Ofelia understood what it felt like to feel hopeless, like every situation was out of your hands.

Though perhaps she looked too deeply into something she manifested inside of her own head. Maverick cared about her, and she damn well cared about him. So much. So all she could do in this situation was pick up the phone when he called. No matter the outcome, she planned to stick by his side and prove to him she didn't care what walk of life he chose, because she *chose* him.

Ofelia stayed after school far past her contract hours. Willow came to check on her before she left, wondering if she was going to leave soon. When she told Willow that she planned to go to the baseball game, Willow offered to go with her. It was a sweet gesture, but Ofelia knew Willow only asked to be kind. Besides, she didn't really want company, unsure of her own emotions at the moment.

Which was how Ofelia found herself alone in the bleachers without Willow or her cheerleaders. She was thankful that her principal's suggestion of cheering at a baseball game was only a one-time deal. Judging by the mood of the crowd and the long faces of McKinley's team, she almost wished she brought her squad though.

Unlike her first game, the bleachers were sparse instead of packed with eager fans. The crowd consisted of a few parents and a few students that came to support their friends or boyfriends. Other people had shown up before the game started, but left when they realized Maverick wouldn't be coaching tonight. Poor Benny was all on his own. He was a nice man, but he was no former MLB player. Seeing people leave in waves made her happy she decided to be an extra body in the stands.

The McKinley boys needed it too. They were playing a school they historically did well against. However, the sixth inning began and the score was 4-0, with McKinley in last place. She could see in their faces how frustrated they were each time they made a bad play on the field. Maverick wasn't there to encourage them, and Ofelia wasn't sure if he had let them know he would be gone.

ON AND OFF THE FIELD

The painful game stretched out for another three innings before the umpire called it in the rival school's favor. She watched as the opposing school jumped in celebration, basking in their win, while the McKinley boys looked like sad, kicked puppies. It was hard to watch. For his part, Benny tried to console and cheer up his team, but not even his lovable personality conjured so much as a smile from their faces. One by one, the players began to trickle out, heads hung low, leaving poor Benny to deal with the rest of the equipment.

Ofelia hurried down from the bleachers and jogged over to the home dugout. Benny saw her as he reached for a discarded catcher's mitt. He smiled but it didn't quite meet his eyes. "Hey, Ms. Mendez. Thanks for coming out tonight, I know these boys appreciated it."

She doubted the boys even knew she was there but nodded politely regardless. "I'm sorry about the game, Benny. You did so well coaching. It was just an off night."

Benny laughed mirthlessly and Ofelia was certain that was the first time she ever heard Benny sound anything less than friendly. There was a certain clip to his voice as he spoke. "You can say that again. Say, have you heard from Mav at all? The boys and I are wondering where he went. I asked Colbie, but you know she's buried under mounds of...whatever the hell principals do." He shrugged.

Although she wondered if Maverick had reached out, she at least assumed Mav would tell Benny where he was, even if he didn't give the specifics. "He's in Chicago, Benny. He's, uh, dealing with some personal things at the moment." She didn't want to put his business on blast if Mav wasn't ready to tell people.

Benny was a smart guy though. She saw the wheels turn in his mind and realization struck. "Ah." He said, his voice carried a hint of sadness as if he had already come to his own conclusions about Mav's future. "I see. Well, I suspect we'd need to be looking for a new coach soon."

"Oh, no Benny. Mav, wouldn't abandon the team. He is just-"

Benny shook his head, putting his hand up to stop her. "C'mon Ofelia. You can't honestly believe that. If this man had the option to go back to his baseball career, you really think he'd give it up to come back here to coach high school boys? Let's be realistic now."

Hearing Benny say it gave power to all the doubts swirling around in her brain. She loved teaching, but she wasn't sure Maverick would want to stay in this career. He never planned on being a high school coach, and she doubted very much this would be something he would want to do in the long run.

Benny picked up the last bat, stuffing it into his bag as he began to walk it back to the golf cart. Ofelia followed behind him silently, still thinking about his earlier words. "Listen," Benny finally said once he heaved the bag into the back seat. "If you talk to him, will you tell him to give me a call? I just want to know what's going on, so I can prepare."

"Yeah, of course."

"Thank you." Benny smiled, getting himself into the driver's seat of his golf cart. "Wanna ride back to your car?"

Ofelia shook her head slowly. "No, I can walk, but thank you."

"Suit yourself, but I'm not leaving this spot until I see that you made it to your car."

She gave his arm a quick squeeze and then made her way back to her car. Her mind was still fogged with questions of Maverick when she unlocked her door and slipped inside. Off in the distance, she heard Benny's cart drive away.

Chapter Twenty-Nine

This wasn't a courtroom.

In his mind, this room would have been a courtroom with a judge presiding over today's hearing. Off to the side would be the jury. On one side Maverick would sit with his legal team and on the other side would sit Grant Adams' team. The scene would play out as a classic trial; both attorneys pleading their cases as they tried to one up the other. It would end with Maverick walking away a free man.

Well, at least that is what they did on murder trials, but he supposed getting banned was a far cry from killing someone.

It shouldn't have surprised him that they waited outside a large conference room, awaiting their moment with the Office of Commissioner. It was a mouthful, but essentially it was a board of people who oversaw the entire MLB operation. Lloyd had mentioned the board was made up of three high executives, a few lawyers, and a judge that dealt specifically with MLB. It had all the fixings of a trial without it feeling like one.

Surprisingly enough, Maverick wasn't nervous, or at least he hadn't been until he noticed a familiar figure in the corner of his eyes. Mav's attention immediately snapped to the newcomers in the room, and he sucked in a deep breath. Grant Adams appeared just the same as he did months ago, only this time he didn't have his pants around his ankles.

He half expected to see Breanna on his shoulder, but he was accompanied by an older, pretty woman. Mav recognized her immediately; his wife. Their postures were stiff, like they weren't comfortable being around each other. Mrs. Adams looked to be here out of obligation rather than a wife concerned about her husband's wellbeing.

Why would she care? This creep cheated on her constantly. Maverick didn't know if Mrs. Adams had other lovers or not, but she could very well be a victim herself in this situation.

Adams looked up, registering for the first time Maverick was seated mere feet away from him. A nearly imperceptible twitch to his jaw gave Maverick everything he needed to know. Grant was nervous. As he fucking should be.

Maverick felt a comforting hand on his arm, and he turned to see Keanon give him a reassuring smile. It wasn't until then that Maverick realized he was clenching his fists so hard, his nails dug into his palm..

The doors to the boardroom opened shortly after that, sparing them further awkwardness. Lloyd got up first and led Mav and Keanon inside. Strategically, Lloyd and Keanon placed Mav in between the two of them, so he'd be boxed in by a friendly face on either side. It was thoughtful, and he gave Keanon a look of gratitude. His friend nodded back, taking his seat.

Adams and his crew came in next, forcing the poor secretary to conjure up a few more chairs rather than forcing some of his people to wait outside. Lord knew he could spare a few.

Once the chair situation was settled and everyone had a

glass of water or coffee in front of them, an older gentleman with a receding hairline cleared his throat. Maverick recognized him from press conferences and online interviews. Every baseball player would know his name. If baseball had a god, it would be this man.

"Good morning everyone. We appreciate your ability to be here on such short notice." The baseball god spoke mechanically. Maverick was tempted to turn around and see if a teleprompter sat behind him, but he forced himself to continue staring ahead. "My name is Jeff Manuelo and I serve as Commissioner of Baseball for the Major and Minor League. We are here today to discuss the recent ban of Maverick Wilson which involved his coach, Grant Adams. Today Maverick's legal team, led by Lloyd Gilmore, would also like to discuss Mr. Adams' history with former MLB players. Is that correct?"

"It is, Mr. Manuelo. We've come with documents I faxed over a few days ago for the board to review." Lloyd said evenly, far more so than Maverick could have sounded in his situation.

Jeff Manuelo didn't comment but nodded his head. He then fixed his stare on Adams and his legal team. "Mr. Adams, you have been an active coach in the MLB for close to twenty years and within that time, five bans were brought forward to us, all petitioned by you. Is that correct, Mr. Adams?"

Adams didn't answer. The young-looking man, reeking of luxury, spoke in his stead. "Good morning, Mr. Manuelo. My name is Timothy Sheppard, part of Mr. Adams legal team. Your assessment is correct. Mr. Grant has rightfully petitioned five players to save the validity and heart of the game, which you are meant to uphold, Mr. Manuelo. These men committed crimes and Mr. Grant made sure that was the case before bringing their offenses to you."

Mr. Manuelo continued to look emotionless, unfazed by

the slight jab Timothy gave him. Was he applying that Mr. Manuelo wasn't upholding his duty to the game? Perhaps he had gone lax over the years, and it finally came back to bite him in the ass. Whatever the reason, Maverick hoped Manuelo and his team would conduct a thorough review.

When Maverick's attention went back to the Commissioner, Mr. Manuelo stared directly at Maverick. He offered no clue as to what he was thinking, nothing but a blank canvas yet to be completed. He appeared to be saving all his emotions for the end verdict, whatever that may be.

"Mr. Wilson," Mr. Manuelo began, gingerly wetting his finger, and flipping to the next page within his folder. His eyes scanned the page before glancing back up. "According to the official records, Mr. Adams stated you attacked him in a fit of rage and jealousy. That you and your fiancée at the time, Breanna, arranged sexual relationships between Breanna and Adams in exchange to get extra playing time. When Mr. Adams tried to deny your fiancée, she threw herself at him and you attacked. Is that correct, Mr. Wilson?"

Of course it wasn't correct! How many times had he tried to set the record straight until he realized that no matter what he did, no one believed him? They avoided him like the plague, as if they too would catch whatever unluckiness fell upon him by association. This was the moment he could change the narrative that had been thrust upon him without his consent, but his throat felt so damn dry. His story was lodged deep inside, and he didn't know how to coax it out.

The silence must have stretched a beat too long; Keanon turned slightly, an unasked question in his expression. Lloyd cleared his throat and leaned closer to Maverick, talking into his ear. "Take a deep breath and tell your story. It's my job to tell the others, but this is your opportunity Maverick. Choose yourself."

Choose yourself.

Could it be that simple? At this point, what did Maverick have to lose? Ofelia was the only name that popped into his mind, which he promptly pushed aside. When he thought of her, his judgment began to cloud, and he couldn't think of anything else. A hard knot began to form in the pit of his stomach as doubt began to form.

Despite the growing tension all around, mostly radiating from Keanon and Lloyd as they held their breath, wondering what Maverick would do, a newfound strength began to take hold.

"No. That is not correct." As soon as the words left his lips, both Keanon and Lloyd exhaled, some tension easing away. It escaped and found a new host: Adams and his legal team. It was their turn to fester under the light of uncertainty. For some reason, that thought made him extremely happy.

Mr. Manuelo cocked a brow and shared a wordless glance with one of his own men. The same man dug through his briefcase sitting on the floor next to him and pulled out a legal pad and a pen, no doubt prepared to write down Maverick's version of the events. "Please go on, Mr. Wilson. My colleague will be taking notes." Mr. Manuelo prompted.

Maverick found that as soon as he began to speak, the words flew out of him like a caged bird escaping. He didn't care that his words were being recorded and would be public knowledge. He shared his truth, taking the Commissioner through his entire day, leading up to the scandal. How he was blindsided by the news and in a fit of rage, attacked after Grant Adams struck first. He didn't know how long the affair had been going on and frankly Maverick didn't care to.

A few times throughout his explanation Maverick was stopped so Mr. Manuelo could ask clarifying questions. None of the man's questions were ever geared towards one side or the other; he was truly a man that straddled the line of neutrality like an umpire.

When he came to the end of his story, Maverick finally felt as if he could breathe a little easier. The pressure didn't go away entirely, but it lessened immensely. His story might not change a single damn thing, it might not even get him unbanned, but it was out and now people could poke holes in Grant Adams' story.

Even though his story ended, Lloyd picked up where Maverick left off. He circled back to the four other men Adams had connections with. Lloyd had filled him and Keanon in on what he would say at the meeting so Mav had a chance to tune him out and check on everyone's body language. The men sitting in front of them were expressionless bobble heads, nodding after every few sentences to prove they were paying attention.

As for Grant and his small army, they appeared completely composed, as most legal teams would be in stressful situations. However, Maverick saw the cracks peeking through, fidgeting with pens, the occasional hushed whisper to one another, white knuckles from clenching a hand too hard. Perhaps it was naïve of Maverick to think this was the start of the collapse of Grant's empire, but clearly he was scared. Why else would he bring in an entire legion of lawyers?

Lloyd seemed to be in his element and Maverick was more than okay with taking the back seat. Lloyd held his own against Adams' team, never wavering or faltering when they would rebuke one of his claims or ask for more proof. Lloyd seemed to have prepared for all the possible scenarios and was always one step ahead of the others.

It was official, Lloyd ranked amongst Mav's favorite humans. He shouldn't have doubted Lloyd, for he had gained quite a badass reputation in the sporting community, but seeing hold his own firsthand was different. He fielded all the questions Mr. Manuelo asked Maverick or tore down any explanation Grant's team had brought to the table. It was like watching a fencing match, but instead of battling with foil, they fought with wit. Far more entertaining, in Maverick's opinion.

The conversation lasted a total of two hours with Lloyd getting the final word in. "Look, Mr. Manuelo, we can discuss until we are blue in the face, but the fact still remains. There was a huge payout for each ban. Money that mysteriously wound up in Mr. Adams' possession when it should have gone to finding and funding a new player to fill the spot of the former. Not only that, but most files from the previous banned players have little to no evidence supporting such a punishment. I know you recently just stepped in as Commissioner a few years back, but Mr. Adams has been pictured multiple times with your predecessor. It's not frowned upon to be friends with the Commissioner, but it does give you pause when you take in account that the two men are in external business together."

"Mr. Adams is not involved in any form with your predecessor, Mr. Manuelo. All tie-"

Lloyd placed a photo out on the table of two men, one very obviously Grant Adams and the other less familiar, but Maverick still recognized him as Darren Jacobs, the man who used to serve as Commissioner. "Unfortunately, that isn't true. This photo is from last week in Mexico. I received this from an anonymous reporter who overheard Mr. Adams and Mr. Jacobs discussing a new business adventure on which they plan to collaborate."

Whatever Adams' team prepared to say was cut off when Mr. Manuelo held up his hand. "I've heard enough for today." He said, his voice leaving no room to argue. "Here is how we will proceed. My team and I will look and read through all the documentation you brought us today, as well as conduct our own investigation into this. Expect an answer within the next few days. Until then, we ask both parties to remain in or near Chicago so we can settle this."

Mr. Manuelo left no room for further comments. He stood and shook hands with both parties before leaving the room while his colleagues trailed after him. Maverick wondered if Grant would say anything, now that Mr. Manuelo left. Grant's team began to trickle out, but Grant and his wife were one of the last to exit. Although Grant didn't speak to Maverick, his former coach shot him a glare so vile, he nearly choked on the animosity. Yet he didn't flinch; he wasn't going to give him the satisfaction.

Lloyd and Keanon stood. Keanon stretched his back while Lloyd gathered his briefcase. Mav stood last. "So, we just wait?" He asked once alone.

Lloyd nodded at him. "We wait. It could be a few days or longer. I don't want to alarm you, just prepare you. However, I do believe we will get an answer sooner rather than later. Can you extend your stay at your hotel?"

"If he can't, Mav knows he can stay with me." Keanon supplied. He was grateful Keanon didn't ask him to stay at his house rather than the hotel. He loved his friend, but Keanon had already done so much. Plus, Mav wanted time to himself just to think and process.

Sometime during the trial he had made the executive decision to keep the trial to himself. He didn't want to share the details or the outcome with Ofelia because he had the sinking suspicion he was going to hurt her if they won. He would have to leave Ofelia in his old life. He couldn't afford another distraction or scandal if he was invited back to play.

"It's settled then." Lloyd said, standing tall once all his possessions were gathered. "I'll keep in contact with you and call you as soon as I hear something. You did good today, Maverick."

Maverick was certain it was the other way around. Lloyd had been the star of the show, but he thanked him nonetheless. "Now I guess we play the waiting game."

Chapter Thirty

The tile in the kitchen sparkled under the bright lights and the air around her smelled of artificial lemon with a dash of bleach. There wasn't a speck of dust to be seen in her too small galley kitchen. No dish clogged up the sink either. Ofelia had forgone the dishwasher and scrubbed the pile completely by hand. She then dried them and stacked the dishes neatly away in the appropriate cupboards.

Ofelia took a step back to assess her work in the kitchen, surveying each inch for imperfections. Damn, her kitchen was completely spotless. Which normally would be a good thing, but now her distraction ended. Maybe a run would clear her head. But she wasn't a masochist and didn't want to put her body through a strenuous activity when her week had been full of cheer practice.

Her cleaning frenzy started early this morning, getting out of bed with enough energy and determination to clean the entire house top to bottom. What else did a tired teacher have to do on a Saturday morning when their boyfriend was gone and not responding to texts? Not that she was thinking about him of course. Nope. Definitely not.

If she were, Ofelia would probably worry that going nearly a week without contacting your girlfriend might be considered a red flag. She might have blamed it on her phone for not sending messages properly, but Maverick had read receipts on, so she knew he was getting all her texts. He simply decided not to respond. Another red flag.

But luckily, Ofelia was definitely not thinking about any of those things or risk feeling a sense of dread begin to stir in her belly. Everything was perfectly fine and, in a few days, when (if?) Maverick returned, he'd probably have a completely logical explanation for his lack of responses and she would feel silly for having over thought it.

She needed to chill out. She couldn't work herself into a tizzy over something she had literally no control over.

"Leila. Stella. Tell momma what she needs to do." Ofelia groaned, looking over at her cats who were both peacefully sleeping atop her dining room table. Leila completely ignored her because she was a bitch (whom Ofelia loved with her entire being), but Stella perked her head up, vaguely interested in hearing Ofelia's voice. But since she was a cat, Stella responded by putting her head down and falling back asleep.

"You both are no help." She muttered under her breath. She supposed she could do some grading, but Ofelia worked hard all damn week and really didn't want to grade during her days off. Besides that, she wasn't in the right frame of mind. Grading essays was stressful enough and she didn't want to add that stress on top of everything else.

There were no rooms left in her house to clean and Ofelia didn't want to be by herself with nothing but her own thoughts to keep her company. She should call Willow and ask her to come over. Typically, her best friend was busy on Saturdays but since Karl just left, Ofelia doubted Willow had much on her schedule.

As if thinking about her name summoned her, Ofelia's phone rang. Her heart lurched as she made a mad dash to grab it. She deflated when she noticed it wasn't Maverick, but then felt guilty because it was Willow.

Ofelia answered the phone, putting extra cheerfulness in her voice in hopes of sounding normal and not a tired mess. "Willow! Hi!" Okay, so maybe she overdid the enthusiasm a bit. Ofelia took an audible breath and started again. "Hi. I was about to call you-"

"Well hell yeah you were! This is freaking headline news, Ofelia. I'm kinda pissed you didn't tell me anything, but maybe for legal reasons you couldn't. You could have at least attempted to tell me. I'm so good at keeping secrets. Also, it is a known rule in the universe that you are allowed to tell your best friend anything because even if someone said, 'don't tell anyone,' they don't mean your best friend."

Willow talked a mile a minute and usually Ofelia didn't mind. Today was not one of those days. Mostly because she had no idea what the hell her friend was talking about.

"Whoa, Willow. I'm gonna need you to slow down." She said, speaking over Willow who blabbered on about the importance of not keeping secrets from your best friend. "Let's pretend I have no idea what you are talking about." She wasn't pretending because she didn't know, but that would only lead to more questions from Willow. "And slowly tell me what you think I'm keeping from you."

"I'm talking about Maverick, of course!" She blurted, sounding like she had been waiting for this moment all day. It felt like an inside joke that Ofelia should be a part of, yet she couldn't think of a single thing about Maverick she kept from Willow.

"Hon, I don't know what you are talking about. I tell you everything and Mav-"

"Oh, don't play coy!" Willow sounded affronted. "I had to find out on the news just now. You know I like my afternoon news, so I turned on Channel 8 and BAM! Maverick in my face. Looking pretty sexy I might add...Ofelia? Hello? Are you still there?"

An icy chill washed over her body and Ofelia found breathing difficult. She felt a light on her feet, swaying from side to side. She reached out to grip the wall to steady herself. When she spoke, her voice sounded shaky, unable to hide the hurt within. "Willow, what about Maverick?"

She heard Willow suck in a deep breath on the other end of the phone, realization donning. "You seriously don't know." It wasn't a question, but Ofelia nodded her head nonetheless, even though Willow couldn't see. "Shit, Ofi. I'm so sorry. I thought he would tell you. Seems like something he'd keep the woman he's dating aware about."

But Ofelia was done with the guessing game. She couldn't continue this conversation without Willow telling her what she knew about Maverick. "Please, just tell me what you are talking about." Deep down she knew. What hurt the most was Maverick didn't want to share the joy in this monumental life moment with her. She would have been happy and cried tears of joy with him because...

Well, because she loved him.

"Turn on your TV now. Channel 8 is airing the story." Willow's voice was soft like a gentle caress. It didn't soothe the knots in her belly though.

Ofelia, in a daze, walked to her living room and dropped

down on her green sofa. The remote was still wedged in between the cushions from last night when she accidentally fell asleep before moving to her own bed.

She turned on the TV and flipped robotically through the channels until she reached the news. The news anchor spoke, looking directly into the camera but Ofelia couldn't hear a thing. All she saw was a photo on the right side of the screen. A photo of Maverick with two other men, all smiling as they left some building. Underneath the picture, floating across the screen, were the words **"APPEAL APPROVED: WILSON'S BAN OVERTURNED."**

"Oh my god." Ofelia's voice cracked. She hadn't meant to say the words out loud and forgot that she was on the phone with Willow.

"Ofi, I'm so sorry. I thought he was keeping you up to date on all this."

The news should be one Ofelia celebrated. The tears that had stubbornly fallen down her flushed cheeks should be tears of joy rather than pity. Her feelings were hurt. She wasn't crying over Maverick; she cried for herself and the doubts forming in her brain.

Yet she couldn't quite voice these insecurities, afraid that by voicing them she would give them life. Even speaking her fears to Willow seemed scary to her.

"Ofi? Are you okay?"

"I'm just...really happy for him." She said. It wasn't a lie; Ofelia *was* happy for Maverick. Mav went through hell and back, had his name shredded in the media, and lost things he loved along the way. She related to loving a sport so much that it became an integral part of you.

"Ofi." Willow said cautiously. "It's okay to be upset with

him because he didn't tell you himself. And also proud because of how badly he wanted this."

Willow spoke the truth, but Ofelia had been blindsided by the news. It was all happening so quickly, and she had no time to take in any of this information. She didn't want to rush into anger when she was already this emotional.

"You should call him." Willow continued. If only she knew how many times Ofelia had tried to call him, only to be met by his voicemail. "Call him and talk. Do you want me to come over, love?"

"No, no. It's okay." It had been what she wanted earlier, but now all she wanted to do was attempt to get Maverick on the phone. She didn't want Willow to see her pathetic attempts to contact him. "I'm fine-"

"Ofi, you are certainly not fine."

"Okay...true. So I'm not fine, but I will be okay. Just let me call him and get answers." Ofelia reached for the remote and turned off the TV. She didn't want to see her boyfriend's name and picture plastered in front of her. She wanted to hear Maverick's voice and get the news from him.

Still, Willow seemed hesitant to leave her in such a state. "Okay..." She spoke reluctantly. "But it will only take a call – not even a call, a text – for me to get my ass in my car and head over. Okay? I'm serious, I don't want you to be all sad by yourself."

She loved Willow so much and was thankful for her gregarious and loving nature. Her resolution to drop everything she was doing to come and sit with a crying friend on her day off. "Thank you, Will." Ofelia smiled, hoping Willow felt her appreciation through the phone. "I'll make sure to request the biggest tub of ice cream if I call you over for a sad party."

"As you very well should! Just a call away, don't forget!" Willow reminded her before they said their goodbyes.

Instead of immediately calling Maverick like Willow suggested, Ofelia got up and headed back to her kitchen. If there was ever a time for wine, it would be now. She didn't typically recommend self-medicating using alcohol, but this seemed like an appropriate time, so she could calm her racing heart. She grabbed one of the shiny glasses she recently washed and grabbed a red wine from her fridge. She poured herself a hearty glass, indulging in her vices.

After grabbing her wine and a snack from the cupboard, Ofelia went back to her couch. She placed her wine on the wooden table beside the arm rest and grabbed her gray Sherpa blanket from behind her, letting the material fan out across her body. Now she was ready to face this phone call.

Ofelia picked up her phone and ran through her contacts, stopping at Maverick. Her stomach lurched; Ofelia shouldn't feel nervous calling her own boyfriend and shouldn't have to question if he would pick up or not. Their relationship was still new and she didn't want to cross any lines with him. She also didn't know where Maverick would be. How old were the pictures the media were using? For all she knew, Maverick could be caught up in press meetings...or something of equal importance former banned baseball players did when they got reinstated to the game.

She was stalling. Ofelia swallowed her pride and clicked on Maverick's name. The phone began to ring.

And ring.

And ring.

And-

"You've reached Mav-"

"Shit!" Ofelia cursed and aggressively hung up her phone.

Her call had gone to voicemail. If he thought she would admit defeat after only one call, Maverick had another thing coming. He was going to talk to her one way or another.

Ofelia did what any other pissed off girlfriend would do. She called again. And again. And again. By the fifth call, she started to believe Maverick was never going to answer and her attempts would have been in vain. Until on the last ring of her fifth time calling, he answered.

"Ofelia."

No greeting, no 'how are you doing.' Just *Ofelia*. His clipped tone bordered on anger, which...understandable. She had called him five times in rapid succession, which was annoying, but it was more annoying to not be updated about a major life event. It was more annoying not to have contacted her for an entire week.

"Really? That's all you have to say to me, Maverick?" So much for not being angry.

"I'm kinda busy right now."

Yeah, no shit. She was barely able to contain her anger but managed to swallow it down. "I understand that Maverick, but I just saw the news. Is it true?" It was a stupid question, considering a major news station was running his story, but she still wanted to hear it from him.

Maverick sighed and she imagined him rubbing his head impatiently. "Yes."

"Then why don't you sound happy? Mav, this is amazing news!" Ofelia tried to cover up the fact he hurt her by not telling her about the news first.

"No, it is great. It is...it's..." Maverick trailed off and Ofelia heard a male voice call out for Maverick. He must have been holding his hand over the speaker because she heard a muffled 'one second!' before he spoke to her again. "Listen, I know I should have told you. There's been a lot going on and I'm trying to sort through some stuff."

"What stuff? Maybe I could help you with it?"

"No, you can't." The words hit like a bullet, hitting their mark perfectly. Ofelia flinched at the coldness in his voice. "Sorry. I mean I'm stuck in my mind and I can't do this over the phone."

"Can't do what? Mav, you aren't making any sense."

"Yeah, I know. I'm sorry." And he truly did sound sorry, but he also sounded like a man who carried too much on his own. "Listen, I'm coming back to Texas tomorrow. Can you meet me at my house, and we can talk? I want to see you when I talk to you."

Ofelia took a little comfort knowing he was coming home and wanted to see her. She couldn't help but feel a wedge grow between them and Maverick was distancing himself from her. Maybe he was also still processing the news and here she was demanding he talk about it. She could wait one day if that meant she got to hear the entire story.

"Yeah, of course. What time tomorrow?"

"Four. Let's meet at four."

"Four it is then." She said and then tried to lighten the mood. "I miss you. I'm excited to see you tomorrow. We could go for dinner and-"

Ofelia didn't get to finish her sentence. Maverick cut her off and sounded like he hadn't been listening to what she had suggested. "Great. I gotta go, Ofi. I'll see you tomorrow. Take care."

Then the line went dead.

Ofelia had never been more confused. She should be excited to see him, but why did it feel like she was about to say goodbye to him? Anxiety. That was all it was. Tomorrow, she would be back with Maverick, and they would get through this patch. That's what couples did. Not everything was happy and perfect all the time. Real relationships had their struggles and problems. It was how they decided to respond to those challenges that made couples strong or tore them apart.

Sunday couldn't come fast enough.

Chapter Thirty-One

Chicago spring was different from Texas spring. Texas had two seasons: summer and hellish summer. There was no in between. Maverick hadn't even lived in Texas long, but he had experienced the scorching hot days and the days that required a light jacket in the morning and a tank top in the afternoon. Unlike Texas, Chicago had seasons. He hadn't been out of the city long, but he forgot that spring still had a chill in the air.

The past few days had been a whirlwind and Maverick still was in a state of shock. It was as if he were having an out of body experience. He could see the smile on his face as he got the news, the joy in his eyes when he learned that Mr. Manuelo sided with Maverick and called his ban "unjust and completely unethical." He saw the calmness wash over him when he did his first interview last night with a big network as he robotically fit back into the role he had known for years.

Yet it still didn't feel real. His time had come to an end, and he could no longer ignore the decision he needed to make. There were only two options. Maverick couldn't have parts of his old life back and integrate it with the new life he had made sans baseball. Those were two different worlds and as far as Maverick was concerned, two different people.

Which is why he needed to head back to Texas and talk to Ofelia. Make her understand the decision he was making had everything to do with him and nothing to do with her as a person. They had fun and he was thankful for their time together, but nothing more could come from it. She didn't belong in his old world and maybe a part of him wanted to shield her from the darker parts of being in a relationship with a professional baseball player. She had to understand. She just had to.

He glanced at his watch, he had two more hours before his flight to Texas took off. O'Hare Airport could be a bitch to get through on a good day, so he needed the extra time to make sure he could get through security. There had also been a surplus of people wanting to come up and ask for his autograph and picture. Suddenly everyone was his fan again because he mattered. It was like everyone simultaneously cut him out of their lives when they thought he soured the name of baseball.

It came with the territory though. Fans would only remain loyal if you didn't fall from grace and could make them happy. That was simple and familiar and that was exactly what Maverick needed right now. There was no room for second guesses. It was the motto he repeated to himself the entire way to the airport.

All through the plane ride and up until the moment he reached Keanon's home in Texas. If he continued to lie to himself, he could believe he wasn't going to regret breaking the heart of the most loving woman he had ever known.

He kept telling himself he was doing this for her benefit. That she would be better off without him. He fed himself these lies until he started to believe them. He had done the right thing not including her in his trial and his decision...hadn't he?

He was a baseball player. He belonged on the field, not at a school teaching teenager. Ofelia was better off without him. She deserved stability and he could not provide her that right now.

Perhaps one day this decision wouldn't cut like a knife.

Chapter Thirty-Two

The cozy one-story craftsman sat snugly at the end of the cul-de-sac. Even in the uncomfortable heat spring days brought, the grass was still a vibrant shade of green, no dry patch in sight. It was also recently mowed, giving off the fresh smell of cut grass. The one tall oak in the front provided a decent amount of shade.

She had been to Maverick's -- or rather Keanon's -- house on numerous evenings when they would cook dinner from scratch and cuddle on the couch as they settled in to watch a movie. Ofelia always got to choose, and Maverick never complained, even when her choice usually consisted of heart-warming romance.

Standing outside now, waiting for Maverick to unlock and open the door felt different. It was exactly four o'clock, the time Maverick suggested they meet. Ofelia clutched her purse tightly to her side, fidgeting with the zipper. She gazed down at her watch. Only twenty seconds had passed since she rang the doorbell, but the seconds were passing agonizingly slowly.

Ofelia moved to ring the doorbell again when the door

suddenly opened. The abruptness of it unnerved her and caused her to jump, nearly slipping on the welcome mat. Before she fell on her ass though, strong hands reached out, grabbed her waist to stop her before she embarrassed herself. Maverick looked just as frazzled as Ofelia felt. His hands lingered on her hips longer than necessary. When he realized he was touching her, he took a step back and put distance between the two of them.

Maverick cleared his throat, rubbing the back of his neck awkwardly. "You definitely know how to make an entrance, baby girl."

The term of endearment had to be a good sign, right? At the very least, it loosened some tightness in her chest. "I guess you could say I'm falling for you." She smiled at her own cheesy joke, trying to lighten the mood. Maverick's delayed smile looked more like a grimace. "Sorry, that was awful."

"It was pretty awful." Maverick said, not unkindly. He then stepped to the side and opened the door wider, allowing Ofelia to squeeze past him and enter the house.

Two suitcases sat in the middle of the hallway, but Ofelia didn't find that unusual since he had just returned from Chicago. What she did find unusual was the lack of *Maverick* around the house. His favorite sweater he hung up on the back of a dining room chair religiously wasn't in its spot. His few baseball caps that hung on the wall were bare. The one family photo Ofelia had seen of Maverick and his parents, that typically sat on an entryway table, had been replaced with a new photo of a cute dog in shades and a sun hat.

"Did your trip inspire you to redecorate?" She asked, her voice sounding strained, even to her. When she turned back around to face Maverick, he looked everywhere but at her.

"Not quite." He mumbled. "Can I, uh, get you something to drink?"

Although her throat had gone dry, Ofelia shook her head. "No, I'm fine. I would rather talk about your big news." *And why you didn't tell me*, she thought but didn't add. They were already dangling off a cliff's edge, one more slip up would plunge them down to the rapids below.

A soft smile, the first real smile she had seen from Maverick since she got here, crossed his features. "Yeah." He said slightly breathlessly, leaning back against the front door. "I'm sure you've heard on the news."

"I heard from Willow. But I'd much rather hear it from you."

"A new investigation is underway with Grant Adams. The board found numerous money links going straight into his account over the years and that was enough to disprove anything he had against me. He'll go to trial soon and the courts will decide his fate."

"I don't understand how the deception went on for so long and nobody knew." Ofelia said, not fully understanding the operation but knowing the ploy couldn't have been easily done.

Maverick just shrugged. "The old Commissioner of baseball was his friend. He was involved too and will also be facing charges. Lloyd found a whole damn chain of people. The baseball world is pretty shaken up and will probably take a bit to recover."

She wasn't sure how an organization recovered after that, but she imagined policies would change as more information came out. She seriously needed to study up on her baseball knowledge because Ofelia had no idea what a Commissioner did, but it sounded really important.

"Wow," Ofelia said after a beat of silence passed between them. "That's incredible, Mav. You helped a lot of future players by doing what you did."

"Nah, it wasn't me. It was Lloyd. The man's a genius."

"No, this was you." Ofelia shook her head adamantly. "It was no easy feat to stand up to those who wronged you and tell your story. That took a hell of a lot of bravery. Don't sell yourself short."

She could have been imagining it, but she swore a new softness in Maverick's expression appeared. He looked like a man who had hardly slept at all this week and was forced into making too many decisions in a short amount of time. Ofelia wanted to reach out and hug him. She couldn't take his worries away, but she could provide comfort. Unfortunately, she didn't know if that would make the situation worse or better.

Ofelia didn't know what to say next. She felt like she was trying to tiptoe through a minefield and hoping her next step wouldn't end in catastrophic destruction. God, she hated feeling this way. Especially with Maverick. Why couldn't they go back to before Chicago -- before things got complicated? She knew where she stood with him then, but now Ofelia didn't even know if Mav wanted to be in the same room as her.

Thankfully Maverick finally spoke up, sparing her. "My old team offered my position back with a pay increase to compensate for lost time. I can finish out the season and renegotiate my contract at the end of the year. I've already got offers from other teams for next year as well. I have options, Ofi. For the first time in a long time, I have full control over my future. Do you know how much I've craved that?"

She thought she did, but maybe she hadn't fully understood the extent of his feelings. At the beginning, she knew how hard the adjustment was for Maverick. She had thought though, over time, it had gotten better. Maybe it was a bit too conceited to believe she was the reason for his happiness in his fresh start and severely underestimated how miserable he had been.

Although she was afraid of what might happen next, Ofelia still tried to smile. Though things were tense between them, she still felt happy for Maverick. "That's incredibly exciting, Mav. I'm so happy for you. You've worked so hard for this and to see it pay off..." She trailed off and reached to squeeze his hand.

Almost immediately as their hands connected, Maverick jerked away. Ofelia flinched as shock and disbelief etched their way across her features. Her eyes followed Maverick as he strode past her, rubbing his hands together. He stopped when he got to the end of the hall and turned back to face her. Nothing familiar remained in his features, only a blank stare as he looked her over.

"Don't you get it, Ofi? Or are you seriously as clueless as you look right now?"

Ofelia stepped back as if he struck her. This wasn't her funny and kind man she had fallen for. This man was quickly becoming a stranger before her eyes. "What the hell is that supposed to mean?" She tried to sound angry, but her voice came out smaller than she anticipated.

"It means I'm taking back what I never should have lost in the first place. I'm not meant to be a high school coach or live in this godforsaken town. This was never meant to be my life, Ofelia. I never asked for it. All I have ever wanted was to play baseball. I'm not going to lose it. Not again."

"You don't have to!" Ofelia shouted back. "No one is asking you to do that! I'll support you in whatever the hell you choose, I just want to be part of that decision-making process. This affects both of us!"

"There is no us!" The words reverberated around them, stopping time itself. Ofelia froze like a statue, her eyes widening as tears pooled in her eyes. Maverick blinked twice, his words settling in. He had the decency to look ashamed and when he spoke again. His voice quieted, but there a new firmness remained. "Look, we had fun. A great time even-"

"Don't."

"-but that's all it was ever going to be-"

"Stop."

"-we have our memories-"

"ENOUGH!" The scream erupting from her was a breaking point she never expected to reach again. "Don't fucking diminish our relationship to a good time. Don't you dare say our relationship is a fling. Not when I fucking allowed myself to love you!"

The word "love" hung heavy in the air between them. Maverick's eyes widened to a comical level and in any other situation, Ofelia would have let herself laugh. But there was nothing funny about handing your heart over to someone and watching it fall and break into a million different pieces at their feet.

"Ofelia...no. You don't lo-"

"Don't you fucking dare tell me how I'm feeling. Don't tell me what I feel is one sided because I know you feel it too. Can you honestly look me in the eyes and tell me you don't feel a damn thing for me?"

Maverick was the man that brought her coffees in the morning. The one who would help her with dinner. The man who would kiss her until she was breathless. The man who went out of his way to make sure she had someone in the audience for her team's cheer competition. That was love. She felt it. He couldn't say he didn't feel the same because Ofelia saw how happy she made him.

This was his chance to take it back. She could forgive him for his outbursts because he had been through an emotional week, but he couldn't push her away because things got hard. He would need to learn to trust her as she trusted him. He could say 'sorry' and all this would be behind them.

But that wasn't what happened. Unfamiliar hazel eyes stared back at her, devoid of all emotions as he said. "I don't love you, Ofelia. I never loved you. I can't love you."

The dam broke and she fought back sobs. The walls were closing around her once again. This was just another failed love story. She had repaired her heart and given it freely to another person, only for it to break all over. But this time was so, so much worse. Because Maverick wasn't leaving her for another woman. No, he was leaving her for a fucking sport.

"Ofelia, I'm sorry." Maverick said, almost looking like the Maverick she loved. He reached out, as if going to hug her when not seconds ago he had been the one to cause this pain.

Ofelia snapped out of his grasp, taking two large steps backwards. "Get my name out of your mouth." Maverick stopped moving, but Ofelia hadn't. Her back hit the front door, and she reached blindly for the handle. "You don't get to leave me. I won't go through this again because this time, I know my fucking worth. You can lie to yourself all you want, but I know you cared for me. I don't understand why you are doing this and when I look back at this moment again in a few years, it won't be me that I pity. You will have to live with the fact that you could have had everything you ever wanted but you decided to throw us away because you were scared."

"Ofelia-"

"I'm not finished!" She hissed, her entire body shaking as she did her best to keep herself together for one more minute. "I love you, Maverick. But you don't fucking deserve me." And with that, Ofelia opened the door and walked out of Maverick's house for the last time.

He didn't follow her and for some reason that stung even more. She managed to get into her car and drive a few blocks before she pulled over and called Willow. The moment her best friend picked up, Ofelia gave in to her misery and openly sobbed for the future she once saw with Maverick. Gone, like the rest of her withered heart.

Chapter Thirty-Three

People said time mended a broken heart and to those people, Ofelia wanted to send a fresh, hot bag of dog turd. Only two weeks had gone by since Ofelia offered her heart to the man she loved as a final effort to save what might have been the best relationship of her life, only for Maverick to say she had no part in the path he chose.

After breaking down in her car minutes after the breakup happened, Willow had tracked her location and found her doubled over the steering wheel. She didn't remember how Willow persuaded her out of her car and into Willow's Buick, but the next thing she remembered was collapsing on her friend's couch as another round of wracking sobs took over her body. Willow had rubbed her hair soothingly, not talking for once as Ofelia cried herself to sleep.

In the morning, Ofelia had found a note saying Willow took the liberty of arranging a sub and the only thing Ofelia needed to do was stay and rest. She didn't possess the energy to care about her classes falling behind with state testing only weeks away.

One would think getting your heart ripped to shred for a second time, only a few years apart, would become easier. It didn't. Not even a little. It came with new regrets and self-loathing. Ofelia blamed herself for letting it go too far. She should never have agreed to their first date or any date that came after. She should have guarded her heart more fiercely and not been so eager to dive into bed with the first man who showed her an ounce of decency.

Javi had called her multiple times over the last two weeks, but Ofelia hadn't had the energy to talk to him. She didn't want to talk about being dumped...again. Eventually Javi had stopped calling and started texting. He knew Maverick had broken up with her because Willow spoke to him. That relieved Ofelia because it spared her from having to talk about it.

Javi started to text her daily, just to check in and make sure Ofelia knew she wasn't alone. She appreciated his efforts and always tried responding, even if it was with an emoji. Some days that was all she was capable of, but her brother never pushed her. Willow didn't either, but she did hover. She knew her friend worried and believed any minute Ofelia might dissolve into a puddle of sad tears, but Ofelia's tears had dried up on Monday night.

It was surprisingly easy to fall back into the work routine. Her body was on autopilot, and she went through the motions of day-to-day life, always trying to keep busy. She feared the sadness and pain that came with breakups would rear its ugly head the moment she allowed herself to relax.

Thank goodness for coffee. Most nights, Ofelia forced herself to stay up and keep busy until she could not physically keep her eyes open. Then and only then did she allow herself to fall into bed and sleep. She worried if she laid down too soon, she would lay in bed and replay the break up over and over.

During this time, Maverick hadn't reached out to her once. Ofelia wasn't sure how to feel about that. She should be happy to never talk to him again and consider that part of her life a lesson learned. On the other hand, she desperately wanted to know why. Why was he pretending he didn't feel the same about her? Why was she not enough for him? She wasn't sure she was in a place to hear the answers to those questions.

Ofelia felt her thoughts slipping into forbidden territory and mentally shook herself as if that would also shake away the darkness settling over her mind.

It was now Friday and school had ended ten minutes ago. All through the day her students had been antsy and full of pent-up energy. That's how they always got before a break, so Ofelia did her best to go with the flow of each class. Nothing major needed to be completed today so if students wanted to share what they were doing for spring break or where they were going, Ofelia would happily indulge.

Hearing their stories made her smile. She took solace in knowing others were feeling happiness and excitement for their upcoming week. She was too, but she pictured her homecoming a little more...celebratory? With losing Maverick and being on shaky ground with her father, the thought of going home didn't hold the same appeal now. Her plane tickets were already purchased and Javi was looking forward to seeing her, so there was no backing out of it now. Not that she would anyway.

A gentle knock on her classroom door nearly sent Ofelia tumbling out of her chair. The door opened slightly, and Willow's apologetic face peeked around the corner. "Sorry! I thought you saw me coming. You were staring right out the window."

Was she? Ofelia had been inputting grades earlier and then blanked after that. "No, it's okay. I'm just spacey today."

Willow nodded understandingly, unable to keep the pity out of her eyes. It wasn't her friend's fault, Willow meant well, but she hated that look of pity. It only reminded her she failed again, and everyone knew it.

Willow stepped further into the room and shut the door behind her. She perched herself up on a student desk close to Ofelia's teacher desk, letting her maxi dress billow out around her. "So, I just got back from talking to Colbie." Willow said after a brief pause.

Ofelia raised a dark brow questioningly. Her principal noticed the change in her and had stopped Ofelia to ask if she was okay, which resulted in complete word vomit and the unfolding of the truth. Colbie had been extremely understanding and checked in on Ofelia from time to time.

Still, she was weary as to why Willow spoke to her.

"I wanted to ask her if we had the funding to send me as an extra chaperone on the next cheer competition. I know it's still a few weeks away, but I didn't want you to go alone. Don't argue with me, Ofi." She said, cutting off any protests Ofelia might have had. "We do; so, I signed myself up to go. It'll be fun!"

"Willow, I'm not fragile. I can handle going by myself." Ofelia said, not meaning to come across as ungrateful. She didn't need Willow tiptoeing around every aspect of her life. "You should have come to me first."

"I know but-" Willow bit her lip, debating on her next words. "Your cheerleaders have noticed a change in you." She admitted. Ofelia's eyes widened. Had her carefully curated mask failed her? It wasn't surprising since she spent a lot of time with her squad, even on non-practice days. They were in her room a lot, either storing personal items, getting prepared for a school event, or simply coming in to talk. She should have known they would see right through her mask.

"And they are worried about you." Willow continued, searching Ofelia's face. "They know you haven't been yourself and a few of them came and talked to me. I didn't tell them anything, only you are going through something personal right now. Then they asked me to come along to their next competition, so you weren't alone. Lacey didn't want you stuck with 'exhausting parents that have nothing better to do than to live vicariously through their offsprings.'"

Ofelia laughed because it was such a Lacey response. She wanted to hug her and thank her entire squad for caring. It was sweet, and she was foolish to think she could hide her pain and fool her cheerleaders, some of whom she had known since they were freshmen. Willow also deserved a hug because she was being the best possible friend she could.

"I appreciate that. Thank you, Will. I've probably been the least fun person to be around these past two weeks, but I want to thank you for everything you've done. I would love it if you chaperoned. It'll make the entire experience much better." And then Ofelia did get up to hug Willow, who seemed surprised at first but hugged her back hard. She had needed that as much as Ofelia had.

When the two finally pulled apart, Ofelia was surprised to see tears in Willow's eyes. Now it was Ofelia's turn to be concerned for her friend. "Will? What's wrong?"

"Nothing." She all but choked out, a tell-tale sign she was

moments away from full-on waterworks. "It's just been so hard to see you so sad and I hate that I can't grab He-Who-Must-Not-Be-Named and shake some sense into him. But it wouldn't matter because dick head doesn't deserve you."

"Oh, Willow." Ofelia couldn't hide the genuine smile that crossed her lips. "What would I do without you?"

"I imagine you would forever live your life in darkness because I'm the light of your life. You are like, my most favorite person in the world. Don't tell my husband."

"Your secret is safe with me." Ofelia assured, crossing her heart to show Willow she met business.

Her phone began to buzz, alerting her it was time to leave. Her flight was set to take off at nine forty-five in the morning and Ofelia had so much laundry she needed to do, not to mention the last-minute errands to pick up her medicine from the drug store and a few toiletries.

"Are you still certain you can drop me off tomorrow? I really don't mind calling an Uber." Ofelia said to Willow, gathering up her lunchbox and purse.

"Uhm, of course. I'm not letting you into an Uber by yourself. You never know what sicko could be driving it. What time did you want me to be by your house again?" Willow wondered. It wasn't as if Ofelia had told her friend numerous times, nor did Ofelia send her several text reminders on when she should be at her house.

"Seven thirty. Seven if you want me to buy you coffee from Starbucks." Ofelia said, knowing Willow would never be able to pass up coffee. It was a teacher's entire life force. Plus, Ofelia craved the lemon pound cake.

"You know my weakness." Willow sighed, following Ofelia out of her classroom. Ofelia set her trash can outside her door and turned off her lights.

She turned to Willow and gave her one last hug. "You're the best. Thank you again." She said before leaving, ready to tackle the mound of laundry waiting for her at home.

Chapter Thirty-Four

The busy streets of Chicago were full of the hustle and bustle of a typical Saturday morning. It was simple to pick out the tourists from the native Chicagoans. Residents of Chicago didn't stop and gawk at any shiny thing the sun touched. There was a sense of ease in their walk that only came from knowing your city like the back of your hand. The tourists traveled in packs, pointing out different shops or vendors as they walked through town.

When Maverick first got to the city, years ago when he was still new to professional baseball, he had been much like the tourists. He and Breanna had spent countless hours exploring their city, neither one ready to believe this was their life. They tried to find places the locals kept secret from tourists and discovered so many amazing restaurants and bars.

Maverick hadn't realized how much he missed the feeling of discovery until it was too late. That was the thing about self-reflection, it only ever happened in the moments one least suspected and oftentimes it was too late to fix the mistakes made in the past. All he could do now was hope he didn't make the same mistakes in his future.

Yet, as he stood by the window in Keanon's high-rise, overlooking the city while only half listening to his friend drone on and on about Maverick's return to the game, Maverick couldn't quite shake the feeling that he had just made the biggest mistake of his life.

Mav didn't regret choosing baseball. It was his passion and a once in a lifetime opportunity to rejoin his old team. What he regretted, even if he couldn't quite admit it to anyone but himself, was choosing baseball *over* Ofelia. The look in her eyes as he watched the moment he broke her heart still haunted him. The utter betrayal and helplessness that radiated from her was almost enough for Maverick to fall to his knees and beg for forgiveness.

He should have begged for forgiveness.

But he hadn't done that. He let her walk away from him, thinking she meant nothing more to him than a quick lay and fun time. Why hadn't he stopped her? What had been holding him back?

"Maverick? Have you been listening to a thing I've been saying, man?" Keanon's voice rang through the fog in his brain. "What's up with you, man? You're not acting like yourself."

Maverick mentally shook himself before turning around. Keanon was sitting on his large symmetrical corner sectional. He had his feet kicked up and resting on the white pillows, looking at Maverick with a hint of annoyance.

Admittedly, he was being shitty company, and he wished he matched his friend's enthusiasm, but he couldn't quite muster it. "Fuck man, my bad. I'm distracted. I'll be good. What were you saying?"

Keanon looked at him like he didn't believe a word he said.

"Is it about that girl? What was her name? It was kinda Shakespearean, yeah?"

"Ofelia. Her name is Ofelia and it's nothing. I'm fine. Or I will be fine." There was no way in hell he'd be able to concentrate on tonight's game if he couldn't force his brain to shut her out.

His friend opened his mouth, no doubt ready to argue with him, but then a phone rang. At first, he thought the sound came from Keanon's phone, but when Keanon didn't make a move to answer, Maverick realized it was his phone ringing. His heart lurched as he read the name. Disappointment came when he realized it wasn't Ofelia trying to call him. Why would she? Maverick thought about sending the unknown number to voicemail when he decided at the last minute to pick it up since he had been getting an influx of important calls from unknown numbers.

"Hello?"

"Maverick."

Everything around him came to an abrupt halt. He couldn't hear anything but his own heart rapidly beating, threatening to jump out of his chest. He knew that voice; had heard that voice for the better part of his life. The reason he had been through hell and back in the first place.

Breanna.

"Don't hang up. Please. I just want to talk."

Anger. Resentment. Hurt. These were all the emotions he was battling, on top of an already emotional past few weeks. He hadn't had 'your ex calling unexpectedly' on his bingo card, and he hated how his breath hitched at the sound of her voice. He didn't love her, not anymore, but the history they shared didn't just go away after a few months. There was a time when this woman meant everything to him and now, she was little more than a stranger.

A stranger he had blocked weeks ago.

"Mav, you good, man?" Keanon sat up, ready to take the phone from Mav if he asked. Although he was tempted, he couldn't help the curiosity starting to form.

He nodded reassuringly at Keanon before excusing himself into the next room, which happened to be the room Maverick had been staying in while he settled back in Chicago. Closing the door to make sure their conversation was private, Mav gritted out. "What do you want, Breanna?" He hadn't guessed she would use a friend's phone to call him, but he should have been prepared for this to happen. He wasn't.

"I saw you were back in Chicago and that you are no longer banned. That's amazing news, Mav."

"No thanks to you." He snarled before he could stop himself. The box he had carefully constructed labeled 'Breanna,' where he filed away every memory and every ounce of pain, finally exploded. There was no stopping the onslaught of harsh words coming out of his mouth. If he were a better man, he'd have the decency to hold back. But he wasn't a better man.

"You turned my world upside down, Bre. The only reason I was banned in the first place was because you slept with my damn coach behind my back, and I was unfortunate enough to walk in on you. If you were so damn unhappy, why didn't you leave? Why did you have to ruin everything? Did you fucking care about my feelings? Or were you so far removed from our relationship you didn't care if you hurt me or not?"

There was a long pause on the other end of the line after his angry speech and Maverick thought for sure he had scared Breanna off. But a moment later, he heard a loud exhale and then Breanna's shaking voice. "I deserved that." She said softly. "That's the reason I called. Will you give me a few minutes to explain? I promise, I won't contact you again, but I owe you an explanation and an apology."

He so desperately wanted to hang up and ignore her as he had done every single time before. But instead he found himself relenting. "Fine. You have five minutes."

"Thank you." Breanna said, sounding grateful. Maverick didn't comment, simply waited for her to continue. "I handled things the wrong way between us and for that I am sorry. For nearly costing you your entire career, I'm sorry. Truly Maverick, I have lost sleep knowing the only reason you were banned was because of me. I couldn't make it right because Grant threatened to sue me if I so much as looked in your direction. I was scared.

"Our relationship had been dying for a while," Breanna continued. "That is not an excuse, just a fact. It had gotten to a point where neither of us could stand to be around each other because it resulted in arguing and resentment. Hell, Mav, we didn't sleep in the same bed half the time. We were falling out of love with each other and both were too scared to do a damn thing about it."

"So you cheated on me because you were scared and didn't love me?" Maverick deadpanned. "Wow, I feel so much better now. Thank you so much-"

"Stop, no. That's not what I'm saying. Or maybe it is, I don't know." Breanna said with a frustrated sigh. "I'm not saying what I did was right, but Grant made me feel like you used to back when everything was new. I got swept up into his fast-paced life and seduced by the lavish presents he rained down upon me. With Grant, I felt like a person. But with you...I just felt like a baseball girlfriend. I didn't know how to be anything different because I had never been anything other than a baseball girlfriend.

"We both deserved to be happy, Mav, and at the end of the day we weren't making each other happy. Were we?" She asked him.

Some anger from earlier slowly started to deflate. Even though he didn't agree with what she did, he understood the reasoning. It just didn't make it right. "No. I suppose we weren't happy anymore."

"We were so afraid of stepping out and trying something new; we decided to stay in a loveless almost-marriage. Mav, we could be married right now and freaking miserable. We both deserve better. I'm so sorry that things happened the way they did. If I could go back and change them, I would. Grant is an asshole, I know that now. I was an asshole for cheating, but at the time I thought you were an asshole for not appreciating me."

"Breanna, I never not appreciated you, I just-"

"Fell out of love with me. I know that now, but I didn't always know that. My biggest regret is hurting you and putting you through so much pain. I can't begin to imagine how miserable and lonely you've been since."

"I wasn't."

"W...what?" Breanna sounded confused. Understandably so.

The truth was, Maverick had been exactly that, miserable and lonely when everything first happened. Having your entire life uprooted would do that to a person, but to say he had been miserable and lonely the entire time would be false. He found a woman who showed him true happiness he had not experienced in a long time. A woman who cheered him on, even though she didn't know a damn thing about baseball. A woman who would text him about the books she was reading or the new podcast she was listening to.

The woman he left in Texas.

"I found love again. I guess I wouldn't have found her if it weren't for what we went through."

Maverick swore he heard sniffles on the other end of the line, and he didn't think Bre cried because she wanted him back. She cried because she was happy for him. The joy in her voice only confirmed it. "Oh Mav, that's amazing. You deserve it. So much. She must be one special woman."

"She was...is." He said, trying to swallow the lump lodged in his throat. "But we're over now. It's for the best."

"Maverick Jarrell Wilson, don't you dare do this to yourself." Breanna's attitude towards him did a complete 180. One minute she seemed over the moon about his news and the next minute she seemed ready to murder him. "You're self-sabotaging. You throw everything into your career and cut people out. It's like you have to be two different people and eventually you get tired of one act and fall back into your cocky baseball routine."

"I don't do that." He said indignantly.

"You do." Bre countered. "I admit to my faults, but you weren't perfect either. You always felt like you needed to pick baseball or a personal life. Like you wouldn't allow yourself to have both. You can, you know. Have both. What's the point of your career if you have no one to share your successes with at the end of the day?"

Breanna sighed and Maverick almost saw her rolling her eyes. "Listen, I didn't call you to lecture you about your new relationship." She said, changing the topic before Maverick could say anything. Not as if he had much to say because, and he deeply hated admitting this, but Breanna was right. "I called to say congratulations on your win. I don't want any bad blood between us anymore. I'm not saying we need to become friends, because I don't think either of us are ready for that, but I would like to leave this phone call with a sense of peace between us. Can you forgive me?"

For so long, he had hated Breanna, blaming her for every single problem he had after their split. Never once did he sit back and reflect on his own shortcomings. It was a lot easier to blame the bad on someone else than coming to terms with his own vices. Breanna was right about something. He was exhausted. Carrying anger and resentment for someone became a burden. One he didn't wish to carry any longer.

There was only one thing Maverick could say. "I forgive you." And he truly meant his words. He was finally ready to let it go.

"Thank you. You didn't have to, so I appreciate it." Bre said and Maverick sensed the smile in her voice. "Oh, and Maverick? One more thing?"

"Sure, but I make no promises."

"Get your head out of your ass and get back the woman you lost."

And damn if he hadn't heard a better idea that entire day.

Chapter Thirty-Five

"Just close your eyes. I'll get you there in one piece. Scout's honor." Willow said, abruptly swerving into the next lane and cutting off the car behind them. The succession of angry honking that ensued afterwards was enough for Ofelia to sink lower into her seat.

When Willow agreed to drive her to the airport, Ofelia hadn't expected she'd need to fight for life. With each abrupt turn and lane switch, Ofelia clutched her seat belt a little tighter, remembering why she never let Willow drive them anywhere. She quite liked living and Willow was apparently hell-bent on killing them both. Of course when Ofelia mentioned this, Willow would take her eyes off the road to glare at her, so she gave up and did as Willow suggested. She closed her eyes.

The airport was thirty minutes away, but Willow made it in twenty. "Southwest, right?" Willow asked as she pulled her car into the passenger unloading zone. In the process, she almost hit an elderly couple crossing the street, earning two very stern glares that Willow dismissed. "We are here, you can open your eyes now."

"Here as in I'm in heaven because my best friend killed us on the way to the airport? Is that what you mean?" Ofelia slowly opened one eye, just in time to see Willow roll her eyes.

"Ha, ha. Very funny. I got you here, didn't I? And you are still very much alive. So you're welcome." She mused, all to please she scared Ofelia half to death. Willow reached for a button next to her steering wheel and the trunk popped open. "No more stalling. Let's get you on your way so Mr. Fugly security guard stops motioning me to go."

Ofelia looked up to see a burly man, dressed in an airport security uniform, stare at the car. They were in a no parking zone, but if the engine was running and you were actively getting your luggage, it was fine to stall to drop off. He probably had seen the reckless abandon in which Willow pulled in and wanted her to leave before she became a liability. Ofelia understood that completely.

Giving him an apologetic wave, Ofelia got out of the car. She heard the driver's door shut, signaling Willow followed her out. "You don't have to grab my stuff." Ofelia argued as Willow dug through her messy trunk to find Ofelia's suitcase and backpack.

"Nonsense. I didn't want you to get lost back there." She said, searching through her messy trunk before handing Ofelia her things. "Okay, you have to promise to call me as soon as you land. I want to make sure you get there alright."

"It will be late. I have a long layover in Denver, but I'll text you when I arrive at the next airport." Ofelia promised.

Willow seemed happy with that answer. After a heartfelt goodbye and a few more promises to keep in touch, Ofelia was on her way to check in. She was thankful they had got there as early as they did because the lines to check in baggage and TSA lines were astronomically long. Clearly she was not the only one who had the idea to travel in April. California would be a popular destination, since it was a hot spot for spring breakers.

It took one hour to weave through both of her lines, giving her exactly one hour before boarding started. She was gate twenty-five and began to maneuver her way down the terminal. Ofelia was thankful she already had her coffee fix once she passed Starbucks and the crowd of people all waiting for their drinks. She couldn't help but notice many of the couples standing hand in hand, in deep conversation as they ignored everyone else around them.

Ofelia's heart ached at the sight, jealous of literal strangers. She walked a little faster down to her gate number, doing her best to avoid noticing anymore couples or families. In a few hours, she would be home with hers and all this silly pain she experienced at the airport would soon be forgotten.

Gate twenty-five bustled with people, as Ofelia assumed it would be. Tired-looking parents attempted to wrangle their rambunctious toddlers, while people in business suits rapidly spoke into their phone about important deadlines needing to be met. It was oddly refreshing to experience such mundane and trivial things, though she couldn't quite place why. Maybe because it made her feel a little less alone in her own problems.

Since seating was limited, Ofelia couldn't be picky and ended up seated between a woman talking amicably on her phone and a man watching something on his tablet. A familiar face caught her attention and Ofelia turned her head to the side so quickly, she nearly gave herself whiplash. The man with the tablet turned to her slightly, raising a brow. "Sports fan?" He wondered, taking an earbud out of his ear.

At first, Ofelia was helpless to do anything other than stare at his screen. Two sports commentators talked excitedly amongst one another. Ofelia didn't need to hear what they said, the man's picture in the corner was a dead giveaway. The picture must have been taken a few years prior because Maverick looked younger, more baby-faced, and he wore his team's uniform.

Today would be his first game and all Ofelia felt was numbness.

"Chicago might actually win a game now. It's been a rocky season without Wilson. You think he's going to whip them boys into shape?" The stranger asked, oblivious to her conflicting thoughts.

The picture should have sparked joy. Maverick was in his element, doing what he loved best. Instead, it reminded her yet again he made a choice and it had not been her. He must be coping a lot better than her.

Realizing the man waited for her to answer, she gave him a half smile that didn't meet her eyes. Coming up with something nice to say about Maverick proved to be more challenging than she initially thought. Finally, she settled on, "I think he's probably happy to be back."

The man seemed satisfied with her answer and nodded. He then proceeded to spend the next hour until they boarded, giving her a full and extensive history of Maverick and his baseball career. If only he knew just how familiar she was with him.

∼

THE MOMENT she stepped into the San Francisco airport, it hit her for the first time in two years, she was home. She had expected to feel like a stranger amongst the sea of Californians, but she didn't. Soon she would be reunited with her brother and the thought of seeing Javi made her giddy. She texted him the moment the plane hit the ground, and he promised to be on his way.

Ofelia followed the crowd until they reached baggage claim. The process was never speedy, but gave her time to catch up on her texts. Or rather text. Willow had sent her a GIF of a confetti bomb after Ofelia had texted her earlier, right before she boarded her final plane. She sent a quick text to her friend, letting her know she made it home. It was the middle of the night back in Texas, so she didn't expect a reply anytime soon.

Once the conveyor belt began moving, Ofelia made her way to the front and watched the luggage go by until she found her bright yellow suitcase. It had been a wise investment to purchase the neon yellow because it stood out. She pitied all the fools who thought black was the way to go.

As she made her way outside to pick up, she watched as families reunited and young couples got into Ubers. She searched the crowd, hoping to see Javi's car pull up, but it was dark and all the headlights were giving her a headache. She reached for her phone again, only to have someone grab her wrist. She shrieked, whirling around, getting ready to hit them with her backpack...and then she heard laughing.

"Javi! You jerk!" Ofelia's fear soon turned to excitement as she jumped into her laughing brother's arms. Javi stood right in front of her. The tears began to fall freely. "I can't believe you are here!"

"I can't believe *you're* here, *chica*." Javi gripped her tightly and didn't let go. If Ofelia looked up, she would bet Javi had tears in his eyes too. Two years was a long time to go between hugs and Ofelia was going to have her fill. Javi smelled like home.

When Ofelia managed to pull herself away from her

brother, she wiped the lingering tears in her eyes and laughed. "I almost hit you!"

"With your luggage, no less. Very dangerous." He teased, and she realized how much she had missed that.

"What are you doing out of your car? I thought you were going to pull up out front?" Ofelia asked, taking another look to see if she missed his car in the lineup, but nope. It wasn't there.

Javi shrugged. "Well, I planned on surprising you inside, but parking was a bitch. When I finally found one, I saw you walking out, so here I am."

"Here you are." She agreed, smiling brightly.

Javi took her suitcase from her and gestured across the street to the large parking garage. "I'm in there. Let's go, I bet you're tired from traveling."

Ofelia was downright exhausted and wanted nothing more than to fall into bed and sleep until she was woken in the morning by homemade breakfast. "I'm so ready to sleep."

"Camilia knows you are coming over, so she is sleeping in the guest room waiting for you. That cool?" Javi wondered, approaching his black pickup truck. She always thought the thing was too big, but since he worked in construction, he needed the truck to maneuver his things to and from workplaces.

"Uhm, duh. I need all the love from my niece. I just want to squeeze her." Ofelia couldn't stop grinning. She hadn't felt this happy in weeks and knew she should have made the trip back earlier. She was here now though and that's what matters.

"Then let's go. Be prepared for the most Mendez crazy spring break you've ever had." Javi grinned, winking at his sister before his expression became serious. "It's so good to have you back, Ofi. We've missed you."

"I missed you all so much. I'm so sorry it took me so long to come back." Her family understood her reasons, but it didn't make separation any easier.

Javi winked. "You are here now." He said before sliding into his car.

Ofelia followed him in, and for the first time in a long time, she was excited to see what the week had in store for her.

Chapter Thirty-Six

"So let me get this straight." Keanon said, rubbing the stubble on his chin. He hadn't moved from his spot on the couch, but mentally Maverick knew he was pacing back and forth as Keanon took in everything. "You don't want to play tonight?"

"No."

"And you don't want to play for the rest of the season?"

"That is also correct." Maverick nodded.

"But you still plan on playing next season, if the team allows?"

"If my plan works out the way I hope it will, then yes." Maverick assured as Keanon looked at him like he was seeing him for the first time.

Honestly, he couldn't blame Keanon for his reaction, considering how hard Lloyd and Keanon worked to clear his name. Maverick would be eternally grateful. It wasn't as if he were deciding to never play again, making all their work for naught; he simply couldn't continue with this season after he royally fucked up his new life.

"I just don't understand, man. Help me understand." Poor Keanon looked out of sorts, rubbing his eyes as if the answer would mysteriously appear in front of him. "I thought this is what you wanted. One call from your ex and suddenly everything has changed?"

"It's not because of Breanna, but she did help me recognize what I wanted and what I didn't." Maverick briefly explained Breanna's call and the impact she had on him. "She's right though, Keanon, I do see in black and white. I can have this, but not that. Or I can be this, but I can't be that and I'm so damn tired of it. My time with Ofelia – god you'd love her – made me the happiest I had ever been in such a long time. Even when playing. I fucked up, man. I fucked up bad."

To his credit, Keanon didn't immediately react and lecture him on the choice he made. Instead, he did something that surprised Maverick. He nodded his head and said, "I agree. You fucked up."

Maverick, too stunned to speak, stood there with his mouth open; something his mom used to lecture him about all the time when he was younger. She said he was bound to swallow a bug one of these days if his mouth was always open.

"Don't look so surprised." Keanon laughed, clearly enjoying himself. "I'm a ladies' man. A romantic. This shit is straight up Hallmark." Normally Maverick would jump at the chance of making fun of Keanon for watching something as sappy as the Hallmark channel, but he decided to let this one pass. Especially since he needed his support.

"Listen, when you first told me of the idea-"

"Thirty minutes ago."

"Shut up." Keanon glared before continuing. "I was hesitant. You've been put through the wringer these last couple of weeks and I wanted to make sure you weren't doing this for the wrong reasons. I'm team love, man. I've never met this girl that has you wrapped around her finger, but I already know she's too good for you." Maverick smirked because he couldn't agree more. Ofelia was entirely out of his league. "As a friend, I want you to be happy. As your agent, I can see the benefits of you starting next season. I can already see the offers coming in. Everybody will be trying to snag you before the season starts. It's brilliant if you ask me. Besides, I think you've outgrown Chicago. You need to set your sights elsewhere."

The tension in Maverick's body eased. He didn't realize how much he needed someone else to affirm his actions. It wasn't exactly a solid plan, there were many factors against him. The biggest one being if Ofelia didn't take him back. She had every reason not to, but he selfishly hoped with enough groveling, she'd at least consider taking him back.

More so than Ofelia, though she was the main reason for his decision, another factor came into play. He was a coach with a real responsibility to his high school baseball team. How shitty would leaving them now be. After all the work he had put into the team, he couldn't give up on them now. Benny and his guys deserved better.

"Alright, I'm fully on board with operation: love, but what the hell is your plan? Going to barge back to Texas and ask for her forgiveness?" Keanon asked.

Well, it *had* crossed his mind until he realized that Ofelia wasn't in Texas. She had mentioned going to visit her family back in California. This complicated things...a lot. How the hell would he find her in California? He couldn't call her and demand her location. Ofelia probably had his number blocked and if she didn't, she wouldn't pick up if she saw his name flash across the screen.

No, if he was going to win her back, it wouldn't be through

a phone call. He had to see her, face to face, and apologize until he was blue. Maverick needed to figure out how to do that. His girl was a romantic, even if she tried to hide it. She liked acts of service, or so Maverick had gathered from their time together.

Then something occurred to him. He laughed because if anyone knew how to track down Ofelia, it was Willow. Keanon looked at him as if he had gone mad, but Maverick shook his head and said, "I know what I need to do. Help me out here because this woman is going to be pissed."

"Who are you calling? Pissed women aren't really my specialty, but I'm a smooth talker." Keanon made a show of dusting himself off, full of himself and his ability to talk to women.

"Her best friend, Willow."

"Fuck, best friends are worse than girlfriends. Alright, let's get this shit done." Keanon sat up straighter, looking like a man preparing for battle. Maverick thought the call would be more of a slaughter but thought it best not to let Keanon know how much tiny Willow terrified him.

Although he didn't have Willow's number saved, he did have access to the faculty directory at school. He pulled up the PDF file the principal sent out and searched through the list until he found Willow's number.

Maverick would be lying if he said he didn't hesitate for a few moments, his pointer finger hovered over Willow's number a beat longer than necessary. Keanon knocked his shoulder against him, his way of telling Maverick to hurry up and call. Keanon would soon realize why Maverick was nervous, and rightfully so.

Before he could chicken out, Maverick touched her number and his phone began to ring. "Speaker. Put her on speaker." Keanon urged in a hush whisper and Maverick listened.

Both men waited in tense silence as the phone rang repeatedly. After the fourth ring, Mav was certain Willow wouldn't answer. He'd have to try later or think of a new plan. Before he could enter panic mode though, his phone stopped ringing and a familiar voice answered on the other end. "If you are a scammer, I will make your life a literal hell."

"I'm a lot of things, Willow, but scammer wouldn't be top of the list." Maverick said in a way of greeting, hoping to ease some awkwardness and hostility that was bound to happen. Which he deserved.

The silence that stretched out between them spoke volumes. Maverick had to tap his phone screen to make sure Willow hadn't hung up on him. She didn't; she just wasn't saying anything. "Erm, it's Mav-"

"I know who it is, dickhead. I'm deciding if I want to take the high road here and hang up on you, or completely rip you to shreds for hurting the sweetest person on the planet."

Keanon snorted, holding back a grin. Maverick shot him a look, but all his friend did was shrug innocently.

"Please don't hang up." Maverick begged. "I would rather you rip me to shreds, but I need to talk to you."

"And I need my best friend to have never met you, jerk face, but both of us are at a loss!" Willow yelled into the phone and Keanon had to grab a pillow to stifle his laughter.

"You aren't helping." He gritted through his teeth, covering up the microphone so Willow didn't think he was talking to her.

"You have some nerve calling me, Maverick. Can you hear how much I want to punch you in the throat? Because there is nothing I like more than some good throat punching, you spineless prick."

If Maverick wasn't so terrified of Willow literally murdering him, he might laugh at her ability to call him every bad name in the English language. There was no use in trying to reason with her. Willow was fired up, and he knew from experience that when she felt passionately about something, there was no stopping the words that tumbled out of her mouth.

Keanon, bless his soul, decided to jump in when he realized Maverick wasn't going to speak any time soon. He cut Willow off mid curse, mustering up all his charm as he said, "Good morning, Willow. I'm sorry to interrupt, because I'm enjoying your monologue, but I wanted to introduce myself. I'm Keanon Jermaine, Maverick's agent."

"Is that supposed to mean something to me?" Willow huffed, her anger shifting courses. For his part, Keanon seemed to handle himself well. "If you are in association with dickwad, then you are also the enemy."

"I like her." Keanon mouthed to Maverick with a grin. Of course he would hit it off with the scary chihuahua-like woman. "I agree that Maverick is a dickwad, as you say, but he's a lovesick dickwad. Which is why he is reaching out to you. This is all part of operation: love. Basically, we are inviting you to be part of that."

Silence remained on the other end as Willow took in his words. Keanon eyed Maverick as if to say, *"see?"* and smugly relaxed back on the couch.

"Is he serious?" Willow questioned after a moment. "I want to hear it from you, Maverick."

"I am. Very serious." Maverick chimed in. "I thought the

only way I could have my old life back was if I left my new life behind. I understand how stupid that sounds now, but things started happening so fast and I felt like I needed to make a decision. I was...scared for what it meant for me and Ofelia. And instead of dealing with our relationship, I broke it off. I was afraid one of us would get hurt."

"One of you did get hurt. Majorly hurt." Willow argued. "Ofelia called me after she left your house. She had to pull over because she was crying so hard and so violently. I held her that entire Sunday while you gallivanted across states to get back to your precious baseball. Now you decide that it's convenient to have a girlfriend? Please." She scoffed and Maverick imagined her rolling her eyes.

Hearing the utter devastation he left for Ofelia to handle on her own, gutted Maverick. How could he fuck something up so horribly and expect her to take him back after all this? But if he didn't try, then Ofelia would forever believe he didn't love her. He couldn't do that to her.

"I'm not making excuses. I was an ass and I acted without thinking. I let the woman I love slip through my fingers because I was scared and rushed into a decision. I hate that I hurt her, more than you'll ever know." Maverick took a long breath, his hand gripping his leg tightly so it would stop nervously bouncing up and down. "I decided I wouldn't play for the remainder of the season. I want to go back and finish my coaching job before I choose where I want to end up. And I need to tell Ofelia that the only life I want is one where she's in it. Because nothing matters if I don't have the girl I love by my side. But I need to make things right with her first. Which is why I need your help in finding her. You know where she is in California. Please, Willow, I'm begging you to tell me. Let me make this right. If she never wants to see me again, I promise I'll disappear. But I refuse to strike out without at least trying to fight for her."

It was up to Willow now. He would be devastated if she decided not to give out Ofelia's information, but at the end of the day he had no one to blame but himself. Even Keanon seemed to be holding his breath, waiting for Willow to put them both out of their misery.

What felt like an eternity later, Willow sighed softly, sounding tired and not convinced she was doing the right thing. "How do I know you aren't going to hurt her again?"

Fair question and it wasn't a flat-out no. His plea hooked her and now he needed to reel her in, sealing their fate. "Because I have never been more sure about a single thing in my life until Ofelia. She made me better, Willow. When I was at my lowest, she gave me a reason to wake up every day and I can't lose that. Not without a fight. I think...she's my person, Willow. Please, let me tell her how much I love her to her face."

For the second time that day, Maverick swore she heard sniffling on the other end of the phone. "Shit, that's romantic as hell. Damn you, Maverick Wilson. Ugh, I can't believe I'm doing this. But fine." A new gentleness laced Willow's words, but hesitation remained. Maverick would have to work hard to get Willow to trust him again.

Judging by the smugness on Keanon's face, Maverick knew he must look like a grinning fool. "Thank you, Will-"

"On one condition."

Her words cut Maverick short as he sucked in a breath. He doubted he'd like this one condition, but he didn't have any other options. "Alright. What?"

"I will give you her brother Javi's number. You talk to him

to get the address. And just so you know, Javi knows everything. So good luck."

Well fuck.

Chapter Thirty-Seven

Last night was by far the best sleep Ofelia had in months. By the time Javi picked her up from the airport and drove her back home it was well past midnight. As soon as Javi brought in her suitcase, Ofelia hugged her brother goodnight and snuck off to her room. True to his words from earlier, a small mound lay in the middle of the bed, curled up with a pillow and a pink stuffed dragon.

After taking care of her business, Ofelia skillfully maneuvered her sleeping niece over, closer to the wall so she could get in next to her. Camilia didn't wake up, not even when Ofelia pulled her close, kissing the top of her little head. She was already thinking about all the fun the morning would bring them when Camilia realized her auntie was finally here.

Unfortunately, Ofelia's body didn't get the memo she was, in fact, on break. So naturally she woke up promptly at seven the following morning. During the night, Camilia had somehow shifted so that laid towards the end of the bed, curled up in her Mickey Mouse blanket. Quietly, as not to disturb her, Ofelia slowly rolled out of bed, needing the bathroom.

Sound from the kitchen soon drifted down the hallway and the familiarity of it made her smile. Vicente Fernández's melodic voice filled the space, and the delicious smell of breakfast made her stomach growl in protest. Ofelia pictured her mother in the kitchen, swaying as she prepared breakfast for the family. Even though she was no longer here, someone carried on her morning tradition.

When she finished in the bathroom, Ofelia made her way to the kitchen. It was surreal to be back in her childhood home after so many years away. There were still touches of her mother's decorating, but Javi had fixed up most of the house and made it his own. Her mother's yoga studio was now Camilia's room, complete with a toddler bed and all the toys a little girl could want.

Ofelia expected to see Javi cooking breakfast this morning, but the man humming along to the music wasn't Javi, but her father. Ruben Mendez finished adding the chopped-up corn tortillas into the hot pan after having sautéed the vegetables beforehand. It took him a moment to realize his daughter stood right behind him. When he saw her, his face immediately lit up and grinned widely. *"Mija."*

Ofelia was conflicted. On one hand, she wanted to run into her father's arms and hug him tightly. She wanted him to rub her hair and tell her how much he missed her and how happy he was for her to be home. On the other hand, Ofelia still held anger with him for bailing on her in San Antonio. The problem was rooted deeper than that one instance, but it had been the tipping point. So as much as she wanted to run into his arms, her anger at him held her at bay.

When Ofelia didn't respond, her father sensed something was wrong, and he dropped his smile. She wondered if he too was thinking about San Antonio and the last phone call they shared. It had been the last time Ofelia had spoken to her father, and she didn't have many pleasant things to say to him. At the time her father deserved her anger, but a lot of the things said were in the heat of the moment. She regretted her tone, but not the words.

"Papa, we have to talk." Ofelia didn't like unresolved problems, and she most certainly didn't want any with her father when they both should be enjoying her time in California.

Her father nodded and gestured for her to sit down at their family table, nestled into the corner of the kitchen. The vintage lace tablecloth her mother had loved still decorated the table. In the center was a large vase of fake poinsettias, another one of her mother's favorites. The beautiful red flowers weren't in season; her mother would put them out during December to decorate the house. Ever since she passed, her father had kept them out year-round because the flowers made him feel like her mother was still here.

When Ofelia sat down, her father sat directly opposite her. He looked so small and too frail. Age hadn't been kind to her father, but she wondered how much of it was grief and how much of it was physical labor he still put himself through. She was tempted to forget the whole ordeal...almost. But if she simply pushed another incident aside, the unresolved problems between them would only continue to stack against them.

Summoning her courage, Ofelia took a deep breath and then began to speak. "Papa, I wanted to apologize for the things I said to you the last time we spoke on the phone. I was angry and hurt. Even though I needed to get those things off my chest, I didn't go about it the right way. You just...it hurt, papa. It hurt so much because I felt like a kid again, waiting for her daddy to show up to my cheer events, but you never did. I hoped with mom gone that I could have you there. Then you completely blindsided me."

This wasn't something she often did with her father; talk about her feelings. He came from an older generation of Mexican immigrants who taught him many things, but never put value on mental health and emotions. It wasn't something they talked about, and her father had followed in their footsteps. When her mother was around, she was able to get him to understand their children had emotions, and they were important. As parents, they needed to listen to them and help guide them through life.

But she wasn't here anymore. Ruben and Ofelia only had each other, and both were sailing uncharted territory.

To her utmost surprise, tears began to roll down her father's face. She had only ever seen her father cry once before and that was at her mother's funeral. Everyone had been in tears, so her father's grief hadn't stood out amongst the rest. His tears now didn't make any sense, and they only seemed to fall harder and faster; his entire body shaking with silent sobs.

Did she manage to break her father?

"Oh, papa." Ofelia moved out of her seat and over to her father's side, pulling his too small frame into her arms. She hugged him tightly, trying to comfort him. His tears opened her own flood gates and soon they both cried while holding each other as they mourned different things.

After ten minutes of silent sobbing, firm hugs, and her father getting up to take the food off the burner, Ruben finally rubbed the last few tears out of his blood shot eyes. She was unsure if she should hug him again or sit back down. Ofelia eventually decided to stay standing, keeping some distance between them but still close enough if they needed another hugging session.

"*Mija*, I..." Her father started but choked on his own words. This wasn't natural for him, and Ofelia appreciated the effort he put forth to save their relationship. "I'm sorry. I'm not always good at showing how much I love you. When you were little and your mother was pregnant with Javi, your mom and I made an agreement. She would be at home with you kids, and I would work to keep a roof over our heads and food on our table. I took every job I found. No matter how exhausted or tired I was. All I had to do was pull out a photo of the three of you and I remembered why I worked so hard.

"I wanted to give you both the best life I could, even if I wasn't in it much. Even if I missed things your brother and you did. The only reason we could afford to keep you in sports was because I worked like a dog every day." Her father looked up and met her eyes. "I know you think I didn't care about your cheerleading, *mija*. I did. But it was expensive, and your mother told me how much you loved it. How good you were. I knew I couldn't be the reason we couldn't afford it anymore."

"You worked constantly because you never wanted us to go without." Ofelia said softly, as if this reason just occurred to her. In truth, it did. As a child, you never thought about money or the cost of things. All this time she had thought her father wasn't interested in her hobbies, but it turned out he had always been her biggest supporter. He just did it in a way she couldn't see at the time.

"I don't understand what that has to do with last month and you not coming down to Texas. If it was about the money, papa, I would have bought your ticket." She still could not understand why he changed his mind at the last minute.

"Your brother is too proud to tell you this. He is a lot like me when I was his age. He took Camilia to a cheer clinic a few months ago and your niece fell in love. Not surprising because she's a lot like her *tía*." Ruben smiled at his daughter and Ofelia's chest swelled with pride. She hoped Camilia would love cheer as much as she does because Ofelia was ready to be the biggest and most involved cheer aunt ever.

"Javi is a good man. Supporting me and Camilia. He works too hard as a single parent and I see how badly he wants to give his baby girl everything, just like I wanted to give you. A love between a man and his daughter is the purest thing in this world, *mija*. I instantly thought about you, and I wanted to help Javi. I can't work much, but I can do some. When I got this job, I took it without thinking how badly you'd be hurt. Your mother would have set me straight." He smiled sadly, still so much pain as he spoke about his wife.

"She's not here anymore to keep me from being a bad father-"

"Oh papa." Ofelia's heart broke. She couldn't have her father thinking he was a bad dad. He was the furthest thing from it. He pushed her buttons, but she never thought he was a bad father. "You are a good man. The best man I know. I don't think you are a bad father."

Ruben reached out to his daughter and squeezed her hand gently. "Thank you, *mi amor*." He said and kissed the top of her hand. "But I am sorry. I didn't think how upset it would make you. I should have gone because it was what your mother would have done. I pride myself on being a man of my word, but I always break it with you, *mija*. You are so much like your mother and sometimes I forget you might still need me."

Fresh tears began to spill from her eyes as she stepped forward and hugged her father. For the first time in a long time, she felt like she understood him. That they were finally on the same page. "I will always need you, papa. Forever. I'm so happy you told me this. I wish you had told me before, but it doesn't matter."

Ofelia got more than she anticipated. She got to see a different side of her father and it made her reevaluate what she thought she knew about him. He had come a long way and it was never too late to make the most of their time now. They could make new memories, and she could put more of an effort into keeping him updated on her daily life. As long as he did the same.

"I love you, *princesa*, and I'm so glad you are here." Her father said and leaned in to kiss the top of her forehead, just like he did when she was little. "Whatever you want to do, just tell me. We'll do it."

"You know what dad? There's nothing more I want than to help you make breakfast. Teach me how to make your special tortillas?"

With the biggest smile she had ever seen from her father, Ruben straightened up and began to explain, in Spanish, how to create fluffy and butter filled tortillas. By the end of breakfast, Ofelia and Ruben were covered in flour, laughing at the mess they created.

It had taken a lot for both of them to open up, but now she felt as if she could reclaim their relationship. She still had one parent left and now more than ever, Ofelia needed her family. She hoped this was the start of the healing her mind and soul needed.

Chapter Thirty-Eight

Spring break at Casa Mendez went off without a hitch after Ofelia and Ruben buried the hatchet. In fact, Ofelia had never felt closer to her father and that filled her with warmth after being so cold towards him for so long. She feared what would have happened if they never had this talk and how much of each other's lives they would miss out on.

When Camilia woke up her niece attached herself to Ofelia's side. It didn't matter they had never met in person; their weekly FaceTime calls had been enough for a strong bond to form and made Ofelia less of a mysterious figure. Hugging her sweet niece for the first time was not something Ofelia would forget anytime soon. The smell of her sweet baby shampoo filled her nose as she nuzzled the top of her head, baby curls bouncing at the action.

The first day Ofelia wanted to do anything Camilia wanted, even though Javi advised against it. "How am I possibly spoiling her? I haven't had the chance!" She argued with him, but her brother just smirked and shook his head.

That was all the permission she needed to take her precious niece out for a fun day. Javi stayed home on Ofelia's insistence since he looked like he hadn't been getting enough sleep. Papa came with, offering up his car, which Ofelia appreciated.

The three of them went to an ice cream shop Ofelia's mother used to take her and Javi to after school on Fridays. She always called their outings a little treat for being so good during the week. It had been their thing for years, even when Javi and Ofelia were too old for ice cream dates. On rare occasions when their father wasn't working, he would join them.

The first time her father had come to their weekly ice cream outings was the first week both Ofelia and Javi had been in school. She remembered how shocked she had been to see her father waiting at their usual table with two brand new backpacks. Hers had been Hello Kitty. She remembered that because she had been obsessed with the cat and brand; she was fairly certain she cried after seeing it. They enjoyed ice cream together after that and remembered going home to play board games, even though her father was absolutely horrific at games and her mother was far too competitive.

It was one of Ofelia's most treasured memories as a family.

She had planned on taking Maverick here to share stories of her mother. How the ice cream shop connected Ofelia to her and she had hoped she'd create new memories with Maverick. Thinking of him sent daggers straight to her heart.

Although Camilia was too young to understand the significance of this simple ice cream place, Ofelia knew her father understood why she brought her niece here. A sad smile crossed his face when they entered the shop. "I haven't been here since your mother passed."

The ice cream shop hadn't changed much since her youth. A new coat of green paint decorated the wall, but the same small circular tables with the rickety wooden chairs still filled up the area. Camilia pointed to four different ice cream flavors she wanted before running off to climb on top of a chair. "I wait here." She said cutely, kicking her little feet up and down.

"She only likes chocolate." Her father whispered and Ofelia ordered a kids cone for Camilia, cookies N' cream for her father, and a rich chocolate shake for herself. After the onslaught of sugar, Camilia's energy spiked, and she bounced eagerly in her seat.

"Is that children's museum downtown still open?" It opened when Ofelia was old enough to babysit. The museum had been a great way to spend a sweltering summer day indoors and all the young kids she brought there had loved it. She was certain Camilia would feel the same.

"Yes, Javi took Camilia there a year ago. She probably doesn't remember." Her father said.

He had been right. When Ofelia pulled up to the large, kid friendly museum, Camilia gasped as if she had just seen a real unicorn and not a pretty building. "We go there?" She asked excitedly, pointing to the horse fountain out front.

"Yes! We're going to go inside to play!" Ofelia was definitely going to win aunt of the year. Camilia's energy was contagious and even her father seemed excited to explore inside.

The museum was set up for smaller children and everything was interactive. There were a few demonstrations going on, one about bubbles seemed exciting, but Camilia didn't seem interested in watching a demonstration. Instead, her niece ran straight to an area set up like a mini grocery store, complete with carts, isles of food, and cash registers run by other little toddlers.

Camilia wasn't shy, despite being an only child. She inserted herself into a group of toddler shoppers and started talking a mile a minute. Whatever they were talking about seemed important. Toddler language wasn't something she was fluent in, but by the looks of it, Camilia was having fun.

After the grocery room, which they spent at least an hour in, Camilia was ready to go on to the next place. They toured the dinosaur exhibit and "extracted" dinosaur bones from a pile of sand. Then they made their way to the insect room where Camilia got to paint her own butterfly. They ended in a diner room where Camilia pretended to be a waitress and served plastic sandwiches to Ofelia and Ruben.

By the time they left, Ofelia was ravenous. Her two companions were fast asleep by the time she pulled out of the parking lot, so she settled on a drive-thru for burgers, picking up extra food for when they awoke. It was nearly 5pm when they got home, and that was only day one.

Day two consisted of the beach. She missed California beaches and yearned to be back in the water. Or more realistically, to lounge in the sand while sunbathing and reading a romance novel.

Javi, now well rested and off from work, decided to tag along. Which was fine by Ofelia. After one day of caring for her niece, she was already exhausted. It amazed her that Javi could do this every single day and never complain. Being a single, working father was hard, but her brother managed to do it with a smile on his face daily.

Ofelia loved watching the two of them interact in the water. Camilia was all smiles and Javi looked at her like she was the very air he breathed. From the corner of her eyes, she watched her father constructing a sub sandwich, big enough to feed an entire army. It only needed to feed the four of them, but her father didn't understand portions.

It was another late evening before they arrived home and

Camilia was barely keeping herself awake. Like her father, she was stubborn and didn't want to miss a single second. "I'll give her a bath. You two relax." Papa said and neither her nor Javi put up a fight.

Javi suggested they sit outside on the porch. Her mother's and father's old rocking chairs sat unoccupied, and Ofelia remembered many late nights her mother or father would rock her outside until she inevitably fell asleep in their arms.

Ofelia didn't notice her brother slipping inside the house until he came back with two blankets, handing the lavender colored one to her. She thanked him and then nestled herself into the rocking chair, humming contently.

Javi glanced over at his sister, a warm smile spreading across his face. "You look happy."

"I am." Ofelia said automatically. Her eyes flickered open, and she tilted her head to see Javi better. "Being home makes me happy. Being back with my family is exactly what I needed."

"After Maverick?" Javi asked softly, stealing the breath from her lips. He was bound to come up at some point. Javi had been just as invested in her relationship as Willow, but unlike her best friend, Javi didn't have the full story. He only knew they were no longer together and whatever Willow told him while she had been inconsolable in her own grief.

"Listen, I don't mean to bring up his name and cause any problems." Javi said. "I know how much he meant to you. Do you think there's a chance you'll get back together?"

Despite her best efforts, Ofelia couldn't help but laugh. It wasn't Javi's fault, he didn't know, but there was no way Maverick would ever come back into her life. He made that perfectly clear. "He made his choice, Javi. I can't keep crying over a man who didn't love me enough. The only thing I am grateful for is that Maverick taught me my worth. If nothing else, I got that out of our relationship."

Javi glanced down at his phone, the screen lighting up with a text message. He seemed to only be half paying attention to her, which was a little annoying since he started the conversation. "Am I boring you with my boy problems?" Ofelia teased, poking his side.

"You're my big sister. You always annoy me." He chided, flipping his phone over to give her his full attention. "What if he asked for your forgiveness? Then what?"

Ofelia wasn't sure where this was coming from. She honestly didn't know what she would do in that situation, but considering it was incredibly unlikely, she simply shrugged. "I guess we will never know." She was done with this weird turn in conversation and wanted to change the topic. "Enough about my pathetic love life. I heard Papa mention that Camilia is interested in cheerleading?"

Her brother's teasing smile faded as he blinked. He retreated into himself, the same thing he always did when the discussion of money wasn't far off. "She's two. She's interested in everything."

"True...but mama started me in cheer when I was about her age. It's a great way to make friends and have fun." She said gently. "Papa said you took her to a free clinic, and she loved it. Why don't you sign her up?"

"Because cheer costs money." Javi answered, forced patience in his voice. Javi rarely got like this, unless she hit a nerve. He wanted to give his daughter everything, but everything cost money. "And before I put her into anything, I want to make sure that this is something she will stick with."

"If it's about the money, Javi, you know I'll help."

"I don't take charity."

"Oh hush." Ofelia smacked his hand lightly. Her brother was so prideful that he couldn't see an act of kindness without strings attached. "This isn't charity. This is my niece and my money. I would love to help pay for lessons on a temporary basis. If she doesn't like it anymore, I'll stop." She shrugged nonchalantly, hoping he'd see the value in her offer.

One of Javi's fears was turning into their father. Working too much and not being able to be there for the little things that meant the most. Neither one of them blamed their father, at least not anymore, but it wasn't a life that either would choose for themselves. Javi worked enough as it was, but he was always there in the evening to play with his daughter and read her to sleep.

A resigned sigh left her brother's lips. "You said temporarily?"

Ofelia did her best to conceal her smile but did a horrible job at it. "Temporarily. Until she decides she doesn't like it or until you can take over the payments."

"Six months."

"Hmm?"

"Six months." Javi repeated. "You pay for six months and if Camilia still likes it, I will take over the payments."

"Javi, we don't have to assign a time frame. It can be for however-"

But Javi cut her off. "Six months. That's my compromise."

It was the best that she would get so Ofelia nodded. "Alright then, six months."

Javi put his hand out to shake, sealing the deal between them. In six months, Ofelia would try to convince her brother again that she was fine with paying. For now, she celebrated that her niece would be following in her footsteps. "I'm going to need a lot of pictures. You are going to be the best cheer dad there is."

Javi's goofy personality came back, leaving the man who stressed about money behind. "Pictures of me or Camilia?"

"Both, of course." She mused, just as Javi's phone went off again. "Damn, you must be pretty popular tonight. Hot date?"

She had hoped that would earn a laugh from her brother, but he didn't hear her. He typed back a message to someone on his phone and then put his phone away in his pocket. "Sorry, that was...dad. Camilia is ready for me to tell her bedtime story."

"Since when does dad text?" Ofelia asked confused, able to count on one hand the times her father had ever texted her. One of those times had been accidental.

"Since now, I guess. I'll be right back."

"Do you want me to read her a bedtime story? Then you can relax."

"No!" Javi said a little too quickly, causing Ofelia to raise a brow in suspicion. Her brother grimaced. "Uh, sorry. I just enjoy this time with her. How about you do it tomorrow?"

"Okay." Ofelia said slowly, still unsure what to think of her brother's outburst. "I guess I'll wait here for you then."

"Okay, yes perfect." Javi said and leaned down to kiss her cheek. "If you need me, text me." Before she could ask questions, Javi went inside, leaving Ofelia on her own.

It was a beautiful night; there were worse ways to spend her evening. The sun was setting, and Javi's active neighborhood of children was finally quiet. No more kids played on the street and cars weren't coming to and from work. It was almost as if she were the last person left on the block, not ready to let go of today's events.

Ofelia pulled the blanket tighter around her, sinking deeper into the rocking chair as headlights illuminated the street. She didn't think anything of it, until the black car came into view. The car nearly drove by the house but pulled over to the curb at the last minute. Ofelia sat up, confused. Had Javi invited someone over? Or was she about to be kidnapped? Also, was it still called kidnapping when you were an adult?

Before Ofelia's brain could finish considering the term adultnapping, a shadow stepped out of the car. It was tall and lean, standing at least half a foot taller than her. She couldn't make out the person's figure, but they were walking this way.

Damn the sun for going down so quickly. Just a minute ago she was admiring the beautiful sunset and now she was sitting in complete darkness as a stranger walked up to the house. It wasn't until he got closer that the shadow triggered the light, illuminating the stranger.

Ofelia heard her breath hitch in her throat as familiar brown eyes stared back at her. The last time she stared into those eyes, they were cold and empty. Now they were full of uncertainty and hesitation. Her body stood without her permission, taking an involuntary step towards him.

For a second, his face looked full of hope. Something in her expression must have made him feel like there was still a chance. But then the pain of the day he left her came rushing back and this time, it was Ofelia's turn to stare at him with cold eyes, keeping the tears at bay.

"Maverick." She whispered. She didn't know how he found her or why he was here, but she told herself she didn't care. "Leave." The words left her lips so quickly that she couldn't take them back even if she wanted to. And a part of her didn't want him to leave, but the logical part of her mind knew his visit meant nothing but more heartache.

If she didn't turn around now, she never would. With great

effort, she turned her back towards Maverick and was prepared to leave him behind. Until she heard his voice.

"Ofelia, please." Maverick said, still behind her. She didn't think he moved at all to allow her space. Smart man. "Please, I only need five minutes. Let me explain and if you still want me gone, I'll go. Please Ofi. I know I don't deserve another chance, but I don't want you to think that I never loved you. That I walked away because you aren't important to me."

"I think you said enough the last time we spoke. There's nothing more to say."

Maverick visibly paled. He looked caught between letting her go and getting down on his knees to beg for time with her. It made her heart hurt, but he had thoroughly ruined her. Made her feel small and unimportant, despite the fact that he knew just how much leaving hurt her. How much it took to open her heart to someone else. She saw a future with Maverick, but he had chosen something else over her. She was tired of being cast aside as if her emotions didn't matter.

"I know I fucked up." There was a slight tremble in his voice as he spoke. She wondered if there were tears in his eyes, but it was too dark to tell. "And I deserve your scorn. I fucked up majorly. Please just give me five minutes, but if you want me gone, I'll go. I'll fucking hate it, but I'll leave you alone if that's what you choose."

His words gave her pause, her hand hesitating over the handle. After a few minutes, she turned to face the man who shattered her heart right before her eyes. Perhaps she should let him suffer like she had suffered. She should turn around and never see him again. It would save her a lot of pain later.

But Ofelia didn't do any of those things. Instead, she crossed her arms over her chest and said, "Fine, speak."

Chapter Thirty-Nine

Throughout the entire plane ride and five-hour layover, Maverick thought about what he would say the moment he came face to face with Ofelia. In his head, he'd rehearsed different speeches where he spoke eloquently and won back the love of his life. Now that he was here and she was waiting on him to say something, anything, all his well rehearsed lines left his brain. Javi had given him the chance to plead his case and he was fucking it up by becoming tongue-tied.

To his surprise, Javi hadn't immediately hung up on him nor had he called him every name under the sun, both of which he would have completely deserved. Instead, Javi listened and agreed Maverick fucked up. "Listen, I'm not her keeper. Ofelia is a grown woman and can make her own choices. Plead your case with her and then accept whatever outcome she chooses." Had been his words right before he sent the address.

That had been his second win, and he held on to that feeling all the way until he landed in California. His mood shifted dramatically. What was once quiet excitement soon changed to dreaded anxiety. Was Maverick doing the right thing? Should he leave Ofelia alone and let her get on with her life? Would she forgive him? Maverick was afraid he might have just lost the woman of his dreams.

Ofelia stared at him expectantly, while his thoughts became a tangled mess of uncertainty and fear. His mouth went dry, and he felt like a middle school kid about to admit his feelings for his crush. Except this was one hundred times worse because her answer would legitimately affect the rest of his – or rather *their* – lives.

"Your brother knows I'm here." He didn't know why he started with that, but it seemed important. Realization washed over her, and Maverick saw the moment she started piecing together the puzzle.

"He was distracted on his phone tonight...I thought it was a friend, but that was you?" She asked, unable to believe it.

"Yeah. Willow-"

"She's involved with this too? Actually, that's not surprising." Ofelia shook her head, looking jostled. Maverick wanted to reach out and hug her. To reassure her that everything was going to be okay, but he didn't think it was his place anymore. At least not yet. "What are you doing here, Maverick? You should be in Chicago at your game."

Clearly she hadn't watched the news this evening. Keanon had fed the media the story of Maverick sitting out for the rest of the season. He'd be back again next year and more than likely with a new team. Keanon said Maverick had affairs he needed to put in order before he dedicated his life back to the game. Which was true, but the biggest "affair" was getting his girl back.

So far he was striking out in that department.

"I decided not to play for the rest of the season. The game

ON AND OFF THE FIELD

will be waiting for me next year. I have more important things to take care of." Maverick said.

Ofelia's brow creased in confusion. "But...why?"

"Do you even have to ask?" Obviously she did because he had done a shitty job at making his feelings known. Maverick sighed and took a step forward. Ofelia didn't back away, but she did tense which made him stop in his tracks. "I was an idiot, Ofi. I was a scared idiot who thought I couldn't have the girl and the dream job. I was so afraid you'd resent me if I brought you into my old life. I was scared that what happened with Breanna would happen again. So I made the cowardly decision to break it off before you could hurt me.

"It doesn't make sense and I took that choice away from you, but baby girl, I have never loved someone as much as I love you. I thought I could walk away from you because I felt like you'd be better off without me. But I'm fucking miserable without you and I shouldn't have made that decision for you. When I was getting ready for my game, which should have been a happy moment for me, all I could think about was you. How badly I wanted you next to me to share this experience.

"I also realized that I have a life in Texas. One that I made for myself and it's a pretty good life. I couldn't just walk away from it without tying up loose ends. I can't leave my team and I most certainly can't let the best woman I had the pleasure of loving think she was nothing more than a fun time to me. I love you, Ofelia. I love you so goddamn much and I was a coward to walk away."

Maverick felt breathless by the time he finished his speech. It had gone so much better in his head; he fumbled over words and wasn't explaining himself well. Being around her made him nervous because he couldn't help but wonder if this was the last time he'd ever get to be close to her.

After a long, stretched out silence between them, Ofelia finally took a step closer. She was still at the top of the porch and Maverick was on the bottom step. They were nearly eye to eye this way and though she closed some of the distance, he still felt worlds apart from her. He desperately wanted to close the gap, but had he done enough?

"Why the sudden change of heart?" She asked and Maverick was unable to decipher her tone.

It was an easy answer though. He didn't have to think about it. "I might have been told that I see the world in black and white. That I make no room for anything to overlap. It has cost me everything, but I finally realized I don't have to choose one thing or the other. I have the ability to make decisions and compromises with people I love and want in my life. I'm the biggest idiot for letting my dream girl walk away and I don't expect you to forgive me, but on the off chance you do, I swear I'll do anything in my power to make it up to you."

"Anything?" She repeated, and he swore he saw the sides of her mouth quirk up into a smile.

"Anything. You name it." Maverick held his breath, anxiously awaiting her answer.

Like a starved fish, she dangled the worm in front of him, too far to reach. It was torture, but the kind that he deserved. If she asked him to walk away, Maverick would. It would be the hardest thing he ever had to do, but he would do it knowing he had put his heart on the line.

Ofelia descended the last two steps, stopping once they were chest to chest. She didn't reach out for him, so he kept his hands trained at his sides, even though everything in him told him to hold her. He had come this far, and he wasn't about to mess it up anymore.

"I want to be an equal partner in this relationship." Ofelia said, eyes fixed on him. "You don't get to make decisions for both of us anymore. I want to be part of them, even if you think I can't handle it. I'm stronger than you give me credit for. I want a relationship that will last a lifetime, so if you aren't in this for the long run, spare us both the heartache and leave now."

Her words were like a challenge, and she waited for his next move. If Ofelia thought her words would scare him off, then she underestimated how deep his feelings ran. He would offer his heart on a silver platter if she asked him too. "Baby girl, I want to be one of those old couples who still does the nasty at the nursing home."

That earned him a genuine laugh. God, it was so good to hear her laughing again. He thought the last sight he would have of Ofelia would be her crying after breaking her heart.

"So, what are you waiting for?" Ofelia's next question caught him off guard. She smirked at him knowingly, but he hadn't a clue what she meant. She saw the confusion on his face because she continued, "Isn't this the part in romance movies where the guy kisses his girl within an inch of their life? I'm feeling a little cheated on that front."

All the nerves, all at once, left his body. He was left with nothing but immense relief and a giddy feeling starting in the pit of his stomach. "How foolish of me."

"How foolish indeed. I'm waiting, Romeo." Ofelia grinned.

There was nothing left to be done other than pulling Ofelia into his arms tightly and crushing his lips to hers as if his life depended on it.

He wasn't fooled into thinking everything was perfect between them now. He still had to make it up to her, but right now, the stars aligned, and the world was perfect.

He was home.

Chapter Forty

Ofelia didn't remember moving, but they must have because the next thing she knew her back hit her front door. How she didn't trip and fall on the stairs would forever be a mystery to her. Her brain still tried to process everything and with Maverick's lips on hers, he made it impossible to do so.

Maverick.

He was here. Kissing her like she was the only woman left in this world, and he needed her kiss like a starving man. So many emotions ran through her mind, but the most prominent one was love. Love for a man who came back and admitted to his faults. Was everything suddenly perfect between them? No, but that didn't mean she wasn't willing to give this another shot. She owed it to herself and their relationship to give them another try.

This time she wouldn't let Maverick walk away out of fear. Not again.

His hand shot up the front of her shirt, hand curling

around her hip. He squeezed, making her involuntarily sigh. This man's mouth was wicked, and she thought of a few other naughty uses for it.

Before she could tell him just what she wanted that mouth to do, the door behind her opened. Ofelia yelped, flailing her arms as she desperately tried to gain her balance. Before she fell on her ass, Maverick's hands shot out and grabbed her, pulling her flush against his chest. "Are you okay?" He asked, and she was pleased to see him slightly breathless from their kiss.

Ofelia assured him she was fine and then whirled around to see who interrupted them. She supposed she shouldn't have been surprised to find Javi, a knowing smile on his face. Nor should she be surprised to see her father only a few steps behind her brother. She was embarrassed all the same and heat rushed to color her cheeks.

"Please tell me you weren't there the entire time." Ofelia groaned, wishing the floor would open and swallow her whole. Even though she was a grown ass woman, there was still something about knowing her brother and father watched her hungrily kiss a man that made her stomach churn in horror.

"You think I'd leave my sister with a man that broke her heart unsupervised? Nah, *princesa*. What type of brother do you think I am?"

"One that stays out of my love life." She said with mock sweetness. She wasn't truly upset with Javi; he was the reason Maverick was here. He could have easily hung up on Maverick and made the decision for her, but Javi wouldn't ever interfere in her life like that. He trusted Ofelia to make her own decisions and if she asked him to escort Maverick off the premises, he would do just that.

"*Mija*, who is this young man?" Her papa said from behind Javi.

Ofelia felt Maverick tense behind her. She reached behind and took his hand, giving it a gentle squeeze to reassure him. To his credit, he didn't back away or wait for Ofelia to introduce him. Instead, he squeezed her hand and then stepped in front of her. He offered his hand to shake, smiling at her father. "I'm Maverick Wilson, sir."

"You look familiar." Her father said, taking his hand to shake "*Hijo*, doesn't he look familiar?"

"*Sí*, papa. He plays baseball for Chicago."

Ofelia was surprised her brother knew that. Both the men in her family were soccer fans; she didn't think they paid attention to anything else. Her father's eyes lit up in recognition though, so evidently they dabbled in other sports as well. "Ah, *sí*." She swore he sounded slightly disappointed, but if Maverick caught on, he didn't show it. "You are dating my daughter then?"

Once again it would be a perfect time for the ground to open and swallow her whole. Javi choked back a laugh, enjoying this far too much. One day she would be able to get him back, but right now she wanted to kick him.

Maverick turned back and smiled at Ofelia encouragingly. It was nice to know that one of them was in control of the situation. "Yes. I am." She heard him say. "As long as she wants me, that is. And if I have your permission, of course."

There was no hesitation in her father's voice. Only pride and happiness when he spoke of his daughter. "If she chose you, then consider yourself the luckiest man on this earth. My girl is perfect."

"That I can agree with." When Maverick turned to wink at her, Ofelia felt weightless.

It took an hour before they escaped into Ofelia's room. Her father refused to let Maverick go to bed without a meal. It was how Mexican families showed their love, so there was no fighting it. Her father made Tostadas, piling it high with beans, shredded chicken, lettuce, tomato, cheese, and topped off with Mexican crema and guacamole.

Both Maverick and Javi managed to eat three while Ofelia and her father settled on one. Thankfully, Ruben was too tired to serve dessert, making escape possible. Ofelia kissed her father goodnight and hugged her brother. Both men seemed eerily calm about allowing a strange man to stay the night, but clearly Willow and Javi had been talking a lot behind the scenes. Ofelia imagined Javi spoke with her dad about it as well.

When she got Maverick alone, Ofelia locked the door and turned to face him. Mav looked over her childhood room, eyes roaming through the photos on the dresser. One caught his interest and he picked it up. It was a photo from ten years ago. Ofelia was a teen, and her mother was beaming at the camera. It had been taken during one of her competitions because she was still in her cheer uniform. "Is this your mother?" Maverick asked softly.

A familiar heavy lump stuck in her throat. Except she didn't feel the need to burst into tears at the mention of her mother. She wanted to share this small memory about her with Maverick. "It is. We had just won in our division and my mother was so excited. This was taken after we accepted our metals."

"She's beautiful. You look exactly like her."

Ofelia had been told all her life that she resembled her mother. It was the best compliment anyone could have given her. "Thank you. She was a wonderful woman. She would have loved you."

"And do you?"

"Do I what?"

"Love me?"

"You know the answer to that." Ofelia said as Maverick slowly closed the gap between them. He cupped her face between his large hands, tilting her head up. His heated gaze was so intense and she almost wanted to look away, but no other man had looked at her with so much. He looked at her like he'd been searching for her his entire life.

"I love you, Ofelia. I love you so damn much. I'm sorry for all the pain I caused. I'm sorry-"

He had apologized enough. Ofelia broke off the newest apology with a kiss. If he wanted to make it up to her, he'd do so now. In this room. It was time for her to take what she wanted, and she wanted nothing more than Maverick. Judging by the smoldering look he gave her once Ofelia pushed him back, he wanted it just as much as she did.

"You're the first man I've ever brought in here." She hummed, lazily taking off her shirt. She was thankful she decided to wear a nice bra today and not one of the old beige bras she sometimes wore. Maverick's eyes burned her skin as he took her in. She liked the way he looked at her, full of desire and need.

"Am I? I'm one lucky bastard." He said, taking the hint and pulling his own shirt off. A body like his shouldn't be covered up but kept on display.

Ofelia was inclined to agree with his assessment. She clucked her tongue, hands moving down to her jeans zipper. She made quick work of the zipper and soon peeled them down her legs, leaving her in nothing but her bra and panties. They didn't match; she didn't know Maverick was going to be here, and she certainly didn't know she'd be having sex tonight. But at least they were cute.

Maverick clearly didn't give a shit if her bra and panties

matched. He reached for her, pulling her towards the small, full-sized bed. Maverick was too big for her small bed, but he made no complaints. Even when he had to wiggle precariously at the edge of the bed to get his own jeans off.

"Can you be quiet?" Ofelia purred, once he rolled back over. It was dark, but she knew he still wore his boxers. If she wasn't mistaken, she could see an impressive bulge in the front, begging to be touched. "Because I have my father and brother on either side of us. I doubt they'd be thrilled to know you are seducing me."

"Says the temptress that brought me in here and locked the door." Maverick grinned. "If anyone is seducing anyone, it's you baby girl. But yeah, I can be quiet."

"Why don't we test that, yeah?" Ofelia didn't wait for a response; she started her descent down his body with kisses. She heard Maverick inhale deeply, his body trembling from the touch of her lips. She flicked her tongue out to tease his nipple on her way down. So maybe she was being mean, but Maverick deserved a little evil in his life.

"You aren't playing fair." He groaned, running a hand through her hair. He gathered up her locks and held it tightly behind her head, which she was thankful for. There was only so much hair a girl could have in her mouth before sexy time turned disastrous.

"Maybe not. But you deserve a little torture." Ofelia finally kissed her way down to his waistband, feeling the heat radiating off his body. She brought her hand up to cup his growing erection and Maverick hissed. "Shh, Mav. You have to stay quiet."

She didn't know where the sudden bravado came from, but she liked being in control of Maverick. He also seemed perfectly fine giving her free-range to do as she pleased. With careful precision, Ofelia began to pull Maverick's boxers down, letting them fall around his feet. He managed to kick them off the rest of the way and Ofelia nestled between his legs, staring down at his massive erection.

Giving head hadn't always been Ofelia's favorite thing to do, but she found herself wanting to please Maverick in this way. He didn't make her feel like a warm mouth to fuck or inferior in any way. In fact, she felt quite the opposite. In her eyes, she felt like the most powerful woman kneeling between the legs of the man she loved. Maverick's next words only confirmed it. "Fucking goddess, baby girl."

Fucking goddess was correct.

She took Maverick's length down in one go, earning a low moan from her man. It spurred her on, giving her an extra boost of confidence she needed to begin bobbing her head, taking him inch by inch. She used her tongue to trace around his pulsing vein, already tasting the saltiness of his precum.

"Shit, Ofi." He panted, pulling the pillow over his mouth to stifle his moans. When he began to buck his hips, Ofelia let her mouth go lax to give him the space to move. Dampness began to pool between her legs as she grew excited for him. Reaching between her legs, Ofelia began to tease herself, circling her clit with her thumb. The added pleasure sent vibrations through her entire body.

"I'm close, baby girl. You gonna take my cum?" He asked, but Maverick control was slipping. Ofelia pulled back just enough to tease his tip while still pleasing herself. They came together in a rush of pleasure. Maverick gripped her bed so hard his knuckles turned white from the force.

Ofelia pulled away, licking the last of him off her lips. "Evil woman." She heard Maverick say, his voice deep from his orgasm. "We proved I can stay quiet, now it's your turn. I also distinctly remember informing you that your clit is mine to take care of." He grinned before grabbing her hips and flipping them over before she registered what happened.

Two thick fingers rubbed her entrance, parting her lips. He dipped his fingers inside of her, gathering up her wetness to lubricate her. "So wet for me, baby girl." He purred happily. Ofelia was extremely turned on and almost frenzied. She needed him desperately. She whimpered impatiently underneath him but that only delighted him.

"Tell me what you want, Ofelia." Maverick said the words slowly. He didn't stop the teasing to her clit, circling his thumb over her lazily. It was pleasurable but his strokes were too slow, keeping her on the edge but never pushing her forward. "Tell me exactly what you want."

What did she want? She wanted him, of course. She wanted to feel the connection between them, to remind herself that Maverick was here and real. That he wasn't going anywhere. How did one put all that into words?

Her face had been an open book because Maverick's face softened, and he stopped stroking her. His free hand came to rest on the side of her face, forcing her to keep eye contact with him. "I'm not going anywhere, Ofi. I love you. I was afraid to say it before and now I'm afraid you don't understand how much I love you."

It was what she needed to hear. Still she needed more. "Show me." She said, her voice barely above a whisper. "Show me how much you love me."

Maverick understood what she needed. Ofelia was almost positive he needed the same thing. He kissed her, in a frenzy, like she would disappear at any moment. Then he was inside of her, taking and giving exactly what she wanted. Her hands roamed his body, touching everything they could reach, imprinting herself on him. It was quick and hard, but exactly what they needed to go over the edge once again.

The second time he made love to her, they took their time, no longer afraid at any moment one of them would disappear. In the single act, more words had been communicated than either could verbally say. But Ofelia had no doubts that Maverick loved her. Only a man who loved a woman as much as he did could make her feel this way.

It was late into the night when they finished for the last time, sweaty and spent in each other's arms. The moonlight flickered in from a gap in her window, illuminating a small corner of her room. Even though she couldn't see Maverick, she could feel him and that was enough for now.

"You don't regret sitting out this season for me?" Ofelia found herself asking, despite the wordless exchange they shared.

To his credit, Maverick didn't seem bothered by her insecurity. "Not even a little. There's always next season. I want to finish out the school year coaching and take the summer to decide what we want to do next year. We have time. We don't have to make decisions now."

And they did have time. She knew there would be many tough decisions ahead of them but those were decisions they were going to make as a team. It included both of their futures and Ofelia didn't want one without Maverick. They could make this work; she just knew it. She could teach anywhere, even online. Or she would become a full-time cheer coach. All those things were possibilities, but none of them had to be chosen now.

For now, she could simply enjoy the man in her bed and

know they had the rest of their lives to make these big decisions. "I love you, Mav."

Not missing a beat, Maverick took her hand in his, lifted it up to his mouth and placed a gentle kiss on her palm. "And I love you, baby girl. Forever."

Forever would have to do.

Epilogue
TWO WEEKS LATER

"Ugh! Ms. Mendez, this stress isn't good for my skin. I read online that stress can make you wrinkle prematurely." Lacey said, obsessively looking at herself in her phone's camera. Tony snickered, earning himself an elbow to the gut.

"Lacey you aren't going to have any friends if this is how you treat them." Willow said, just as nervous as Lacey.

Ofelia would be forever grateful for Willow who agreed weeks ago to accompany Ofelia and her cheerleaders to nationals, their final competition of the year. Willow threw herself into the assistant coach role with ease, going as far as leading some warmups allowing Ofelia an extra thirty minutes to get ready in the morning.

"Oh, we aren't friends, Mrs. Clarke. Lacey and I tolerate each other at best. It's more of a reluctant friendship, if you will." Tony said.

Willow shook her head. "I will never understand teenagers."

"Well, I'll never understand teachers. Like, why would you

willingly go back to high school? It's like a never-ending nightmare." Tony shuttered, like the thought was too grim to bear.

"With all due respect, Mrs. Clarke, and no respect for you at all Tony, I need you both to stop talking so I can panic in silence." Lacey stressed, peering from backstage to look at the judges table. They were still deep in conversation and Ofelia understood the apprehension from her seniors.

This was their last competition as high school students. Not only that, but a hefty scholarship was on the line for the top five schools. Ofelia knew how much that money would help a lot of her seniors. At the very least, it would cover a semester at their chosen institute.

"Any news?" A voice came from her phone. Ofelia shook her head, looking down at the tiny screen where Maverick, along with a few of the other baseball players, stood on a field.

"Not yet, they are still debating. There are tons of teams here, so it could take a while." Ofelia said, biting her lip. The anxiety wafted off her cheerleaders and settled in the pit of her stomach. She wanted this win just as much as her squad.

"Damn, does it usually take this long? I feel like this is the longest Maury show ever, and we are waiting to hear if we are the father or not." One of Mav's boys said. She thought his name was Garrett, and he was dating one of her cheerleaders.

Upon coming back from California, Maverick had taken back his position as head baseball coach. Surprisingly enough, it had not taken near enough groveling and apologizing as Ofelia initially thought it would to win the boy's trust back. They seemed happy to have their coach back; Benny most of all. His coaching assistant didn't know how he would survive the rest of his season alone, especially when tournaments were just around the corner. He all but kissed Maverick's feet when he returned.

The tournaments were the reason Maverick couldn't join her. Ofelia was bummed she was missing his games as well, but they had video chatted an exuberant amount this weekend, making it feel as if they were truly taking part in the other's events.

Maverick would be there when she returned home. Considering he moved in with her after California. They hadn't planned for that to happen, but after Maverick stayed a few nights at her house, Ofelia wasn't about to tell him to leave. It was more fun to have him there.

"What about y'all? Still in the bracket?" She asked. It was a new term she learned from Maverick. The more they won, the further they moved in this imaginary bracket until only two teams remained. Then the final two teams would play off and the winner would be crowned champion.

"Yup. Next game is in two hours. They should be at lunch." Maverick glared at the few guys around him, but none of them seemed intimidated by his stare.

"Hey, my girl is on the other side of that phone. I gotta hear what happens." Garrett said.

"Yeah, well my girl is holding the phone and you all are ruining our call." Maverick shot back and was meant by a chorus of whistles and jests.

It was now common knowledge that Maverick Wilson and Ofelia Mendez were dating. If it was up to her, she wouldn't have put their relationship on blast since her students were insistent with their questions. Unfortunately, that choice was taken from her when the press caught wind of them and a few articles about her surfaced online. Nothing bad, but Ofelia was still new to this world, and she was adjusting to public scrutiny. She felt as if she were handling that public side of their relationship better though.

"Oh my god!" Lacey suddenly shrieked and Ofelia nearly dropped her phone as a chorus of "whats!?" rang out through her phone. "He's moving! The balding judge is moving. Oh my god they are about to name the top five squads. Somebody hold me-not you Tony!"

"We want to see!" A voice hissed from Ofelia's phone, but she barely paid attention. She looked towards the stage and watched the judge meet the announcer with a sealed envelope. The whole auditorium went quiet, as if everyone collectively held their breaths. Her squad should really be in their seats, but she couldn't stop them from coming behind the stage and no one had kicked them out yet.

There was another long pause as the competition announcer broke the seal on the envelope. He didn't look at the card immediately like anyone else would have in his situation, instead he launched a drawn-out speech on the importance of sportsmanship and hard work. Ofelia swore Lacey's head was going to explode at any minute. That or she would run up on the stage and snatch the envelope from him.

Just when Ofelia thought she'd have to hang up the phone to keep Lacey at bay, the long-winded announcer finally began to call out the top five schools, starting with 5th place.

"Bayview High school!"

Bayview stormed the stage accepting their metals while their seniors veered left to hold the large check of scholarship money.

"I'm going to have a heart attack." Willow whispered, gripping Ofelia's free hand tightly.

"It's okay. There are still four more-"

"Deer Valley High School!"

"Okay, make that three." Ofelia muttered as the announcer

ON AND OFF THE FIELD

named another school. The tension between her squad was palpable now.

These were the hardest moments as a coach. Her squad did an absolutely amazing job, but the competition was fierce. Everyone here was looking for a win and the reality of the situation was not everyone here would be leaving a winner. She didn't want to have to end the season off on a bad note, but she would remind her team how amazing they did this year. It was a successful season they should feel proud of.

Two more schools were called, leaving one left. Mentally, Ofelia already thought of the speech she would give her squad and parents if this went south. She turned to Willow, but her friend looked to be at her breaking point and Ofelia didn't want to add another layer of stress. She could deal with this. They had never not placed, but this could be a humbling experience. There had to be a way to turn this around.

Ofelia was deep in her own thoughts, so she didn't hear the announcer say the last school. What she did hear was the loud screams coming at her in every direction, including from her phone. At first, she thought someone had gotten murdered until Willow began to shake her and jump around in a little circle. "Why aren't you celebrating!?" Willow yelled, clearly mystified as to why Ofelia wasn't reacting.

"Celebrating what? What happened?"

"You didn't hear? Oh my god, look!" Willow pointed, causing Ofelia to notice her team was no longer standing around her anymore. That was because they were now on stage accepting their trophies while the seniors got a huge scholarship check.

"Oh my god!" Ofelia repeated Willow's words, nearly sinking to the ground.

They did it! Her squad won! The long months of practice,

dealing with whiny parents, and all the fundraising had finally paid off.

Willow had run off to celebrate with the parents, leaving Ofelia alone with Maverick. Through the chaos of the last minute, she had accidentally dropped her phone on the ground when Willow hugged her, so she quickly retrieved it. Maverick was alone now, smiling widely at her. She didn't know how he ditched the rest of his team, but they were no longer in the frame.

"You did it, baby girl!" Maverick grinned and his happiness was genuine. He was proud of her and that made Ofelia melt a little inside.

"They did so amazing! Oh, Mav, they worked so hard! They deserve this."

"And you deserve a warm bubble bath and a nap."

Ofelia laughed. Those things sounded heavenly to her. "Are you offering to run me a bath?"

"Hell yeah. As soon as you get home. I'll be your bath boy."

She liked the sound of that. It was a five-hour drive home, but she had Maverick's upcoming game to keep her entertained on the ride back. "I'll meet you on the field in two hours?" She asked since he always propped up his phone so she could take in most of the infield.

"And off, baby girl. Get your sexy ass home as soon as you can, and we will have our own celebration."

Ofelia didn't have to ask what his celebration would entail. She knew and her body grew hot at the thought of it. Sometimes when she thought about her life, she couldn't believe this was the path she was on. She wouldn't change it for the world, not even the small breakup they went through. Because even that taught her what she was worth and what she deserved in a man. It taught Maverick to trust and not to let fears or insecurities get in the way of a good thing.

Her love story wasn't a typical fairy tale, but it felt like the only story worth reading about. So much was still left unwritten, but together, they would create their own happily ever after. Ofelia couldn't ask for anything better.

Afterword

Need more from a New Beginnings Romance? Javi's story is coming in 2023! Make sure you keep up to date by signing up for my newsletter.

Acknowledgments

There are so many people who have helped make On and Off the Field possible. First and foremost I want to think my grandma who has always been my biggest supporter. I'm truly lucky to have such an amazing person in my life, encouraging me every step of the way, (even though I won't allow her to read this book, lol!)

Thank you to Emmaline for being the first person to ever have their eyes on this manuscript. For the countless phone calls, texts, tears, and editing sessions you put up with. I'm so lucky to have you as a friend and critique partner!

For Brad and L.R. Friedman for encouraging me and answering any questions I had.

Huge shoutout to my besties, Candice and Shelby. Girls, you know I absolutely love and adore you both. I truly lucked out in the best friend department and I can't thank you enough for loving this book as much as I do.

Thank you to the wonderful authors, bookstagrammers, and booktokers who have supported me throughout this process. I hope you love Mav and Ofi as much as I do.

And finally, thank you to the readers. To those who took a chance on a new author. Whether you came here from my fantasy book, social media, or simply happened to stumble across me, I appreciate your support.

Also by Anastasia Dean (pen name for Tati B. Alvarez)

A New Beginnings Romance

On and Off the Field

Javi's book coming 2023

BY TATI B. ALVAREZ

Dawn of Dasos

1. The Ambrosia Throne
2. The Ambrosia Deception - Coming Soon
3. The Ambrosia War - Coming Soon

About the Author

Anastasia Dean is a pen name for Tati B. Alvarez. This is her second book, but first romance. Anastasia Dean lives in Austin, Texas, where she spends most days lost in her own head, creating stories. When she is not writing, you can find her vacationing at Disney World.

instagram.com/heyanastasiadean
tiktok.com/@anastasiadean.author